W9-BVF-615

"Sex, murder, madness, and medicine. What more could any thriller reader want? A disturbing, riveting read, *Denial* is written with insights only a forensic psychiatrist could have, with characters vividly human because they're humanly flawed. Keith Ablow has written the prescription for terror. Readers should fill it only if they are caught up on their sleep."

—Michael Palmer, bestselling author of *Fatal*

"*Denial* placed the reader on the cutting edge of psychiatric thrillers, and in the hands of an author whose expertise as a psychiatrist make this story as authentic as it is compelling."

—Bestselling true crime writer Jack Olsen

"Wonderful inside detail . . . the psychological thriller has gotten some professional help, and it works."

—*Newsday*

"*Denial*, which is a perfect title, is not easy to read, but it is harder to put down. The characters are compelling for all their flaws, the story is tightly told, and the outcome is anything but predictable."

—*The Cleveland Plain Dealer*

"A first-rate debut thriller involving forensic psychology . . . A distinctly unusual hero . . . A novel for the self-destructive in all of us."

—*Kirkus Reviews* (starred)

"A convincing, seductively fascinating portrait of a man and a milieu obsessed with sensation and trapped in denial of that obsession."

—*Publishers Weekly*

PRAISE FOR THE NOVELS OF KEITH ABLOW
COMPULSION

"Compelling, graceful, and nearly impossible to put down."
—Robert B. Parker, author of *Widow's Walk*

"No one burrows into the darkest recesses of the human mind as deeply as Keith Ablow."
—Tess Gerritsen, author of *The Surgeon*

"Keith Ablow is a master of psychological suspense. This is a dark, taut, terrifying novel, driven by a talented psychiatrist's insights into the human condition. Stoke up the fire, curl up with *Compulsion*, and be prepared for a sleepless night."
—Michael Palmer, author of *Fatal*

"Frank Clevenger is a wonderfully flawed hero, as haunted by his own demons as the sociopaths he faces, and Ablow writes like a man possessed—with a pace so blistering the pages will all but singe your hands."
—Dennis Lehane, author of *Mystic River*

"Fast-paced and frightening, *Compulsion* is a novel that explores the very nature of evil itself. Psychiatrist Frank Clevenger is a hero with heart, soul—and brains."
—Janet Evanovich, author of *Hard Eight*

"From the first sentence to the last, *Compulsion* is mesmerizing. A tense and sexy thriller stocked to the brim with juicy characters . . . featuring an utterly shocking, yet thoroughly convincing family of fiends . . . with deft intelligence, Ablow maps the torturous terrain of the darkest regions of the human heart."
—James W. Hall, bestselling author of *Blackwater Sound*

More . . .

"This series just keeps getting better. Frank Clevenger is a real original: a jeans-clad, black-turtleneck-wearing head-shaven loner whose compassion for victims of violent crimes—and the perpetrators of those crimes—threatens to destroy him. Whether Clevenger is entirely fictional, or a re-flection of his creator's dark side (Ablow is a practicing forensic psychiatrist), the upshot is the same: He's a brilliant creation and this is a brilliant novel."

—*Booklist* (starred reviews)

"The present is wounded by the past in an expertly judged psychological thriller . . . a solid, satisfying case."

—*Kirkus Reviews*

"The author, a practicing forensic psychiatrist, uses his ex-tensive knowledge of mental illness and violence to lend au-thenticity to *Compulsion*, weaving a suspenseful mystery around riveting insights into the criminal mind. An engross-ing thriller that belongs on your summer reading list."

—*Bookpage*

"Action nimbly shifts from gritty urban Boston to window-dressed Nantucket, and the people and politics are realisti-cally portrayed, including the ballsy but deeply flawed protagonist . . . this one scores as a great psychological mind-bender."
—*Publishers Weekly*

PROJECTION

"*Projection* is a crime novel like no other. It's a week in the loony bin; it's a psycho tour de force. Keith Ablow has the expertise and an overachiever's grasp. Ablow has . . . the in-stincts of a Zen Thomas Harris."

—James Ellroy, bestselling author of *L.A. Confidential*

"This realistic and suspenseful story should please laymen and experts alike."

—*Booklist*

Compulsion

Keith Ablow

St. Martin's Paperbacks

COMPULSION

Copyright © 2002 by Keith Ablow.
Excerpt from *Psychopath* copyright © 2003 by Keith Ablow.

Cover photo © Steve Dunwell / Getty Images

Library of Congress Catalog Card Number: 2001058861

ISBN: 0-312-98824-9

Printed in the United States of America

St. Martin's Press hardcover edition / July 2002
St. Martin's Paperbacks edition / June 2003

St. Martin's Paperbacks are published by St. Martin's Press, 175 Fifth Avenue, New York, NY 10010.

10 9 8 7 6 5 4 3 2 1

For Deborah Jean,
Devin Blake,
and Cole Abraham

ACKNOWLEDGMENTS

Thanks are especially due my extraordinary editor, Charles Spicer, my gifted agent, Beth Vesel, and my publishers, Sally Richardson and Matthew Shear.

A number of people read drafts of this book and gave me valuable feedback. They are: Helena LeHane, Jeanette and Allan Ablow, Dr. Karen Ablow, Christopher Burch, Charles "Red" Donovan, Holly Fitzgerald, Marshall Persinger, Dr. Rock Positano, Dr. John Schwartz, and Emilie Stewart.

Nantucket's own David Goodman of the *Inquirer & Mirror* and Nantucket Chief of Police Randy Norris made me feel at home on the island and shared with me a native's eye for detail.

Finally, I thank artist George Rodrigue for showing me the way.

Compulsion

Come away, O human child!
To the waters and the wild
With a faery, hand in hand,
For the world's more full of weeping
  than you can understand.

—William Butler Yeats
The Stolen Child

1

Lilly Cunningham looked up. I melted. She was twenty-nine years old, with pale blue eyes to get lost in. Her blond, curly hair would make any man want to touch it. Her strong forehead predicted intelligence and was perfectly balanced by the gentle slope of her nose. Then there were her full lips, dimples in her cheeks, her long, slender neck. A simple gold cross on a delicate chain pointed toward the curves of her chest and abdomen, rising and falling under a white sheet.

Part of me wanted to let my attention linger on Lilly's beauty, but the bigger part of me loves truth, which is almost always about something ugly. My eyes moved to her exposed thigh.

The flesh was inflamed from groin to knee. The skin had broken down in places, spreading like wet parchment, weeping pinkish fluid. Two serpentine black lines, in Magic Marker, each running twelve or fourteen inches through the muck, showed where her surgeon would make incisions to promote drainage.

A war was being fought. Battle lines had been drawn.

"I don't believe we've met," Lilly said, her voice straining.

"Dr. Clevenger," I said, still focused on her thigh. I

stayed several feet from the bed, which is my habit when first seeing patients.

"Hmm. Shaved head, jeans, cowboy boots. You don't look like any doctor I've ever seen. Certainly not at Mass General."

I met her gaze. "What do I look like?"

She worked at a smile. "I don't know. An artist, maybe . . . or a bartender." She laughed, but weakly. "You have a first name?"

"Frank."

"Okay, then, Dr. Frank Clevenger. What's your line? Surgery? Internal medicine? Infectious disease?"

"I'm a psychiatrist."

She shook her head and turned toward the wall. "This is un-*fucking* believable."

I stood there a few moments, staring through the tangle of IV tubing that dripped amphotericin and vancomycin into Lilly's subclavian vein. A window just beyond the hanging bottles looked onto Boston's Charles River at dusk, its waters blue-gray and utterly still. I tried again. "Do you mind if I ask a few questions?"

"You can do whatever you want. I don't care."

I heard a fusion of anger and surrender in her voice. And I sensed something more in the way she half-whispered, half-swallowed the word *care*. A hint of seductiveness. Her tone made me imagine that I could, quite literally, do whatever I wanted to her. I took a mental note of that feeling, wondering whether she provoked it in others—and why. I stepped closer to the bed. "Do you know why your doctors asked me to see you?"

"Probably because they keep screwing up," she complained, shaking her head and exhaling in exasperation. "They can't figure out what's wrong with me, so they're calling me crazy."

That was half right. Her doctors *were* calling her crazy, but they had figured out exactly what was wrong with her—at least, physically.

Drake Slattery, chief of the internal medicine department, had filled me in. He is a lumberjack of a man who wrestled for Duke, and the muscles of his crossed arms had begun to ripple as he spoke. "She presented about four months ago, fresh from her honeymoon on St. Bart's. Mild fever, red blotch on her thigh. I'm figuring some tropical insect took a bite out of her, left her with a little cellulitis. Nothing to write home about. Like an idiot, though, I trash my whole schedule to get her worked up and started on antibiotics right away."

"Is she that pretty?" I had asked.

He looked offended. "Professional courtesy; she's a nurse over at Brigham & Women's."

"Fair enough."

"And she happens to be gorgeous."

I smiled.

"So I dose her up on ampicillin, which seems to work," he said. "But then, two weeks later, she's back in the emergency room. The leg is puffed up twice normal size. She says she feels like someone's jamming a red-hot knife into her thigh. And she's running a fever of 103." His arms started rippling, again. "The ampicillin doesn't seem to cut it anymore, so I add a chaser of Rocephin. And the swelling goes down pretty quickly. All's well that ends well, right? Sometimes you have to go after the bugs with bigger guns."

Slattery was an avid hunter, which made it hard for me to like him, despite his rare combination of genius and dry wit. "You're the shooter," I said.

He winked. "Five days later, she's down in the ER again, bigger and redder than ever. Shaking like a leaf. Fever of 105. Now I'm worried. I don't know what to think. Lymphatic obstruction from a malignancy? Sarcoidosis? I even wondered about some weird presentation of AIDS. I never guessed what was really going on."

Over the next few months, Slattery admitted Lilly to Mass General four times, treating her with a dozen different antifungal and antibiotic agents. Some seemed successful, dropping her white blood cell count and stopping the chills and sweats that plagued her. But, inevitably, she would return to the emergency room within days, infected and feverish again.

A CAT scan of her leg showed no tumor. A bone scan revealed no osteomyelitis. Repeated blood cultures failed to turn up any offending bacterium. So Slattery finally had a surgeon biopsy the semitendinous and biceps femoris muscles of Lilly's leg. He forwarded the tissue samples to the bacteriology laboratory of the National Institute of Infectious Disease in Bethesda, Maryland. The report came in a week later: *Pseudomonas fluorescens*, a pathogen generally found in soil.

"We gave her husband the news first," Slattery had told me. "He broke down and admitted he'd found a frigging syringe caked with mud at the back of one of her drawers. Wrapped in a pair of her panties."

That image turned my skin to gooseflesh.

"Here we are busting our asses trying to keep this mental case from losing her leg," Slattery went on, "and it turns out she's been injecting herself with dirt."

"That might say something about how she sees herself," I said.

"To you, maybe. To me, it says she has no business being in the hospital. She's stealing—my time, not to mention the hospital's resources."

"I'd bet this case is all about stealing. But the key is to figure out what was stolen from *her*."

"You're the poet," Slattery had said wryly. "That's why I called you in."

I looked at Lilly lying in bed, still facing the wall. The technical term for her condition was Munchausen syndrome, intentionally creating physical symptoms in order to get attention from doctors. The name derives from Baron Karl Friedrich von Münchausen, a Paul Bunyan–like storyteller. Research studies have shown that a high percentage of patients with the disorder have, like Lilly, worked in the health care field.

Many patients with Munchausen syndrome were also hospitalized when they were children. One theory is that they faced terrible abuse at home and were so relieved by the kindness shown them by doctors that they came to associate being sick with being safe. As adults they became dependent on using the sick role to numb their underlying emotional pain and keep distressing memories from surfacing—the same way drug addicts use heroin.

To treat Munchausen's, a psychiatrist must coax the patient to confront the original psychological trauma he or she has repressed. If that sounds simple, it isn't. People with Munchausen's will generally flee treatment to avoid any exploration of their underlying problems.

Trying to get Lilly to admit she had caused the infection would just make her shut down. The important thing was to let her know I understood that she *was* infected. Only one of the pathogens lived in dirt. The other—more toxic and invasive—lived in the remote recesses of her unconscious.

I pulled an armchair to the edge of the bed and sat down. "No one doubts that you're ill," I said. "Dr. Slattery least of all. He told me the infection is very severe."

Lilly didn't move.

I decided to tempt her by bending the professional boundary between us, offering her a little of the physicianly warmth she craved. I reached out and touched one of the black lines her surgeon had drawn on her thigh. "Stress affects the immune system. That's a fact."

Still no response.

I moved my hand to Lilly's hip and let it linger. "As a nurse, I would think you'd agree."

She rolled onto her back. If I hadn't moved my hand, it would have traveled to the lowest part of her abdomen. "Look, I'm sorry I jumped down your throat," she said, staring up at the ceiling. "I'm worn out. There's been one doctor in here after another. Medication after medication. I don't think I've been home five days in a row, between admissions." She let out a long breath. "Not exactly an extended honeymoon."

"You're newly married," I said. "I read that in your chart."

"I guess my life's just an open book," she said.

"I would guess you're as far from an open book as they come."

She looked at me.

"How long ago did you marry?" I asked.

"Four months."

"Is it everything you expected?"

She stiffened, maybe because I sounded too remote, too analytic, too much the psychiatrist come to diagnose her.

I offered up another bend in the doctor-patient boundary. "I've never tried the marriage thing myself."

"No?"

"Engaged once. It didn't work out."

"What happened?"

I pictured Kathy the last time I had seen her, in her room on a locked psychiatric unit at Austin Grate Hospital. "She wasn't well," I said. "I tried to be her husband and her doctor. I made a mess of both."

"I'm sorry," she said.

"Me, too."

Lilly relaxed visibly. "Paul's been a dream. He's been so understanding about this whole thing. About everything."

"Everything . . ."

She blushed like a schoolgirl. "We didn't have much time to be, you know . . ."

I shrugged and shook my head, even though I did know.

"Well, time to be"—she giggled—"newlyweds."

"Did you have any time at all?"

"The problem with my leg started right after we left for St. Barth. We ended up flying home early."

"But he understood."

"He's never pressured me," she said. "He's a very patient man. He reminds me of my grandfather that way. I think that's the reason I fell in love with him."

Sometimes a voice speaks at the back of my mind as I

talk with patients. It is my voice, but it comes from a part of me over which I do not have complete control—a part that listens between the lines, even my own lines, then plays back what has gone unspoken. "*Sex, pain, grandfather. When making love feels like being injected with dirt, you cut the honeymoon short and head for the hospital.*"

"Tell me about him," I said, wanting to let her decide which man to talk about.

"Grandpa?"

I just smiled.

"He's quiet and strong. Very religious." She paused. "My father died when I was six. My mother and I moved in with my grandparents."

"Are they still living?"

"Thankfully," she said.

"Do they know about the trouble you're having?"

She shook her head. "I haven't told anyone in my family."

"Not even your mother?"

"No."

I felt as though I had found a path into Lilly's psyche. I could speak of the infection in her leg as a metaphor for her childhood trauma. "Keeping a secret—especially a big one, like this—can add to your level of stress," I said.

"My grandparents are old now. And my mother's got her own problems to worry about. I don't want to burden them."

"But they care about you, and you're in pain."

"I can handle it," she said.

"*After you've lost your father,*" the voice at the back of my mind said, "*you don't risk losing your grandfather, no matter what it costs to keep him close. Even if it costs you your innocence. Or your leg.*"

I kept speaking in metaphor. "It could be a long haul, getting to the bottom of this infection. You might want someone you can open up to. Someone outside your family." I glanced at the skin of her thigh where it stretched, tight and shiny, over the inflamed tissues below. "To release some of the pressure."

"They do the incision and drainage tomorrow afternoon," she said.

"Otherwise the infection has nowhere to go but deeper."

She gazed down at her leg. "I guess it's going to look pretty ugly once they open it up."

"I've seen . . . and heard . . . just about everything," I said.

She studied the leg a few seconds longer, then looked at me.

"If it's okay with you, I'll stop by after the procedure."

She nodded.

"Good." I squeezed her hand, stood up, then headed for the door.

That's what a little victory in psychiatry looks like. You slip into the shadows, dodging the mind's defense mechanisms, glad enough to take a half-step toward the truth. Behind the next word or the next glance may lurk the demon you seek, all in flames, desperate to be held, but set to flee.

As I left Lilly's room I caught the "-venger" part of my name being paged overhead. I stopped at the nurses' station, picked up the phone, and dialed the hospital operator. "Frank Clevenger," I said.

"Outside call, Doctor. Hold on."

There was dead air, then a deep voice said, "Hello?"

Even after two years I recognized North Anderson's baritone. He was a forty-two-year-old police officer from Baltimore, a black man as intimate with the dark city streets as with the veins coursing through his perfectly muscled, weight trainer's body. We had become fast friends working the forensic case I had sworn would be my last. Plumbing the minds of murderers had finally worn my own psyche paper-thin. "It's been too long," I said.

"I would have called sooner, but . . ."

But we reminded each other of carnage. We reminded one another of Trevor Lucas, a plastic surgeon gone mad who had taken over a locked psychiatric unit, performing grisly surgeries, including amputations, on select patients and staff. Before we could convince him to surrender, which only happened after I went onto that locked unit with him, he harvested a grotesque sampling of body parts that still floated through my nightmares. Anderson couldn't be sleeping any better himself. "You don't need to explain," I said.

A few seconds passed. "You'll never guess where I'm working now."

Anderson was as tough and streetwise a cop as I'd ever met. "Gang unit?"

"Not even close."

"Vice Squad," I said.

"Nantucket," he said.

"*Nantucket?*"

"You remember how I like the ocean," he said. "They advertised for a chief of police; I sent in a résumé. Been here sixteen months. I actually sailed *North's Star* up here myself."

North's Star was Anderson's thirty-two-foot Catalina sloop, one of the loves of his life. The only greater ones were his wife, Tina, and his daughter, Kristie.

"I figure I did my time on the front lines, you know?" he said.

I knew. All too well. Anderson had retreated to an island. I had retreated to the halls of Harvard medicine. "You did more than your share," I said.

He cleared his throat. "I could use your help."

His tone made me wonder whether he was battling a depression of his own. "I'll do anything I can. What's up?"

"The Bishop family," he said, as if that would explain everything.

"Who are they?"

"Darwin Bishop."

"Never heard of him," I said.

"The billionaire? Consolidated Minerals & Metals—CMM? It's publicly traded."

"Hey, you may live in that world now, but I don't hang in Nantucket," I said. "And I don't play the market. I always liked the track better."

"They made national news last night," he prompted.

"I try to stay away from the news, too."

Anderson got to the point. "One of his little twin girls was found dead in her crib. Five months old."

I closed my eyes and leaned against the wall. I had worked with other families stricken by SIDS, an unpredictable condition that cuts off breathing in infants, taking them in their sleep. "Sudden infant death syndrome," I said.

"Maybe . . . We're not so sure. There are two older, adopted sons in the family—sixteen and seventeen years old. The younger one has a history of violence. Really ugly stuff, including strangling a few neighborhood cats."

I knew where the discussion was headed. And I knew that Trevor Lucas had left me without the heart to go there. "I don't do forensic work anymore," I said.

"So I hear. The chief back in Baltimore said he tried you once or twice," he said.

"Four times."

"Can't blame him. You have a gift."

"That's one way to look at it," I said.

"I'm not expecting an investigation," he said, "just an evaluation."

"The answer is still no."

"I'll sign a purchase order for whatever you think is fair."

"Christ, North, you know it's not about the money."

"Look," he said, "the D.A. here is leaning on me. He wants the younger brother arrested and charged with murder. He'll try him as an adult and aim for life in prison, no parole."

Few things outrage me more than a judicial system that bends chronology in service to vengeance, and Anderson knew it. I stayed silent.

"He's only sixteen," Anderson went on. "The Bishops adopted him from a Russian orphanage at six. Who knows what kind of hell he went through before that?"

"I've got my work cut out for me right here," I said, half to remind myself.

"I don't want to push you, but there's something that bothers me about this family—especially the way the father laid out a red carpet for me to question his son. You're the best I've . . ."

"I'm trying to stay focused." I was also trying to stay sober, not to mention sane. "Why don't you call Ken Sklar or Bob Caggiano at North Shore Medical Center? They work with Judith David. You know the group. They're world class."

"One interview with the boy," he pressed. "That's all I'm asking."

I didn't want to let Anderson down. But I didn't know how far into darkness I could walk without losing my way forever. "If you want me to call Sklar myself and ask him the favor, I will."

"I want you."

"No," I said, "you want part of me I left behind two years ago, the part Trevor Lucas took." I didn't give him the chance to respond. "Listen, I got to finish up rounds."

"Frank . . ."

"I'll give you a call some time." I laid the receiver back in its cradle.

2

I drove my black Ford F-150 truck out of the Mass General parking garage, took a right onto Storrow Drive, and headed toward the Tobin Bridge to Chelsea and East Boston. I wanted to chase North Anderson and the Bishops out of my thoughts, to keep my distance from death. That used to mean half a bottle of scotch and a gram of cocaine, but I knew I would have to settle for my ritual coffee at Café Positano, an unexpected collage of mahogany, marble, and brass in the middle of a run-down row of storefronts, sandwiched between a discount packie and a variety store.

I pulled up in front of the place, went inside, and stepped up to the espresso bar. Mario Graziani, a broad-shouldered, perpetually tanned, fifty-something-year-old, who wore a tattoo of the Colosseum on his forearm, was bantering in Italian with the bricklayers and bookmakers and judges who were his regulars. Without my asking him to, he steamed my milk to a cottony froth, spooned it over a couple ounces of ink-black espresso, and dusted the top with cinnamon. He slid the mug across the bar. *"Qualcuna ti vuole,"* he said, nodding discreetly over my shoulder.

I had picked up a bit of Italian about five years before, treating an eighty-four-year-old Sicilian man with Alzheimer's disease. His name was Maurizio Riccio, and his cortex was so full of the tangled neurons of dementia that he had become unshakably convinced he was back in Sicily with his teenage sweetheart. This break with reality was distressing to his children, who wanted their father to know for sure that he wasn't nineteen and frolicking in the Mediterranean, that he was slowly wasting away from prostate cancer, in the Cohen, Florence, Levine Assisted Living Center, right in Chelsea. They insisted I prescribe him an antipsychotic like Thorazine. I refused, and they took his case away from me. I held on to what I'd learned of his language—and what I'd learned from him about the agelessness of the human soul.

Qualcuna ti vuole—Someone wants you. I lighted a cigarette, sipped my coffee, then turned slowly and glimpsed Justine Franza sitting alone toward the back of the place, reading a book. She was resting her head on her palm, her elbow on the table, so that her long, golden hair hung to one side, like a curtain. She was a thirty-two-year-old, upper-crust Brazilian photographer touring the United States. I had met her the night before when she'd come in with a few friends. We'd spent twenty minutes talking about the Amazon and Rio de Janeiro and the seaside resort town of Buzios, all of it a pleasant enough cover for what I really had to say. *If I were alone with you on the beach in Rio or in a cliffside cottage in Buzios or down the street in my loft* . . .

"*Molto bella,* no?" Mario purred.

I drank enough of my coffee to be able to walk with the mug, then started toward her table.

"Clevenger!" someone shouted.

I stopped and turned toward the door.

Carl Rossetti, a local defense attorney who looked more like a drug dealer, bounded in. He had straight, jet-black hair to the small of his back, gold bracelets on both wrists, earrings in both ears. He also had one of the sharpest legal minds in or around Boston. "You think you could analyze *me,* doc?" he announced. "Let me tell you: You ain't got that kind of time."

Men and women seated at the tables around me looked up at him. He threw waves and smiles back at them.

I *had* analyzed Rossetti, but he could count on my never telling a soul.

He walked up to me, kept shifting foot-to-foot, as if still on the move. "How about that adopted lunatic on Nantucket?"

My heart sank.

"I guess he's some piece of work. Strangled a couple cats around the island a year or so back. Nearly burned down the Bishop estate. And he's got a history of breaking and entering every place within walking distance." He grinned. "From Russia with love, huh?"

"The way I heard it," I said, "nobody has any idea whether he's involved. They haven't ruled out sudden infant death syndrome."

"C'mon. The kid's got the whole profile. What odds you want to give me he's a bedwetter?"

Rossetti was referring to the triad of bedwetting, fire setting, and cruelty to animals typical of budding psychopaths.

"He's a juvenile," I said. "And he hasn't been charged. Who's leaking his life story?"

"Who else? Harrigan—the D.A. This case is a rocket ship, and he knows it. He could ride the publicity right to the Attorney General's office."

"So I heard."

He put a hand on my shoulder, looked at the floor. "Listen," he whispered, "if I wanted to come in for a tune-up, like . . . You know, no major overhaul. I'm basically good. A couple sessions, maybe. That kind of thing."

"No problem," I said automatically. I was having trouble dragging my mind away from Nantucket.

He dropped his voice even lower. "I don't want to ask any special favors. But I know you been some of the same places I been in life, and I don't want to go there no more, if you get what I'm saying."

"Give me a call. We'll set something up right away." Out of the corner of my eye I noticed Justine watching us.

She noticed me noticing her and went back to reading her book.

Rossetti slapped me on the shoulder, took a couple steps back. "You look friggin' fantastic," he half-shouted. "Still got the bike?"

We'd taken our Harleys to the White Mountains after our last session. I nodded.

"They'll throw mine in the box with me, Doc, 'cause I'm ridin' till the light turns red for good." He pointed at my head, winked. "What about one of them weaves? They're good now. You can hardly tell." He started toward the bar, where Mario, no doubt, was already steaming his milk.

I walked the rest of the way to Justine. She was reading *Angela's Ashes.* "Light reading?" I said.

She lowered the book. "So sad, Frank. What they went through." She pulled out a chair.

I sat down. Her olive skin, full lips, and deep brown eyes steadied me. Something ugly inside me has always retreated in the face of feminine beauty.

"You look tense. What is the matter?" she asked.

"Rough day," I said, and left it at that.

"What? What was rough?"

I'm used to asking the questions. Answering for a change felt uncomfortable and inviting at the same time. I pointed at her book. "People. Their suffering. Knowing what you can do for them, and what you can't."

"Yes," she said. The look in her eyes made me feel she might actually understand. "This has to be very difficult." She drank the last of her coffee. "For me this would be too much."

I motioned to Mario for a refill, took a drag off my cigarette. "Why do you think that?"

"I could not keep myself . . . how do you say? . . . apart from it."

"I've got the same trouble."

Justine used the tip of her finger to steal a bit of the froth off my coffee, licked it away. "But you see patients even knowing this. You don't worry for yourself?"

"Every day."

A few seconds of silence passed. "My day," she said, "was mostly thinking of you."

The last of the tightness in my jaw and neck melted away. I took her hand and felt my pulse slow.

I took her home. My place. A nineteen-hundred-square-foot Chelsea loft with floor-to-ceiling windows looking out on the steel skeleton of the Tobin Bridge as it arches into Boston. The building had been constructed as a factory when the Industrial Revolution transformed Chelsea from farm-land and summer homes to coal yards and textile mills. It had stood through two fires that burned most of the city to the ground, in 1908 and 1973. It had stood as the city welcomed wave upon wave of immigrants—the Irish speaking Gaelic, Russian Jews escaping anti-Semitism, Italians, Poles, Puerto Ricans, Vietnamese, Cambodians, El Salva-dorians, Guatemalans, Serbs.

My view was as raw and beautiful as a heavyweight bout. In the foreground: triple deckers, smokestacks, tug-boats driving full throttle against the massive hulls of oil tankers on the Mystic River. In the distance: the shimmer-ing skyline of Boston's financial district.

Justine, elegant and slim in tight black cigarette pants and a fitted black sleeveless shirt, stood facing one of the windows as I poured her a Merlot and myself a Perrier.

"Cheers," I said, handing her the glass.

She noticed I wasn't joining her. "No wine?"

"I can't drink." I paused. "Actually, I can drink more than anybody I know. I just can't stop."

"Why not?"

"Why not what?"

"Why can't you stop?"

For a moment I thought we were separated by a lan-guage barrier, that she wasn't getting the fact that I was in recovery from alcohol, among other things. But then she looked at me in the same knowing way she had at Café

Positano, and I realized she had intended the question—and wanted the answer. I nodded. "I can't stop because I lose myself in the booze. And I end up never wanting to find myself."

"Right."

"Thanks. I hate being wrong about my own disease. It makes me wonder whether I'm worth my hourly rate."

She laughed. As she moved, her collar gaped open enough for me to glimpse her cleavage and the top of her black lace bra. "No," she said. "I mean, I understand." She sipped her wine.

I still felt the need to explain. "It's like having a headache that finally goes away with a pill. You might have struggled through the pain before, but now you know relief is just a swallow away. So you keep swallowing. And meanwhile, underneath the waves of calm, your life is unraveling."

"I understand. My mother died of this."

I felt like an idiot. "Of alcoholism."

"Yes. They have this even in Brazil."

"I'm sorry. I . . ."

She left me at the window and walked over to the largest of five paintings I had hanging on a brick wall that ran the length of the place. It was a six-by-nine-foot canvas by Bradford Johnson depicting the rescue of the crew of a sailing ship by another vessel. A rope is tied between their masts, high above the raging seas, and a man dangles by his hands as he traverses the fragile connection. "I like this very much," she said.

I walked to her side. "What do you like about it?"

"Taking a risk to help someone." She pointed at the ship that was still in one piece. "That one could have kept sailing."

Her comment made me think again of the sixteen-year-old Bishop boy, probably headed for trial as an adult, facing life in prison. Would the system stop long enough to listen to him? Then I thought what it would be like to hear about the animals he had tortured, about *his* torture in Russia, about Darwin Bishop finding one of his baby girls dead in her crib. I thought about having to feel all the jealousy and fear and anger coursing through the family, in order to understand whether it could have added up to murder. "What if both ships end up sinking?" I half-joked.

"Then taking the risk was even more beautiful," she said.

In my heart I agreed. But coming close to drowning in the undertow of Trevor Lucas's terror had left me with deep respect for solid ground. I pushed the Bishops out of my mind and reached for Justine, using her beauty to anchor me in the moment. My hand found the soft curve of her arm, just above the elbow, then moved down her rib cage, not stopping until my fingers were curled under the waistband of her pants.

She touched her lips to mine, then leaned back. "Perhaps we should not start," she said. "I am in this country only one more day."

I have seen lives saved and others destroyed in less time. I tightened my grip and pulled her to me.

I took her to bed, a king-sized Italian creation with chrome legs and a gray flannel, upholstered headboard, all done up with pearl gray linens. She sat at the edge and lifted her arms so I could help her with her top, but I gently pushed her onto her back, moved my hands to her ankles, and pulled off her pants. The scantiest black lace thong covered her. A vertical fold in the cloth was enough to make me lightheaded.

Five or so years back, my own psychiatrist, Dr. James, then eighty-one and still razor-sharp, had challenged me to consider whether my sex life was actually driven by addiction. He was a Freudian analyst and a Talmudic scholar, and I am eternally in his debt for partly filling the holes left in my personality after it developed without a real father.

"How would I know if I'm addicted?" I had asked.

"Are you seeking the woman or the act?" he said. "Do you want her soul or her body?"

"Both," I said immediately.

"For what purpose? To what end?"

"To feel love."

"You can fall in love in a day?"

I thought about that. "In an hour."

"Again and again?" he said.

"Dozens of times. A hundred times."

"You believe these women seek this also? This union? What you call love?"

"I do."

"And you believe this is Nature's design?" he asked.

"Yes."

He took a deep breath and let it out slowly. Then he sat there looking at me, without speaking.

The quiet began to weigh on me. "What do you think?" I surrendered. "Do I add sexual addiction to my list of diagnoses?"

"I'm afraid not," he said. "The case is worse."

"How so?"

"You have a touch of the truth." He smiled, but only for an instant. "God help you."

Tonight my truth was Justine. In a world of artificial intelligence, transplanted organs, and cloned sheep, I knew it was my heart pounding in my chest as I looked at her, my lungs working like a bellows, my blood feeding my excitement. I reached and pulled the cloth triangle up between her lips, watched the cloth dampen, listened to her groan as my fingers moved inside her panties, then inside her. I knelt in front of her and traced her smooth lips with my tongue, moving her thong first this way, then that, teasing. When I could feel her muscles starting to tense for complete release, I stopped and stood up. I pulled her thong off. Then, never taking my eyes off her, I freed myself, lifted her knees, and spread them apart. I moved inside her, reveling in the way her flesh resisted then yielded to my thrusts, resisting less and less each time. And then I yielded,

abandoning control, moving now as one with Justine, as
Nature dictated, with no more thought of it than waves
rolling onto a beach, soaking into soft, moist sands.

Sunday, June 23, 2002

My eyes snapped open, flicked to the bedside clock—7:20
A.M. I had the feeling we were not alone. I dropped my
hand to the Browning Baby semiautomatic I keep between
my bed frame and mattress, a vestige of my days tracking
killers. I lay still. I had almost convinced myself I could
hear the intruder's footsteps when the lobby buzzer
sounded two insistent blasts, vaguely reminding me that I
had heard the same sound in my sleep. I realized I had
probably been awakened by something closer to a Federal
Express delivery than an attempt on my life.

"Make them go away," Justine said, still half-asleep.

I got up and headed to the door. I pressed the SPEAK
button on the intercom panel. "If it's a package and it isn't
ticking, leave it," I said. I hit LISTEN.

"It's North."

I squinted at the intercom. I thought I had gotten more
distance on my past. I should have known better. Anything
you run from turns up in front of you, usually sooner rather
than later.

"Frank?"

"I'll be right down," I said.

"Who is it?" Justine asked.

"An old friend," I said, getting into my blue jeans and
black turtleneck.

She sat up, gathering the comforter around her. "So
early?"

I slipped on my boots. "He needs some advice."

She swung her legs to the side of the bed and got up.
She was naked. She reached for her clothes where I had
left them, draped over a leather armchair.

I stood there watching her.

"What?" she asked, noticing my stare. She pulled on her pants, nothing underneath.

"You're magnificent."

"Your friend's waiting," she said, feigning irritation. She put on her top, glanced at me. "Do you have food? Eggs, bacon? I could make breakfast."

"Pop-Tarts, if there are any left." I wanted her to stay. "There's a 7-Eleven up the street. I'll be back with everything in thirty minutes."

"No. I'll go. That way everything will be ready when you're finished with your friend."

"Perfect."

We took the elevator to the lobby and walked outside.

North Anderson stood on the sidewalk in front of the building, in black jeans and a black T-shirt. He looked pretty much the way he had two years before. His shoulders, chest, and arms were still overbuilt from working out. He still had the habit of planting his feet far apart and clasping his hands behind his back, as if his wrists were cuffed. The only change in him was a three-inch, jagged pink scar over his right eye. On a white man, the wound would have been less noticeable. Against Anderson's black skin it was arresting.

"Jealous husband?" I asked, running a finger along my own brow.

He acknowledged Justine with a nod, then looked back at me. "My life's not that interesting. Run-of-the-mill car thief. Just before I left Baltimore."

"Some souvenir." I extended my hand. He shook it. Then we pulled one another close, holding on long enough to respect what we'd been through together. "This is Justine," I said, as we broke.

"My pleasure," he said.

"And mine," Justine said. She navigated the moment effortlessly. "I'm off to the store. Will I see you later?" she asked him.

"Probably not this visit," Anderson said.

"Next time, then." She smiled and walked away.

He glanced after her. "I should have guessed I wouldn't find you alone. Some things don't change."

"You want to grab coffee?" I said. "There's a place not too far."

"Let's just walk."

We started down Winnisimmet, toward the Fitzgerald Shipyard, a stretch of asphalt and seaworthy docks where Peter Fitzgerald worked magic on injured ferries and Coast Guard cutters. I noticed that the limp Anderson struggled with, the result of taking two bullets from would-be bank robbers several years before, was more pronounced than I remembered. There was a new outward arc to the swing of his right leg. That quirk, combined with his new scar, made me glad he'd left Baltimore before dissolving completely into its streets.

We sat on a stack of lumber at the water's edge. A lone barge made its way toward Boston Harbor, carrying a mountain of silt from a dredging operation downstream. "How are Tina and Kristie?" I asked.

"Great," he said, without much conviction. "The island's good for a family, you know? Different than the city."

"Night and day," I said.

"We're in a little place in Siasconset, right near the beach. Sunsets. Clean air."

"Nothing better."

He smiled, but tightly. "She's pregnant again. Tina is."

I kept watching his face. "Congratulations. How far along is she?"

"Six months."

"Boy or a girl?" I asked. "Or don't you know?"

"A boy," he said. His eyes narrowed, as if he was trying to see his future through the mist.

Anderson was both brave and sensitive, and I liked thinking of him fathering a son. But I couldn't tell how much *he* liked the idea. "How do you feel about it?" I asked.

He focused on me. "Feel about what? What do you mean?"

"I mean, about having a child. Are you happy?"

"Of course." He shrugged. The tight smile reappeared. "How could I not be happy about it?"

"*A whole bunch of ways*," the voice at the back of my head whispered.

"People feel all kinds of things about having kids," I said.

He shook his head, looked out across the water. "I didn't fly here to lie on your couch, Frank. Do you ever turn it off?"

I never do, which has cost me more than one friend and countless dinner invitations. At some point during my training in psychiatry, I lost the ability to stay on the surface of things. I became a relentless burrower—so much so that even after Anderson's plea to let his unconscious off the hook, I was wondering whether ambivalence about his unborn child was driving his interest in the death of the Bishop baby. "Sorry," was all I said.

He turned to face me. "I didn't mean that the way it came out. I'm running on empty. I was up all night."

"No apology required."

"So how about you? Mass General's the end of the line. Impressive stuff."

"You definitely didn't fly here to flatter me about my job."

He leaned a little into my space. "Look, I heard everything you told me on the phone yesterday. Believe me, I still get nightmares from that case myself. I can still see—"

"—Then you're still human," I interrupted, not needing a recap of the carnage.

"And I don't blame you one bit for not wanting to get involved this time."

"Good. Because I'm not planning to."

"Can I tell you what's bothering me?" he said.

"Didn't you just say you wanted nothing to do with my couch?"

Anderson didn't break stride. "Like I said on the phone,

with all his millions, Darwin Bishop pretty much invited me to question his son. Right in the house. No attorney present. No nothing. He could have pulled a Ramsey, tied the department in knots for months until we proved probable cause." He shook his head. "The kid wouldn't talk, but even so . . ."

"Maybe he's got no reason to get in your way. Maybe his little girl died of SIDS, after all."

"But she didn't."

"You know that for a fact," I said.

"We got the autopsy results late last night," Anderson said. "Brooke Bishop died of asphyxiation due to airway obstruction." He dropped his voice, maybe to take the edge off his words. "Her nasal passages and trachea were filled with plastic sealant, like you'd use to caulk up a window."

My stomach fell. I tried not to think of little Brooke's last minutes of life, but unwelcome images and feelings crashed through my resistance. I imagined her watching the person approaching her, maybe even smiling expectantly, cooing, then opening her eyes wider with curiosity at the white tube of caulk. I felt her laugh as the plastic tip tickled the rim of one nostril, then fall silent and begin to squirm as the tip moved deeper inside. I felt her begin to gag and strain, mouth open, lungs sealed. Cut off. Did she, I wondered, wish some last, infantile wish to be held? Did her mind flee to a memory of her mother's face or smell or touch?

"*Frank?*" Anderson said.

I focused on him again. "I'm listening," I said.

"Like I was saying," he went on, "if I'm Darwin Bishop, loaded to the gills, I get Billy the best lawyer money can—"

"Billy?" I broke in.

"They obviously renamed the kid when they brought him over from Russia," Anderson said. "American as apple pie, huh?"

I had lost one patient to suicide in my seventeen years as a psychiatrist. He was a depressed teenager named Billy

Fisk. I had never stopped feeling responsible for his death. "Right," I said.

"Right?"

I closed my eyes, remembering Fisk.

"There are no coincidences," the voice at the back of my mind prodded me. *"Take it as a sign."*

"You still with me?" Anderson said.

I looked at him. "What else do you know about the family?"

Anderson relaxed visibly and let out a sigh.

"I'm just asking a question," I said. "I'm not signing onto the case."

He held up a hand. "Of course not." His tone said he thought otherwise. "It turns out Darwin Bishop grew up in Brooklyn," he said, "even though you'd never know it from his voice or the way he carries himself. He's all Park Avenue and Nantucket now. Fifty-one years old. His wife Julia is a former model. It's his second marriage."

"Much younger?" I said.

"Mid-thirties," Anderson said.

"How's she bearing up?"

"What would you expect?"

"I don't. Ever," I said. "That way I'm never surprised."

"She's a basket case," Anderson said. "She hardly leaves the twins' bedroom."

"And the older adopted son? The seventeen-year-old. What's he like?"

Anderson shrugged. "I only got about ten minutes with him. His name is Garret. Bishop adopted him a year before his divorce. He's a golden boy. Good-looking. Straight A's at Andover Academy. Varsity tennis and lacrosse. Headed for Yale in the fall. You know the pedigree."

"Did you learn anything from him?" I asked.

"I'd say he's in shock," Anderson said. "He kept holding his head in his hands, saying, 'I can't believe this is happening.' He was worried about his mother, mostly—whether she'd hold up. She's got a history of depression."

"Why did Bishop adopt the two boys in the first place?" I asked.

"I don't know. I was focused on the kids themselves."

I nodded. "So there's Garret, then Billy, then Brooke and . . . what's the surviving twin's name?"

"Tess."

"Garret, Billy, Brooke, and Tess."

"Right."

"Was anybody else in the house the night before they found Brooke dead?" I asked.

"A nanny. Claire Buckley. She summers on the island with the family. Takes care of the kids, gets a place to stay, half her nights and weekends free—that type of thing."

"Young and pretty," I said. "Sticks close to the wife."

"You got it."

"Any guests that evening?"

"No," Anderson said.

I looked out over the water, its surface speckled with white, electric jewels of light. "So why do you figure Mr. Bishop flung the door wide open for you?"

"I don't know. Like I said, that's what bothers me."

"It was before the autopsy results," I said.

"Still . . ." Anderson said.

"Maybe he's burnt out," I said. "He's gone to bat for Billy over his firesetting, his cruelty to animals—now this. Maybe he finally gets the picture that Billy's a dangerous kid."

"Could be."

"Or it could be something else."

"Like . . ." he said.

"Like maybe he'd rather have Billy take the fall than somebody else," I said. "Like his golden boy. Or his wife. Or himself."

"Also possible," Anderson said. He paused. "If I had a psychiatrist working with me, I might actually be able to find out which answer is the right one."

I took a deep breath, let it out.

"I really need you on this," Anderson said. "My gut tells

me Billy Bishop isn't guilty. And if I'm right, that's only half the problem. Because then I've got to find out who is. There's another baby girl in that house."

Anderson was right to worry about Tess. In the dozen or so recorded cases of infanticide in families with twins, the surviving baby eventually dies mysteriously over seventy percent of the time, usually due to sudden heart or respiratory failure. Some researchers have theorized that the jarring loss of one twin spawns a toxic grief reaction in the other that mysteriously shuts down cardiac conduction or short-circuits the respiratory drive. An immeasurable connection of souls has been abruptly severed, sapping the will to live. But the most convincing explanation is that the killer has simply been given time and opportunity to claim another victim—probably by suffocation—either because the wrong person was arrested or because lack of evidence precluded any arrest.

I looked up at the sky. For some reason I pictured my father in a drunken rage, ready to mete out one of the beatings that were my childhood. I thought how nice it would be to keep myself safe, for a change. I thought how no one could blame me if I did. Because I already had wounds crisscrossing my psyche like a map to hell. And some of them had never stopped bleeding.

"*No one could blame you,*" the voice whispered, "*except yourself.*"

Justine had breakfast nearly ready when I got back to the loft. Omelets and bacon sizzled on the stove. Still-warm bagels from Katz's, a sixty-five-year-old shop just beyond the 7-Eleven, were sliced and spread with cream cheese. A deep red, sparkly liquid filled the blender.

"Strawberries, ice, and sugar," she said, without my asking.

"Everything looks wonderful," I said.

"So you will leave this minute or later today?" She flipped an omelet.

I wasn't expecting the question and didn't answer.

She glanced at me. "I know you have to go. I could see it in your friend's face."

"I told him I'd meet him at the airport in four hours. He's got a tough case on Nantucket. A little girl was murdered."

"Oh, God," she said. "How old?"

"Five months."

She looked at me in that searching way people sometimes do when confronted by man's limitless capacity for cruelty.

"They're saying her adopted brother did it," was all I could think to say. "He's not well."

She shook her head. Without another word she turned off the burners, arranged our food on plates, and poured the strawberry concoction into two glasses. We sat on stools at the granite center island, eating in silence. "You can visit me in Rio or Buzios," she said finally.

"Buzios," I said. "As soon as I can get there." I meant it.

She took another bite, pushed her plate away. "This is a waste of time," she said.

I figured she was upset about my abrupt departure. I expected a scene.

She shrugged. "I don't even like eggs." She peeled off her shirt, tossed it on the floor, and walked over to the bed.

I followed. I could not have predicted how close to losing everything the Bishop case would bring me, but I must have sensed it. Because as my eyes and hands and mouth traveled over Justine, I felt more than passion. I felt the need to tap her spirit, to somehow use her aliveness to inoculate myself against death.

3

Anderson and I took the forty-five-minute Cape Air flight out of Logan at 1:15 P.M. The nine-seat, single-pilot Cessna bounced a little in the wind, but gave us no big trouble and a pretty view of the sapphire-blue Atlantic on approach. We came in low enough to glimpse the surfers at Cisco Beach and got an eyeful of the island's sprawling, gray-shingled estates.

Nantucket, nicknamed the "Gray Lady," is actually three islands shaped like a fat boomerang, with a couple spits of land broken off one end. Legend attributes its formation to ashes which floated out of the pipe of the Indian giant Moshup, mythic guardian of the natives living on Cape Cod. But if Moshup was charged with protecting his creation and his people, he failed. During the 1700s, Quaker settlers from Massachusetts prevailed upon the kindly Wampanoag Indians to teach them how to fish Nantucket's waters, hunt its fowl, and farm its soil. In turn, the settlers taught the Indians just enough reading, writing, and arithmetic to sell their land. The Indians learned so well and conveyed so many tracts that their livestock had nowhere left to graze. That loss, together with mainland imports of whiskey and tuberculosis, left Abraham Quary as the last male Nantucket Indian, when he died in 1854.

Whaling was the life blood of Nantucket through the 1800s. Herman Melville used the tragic voyage of Nantucket captain George Pollard, whose ship was rammed by a whale in 1820, as the basis for his masterpiece novel *Moby-Dick*. Though perilous, whaling was well suited to the Quaker work ethic—and very profitable. Money poured into the island, fueling a building boom that stripped most of its trees, but lined Main Street with mansions, one of the later and most prominent of them being Jared Coffin's three-story home of English brick and Welsh slate.

In every chapter of its modern history, commerce has driven Nantucket's growth while exacting bigger chunks of its soul. So it should have come as no surprise when the decline of the whaling industry, accelerated by the fleet's heavy losses during the Civil War, was followed by the ultimate devil's bargain: the growth of tourism. The island slowly evolved into a playground of leisure, wealth, and reverie—enough to make any Quaker blanch. Captain George Pollard's home became the Seven Seas Gift Shop. Jared Coffin's mansion was turned into an inn filled with Colonial-style reproduction furnishings.

The working soul of Nantucket, the part that churned with native instinct and courage at sea, was buried under so much glitter as to be, for all intents and purposes, dead as the last Wampanoag.

On the flight over, North Anderson had told me that Darwin Bishop purchased his Nantucket estate in 1999, just after the IPO of Consolidated Minerals and Metals netted him $1.2 billion. With that kind of windfall, $9.6 million for an eighteen-room spread on about five acres off Wauwinet Road, with views to the ocean and the harbor, must have seemed like petty cash.

CMM mined iron and copper from rich reserves in Russia's Ukraine. Even with the political instability in that region, the company continued to net massive profits exporting ore to other European nations, Asia, and the United States. Consolidated had hinted at expansion into oil and natural gas, which would propel profits into the stratosphere.

"Does he know we're coming?" I asked Anderson as we took the turn onto Wauwinet.

"If he didn't, we wouldn't make it to the door," Anderson said. He motioned toward a pristine little cottage by the side of the road, with a slate roof, white shutters, and window boxes overflowing with flowers and vines. "He calls that his 'watch house.' "

I noticed two white Range Rovers with smoked windows parked next to the cottage. "Why does he need someone to watch over him?" I asked.

"About a billion reasons, I'd guess," Anderson said.

The house looked very much like the clubhouse of a country club, with two dozen canopied windows running along its curved facade. The exterior had weathered to the gray-brown of well-oiled leather. Off to the right of the driveway stretched a pool of Olympic proportions, surrounded by twenty yards of mahogany decking. A grove of green cloth umbrellas sheltered a half-dozen white tables at poolside. Just beyond them, nearer the ocean, I saw a man and a boy playing tennis on a clay court, running hard and raising clouds of dust.

I nodded at the court. "Who are they?" I asked.

Anderson squinted at the players. "Garret, the older son," he said. "I don't know the other guy."

"Garret's not in shock anymore," I said.

"The games must go on," Anderson quipped.

We parked and started toward the house. When we were still several feet from the front door, it opened. An attractive woman, about twenty-five, with a velvet complexion and long brown hair pulled into a ponytail, stood in the doorway. She was wearing a pained expression and a short linen dress that hugged her everywhere it should, showing off a Victoria's Secret figure. Her chestnut eyes were bloodshot, as if she'd been up all night.

"Captain Anderson," she said. Her voice was surprisingly warm.

"Good afternoon, Claire," North said. "How are you holding up?"

She shrugged.

"This is Dr. Frank Clevenger, from Boston. I called Mr. Bishop earlier about bringing him by."

"Of course." She extended her hand. "Doctor," she said, summoning an especially cordial tone, "I'm Claire Buckley."

I reached out and shook her hand. Her skin was as soft as a child's. I noticed she wore a channel-set diamond pinkie ring and a Cartier love bracelet, the bangle style with screw heads around it. The bracelet alone runs almost four grand. I knew because I'd bought one for Kathy before she got sick and our lives went bad. Claire Buckley was very well paid, for a nanny. "I'm sorry to hear what happened," I said.

She nodded, stepped aside. "Come in."

The interior of the house was impressive, in an intentional way. The ceilings were twelve feet high, with smooth, whitewashed beams. The furniture was perfectly arranged, overstuffed and covered in woven fabrics that wouldn't last a single summer of careless living. The walls were hung with oil paintings of beaches and ships and whaling scenes, most of them American, a few of them French, all of them very valuable. Walking through the great room, I noticed one canvas by Robert Salmon and another by Maurice Prendergast, each of them worth millions, and each forever fixing in time a moment of Nature's magnificence. What ruined them for me were the showy brass plaques affixed to the frames and engraved with the artists' names.

"It's like a museum," North said under his breath.

Claire Buckley brought us to the door of Darwin Bishop's study. He was seated in a high-back, tufted leather chair, in front of a long, Mission-style desk, staring out French doors that looked toward the pool, tennis court, and ocean. He wore a crisp white button-down and pleated khakis. "I don't have a preference whether you haul them to Palm Beach or Myopia," he was saying, in a regal voice that left no hint of his roots in Brooklyn. "Keep them stabled right there in Greenwich, if you like. Packer can play them at White Birch. I'm obviously out of commission for now." He noticed us and motioned for us to come in.

We hesitated at the door.

"Go ahead," Claire said. "He'll be right with you." She turned and walked away.

We took seats on a couch to one side of the room, opposite two armchairs.

Bishop swiveled in his chair and watched us while he finished his call. He was a striking man. His hair was silver and swept straight back, revealing a prominent brow that sheltered eyes the gray-blue of steel. His skin was perfectly bronzed. I could see from his wide shoulders, muscular forearms, and thick wrists that he was still, at fifty-four, physically powerful.

I took in the rest of the room. An Oriental carpet of subtle green, rose, and beige hues covered the floor. Recessed shelving, painted high-gloss white, ran along two walls, each shelf lined with leatherbound volumes that looked as though they had never been opened. A round table of burled walnut, with claw feet, held a dozen or more silver-framed family photographs. One showed Bishop and two boys racing a sleek sailboat. Another showed Bishop in black tie, arm-in-arm with a radiantly beautiful, younger woman with black hair who I took to be his wife Julia. In a third photograph Bishop was decked out in jodhpurs and riding boots, astride a sinewy horse, pointing a polo mallet toward the horizon.

Bishop had obviously been discussing where to stable his polo ponies on the phone moments before. The Palm Beach Polo Club and Myopia Hunt Club were hubs of the sport. Gary Packer, partner of legendary media mogul Rupert Murdoch, was one of its patron saints.

I noted that none of the photos on the table was of Bishop's baby girls.

"I appreciate that, Pedro," Bishop said, finishing up. "We'll get through it." He hung up, stood, and walked over to us. He looked even more imposing on his feet than he had seated at the desk. He had to be six foot two, maybe six three. "Sorry to keep you waiting," he said. "Win Bishop," he said, extending his hand. "You would be Dr. Clevenger."

We shook hands, if you can call it that. He put nothing into his grip, as if he were a Lord offering the rare chance to touch him.

"I'm sorry for your loss," I said.

He took one of the armchairs across from Anderson and me. "We'll get through it," he said again.

A few uncomfortable moments passed, with Bishop looking straight at us, showing no sign that he would speak another word, his expression that of a hitter waiting for a pitch to cross the plate. It occurred to me that Win Bishop had grown very comfortable wielding power over people.

"It's probably best I leave Dr. Clevenger here to interview . . ." Anderson started.

Bishop held up a hand. "An apology. With all the planning it took to make it happen, I neglected to bring you up to speed: Billy is no longer here."

"Not here?" Anderson said. "Where is he?"

"I arranged for his admission to the Payne Whitney psychiatric unit, in Manhattan," Bishop said. He looked at me. "They tell me it's a well-regarded place. Part of Cornell."

"It is," I said. "What was your hope in admitting him there?"

Before Bishop could answer, a baby's shrill cry—presumably that of his surviving twin girl, Tess—drifted into the room.

Bishop grimaced.

"Coming, sweetheart," Claire Buckley called out, from somewhere not too far away. I heard her footsteps on the staircase as she headed up.

Bishop stood, strode over to the door, and closed it. Then he sat opposite us again, crossing his legs. He was wearing no socks, and I couldn't help staring at his ankle, decorated with a crudely tattooed green-black peace sign. "Vietnam," he said, answering the question that must have been showing on my face. He didn't give me any time for a follow-up. "Let me be clear about Billy," he said. "My wife and I feel we have done everything possible to salvage a very damaged young man. After Officer Anderson informed me of the autopsy results, I had to face reality. Billy can never live with us again. I have to keep my family safe. I have another infant to think about."

"I understand," I said.

Anderson leaned forward in his seat. "The D.A. will see the admission to Payne Whitney as a strategy to avoid your son's arrest."

"The state can order Billy back to Massachusetts to stand trial, if it wishes to do so," Bishop responded.

"Unless I'm misreading something," Anderson said, "that's exactly what will happen. A court order for his extradition can be issued within hours."

Bishop nodded. "I can't control that," he said. "It would be a waste of resources, however. The D.A. will never prove Billy is responsible for his sister's death. There were five people at home the night my daughter was murdered. Any one of us could be the killer." He paused. "And none of us will be testifying."

So much for Darwin Bishop's open-door policy. I glanced at Anderson.

"I hope you'll cooperate with my officers searching the house later today," Anderson said. "We'll need to look for anything that could be relevant to your daughter's death."

"Any time you like," Bishop answered. "I assure you, you'll find nothing."

"The tube of plastic sealant, for instance," Anderson pushed.

"My guess on that," Bishop responded, "is that your crime lab will find that everyone in the house has touched it at one time or another."

"By chance, or design?" Anderson said.

Bishop didn't answer.

I didn't want the meeting to degenerate into confrontation. "What would you like to see happen to Billy?" I asked Bishop.

"It isn't about what I'd *like to see*. As his father, I'll *see to it* that he remains at Payne Whitney—or an equivalent facility—until at least his eighteenth birthday. Thereafter, I can create a very structured and safe environment for him in the community."

I thought back to the "watch house" on the road leading to the Bishop estate. "House arrest?" I asked, taking the edge off the words with a half-smile.

"If that's what it takes," Bishop said. "But not this house."

It suddenly registered fully with me that I was sitting with a man who had lost his infant daughter to murder. I wasn't seeing much in the way of rage—or grief. "You still want to be supportive of Billy," I led.

"Certainly."

"Even after hearing the autopsy results," I said.

Bishop didn't hesitate. "Billy isn't evil," he said. "He's ill. And he has good reason to be ill. He's a victim himself."

That vision fit with everything I believe about violent people. Yet Bishop's evenhandedness, in the wake of his daughter's death, bothered me. He seemed detached rather than empathetic. "Do you mind if I ask a few questions about Billy?" I asked.

"Not at all," Bishop said.

"You mentioned Billy was damaged when you adopted him. In what way?"

"I don't know how much Captain Anderson has shared with you," Bishop said.

"I like to hear things myself," I said.

"Very well. We adopted Billy from an orphanage in Moscow at age six. That was ten years ago. He had a history of severe psychological trauma."

"What had happened to him?" I asked.

"His parents were murdered," Bishop said flatly.

"How?" North asked.

"Each of them was shot once in the head, execution

style. Billy was found with their corpses, in the family's apartment."

"Was the case solved?" North asked.

"I'm not sure it was ever investigated," Bishop answered. "We're talking about a time of tremendous upheaval over there—government corruption, organized crime influence. The police were busier collecting protection money from business owners than protecting the good citizens of Moscow." He cleared his throat. "I'm certain the orphanage only added insult to injury. When Billy first arrived in the States, he was badly bruised and malnourished. He weighed thirty-four pounds."

"And emotionally?" I asked.

"Seemingly a very gentle, fragile child. Terrified of loud noises, new places, new people. Even me. The biggest problem he had was with nightmares. He would wake up hysterical. His sleep has never really stabilized." Bishop laced his fingers together. "Some of that might be due to a problem he's had with bedwetting."

I thought back to Carl Rossetti's wager, at Café Positano in East Boston, that Billy would turn out to have the full triad of risk factors for psychopathy—cruelty to animals, firesetting, and bedwetting. "How did he do over time?" I asked.

"His fear certainly receded," Bishop said. "Unfortunately, in its place came aggression. He would strike out at me and his mother, unpredictably. We wondered for a time whether he was angry with us for bringing him to this country—or for trying to replace his natural parents. But his destructiveness was never exclusively focused on Julia and me. It attached itself to almost anything: property, animals, even himself."

"Cutting himself?" I asked.

"Yes. And he would bite himself," Bishop said. "He also had a rather nasty habit of pulling out his hair. The self-abuse stopped; the violence toward others never did."

"Has Billy been treated by a psychiatrist?" I asked.

"More than a few. He's been admitted to half a dozen

psychiatric units, starting with the first problems he had hurting neighborhood pets at age nine."

"And has he had a steady psychiatrist outside the hospital?"

Bishop shook his head. "The Department of Youth Services tried to make outpatient care a condition of Billy's release on several occasions. He would comply with the letter of the law—ten sessions, fifteen, whatever it took to get out and stay out of detention centers. Then he'd utterly refuse to go to the clinics. If we forced him, he would sit in silence the entire hour. There was a brief trial on Prozac after he tried to set fire to the house. But, if anything, the medication seemed to make him more impulsive."

I studied Bishop a few moments. He looked as staged as his surroundings. Elegant and unflappable. Maybe a little confrontation, I thought, wouldn't be such a bad idea, after all. It might wring a little emotion out of him. Guilt. Anger. Anything. "Why did you make the mistake of adopting Billy in the first place? Foreign adoptions are notorious for trouble, even without a catastrophic personal history like his."

He didn't take issue with the word *mistake*. "I had had a very positive experience with my first adoption, of Garret. I was building a company in Russia, having extraordinary success," he said. "I wanted to give something back. I'm sure I underestimated the emotional hurdles in Billy's way."

I noticed that Bishop spoke of the adoptions as if he had undertaken them alone. "The adoptions were both your idea," I ventured.

"Yes," he said. "I like the idea of leveling the playing field for people with odds stacked heavily against them. Especially young people. Especially children."

"And how did your wife Julia feel about Billy joining the family?" I asked.

"She was supportive," he said.

"Sounds like a long way from ecstatic," I pressed.

Bishop's hands remained folded on his lap. His voice

stayed steady. "I've asked a great deal of Julia," he said. "She welcomed my son Garret into our household from the day we were married. Integrating another child after seven years was no small challenge—especially a boy with Billy's past."

"Your ex-wife didn't win custody of Garret," I said.

"She didn't sue for custody," he said.

"Why?" I asked.

"It's a complicated story. Nothing worth going into right now."

His tone of voice told me the topic was off limits. I took a mental note of his discomfort and pushed in another direction. "Who found your daughter after . . . the crime?" I asked.

"I did," he said, without hesitation and without emotion.

"When?"

"Friday, a little before four A.M."

"You just happened to be awake at four in the morning?" Anderson asked.

"I was reviewing financial data prior to the opening of the markets in the Far East," Bishop said.

"Did you follow the markets yesterday, as well?" I asked.

"Yes," he said.

I took a more direct shot at piercing his armor. "How is it that you were able to conduct business," I said, "after finding your daughter the way you did?"

Bishop's eyes locked on mine. He didn't respond.

Anderson looked at me with an expression that telegraphed he thought I had gone too far.

I worried he was right, that I had pushed the needle into Bishop's soul and pierced something that would bleed uncontrollably. But when he finally spoke it was with the same cool certainty he had displayed throughout our meeting. "If I could pay a ransom to bring my daughter back," he said, "I would happily surrender every dollar I have. But that isn't possible. And I've worked very hard for my money. I intend to keep it." He smiled a fake smile and checked his watch. "Gentlemen," he said, "we're out of time. I promised Julia an early dinner."

"Would it be possible for Dr. Clevenger to interview Billy in New York?" Anderson asked.

Bishop's face remained a mask of affability. "To what end?" he asked.

"I could be helpful to your son if he's ultimately charged with murder," I said. "There may be issues of diminished capacity."

Diminished capacity is a legal doctrine that allows judges and juries to be more lenient with defendants who are sane at the time of their offenses, but still significantly mentally disturbed. Such defendants are sometimes convicted of lesser crimes—manslaughter or second-degree murder, for example, rather than first-degree murder.

"I can see how that might be of value," Bishop said. "I'll make the arrangements." He stood up. "Is there anything else I can help with?"

"Not just now," Anderson said.

We got to our feet and started out of the office. A grouping of three oil paintings mounted just inside the door caught my eye. They were portraits of three polo ponies, dressed with fancy saddles and stirrups, ankles wrapped in bright purple bindings. I stopped in front of them. I wanted to see how easily Bishop could shift from a discussion of his daughter's murder to a topic of infinitely less gravity. "Yours?" I asked him.

The transition seemed effortless for him. "Yes," he said, with real pride. "They're all mine." It was the most emotion he had shown. "I keep a string of twelve."

"Beautiful animals," Anderson said.

"They are," Bishop said.

"I've never played the game myself," I said. "I've always had it in mind to learn."

"I hope you'll be my guest, someday," Bishop said. "Perhaps Myopia. It's so close to Boston." His tone told me I shouldn't hold my breath for an invitation.

"I'd like that." I looked back at the portraits. "Are these

your favorites? Of your string of twelve, I mean."

"Not really. They happened to be available for the artist."

"You haven't fallen in love with any one as opposed to another?"

Bishop smirked. "I feel the same way about each of them."

"Is it like loving a pet?" I asked. "A dog or a cat?"

"No," he said. "It's more like loving a tennis racket or a golf club."

"I'm not sure I follow," I said.

"You love them," he said, "as much as they help you win."

Claire Buckley showed us out. As we walked into the driveway, Garret Bishop and his mother happened to be walking toward the house from the tennis courts. We slowed so I could meet them.

The older Bishop boy, in white shorts and a white T-shirt, was already, at seventeen, close to six feet tall and broadly built, like his father. But where his father's gait was certain and aggressive, leading with his right shoulder like a running back, his son's was more tentative—shoulders turned inward, a slight bend in each knee, a momentary shuffle with each step.

Julia Bishop, wearing a black pareo and white T-shirt, was a little shorter and slighter than I would have guessed from her photograph in the study. She was walking with her head hung.

From twenty yards away, mother and son looked like a college-aged couple fresh from a tennis tournament. But as they came closer, it became clear that Julia looked her age—mid-thirties—and that she was taking the loss of her daughter hard. Her cheeks were a bit puffy and her throat was blotchy in places, suggesting she had been crying a long time. And yet, her beauty was undeniable, a spotlight burning through fog. I noticed her emerald eyes first, a deep green made more remarkable by a frame of silky black hair cut shoulder-length—the hair of a geisha. Then my gaze traveled to her high cheekbones and full lips, the slender neck that blended gracefulness and raw sexuality into something more potent than the simple sum of the two, something magnetic and irrepressible, created by their fusion.

I couldn't take my eyes off her. They cheated lower, taking in Julia's short-sleeved, scoop-neck white T-shirt, the Hanes kind I wore as a little boy. Hers was tight enough to show the outline of a lace, underwire demi-cup bra, and short enough to expose her navel and three or four inches of her tanned abdomen. Lower still, the skinny sides of a black bikini bathing suit bottom peeked over her pareo of black linen, tied on one hip, completely exposing one perfectly toned leg.

I held out my hand as Anderson made the introductions, and Julia took it.

"I'm sorry you had to come all this way, Doctor," she said in a voice full of vulnerability, as if she might ask to be held at any moment.

"She would ask or you would offer?" the voice at the back of my mind interjected.

I silently conceded the point. The impulse to hold her was mine. As I kept looking at her, the luminosity she emanated seemed to envelop me. An azure haze. I felt the loss of her hand as she withdrew it. "I was able to talk with your husband," I said. "I'm glad I made the trip."

Julia looked at Claire. "How is Tess?" she asked anxiously.

"Just fine," Claire said. "She had a little crying jag earlier . . ."

Julia sighed and looked up toward the second floor of the house. "I knew I shouldn't have left her. Is she . . . ?"

"She's fine," Claire said, a soothing lilt in her voice. "She stopped right away with a bottle. Now she's napping."

Julia nodded to herself, twisting her engagement ring and wedding band nervously. The diamond shimmered in the light. It had to be eight or ten carats. A skating rink.

Garret looked even more fidgety. Occasionally, he'd kick at one of the pebbles on the ground. He was not a handsome young man, but he had a Roman nose and Lincolnesque, prominent cheekbones that made him look sturdy and serious. "I want to go inside," he said. He pulled at the braided leather bracelet around his wrist.

Julia forced a smile, but the sadness never left her eyes. "Garret nearly beat his tennis instructor today."

"I don't care about any of that," the boy objected, directing the words at Claire. "I didn't want to play in the first place. I just want to be alone."

"My husband wants him to keep his routine," Julia said, looking at me plaintively. She obviously felt the need to explain why Garret would be taking a tennis lesson a couple days after his sister was murdered and several hours after his brother was shipped off to a locked psychiatric unit. It wasn't a bad question. "It's not just Win," Julia added. "Our family doctor said to keep things as normal as possible."

Garret shook his head. "Whatever," he said.

I didn't want to be a bull in a china shop, but I didn't want to leave without learning as much as I could about the family's emotional dynamics. "Garret," I said. "How are you handling what's happened here over the past forty-eight hours?"

He stopped fidgeting and made fleeting eye contact with me. For an instant, he looked as if he might cry. But then his expression hardened. "Fine," he said defiantly. "I'll get through it."

Julia winced.

I reached out and gently touched her arm. "If you—or anyone else in the family—want to talk about what happened, I'd be happy to take the time," I said. I noticed Anderson staring at my hand lingering on Julia's soft skin and withdrew it.

She swallowed hard. "Thank you," she said. "I don't suppose we can all be expected to 'get through it' by ourselves."

• • •

"What do you think?" Anderson asked as we started down the driveway, heading back toward Wauwinet Road.

"I'll tell you what I *don't* think," I said. "I don't think Darwin Bishop forgot to let you know Billy was hospitalized in New York."

"Meaning?"

"Anyone who can trade stocks on the Nikkei twenty-four hours after he finds his daughter dead in her crib doesn't forget that the chief of police is stopping by with a shrink from Boston. He wanted us at the house."

"Why? Why drag us out here when Billy wasn't available?"

"Maybe to check me out, maybe to deliver a message. He certainly got his points across: How damaged Billy is; how he, Julia, and a half-dozen psychiatrists have tried to help him; even how Billy fits the portrait of a psychopath to a tee. He didn't miss a beat: Firesetting. Cruelty to animals. Bedwetting. He even threw in self-mutilation, for good measure—the biting and hair-pulling."

"He was answering your questions," Anderson said. "He didn't volunteer a thing."

"A man like Darwin Bishop communicates the same way a black belt fights," I said. "He harnesses your momentum to take you where he wants you to go. If he wanted to tell you something about his company, he wouldn't blurt it out. He'd make you think you were dragging the information out of him." I nodded to myself. "He's handling this the way he would handle a business deal. Strategically."

"Well, it isn't a great strategy," Anderson said. "He's backing the D.A.'s office against a wall. Once the media gets hold of the fact that Billy is out of state, Tom Harrigan almost has to charge him with the murder. Otherwise, he looks weak."

"That could be exactly what Bishop is hoping for."

"To force Harrigan's hand, make him go after Billy before he's really ready to?"

"Or," I said, "to make him go after Billy instead of someone else."

4

The last Cape Air flight landed me back in Boston just after 8:00 P.M. Anderson and I had decided I would shuttle to New York the next morning, provided he could get me clearance that quickly to meet with Billy Bishop at Payne Whitney.

On my way back to Chelsea, I stopped at Mass General. I wanted to make good on my promise to see Lilly Cunningham after the incision and drainage of her leg abscess.

She was sleeping when I got to her room, but her bedside lamp was on. Even from her doorway I could see that the surgery had been more extensive than planned. Her leg was in traction, bent at the knee and suspended six, eight inches off the mattress. Her thigh was covered with a wet gauze dressing. Two thin steel rods had been screwed into each side of her femur.

I knocked on the door frame, but she didn't awaken. I walked into the room. I stood there half a minute, listening to the tired electronic beeping pulse of the ward at night, and watching Lilly breathe. I tried to imagine the emotions she might have experienced each time she buried a hypodermic needle in her flesh, soiling her insides. I didn't settle on rage or panic or even sadness. I thought she probably felt relief. Maybe even euphoria. For the moment, she could shed the pretense of normalcy. Her sham self-esteem and self-confidence could melt away, yielding to her real unconscious vision of herself as dirty and infected. Trash. Like someone finally allowed to drop her arms after holding them aloft for hours, she could give up the struggle to fend off her demons and, instead, let them spirit her away.

"Lilly," I said softly.

She didn't stir.

A little louder: "Lilly."

She slowly opened her eyes, but didn't respond.

"It's Dr. Clevenger," I said. "I told you I'd stop by after the procedure."

She took a dreamy breath, then closed her eyes again. "They gave me something for the pain."

"Would you rather sleep? I could try to stop back tomorrow."

She looked at me, squinting to focus. "No. Stay."

I walked the rest of the way to her bedside, pulled up a chair, and sat down. "How did it go?" I asked.

"Dr. Slattery says the infection had gotten into the bone. They had to take a piece of it."

I nodded, looking at the steel rods holding her leg together. "Opening the wound and letting the bad stuff out should prevent that from happening again," I said, picking up on the metaphor for her psychological trauma that I had started to build during our last meeting.

"Right," she whispered, obviously unconvinced.

I remembered telling her that I wasn't afraid to see the truth—even if it was ugly. I needed to prove that that was true in the physical realm, in order to coax her to reveal her emotional wounds. I leaned forward and touched one corner of the gauze bandage. "Do you mind if I take a look?" I asked.

She shook her head. Her gaze focused intently on my hand.

I gently pulled the gauze back far enough for me—and Lilly—to see the incision. She turned her head immediately and stared at the wall. I kept looking at the dissected layers of skin, fat, and muscle. Sterile gauze, soaked with bloody drainage, filled the base of the wound, which clearly went bone-deep. "Good," I said.

"Good?" she said bitterly.

"All the tissue they left looks healthy," I said.

She rolled her eyes.

"The last thing you'd want," I said, "would be a surgeon who wasn't willing to follow the infection all the way to its source." I noticed a tear start down Lilly's face. I grabbed a tissue from the nightstand and blotted her cheek dry.

She turned her head toward me, but said nothing.

"It's really no different than what I try to do," I said. "I have to help my patients trace the roots of their pain as deep as they go."

A few seconds passed. "What if your patient doesn't know what caused the pain?" she asked.

"*Asking the question is half the answer*," the voice at the back of my mind said. "*She wants to take the journey. At heart, everyone wants the truth.*"

My breathing slowed. My eyes closed an instant, then reopened. "If you don't know, then we both have to find the courage to figure it out," I said.

Lilly blushed. "I have trouble talking about myself," she said.

"Why is that?" I asked.

"I guess I think it's safer to keep things inside."

"Safer?"

She didn't respond.

"What's the danger in opening up?" I asked.

"People who tell too much about themselves end up . . ." She stopped short.

"End up . . . what?" I asked.

"I don't know." Her brow furrowed. "Alone, I think."

That statement spoke volumes about Lilly. Fabricating an illness—lying—had brought her close attention from a team of doctors. Coming to terms with the real source of her suffering, especially if that source was abuse at her grandfather's hand, would end her relationship with him, and possibly with other family members as well. The risk of abandonment was real and had been with her since her childhood. There was no sense candy-coating the stakes. "I know how frightening it is for you," I said, "but you have to be willing to be alone, for a while. At the very least, you have to be willing to be alone with your own thoughts."

She nibbled at her lower lip, like a timid little girl. "I can't stand being by myself."

That was a pretty clear message. She needed something—*someone*—to count on, no matter what she divulged. I touched her thigh, just above the incision. "I promise to stay with you every step of the way," I said.

"But how can you say that?" she asked. "You don't even know me. How am I supposed to trust you?"

I could have come up with a platitude to sidestep that question, but only an honest response would count with a person whose life had become a lie. "You can't be sure that I'm trustworthy," I said. "You can never be certain—not with anyone. Eventually, you'll have to take a leap of faith. You'll have to go with your gut."

"I don't know," she sighed. "I'm so confused."

Another small victory; confusion is often the first sign of weakening in the mind's defense mechanisms. I didn't want to seem too eager to breach them. "Shall I stop back in a few days, then?" I asked.

She stared at me several seconds. "Okay," she said. "Yes."

I made it home just before 11:00 P.M. A message from North Anderson on my voice mail told me I was scheduled to interview Billy Bishop at 10:30 A.M. the next day. Judging from my experience flying to Manhattan on other cases, that would mean taking the 7:30 A.M. shuttle, planning for it to be late by a couple hours, which it pretty much always is.

I decided to hop on the Internet and learn what I could about Darwin Bishop. Yahoo! came up with 2,948 refer-

ences, from sources like the *Wall Street Journal,
BusinessWeek*, and *CNN Financial News*. The pieces told
me Bishop had founded CMM with over $40 million of
venture capital, that he had recruited engineers and metal-
lurgists out of MIT, CalTech, and the University at St. Petersburg, and that his company had grown to one thousand
employees within eighteen months. A mention in the *New
York Times* noted Bishop's winning bid of $4.2 million for
a Mark Rothko oil painting that had been predicted to bring
$800,000 at auction at Sotheby's. His lavish lifestyle caught
the eye of *Vanity Fair*, which published photographs of his
vintage car collection and his nineteen-thousand-square-
foot River House penthouse, as large as a quaint hotel. The
property, located on 52nd Street, on a cul de sac between
First Avenue and the East River, was also home to Henry
Kissinger and Sir Rothschild. The penthouse had itself been
owned by the Astor family before Bishop picked it up for
a mere $13 million. And that was before Manhattan real
estate really went through the roof.

I lingered over an archived, older piece from *New York*
magazine entitled "Bishop Takes Bride on Ride of Her
Life" that focused on Bishop's marriage to "socialite and
Elite model Julia Oakley." A photo captured the Bishops
in tux and wedding gown, driving a red Ferrari Testarossa
down Fifth Avenue. Julia looked ravishing.

Midway through the article, Bishop commented on his
first marriage. "Lauren and I had two great years," Bishop
had told the reporter. "I wouldn't trade our time together
for anything. We just sort of woke up one day and said,
'We're better as friends than we are as husband and wife.'
And let me tell you something: I couldn't have a better
friend."

I chuckled. You had to figure there was a lot more to
that story.

I scanned dozens of entries, flew past a couple hundred
others, then stopped short when my eye caught one that
seemed out of sync with the rest. It was a 1995 article in

the *New York Daily News*, headlined "Trouble at the Top," that described Bishop's arrest for drunk driving.

STUART TABOR
SPECIAL TO THE DAILY NEWS
MANHATTAN

A Manhattan man was arrested shortly after 2:00 A.M. yesterday when his Porsche Carrera slammed into two other cars on the Triboro Bridge, and he then fled the scene.

Darwin Bishop, age 45, of 32 East 49th Street, was charged with driving under the influence, driving to endanger, leaving the scene of an accident and resisting arrest. Police apprehended him after a high-speed chase that ended in Astoria, Queens.

Despite a prior 1981 conviction for assault and battery, Bishop was released today on personal recognizance after posting $250,000 cash bail.

Estelle Marshfeld, 39, was transported from the scene of the crash to the Columbia Presbyterian Hospital, where she is listed in guarded condition, with injuries to her chest and abdomen. There were no other reported injuries.

A photograph showed a very different Darwin Bishop from the unflappable man I had seen earlier in the day on Nantucket. His head was down and his hands were cuffed behind him as two police officers escorted him into the Twenty-third Precinct station. Bloodstains covered the front of his blue and white pinstriped shirt.

I kept looking at the image of a drunken Darwin Bishop with bowed head. He had seemed so starched and buttoned-down in his Nantucket digs. Invulnerable. The picture made him real to me because it confirmed what I had long believed: Everyone—rich or poor, black or white, educated or not—is in emotional turmoil, in some sort of pain. For years I had doused mine with booze and cocaine. Bishop obviously had had his own trouble with alcohol. Now he was high on money, a drug at least as intoxicating.

But maybe that meditation on humanity was only part of what kept me looking at the photograph. Maybe I *liked* seeing a humbled version of Bishop because the thought of him with his new bride, Julia, irked me.

I wondered why Julia Bishop had made such an immediate and powerful impression on me. She was stunningly beautiful, but that didn't feel like the whole reason. It didn't even feel like half the reason. I thought back to our conversation in front of the Bishop estate and realized that, within those few minutes, I had come to feel that she was suffering and that she might need my help. And, for me, a woman in distress is the ultimate motivator.

My mind wandered to my mother, a weak person who had the unattractive habit of locking herself in the bathroom when my father was three sheets to the wind and looking for somebody to hurt, no doubt to avoid the hurt festering inside himself. I was the only other one in the apartment, the top floor of a run-down tenement house in decaying Lynn, Massachusetts, and my father invariably spent his rage on me, until *he* was spent and fell down, or fell off into a drunken slumber. And even though my mother was not a loving person, nor brave, nor responsible enough to get us out of that house and out of harm's way, she was my mother and I loved her. And that made me feel a little bit like a hero as the blows landed. And with all the time I spent on Dr. James's couch, untying the knots in my psyche, I was never able to free myself from that double bind of pride and pain. I am still happier to suffer than to watch a woman suffer.

I shook my head and refocused on the computer screen image of Darwin Bishop being led away in cuffs. I wanted to find an article that would fill me in on what sort of sentence he had received for his crime. I spotted one entry slugged *Bishop's Day in Court*, clicked onto it, and got a nice glimpse of how money speaks in the courts—or whispers behind the scenes. The entry was for coverage in the *New York Post* six months after Bishop's arrest, buried as the second-to-last item in the "Local Notes" section of the paper. It told of the case against Bishop being dismissed. He didn't get a day of probation, let alone jail time.

BISHOP'S DAY IN COURT

> A Manhattan court dropped charges of driving under the influence, driving to endanger and resisting arrest lodged against Darwin Bishop, 45, of 32 East 49th Street, citing questions about the validity of the field sobriety tests administered to him at the scene, a lack of credible eyewitnesses and the unavailability of key police testimony. Defense attorney F. Lee Bailey stated, "No one came forward in this case because everyone knows Mr. Bishop had an accident, plain and simple. Then things got out of control, as much due to overreaction on the part of law enforcement as anything else." Bailey said he has not decided whether he will file litigation against the city or against any of the officers involved.

I tried to find information about Bishop's prior conviction for assault and battery in 1981, but couldn't come up with any other reference to it.

I looked at the clock—12:54 A.M. That didn't leave much time for sleep. I turned off the computer and headed to bed. But as tired as I was, my mind kept racing as I lay there. Because I had the growing suspicion that Darwin Bishop was playing me. I just didn't know exactly how—or precisely why. And while shielding a woman from harm can fill me with mixed-up pride, it is nothing compared to the energy that fills me when a man tries to use me, or bully me, or make me the fool. Maybe that surge of determination is all tied up with the rush of adrenaline that used to course through my bloodstream every time my father came up with some cockamamie reason to take his belt to me. Maybe my inability to step away from trouble, to retreat one inch from aggression, is irrational—rooted in a boy's shame for yielding so much to a brutal father. But Dr. James never managed to untie that knot in my psyche, either.

Monday, June 24, 2002

The shuttle into LaGuardia was only eighty minutes late, so I arrived shortly before ten at Payne Whitney, a nondescript building at 68th and York, on the New York Presbyterian Hospital–Cornell Medical Center campus. Billy Bishop was a patient on the third-floor locked unit for children and adolescents. I took the elevator up, followed signs down a long white hallway, and pressed the buzzer at the side of a gray steel door labeled "3 East." Through a security glass window in the middle of the door I could see girls and boys of various ages milling about the unit, while staff members circulated among them.

"Yes?" a female voice emanating from a speaker next to the door asked.

"I'm Dr. Clevenger," I said. "I'm here to interview Billy Bishop."

"We were expecting you at ten-thirty," she said.

"I'm early."

"Did you want to get a bite in the cafeteria?"

Psychiatry units are all about establishing boundaries and maintaining control. Patients whose minds are unraveling are comforted by the rigid structure. The trouble is that the staff can get addicted to it, unable to budge an inch, on anything, for anyone. "No," I answered. "I already ate."

"There's a very nice coffee shop across the street."

"I'd rather get started with the interview."

"I'll find out whether that's possible," the voice said coldly. "Please wait."

Five minutes passed before a portly woman about my age, wearing half-glasses and a blowzy Indian print dress, walked to the door, unlocked it, and let me in. Her graying hair was long and unruly. She wore half a dozen strands of pearls. "I'm Laura Mossberg," she said, in an unmistakable New York accent, "Billy's attending psychiatrist."

I shook her hand. "Frank Clevenger."

"I'm sorry if the ward clerk put you off," Mossberg said.

"No problem," I said. "I'm forty minutes early. I know something like that can turn a locked unit inside out."

She laughed. "Why don't we take a few minutes together in my office, then I'll get Billy for you?"

As we walked through the unit, we passed patients as young as four or five years old and others who looked closer to seventeen or eighteen. They seemed perfectly normal as they spent the weekend chatting in the hallway or playing board games in their rooms or watching television in the lounge. But I knew from my own rotation in child and adolescent psychiatry, back when I was a resident at New England Medical Center in Boston, that only the sickest young people got access to inpatient units, the ones at risk of committing suicide or homicide. Managed care insurance companies indiscriminately shunted the rest to outpatient treatment. The patients here were on multiple psychoactive medications. Any one of them could fly into a rage or be overwhelmed by hallucinations, without warning. Their minds had already veered into chaos—whether due to trauma, abuse, or addiction to drugs or alcohol. They might never live normal lives, no matter how much help they got. Kids are less resilient than people think.

I thought of the murderous violence Billy had witnessed in Russia and the trauma he had, no doubt, suffered in the orphanage. Was it at all surprising that a boy whose world had been destroyed would come to be destructive? Wasn't it obvious that the ruinous potential of fire would feel as warm to him as returning home after a long journey?

Would he not be drawn to revisit his private terrors by looking into the eyes of a neighbor's terrified pet? And then this more disturbing thought came to mind: Would watching his baby sister struggle for her last breaths speak to him of his own emotional suffocation?

We walked into Mossberg's office, an eight-by-ten-foot space piled high with books and medical journals. "Please," she said, pointing to a chair next to her desk.

I navigated my way to the chair, careful not to knock over any of the stacks of reading material. I moved a bunch of *New York Times* newspapers, two volumes of Tennyson's poetry, and a copy of Harry Crews's *A Childhood* off the seat, and sat down. Once I did, I was nearly face-to-face with the only thing hanging on Mossberg's walls: a three-by-four-foot painting of a dog with electric blue fur, a white snout, and big, pointy ears. Sitting amidst rolling green hills and blue-black oak trees, the dog had a questioning expression on its face and big, golden eyes that stared into the room, seemingly waiting for something.

"Interesting painting," I said.

"Blue Dog? She helps the kids talk. Sometimes they tell her things they can't tell me, and I just listen in."

"She looks like she's heard a lot of stories," I said.

"Those big ears," Mossberg said. She smiled.

I felt comfortable in Mossberg's space, and with her. The ability to inspire that kind of feeling in people is essential—and rare—in psychiatrists. One in fifty might have it. "You like pearls," I said, nodding at her.

"I like the lesson they teach," she said. She reached to her neck and rolled one of the pearls between her thumb and forefinger. "The grain of sand is an irritant, but the oyster turns it into something beautiful. An oyster without a grain or two of sand doesn't have much potential. Same with people, if you ask me."

"Agreed," I said. "I feel like I'm sitting with a friend."

She smiled. "Maybe you are," she said. "I know of your work. You've had fascinating cases."

Every so often I bump into someone who's read one of

the profiles of me that ran in publications ranging from the *Annals of Psychiatry* to *People* magazine when I was taking one forensic case after another, each more chilling than the last. But that was a different time, and I was a different person, and I didn't want to get into any of it with Mossberg. "I gave up my forensic practice a couple years back," I said. "I wouldn't normally be involved in Billy's case. I'm interviewing him as a favor to a friend in law enforcement."

She didn't take the hint. "I've never heard anything like the case of that psychotic plastic surgeon," she led. "Where was it? Lynn, Massachusetts? The state hospital?"

"Right," I yielded.

"Dr. Trevor Levitt."

I really wished she would stop.

"No. Lucas," she said. "Trevor Lucas. He had taken hostages. Nurses, patients, and so forth."

"Yes."

"And you negotiated their release," she said.

I could feel my pulse in my temples. "Not all of them," I said. "Lucas butchered a few of them before I declared victory and had my picture taken for the papers. It's a minor detail people tend to forget."

"I'm sorry," she said. "I do recall reading about an elderly woman. Her body had been disfigured—with a knife."

I didn't respond.

"And if I remember correctly, Lucas performed some sort of crude *neurosurgery* on another hostage?" She shook her head. "It was very brave of you to go onto that unit in the first . . ."

My brow was damp. I wiped it with my shirtsleeve. "These memories are very painful to me. I don't talk about them."

Mossberg leaned back in her chair, then sat there, watching me intently. "I see," she said, a therapeutic strain of kindness in her voice.

I knew what she was thinking. I would have been think-

ing the same thing: That not being able to talk about a
memory means your mind is still enslaved by it. But I
wasn't ready to do the work of freeing myself, and I hadn't
come to Mossberg for that kind of help, anyway. I had
come for clues to help solve the murder of an infant girl—
and to make sure that her twin sister stayed alive. I sat
straighter in my chair. "What can you tell me about Billy
Bishop?" I asked her pointedly.

Her eyes narrowed, and she pressed her lips together, as
if finalizing her diagnostic impression of me. If she was as
sharp as I thought she was, she'd get it right: something
just shy of full-blown post-traumatic stress disorder. A few
moments passed. "Very well," she said. "I'm sorry to in-
trude. I tend to wander places I haven't been invited."

"No offense taken," I said. "I understand."

She nodded. "About Billy . . ." she said, reorienting herself. "I can tell you he's a very dangerous person. He seems
to be a young man without conscience. I'm not surprised
that he lashed out at his sister."

"Why do you say that?"

"Certainly not because of anything he's told me," she
said. "He's happy enough to talk about Nantucket, Manhattan, sports, television, and anything else unrelated to the
Bishop baby's death—or to his life in Russia. He avoids
those topics like the plague."

"I can understand that," I said.

"Of course you can," she said. She paused to underscore
her point.

"Let's stick to Billy," I gently reminded her. "I promise
to work on my own avoidance another time."

"You're right. I lost my head." She winked. "My main
concerns about Billy," she continued, "come from the psychological testing we conducted yesterday, shortly after he
arrived on the unit."

Psychological testing involves a variety of evaluations,
including the Minnesota Multiphasic Personality Inventory,
the Bender Gestalt Intelligence Test, and the Rorschach series of inkblots. The goal of the testing is to determine

whether the examinee suffers from any major mental illness, as well as to assess his core character traits, how he thinks about himself, and how he responds to the world around him.

"He cooperated with the testing?" I asked.

"Not really. The deception scale shows he gave untruthful answers to many of the questions. He was trying so hard to appear absolutely healthy psychologically that he didn't endorse a single sign or symptom of psychic distress. He rated his mood at ten out of ten. He insisted that he saw only happy scenes in the inkblots. No blood. No monsters. No storms. He said he 'always' gets along with people and that they do nothing to irritate him."

"So did the testing yield any useful data?" I asked.

"It did." She picked up a set of sheets from her desk and turned a page. "First things first: Billy is highly intelligent. His IQ tested full scale at 152. He's in the extremely gifted range. In his case, that's good news and it's bad news."

"What's the bad part?"

"The bad part is that his intelligence seems to exist in a moral vacuum. It may just make him a more cunning predator. On the projective sections of the test, his responses were highly egocentric. He saw people almost exclusively in terms of what they could do to satisfy his needs." She flipped a few more pages. "Billy was asked, for example, to tell a story about a drawing of a police officer chasing a man. The man is holding a fistful of money. Billy's only comments were, 'I wish I had that money. He'd never catch me.' When the examiner coaxed him to say more about the scene, all he added was, 'I want a gun like that someday, too.' "

"He didn't say anything about what the man had done wrong?" I asked. "He didn't offer any thoughts about what would happen to him if he were caught?"

She shook her head. "Nothing related to law, morality, or punishment." She looked at the report again. "A drawing of a baseball player lying on the ground between bases, clutching his knee, yielded, 'I didn't want to play baseball this summer, but my father made me. It's a stupid game.' "

"He showed no interest in how the man had been injured?" I asked.

"None whatsoever," Mossberg said without looking up. "A third example: When he was asked to describe what was happening in a picture of a man leaving a room, obviously angry, with a woman in tears looking after him, he said, 'She should stop crying. She's loud, and it's hurting his ears. He should go back and *make* her stop.' "

I cringed at that narrative, remembering how Tess, the surviving Bishop twin, had cried out while North Anderson and I were with Darwin Bishop in his study. Could little Brooke Bishop's wailing have annoyed Billy enough to seal off her windpipe? "Did you question Billy directly about the loss of his sister?" I asked.

"In a general way," Mossberg said. "I asked him what had happened to Brooke."

"And?"

"He said she had stopped breathing."

"Did he show any emotion when he answered?" I asked.

"No."

"Did you sense he was suffering any guilt?"

"He insists he had nothing to do with it," she said.

"But you don't believe him," I said.

"Well . . . no. Of course not."

"Why not?" I asked.

Mossberg looked at me askance. "I hadn't heard anyone express doubt that Billy committed the crime. Mr. Bishop's wishes were for a secure setting where his son could be held—away from the glare of the media—until trial. I assumed you would be helping to craft an insanity plea."

"Did Bishop say that? He expects Billy to stand trial for murdering Brooke?"

"Very clearly," Mossberg said. "Am I missing something? Is there confusion on Nantucket about whether Billy killed his sister?"

I took a deep breath, let it out. "Less than you might expect," I said.

5

Laura Mossberg walked me down the hall to Billy's room, a space about the size of her office, but furnished with a smaller wooden desk, a desk chair, and a platform bed. Billy was lying facedown on the mattress, apparently asleep. He was wearing blue jeans and a white T-shirt. A young man about college age sat outside the room, reading a textbook.

"We have Billy on one-to-one observation, around the clock," Mossberg explained. "I should tell you that this unit wouldn't normally provide services to someone with a history of violence like his. We admitted him at the request of our CEO. Mr. Bishop is a major donor to the medical center."

That didn't surprise me. Darwin Bishop's influence obviously reached far and wide. "I won't need more than half an hour with him," I said.

"Feel free to ask for me when you're finished," she said. She started back down the hallway.

I walked into Billy's room. He rolled onto his back, flipped his straight, dirty blond hair out of his eyes, and stared at me. He obviously hadn't been sleeping. "You would be *who*?" he demanded.

"Frank Clevenger," I said, staring back at him. "I'm a psychiatrist."

Billy's ice-blue eyes sparkled. He was sixteen and

looked like a prototype adolescent, at the edge of boyhood
and manhood, with fine features that promised to become
handsome. The lines of his nose and jaw were almost feminine, suggesting fragility, but in another year or two, as
his wiry body filled out, his broad shoulders adding impressive bulk, that hint of femininity would be the very
thing that reassured women they could immerse themselves
in him, rather than fear him—this Russian-American, bad-
boy billionaire's kid. That is, if he wasn't in prison for life.
"My dad sent you," he said.

"Not exactly," I said. "Your father gave me permission
to see you. I'm working with the Nantucket Police Department."

Billy sat up, smiled. "He gave me your name before I
left home," he said. "Trust me. He sent you."

The bravado in his voice reminded me of Billy Fisk, the
teenager I had lost to suicide. I pictured Fisk sauntering
around my office during his first visit, talking trash about
how much respect he got on the streets. It took me months,
and fifty or so meetings together, to get him to back off the
tough-guy routine and talk to me about how tough his life
had been. I should have taken things even slower. Because
I had lost him somewhere on the journey into his pain. I
closed my eyes, remembering the call I'd gotten that he had
hung himself.

"Still with the program, Doc?" Billy asked.

I opened my eyes. "I'm fine," I said. I noticed Billy's
forearms were marred by faded, haphazard scars where he
had slashed at himself. "And maybe you're right. Maybe
your father sent me, after all." I pulled out the chair from
under the desk, turned it toward the bed, and sat down.

"This should be fun," he said.

"Really. Why?" I said.

"I've never seen a police psychiatrist before, just the
regular ones."

"And what were they like?" I asked.

"Mossbergs. Every one of them," he said, with a smile
full of disdain—his father's smile. "Nice, soft people, who

felt very powerful holding the keys to their little locked kingdoms. I keep every one of their names right here." He pointed at his head, made a mock gun of his fist, thumb, and forefinger, and pointed it at me. He pretended to drop the hammer, then winked and let his hand drift to his side.

I hadn't forgotten that Billy was a predator, whether or not he had murdered Brooke. His firesetting and cruelty to animals showed he was intoxicated by his own power—the power to destroy. I wanted him to know that I wouldn't be scared off. "Let's not waste our time on threats," I said. I stood up and walked toward the door, feeling Billy's eyes on me. I reached for the door, pushed it shut. Then I turned around, facing him again. "I know exactly who and what you are," I said.

He rolled his eyes. "You're clairvoyant *and* over-educated."

"I know about the feeling in your gut—the emptiness."

"Actually, I had a big breakfast this morning," he said. "Courtesy the hospital cafeteria. I'm full."

"Even when you joke about it, it's there. It's always there, gnawing at you," I said.

He looked away, tilting his head. "Let's see . . . two eggs, sunny-side, hash browns . . ."

"Some days are worse than others," I pressed. "Some days, you feel so empty it actually hurts."

He flashed that Bishop smile again, but said nothing.

"Maybe you light up a joint and get yourself two, three hours of relief. It never lasts. You've tried cutting yourself, biting yourself, pulling out your hair, probably making yourself vomit now and then, to start feeling something. *Anything*. Nothing works."

Billy's expression shifted a few degrees away from mockery, toward uneasiness.

I kept burrowing. "There are times you feel so much dead space inside, such a cold, black hole, that you wonder whether you even exist. You look around at other people and wonder if they're real. Maybe they're just pretending to be alive, too."

He shook his head, squinted at me. "How much is my father paying you for this crap?" he asked.

"He's not paying me," I said.

"Then you're an idiot," he said.

"Why's that?"

"Because," he said, "you're doing exactly what he wants you to do. You may as well cash in."

"*He's projecting*," the voice at the back of my mind interjected. "*He's the one who feels bought and paid for.*"

I listened to that voice and decided to reflect Billy's comment back onto whatever fragile part of his psyche it had come from. "Your dad owns *you*, champ," I said, "not me."

His face lost every trace of gaminess. "No one owns me," he said, a new loathing creeping into his tone.

I had struck a nerve. I wanted to follow it toward its root. "The way I understand it, you're bought and paid for, buddy."

"Wrong, Sigmund." His face flushed.

"F.O.B. Moscow," I said.

His upper lip started to twitch.

"And now," I said, "it looks like your dad's finally convinced you're damaged goods. He's cutting his losses."

Billy shrugged, but the movement looked weak and artificial. He knew he couldn't shrug me off. "Leave," he said, his voice thin with rage. "Get out." He stood up. He was nearly six feet tall. The muscles in his arms were ropy and tight. His hands were balled into fists.

I wasn't about to back down. Not when we were getting closer to the truth. "I'm not ready to leave," I said.

He took a step toward me.

I instinctively focused on the point where I would plant the ball of my foot to drop him if he lunged at me—just where his ribs met, at the lowest point of his sternum. "Why can't you admit it?" I prodded. "All you cost Win Bishop was a one-way ticket."

He took another step. "I've cost him a lot more . . ." he sputtered, then stopped himself short.

A new quiet filled the room—the pure silence that heralds the arrival of the truth.

"Tell me," I said. "Just how angry are you at your father?"

He stared at me for a few moments, as if he might answer, but then took a deep breath, spread his fingers wide, and stepped back toward his bed.

"You're mad enough to take it out on a few cats, from what I heard." I shook my head. "I love cats, by the way."

"You heard what you heard," he said.

"Mad enough to try burning his house down."

"If I had wanted to burn his house down," he said, "it would be gone."

"But none of that was enough," I continued. "So you moved on to your baby sister, Brooke. You had to cost him a child. One of his *real* children."

He looked away from me, toward the room's single, grated window. With the light falling on his face, he suddenly looked more like a lost boy than a violent young man.

"I think I get it," I said, not letting up. "It's the old cliché: 'Misery loves company.' You're so dead inside that you feel a little better watching the life drain out of something else. And you're not brave enough to go after your father—who you'd really like to kill—so you pick on things that can't fight back. Kittens, babies, real brave stuff like that." I got up. "I don't need to hear anything else." I walked to the door and opened it.

"You don't know the first thing about me," he seethed. "Or my father."

"*Let him tell you the first thing*," the voice at the back of my mind said.

My skin turned to gooseflesh. A crown of shivers made my scalp tingle. Billy seemed about to invite me into his suffering. And I have never felt closer to God than when journeying into a damaged heart. I pushed the door to the room closed again and slowly turned to face him.

"I'll let you in on a little secret," Billy deadpanned. He pulled his shirt off, tossed it on his bed, and stood there, the taut muscles of his chest and abdomen twitching.

I wondered if he was baiting me while he gathered the courage to rush me. I shifted most of my weight to my left side, freeing up my right foot in case I needed to deliver the blow I had planned. But all Billy did was turn around. And that was enough to make me nearly lose my balance. Because I saw that his back was covered with welts, from his shoulder blades to his waist, as if he had been savaged with a strap. Some were raw and open. Others had healed into thick scars.

"If you want to figure out what happened to little Brooke," Billy said, "maybe you should figure out why good old Win gets off on doing this to me."

My head was spinning. I tried to picture Darwin Bishop wielding a strap as Billy cowered in a corner of the family's Nantucket mansion, but my mind kept serving up my father, in the tenement house we called home. His belt was black, two inches wide, thirty-eight inches long, with a square, brushed silver buckle. He wore it every day, whether he was drunk or not, which left me with a tinge of terror even when he was sober and kind and picking me off my feet with a bear hug, telling me how much he loved me. Standing there with Billy, I could actually smell the stench of alcohol that came off my father's skin. I could feel the mixture of nausea and fear that I lived with until I had lived long enough to get myself out of that house and out of his way.

"Your father did that?" I quietly asked Billy.

He didn't respond. But his scarred shoulders seemed to sag under the weight of his revelation.

I walked closer to him and reached out, almost touching his back. I let my hand fall. "When?" I said.

He turned around, the fake smile back on his face. "Whenever he feels like it," he said. "When I got to this country, I tried being good, because I thought I might get sent back to the orphanage, but he seemed to like punishing me, anyhow, especially when he'd had a little bit to drink, so I figured, Why try to please him? Why give a fuck—about anyone?" He shrugged. "Then something strange happened," he said.

"What was that?" I asked.

"It stopped hurting," he said, simply. "He could whip me as hard as he wanted, and it didn't get to me."

"Is that when you started to hurt yourself? The biting?"

He turned his arms over, revealing more arc-shaped scars here and there on the undersides of his forearms. "It felt good for a while," he said.

"It felt good?"

"Well, I could *feel* it. And that was good. You know?"

I did know. "The cats? The house?" I said. "Talk to me about those."

He sat on the edge of his mattress, looking away. "I don't know why I did that stuff," he said. "Maybe it was what you were saying before, how I wanted to hurt something or destroy something because I was feeling destroyed myself. Maybe I wanted to see *them* suffer. Maybe because I couldn't, anymore. I don't know. I'm all mixed up about it." He looked at me. His eyes were filled with worry. "I'm not right in the head. I'm not . . . normal. I never will be."

I didn't want to get distracted by how badly I felt for Billy. I needed more information. "What about Brooke?" I said. "Be straight with me. I'll try to help you either way. Are you the one who killed her, or not?"

"No," he said emphatically. He sat down on his bed. "I would never do that. You've got to believe me."

"You know that's why you're here," I said. "You know that your father believes you're guilty."

"I'm here because of my father," Billy said, flipping his hair out of his eyes again, "but he doesn't believe I hurt Brooke."

"Then why would he send you?" I asked.

"Why? Probably because he's the one who did it. And he isn't about to take the blame. He never does."

"Why would your father kill your sister?" I asked.

"He never wanted one baby girl, let alone twins," Billy said. "He wanted my mother to have an abortion."

"How do you know that?"

"He was always screaming at her to get one." Billy squinted at me, as if remembering. "I'd wake up in the middle of the night and hear him yelling, 'Get rid of them! Stop thinking about yourself all the time! Get rid of them or get out!' Mom would cry and curse him and say she'd do it. I think she even went to an appointment once at one of those family planning places. But she never went through with it."

I remembered Laura Mossberg's comment that Billy's extraordinary intelligence might just make him a more cunning liar. "Why tell me all this?" I said. "Why didn't you tell Dr. Mossberg or the police?"

"You're the only one who asked," he said. He swallowed hard. "I got to take a chance, sometime, on somebody." Our eyes locked. "Also, I figure I got just about nothing left to lose."

I found Laura Mossberg back at her office. She invited me in. I took the seat near her desk.

"Well," she asked. "Any breakthroughs?"

"Only one, if you want to call it a breakthrough," I said. "He insists he didn't hurt his sister."

"He answered you directly about that?"

"Yes," I said. "He did."

"Did he point a finger at someone else?"

I couldn't be sure whether what I told Mossberg would stay with her or be passed on to Darwin Bishop. Billy was a minor, after all. His medical records were officially the property of his parents. And Darwin Bishop probably had an even more immediate pipeline to the goings-on at Payne Whitney, through his friend, the medical center's CEO. "No," I said. "He didn't have any theory about Brooke's murder."

She nodded. "So, let me ask you the same question you

put to me: Do you believe him? Could someone else be responsible?" She toyed with the pearls hanging around her neck.

"I have no reason to believe him right now," I said. "His psychological profile, his prior history of violence, his lying on the standardized tests you administered here—all of it puts whatever he says in grave doubt. I suppose the shocking thing would be if he admitted the crime."

"Agreed," she said. "But you seem troubled. What's on your mind?"

I knew I was sitting with someone trained to listen to the music between spoken words. "I feel for him," I said, hoping that would be a sufficient explanation. "Like his father told me, Billy isn't evil, he's ill."

"And on that score, could you be helpful to him in court? Does he meet the criteria for an insanity plea?" Mossberg asked.

"He certainly has a history of terrible trauma," I said, "going all the way back to his childhood in Russia, witnessing the murder of his parents. A case could be made that he lost the emotional ties that bind the rest of us. Without empathy, without conscience, he might not have any brake on his primal feelings—including being pathologically jealous of new children in the family. He may have lashed out as a reflex, rather than a premeditated act. To put it in legal terms, he may 'lack the substantial capacity to conform his behavior to the requirements of the law.' "

"That rings true," she said. "His psychological testing would support that."

I looked into Blue Dog's golden eyes. "Just out of curiosity," I asked, "did Billy have a physical examination when he was admitted?"

"He refused," Mossberg said. "We didn't see a reason to press him on it. He's been quite healthy—from a medical standpoint—according to his father." She paused. "Is there anything in particular you're concerned about?"

"Billy has quite a few welts on his back," I said, looking at Mossberg. "Some are scarred over. Others are fresh."

She nodded. "That would be consistent with what Mr. Bishop told me," she said. "Apparently, Billy has the habit of whipping himself with a belt—along with his cutting, biting, and hair-pulling. I've understood all of that as an outgrowth of his self-hatred. He makes attempts to channel his violence inward, but it inevitably spills over, and he strikes out at others."

"Mr. Bishop hadn't told me about the belt," I said. "Just the other behaviors."

Mossberg shrugged. "Maybe it slipped his mind. He may not have thought it was as important to let you know, given that you wouldn't normally be doing a physical examination."

"That's probably right," I said. It was equally possible that it had "slipped" Darwin Bishop's mind because he didn't think I would find out about it.

"How did he come to show you his back to begin with?" Mossberg asked.

"Very much by accident," I fibbed. "He took off his shirt to intimidate me. He's a strong kid and he looks it. For a minute there I thought he might attack me."

"I'll keep that at the front of my mind," she said. "I bruise easily." She winked. "Is there any other way I can be helpful to you?"

"Will you be assembling Billy's other medical records?" I asked. "I understand he's been treated by other psychiatrists."

"We've sent out the relevant requests," she said. "I'll be sure to call you with anything we get our hands on."

"That could be a big help," I said.

I grabbed a quick lunch at a greasy spoon and hailed a taxi. I was anxious to get my hands on information about Darwin Bishop's 1981 conviction for assault. I'd had luck getting case records before at the Office of Court Administration, way downtown on Beaver Street, just below Wall Street, a couple blocks from Battery Park.

"Let's take Second Avenue, headed downtown," I told the cab driver. I opened the window a few inches to let out the odor of stale smoke that was making me hold my breath.

"Why Second?" he said, without turning around. "The FDR. Faster." He had a European accent I couldn't quite place. Maybe Russian.

I glanced at his photo ID, mounted to the dash, next to a white plastic Jesus. His name was Alex Puzick. He looked about sixty years old. His eyes were weary. His face was half-shaven. He wore a white shirt that had yellowed at the collar and along the shoulder creases. "I want to make a quick stop at the River House," I said. "It won't take me more than a minute."

He answered by throwing the car into drive and barreling across 67th Street, then down Second Avenue.

As I half-watched the endless parade of copy shops, boutiques, groceries, and electronics stores, my mind kept wandering to Tess Bishop, Brooke's surviving twin. Because I wasn't more than fifty-fifty on Billy's guilt. And that left even odds that a killer was still loose on the Bishop estate.

I wondered if I could move the Department of Social Services office on Nantucket to take custody of the child until the murder investigation was further along. But the likelihood of DSS intervening, given the District Attorney's exclusive focus on Billy, was slim.

The key might be a direct appeal to Julia Bishop to place her daughter in a safer environment. I knew that wouldn't be without risk; if she shared my suspicions with her husband, he would almost certainly shut the door completely on me—and North Anderson.

I was still weighing the idea of talking openly with Julia when the cab driver glanced over his shoulder. "Live here?"

"No," I said. "I live outside Boston."

"What brings you?"

"I'm a psychiatrist," I said. "I have a patient in town."

He stared into the rearview mirror, studying me several seconds. Then his gaze settled back on the road. "They bring you in from Boston," he said, "you must be good."

"I've been at it a while," I said.

He nodded to himself. A few more seconds passed. "You treat schizophrenics? You've had schizophrenic patients?"

"Many times."

He nodded to himself again, but said nothing.

"Why do you ask?" I said.

"I have a daughter," he said. "Twenty-six years old."

"She has the illness?"

"Since seventeen," he said. He took a hard left onto 52nd Street. "My only child."

I stayed silent. I was feeling the reluctance I always feel before embracing another life story—as if mine might finally slip its binding and get lost amidst the thousands of disconnected chapters floating free inside me. I looked out the window again.

"Her name is Dorothy," Puzick said. "She's in Poland, with her mother. Warsaw."

Now the life story had a name and a hometown and a mother and a father. And those slim facts were enough to dissolve my reluctance to hear more. If I were a rock, I would be pumice—rough on the outside, permeable to the core. "How do they come to be there, and you here?" I asked.

"I left them," he said simply. "Bitch!" He swerved to avoid an old woman stepping off the curb. "I left them," he said again.

"Why?"

"I fell in love with an American. I didn't want to be married anymore." He shrugged. "I left, and Dorothy was nine years old." He suddenly pulled the car over to the curb. "River House."

I opened the door to the cab, but sat there. "Nine years old," I said.

His brow furrowed. "Go. See what you have to see. I wait here for you."

I pulled myself out of the cab. I walked to the sidewalk,

lined with black, chauffeured limousines, and looked through the open gates of the River House, their immense wrought frames anchored in limestone pillars marked "Private" and capped by carved eagles, heads turned, staring at one another. Past the eagles, a cobblestone driveway separated a magnificent courtyard with flowering gardens from the entrance to the building, flanked by two doormen standing under a massive, hunter green awning.

The scene spoke of timelessness, security, elite tranquility.

I looked up at the building itself, which ran an entire city block. It was about fifteen stories high, the first three stories of limestone and the rest of brick, covered with ivy in places. The corner penthouse Darwin Bishop and his family called home was a duplex that boasted a series of two-story pillars and a terrace that had to be a thousand square feet or more, its innermost wall lined with enormous slate slabs.

I walked down to the East River and took in a view framed by the Queensboro Bridge to the left and the Williamsburg Bridge to the right. Between them stood epic symbols of American industry—giant smokestacks, the Citibank Building, a landmark neon Pepsi-Cola sign. My eyes skated past them and lingered on the mesmerizing ruin of a castle on Roosevelt Island.

Standing there, I got what I had come for: a hint of the majesty Darwin Bishop must have felt the moment he purchased his home, laying claim to real estate at the epicenter of the civilized world, a safe haven not one mile from the Waldorf-Astoria, St. Patrick's Cathedral, Radio City Music Hall, and Central Park. Nobody would ever peg him for a guy from Brooklyn, with a criminal record. I walked back to the cab.

"So?" Puzick said. "You saw so fast everything you needed to?"

"Pretty much," I said.

"Garbo lived right there," he said, pointing to the building across the street from the River House.

"Garbo," I said. "Really."

"That's what they say." He started back toward First Avenue, heading toward FDR Drive for the rest of trip downtown. He glanced at me twice in the rearview mirror, without saying anything.

"You visited her in Poland?" I prompted him. "Your daughter?"

"Every year, as God is my witness," he said. "But it wasn't enough." His voice trailed off.

I knew exactly what Alex Puzick was looking for. Forgiveness. I stared at the little plastic Jesus glued to his dashboard. "Leaving your wife didn't make your daughter sick," I said.

He didn't turn around, didn't even look at me in the mirror. "How can you know?" he said, in a voice as solemn as a prayer.

"Because you worry over it," I said. "You worry about her."

He sighed. "Probably I should have stayed with them," he said, as much to himself as to me.

Maybe he should have. And maybe staying would have made things worse. All I could say for sure was that a man I had known barely fifteen minutes was in so much pain that it was flowing freely from him to me. "You left because you were in love," I told him. "That means you acted on your heart. You were true to yourself. I don't know what made Dorothy lose control of her emotions, but I can tell you it wasn't that."

"You sound so sure."

"I've done this work a long time," I said, leaning toward him. "I am sure."

He relaxed visibly. "I'll see her in another month," he said. "Five weeks."

I sat back in my seat. "Good."

Neither of us spoke another word until we had pulled over in front of 25 Beaver. I got out of the cab and stepped up to Puzick's window.

"On the house," he said.

The meter read $11.30. I held out a twenty. "You don't need to do that," I said.

"I don't need to. You didn't need to," he said. "We're even."

I took an elevator to the eighth-floor Criminal History Search office. There were two clerks and about a dozen people in line, so I waited my turn, which meant waiting about an hour. When I got to the desk, a young Asian woman, with a very serious expression on her face and very large silver hoop earrings, reminded me that I would need to pay sixteen dollars to do a computerized criminal background check on Darwin Bishop. The search would yield the docket number and disposition of any case against him since the mid-1970s. I was happy to hand over the money, but unhappy when she told me to come back the next morning for the results.

"I'm working with the police on a case," I said. "I could really use the information today."

"You're a police officer," she said skeptically.

"A psychiatrist," I said. "I'm working with the police on a case involving the Bishop family."

"A psychiatrist. That's a first." She almost smiled. "You don't look like a psychiatrist."

"I've been told that," I conceded. "More than a few times." I pulled out my wallet and showed her my medical license.

"It says here, 'Massachusetts,' " she said, pointing at the card.

"That's where my office is, but I take cases in other states," I said.

"This one case," the voice at the back of my mind chided me. *"This case, then no more."*

I silently agreed. Forensic psychiatry had nearly cost me my sanity. I didn't want to gamble it away.

The clerk looked at me, as if to check whether I was on the level, then shook her head. "If you're a liar, you're a

good one." She turned around and disappeared into an office. Ten minutes later, she came back to the counter with
a computer printout. She folded it and placed it in an envelope. She held it out to me, but pulled it back before I
could take it from her. "We can't do this all the time," she
said. "Doesn't matter who you are."

"I appreciate this one time," I said.

She handed over the envelope.

I took the report to a bench just outside the office, sat
down, and started to read:

Adult Record Information as of 06/24/2002   Page 1 of 1

Name: Bishop, Darwin G.   DOB: 05/11/1948
PCF# 507950C0   POB: Brooklyn
Sex: M SS#: 013-42-1057   Mother: Norma Erickson
                                   Father: Thomas

Home Address: 829 Park Avenue Ethnicity: White
               NY, NY 10021
Alias Name(s): None

Date: 05/22/95 Manhattan   Docket #6656 CR952387
   Criminal
Offense: Operating to Endanger
   Lives and Safety
Disposition: Dismissed

Date: 05/22/95 Manhattan   Docket #6656 CR952388
   Criminal
Offense: Operating Under the
   Influence of Alcohol
Disposition: Dismissed

Date: 09/06/81 Manhattan   Docket #7513 CR811116
   Criminal
Offense: Domestic Assault
Disposition: Convicted
   (Probation)

Date: 07/23/80 Manhattan   Docket #4912 CR800034
   Criminal
Offense: Violation of Restraining
   Order, Abuse Prevention Act
Disposition: Convicted
   (Probation)

Nothing about the rap sheet gave me any comfort. Bishop's 1981 conviction for assault obviously had been for smacking his first wife, Lauren, around. And that episode had apparently followed another worrisome event during 1980—something threatening enough that the court had issued a restraining order against Bishop, an order he then violated. So much for the "I couldn't have a better friend" line that Bishop had fed the *New York* magazine writer who asked about his and Lauren's divorce.

For all his Manhattan and Nantucket cachet, Bishop was starting to look like a garden variety alcoholic and domestic abuser—something I knew more than a little bit about, firsthand. I'd grown up with one. It didn't seem like much of a reach to think Bishop could be beating Billy, or that he could have killed little Brooke.

I called North Anderson's mobile phone from the lobby. He answered right away.

"I just picked up a copy of Darwin Bishop's criminal record in New York," I told him.

"What criminal record?" he asked.

"I found a newspaper article that referenced an assault charge against him during the early eighties, so I pulled his whole sheet."

"And?"

"Not good. He was convicted of a domestic assault on his wife Lauren during 1981. He also violated a restraining order the prior year. That's on top of charges of driving to endanger and driving under the influence during the mid-nineties that he managed to get dismissed, with the help of F. Lee Bailey."

"That puts Sir Bishop in a whole new light," he said.

"How about Billy? What did you learn from him?"

"He says he's innocent."

"What do you think?"

"I'm not sure what to think. Billy says his father's been beating him, badly. He has welts all over his back to prove it. He also seems convinced that his father is the one who killed the baby. He even suggested a motive: According to him, Darwin never wanted the twins. He pressured Julia to get an abortion. Ranted and raved about it, all hours of the night. But she wouldn't give in."

"And Bishop's used to getting his way," Anderson said.

"Probably in any way he has to," I said. I took a deep breath and let it out. "We've got to remember, though: Billy's no saint. He's a sociopath, whether he murdered Brooke or not. He may be lying about his father's feelings toward the twins. The wounds he showed me could even have been self-inflicted."

"This case keeps getting more complicated," Anderson said. "There's another wrinkle."

"What's that?"

"My friend Sal Ferrera, a private eye out of Brooklyn—used to teach at Xaverian—did a little research for me. Turns out Claire Buckley's job description must be something more than the traditional nanny. She and Darwin traveled together to San Francisco, Chicago, Palm Beach, London, and Buenos Aires, just this year. No other family members had reservations on any major airline for any of the dates they were away."

"She could be an executive assistant type," I said, even though I didn't really believe it.

"According to Sal, they only booked one room at each of the hotels where Bishop checked in," Anderson said. "There were plenty of room service charges for two meals. And there was a hell of a lot of wine and champagne on the tab."

"The man has his needs," I said.

"So, if I'm Darwin Bishop," Anderson said, "looking to hook up with my nanny, maybe make her Mrs. Bishop number three, I might not like the idea my present wife is saddling me with twins. I might see that as a direct threat to my future."

I winced, wondering whether Anderson's own conflicted feelings about his unborn child might be coloring his perspective. But I went with the theme he was developing, because it did seem powerful. From my perspective, Darwin Bishop was starting to eclipse Billy as the lead suspect in Brooke Bishop's murder. "Bishop is a man who has re-created himself," I said. "He's Jay Gatsby. He rises out of poverty, sheds his Brooklyn roots and accent, plants his flag on the Upper East Side and Nantucket. He's at the top of the world. He wouldn't take kindly to anyone telling him that he can't go forward with his plans. In fact, he may experience people who get in his way as, quite literally, trying to do him in, trying to kill off his vision of himself. Then he's psychologically prepared to defend himself—by lethal means, if necessary." I paused. "What do we do to protect the other baby?" I asked.

"I'm not sure there's much we can do," Anderson said. "The D.A.'s office has decided to charge Billy with the murder. Tom Harrigan is in court today seeking an order to arrest him and bring him back to Massachusetts. New York seems to be cooperating. Making the case that Tess Bishop could be in danger from another family member isn't going to fly."

"Even if it's true," I said.

"I wish it were always about that, Frank," he said. "Welcome back to my world."

6

I flew to Logan and got to my loft at about 9:30 P.M. I listened to my phone messages and found one from Julia Bishop. My pulse started to race, partly because the message took me by surprise, partly because Julia's voice took me back to feelings I hadn't felt since splitting with Kathy. It was a voice full of intelligence and worldliness at the same time as it brimmed with vulnerability. She said she needed to meet me, alone, but didn't say why. And I found myself not only willing but *wanting* to see her, something I should have pegged as trouble right off the bat.

The phone number Julia left on my machine was different from the one directory assistance gave me for the Bishops' home in Nantucket. I dialed it, taking the chance she would be somewhere she could talk.

"Yes?" she answered.

"Frank Clevenger," I said.

"I'm glad you called."

"Where are you?"

"A friend's house. Here on the island. But I have to get back home."

"Are you all right?" I asked.

"Can we meet?" Her tone had urgency and a hint of fear in it. "I could come to Boston tomorrow. Win has a full day of business meetings at the house."

"Of course," I said. "Did you have a specific place in mind?"

"Wherever you like," she said. "I can be in the city by one."

"Bomboa Restaurant," I said. Bomboa was tucked in an alleyway, and quiet in the afternoons. "It's right downtown on Stanhope Street, around the corner from Mistral, if you know that place. I'll wait for you at the bar."

"I'll wait for you at the bar—another sign of trouble," the voice at the back of my mind said.

"I'll see you then," she said. She hung up.

I didn't know exactly why Julia wanted to meet, but I knew I was being invited deeper into the Bishop family's psyche. That reassured me I was burrowing toward their truth. It also worried me because I sensed that the journey would end in a very dark place.

I felt tired enough to sleep. I undressed and laid down, but my mind wouldn't shut down. I kept going over what Billy had told me about being beaten by his father, what I had learned from Darwin Bishop's rap sheet, and what North Anderson had told me about the romance between Bishop and Claire Buckley. If Bishop was hiding behind gentility, if he was someone who had tried desperately to extinguish parts of his life, then he would find it that much easier to extinguish another life. The dying embers of a man's repressed pain have the unwieldy habit of catching fire, spreading underground, and burning down everything nearby.

Billy might even have been expressing his father's destructiveness when he torched property and tortured animals. He could be what psychiatrists call the *designated patient*—the family member everyone points to as the insane one, the black sheep—when the truth is that that person is simply less able to resist acting on the pathological dynamics alive elsewhere in the household.

But then there was Claire Buckley. A wild card. I knew almost nothing about her, other than that she was playing confidante and counselor to Julia while sleeping with Julia's husband. And she was the one Julia relied on to help care for Brooke's surviving twin, Tess. I felt glad I would be seeing Julia the next day. Maybe there was a chance I could move her to let the baby stay with grandparents, or somewhere else off the Bishop estate.

After half an hour lying there awake, wrestling with my suspicions, I realized a good night's sleep wasn't in the cards for me. I got up, pulled on my boots, jeans, and black T-shirt, and headed out to the truck. I felt like grabbing a drink, so I decided to grab a coffee at Café Positano.

Carl Rossetti, my renegade attorney friend (and onetime patient), was standing at the espresso bar when I walked in. His long black hair was tied in a braid. I took the space next to him and nodded at Mario.

"What's new, chief?" Rossetti asked. Before I could answer, he held out his pinkie, showing off a diamond solitaire that had to weigh over two carats. "What do you think?" He took a drag off a cigarette.

"I guess it's okay," I said. "I mean, if you're planning to get engaged and give it to your girl."

He smiled and spewed a thin stream of smoke up toward the silver tin ceiling. He probably thought I was kidding. "I got it off Scotty Deegan as a fee," he said. "I handled a drug case for him before Judge McClure in Federal Court. Possession, intent to distribute five hundred pounds of weed. We did good. Thirty-six months in Allenwood. Easy time. Maybe a halfway house after two years. So it was a score."

"He came to the right person," I said. I meant it. If I were in trouble, my first call would be to Carl Rossetti.

He waved his hand back and forth, admiring the stone as it caught the light. "I would never cough up the cash for something like this, but when it falls in your lap, what the hell, right?" He shrugged.

"It's a little flashy for my taste," I said. "It may even be a little flashy for your taste. And that's saying a lot."

"Sometimes you got to stretch," Rossetti said. He slapped my shoulder. "So tell me, already, what's happening in your world? You still hanging around that beautiful Brazilian from the other night?"

It seemed like more than a few nights had passed. I pictured Justine getting dressed in my apartment the morning North Anderson had rung my doorbell. "She's back in Brazil," I said. "I'd be over there myself if I hadn't gotten called into the Bishop case. You remember: the baby on Nantucket."

"Of course. The Russian kid," he said. "He's pleading insanity?"

"It doesn't look that way. He says he didn't do it."

He smiled. "What else is he gonna say? Does he have a lawyer?"

"Not that I know of," I said.

"Put in a good word for me, if you get the chance."

"Two nights ago you told me the kid was guilty, for sure."

"He's still gonna need an attorney," Rossetti said. "And I could use that kind of payday. My other clients aren't billionaires."

Mario delivered my coffee. I sipped it. Then I bummed a cigarette off Rossetti, lighted it, and inhaled as much smoke as my lungs would hold.

"Can you share anything you've learned about the case?" Rossetti asked.

Rossetti was peculiar-looking, but he was also peculiarly brilliant. I welcomed the chance to run some of what I knew about the Bishop case by him. "One of the things I dug up," I told him, "is that Darwin Bishop—the father of the suspect—has a record of domestic assault. He beat his first wife. He also violated a restraining order she took out against him."

"You're joking," Rossetti said.

"I pulled his rap sheet. It's all right there in the public record."

"Then I respectfully withdraw my previous opinion."

"On?" I asked.

"The Russian kid," Rossetti said. "I hereby rescind his conviction."

"Why?"

"Because, until further notice, the father's your man, Doc. I don't care how many cats the boy strangled, or how many times he pissed his bed."

"But why do you say that?"

Rossetti held both hands in the air, like a conductor. "As if you don't already know all this, men who beat up on women are different than the rest of us. Okay? They're unhinged. Out there. Without feelings. And anyone arrogant enough to violate an order of the court, when it could get him a year or more in jail, is different, too. He doesn't get the idea of boundaries—like, where his life stops and other people's start." He let his hands settle back to his coffee cup. "If you or I were the subject of a restraining order, we'd be twenty miles from ground zero at all times. We're not gonna screw with the justice system once it buries its teeth in us." He paused, sipped his coffee. "Add up the two charges, and what you have here is a violent crime occurring in a household where the father is a violent offender with no regard for the law. Ten to one, he did it."

"Not every domestic abuser graduates to murder," I said.

"That's why it's ten to one and not a million to one. If it was open and shut, the police wouldn't need you. The friggin' department could buy another cruiser with what you're gonna charge 'em."

"There were five people at home the night the baby was killed," I said. "Darwin Bishop and his wife Julia; their two sons, Billy and Garret; and the nanny, Claire Buckley. The D.A. is going to arrest Billy and try to prosecute him. What do you think of his chances for a conviction?"

"Pretty good, with the father's testimony," Rossetti said.

"He's *not* testifying," I said. "He said he'll do anything necessary to protect Billy from a jail term."

"Very noble. Watch what happens when they call him to the stand, though. My guess? He suddenly *remembers* something important—and very incriminating—about his son's behavior that night. He may even get all broken up about having to divulge it." He nodded to himself. "Look for tears. You won't find any. Unless the guy's even better than I think."

"I'll keep my eyes open."

"I'd put a pair in the back of your head, too," he said.

"Meaning?"

"You're playing in the big leagues now. Bishop is a billionaire. I don't think you fully understand what that implies. He has one thousand million dollars. That buys him reach you can't imagine. He's got police, politicians, and judges he can call for favors. He has powerful investor friends who rely on him to keep generating money for them. If you're a threat to him, you're a threat to them. They can come for you in a dozen different ways. You're expendable."

"I've been against the wall before," I said. Strangely, what I had in mind wasn't my having joined Trevor Lucas and the hostages he had maimed on the fifth floor of Lynn State Hospital—the case that had all but ended my work in forensics. I had my own childhood in mind—my having been held hostage on the third floor of a Lynn tenement house with a violent alcoholic. Making that connection bothered me. I had to wonder whether any of my suspiciousness of Darwin Bishop could be grounded in the ill will I felt for my father.

Rossetti blew out another long stream of smoke. "Don't get me wrong. I know you can take care of yourself, Franko. But you haven't been up against anything like Darwin Bishop. If you think you have, that's just another advantage he's got over you."

I took a deep breath. "I'll keep looking over my shoulder," I said. After a year away from forensics, just forty-eight hours back in it had put me in harm's way again. But I wasn't about to raise any white flag. "If this kid isn't guilty, he's not going away for life," I said. "I'm not going to let it happen."

"This one's important to you," Rossetti said. "Personally."

"Yes," I said.

"You want a hint where to look for the real Darwin Bishop?" Rossetti asked.

"Shoot."

"Russia. It's the Wild West over there. If this guy successfully adopted a kid out of that country, then he's connected to some very tough people."

"He built and sold two companies in Russia," I said.

"Then he's got loads of dirty laundry hanging out over there. I could put in a call to my buddy Viktor Golov. He runs an oil refinery outside St. Petersburg. He's got his finger on the pulse of business across Russia."

"I'd owe you one." I finished my coffee and put down a ten to cover Rossetti's as well. "I'll take care of us this time," I said. I turned to leave.

Rossetti caught my arm. "Thanks for the round," he said. "Just promise you'll take care of *yourself*." His face lost every trace of humor. "I mean it. Be careful."

I nodded. "I'll talk to you soon," I said. "Call me with anything from your friend Viktor."

I drove back over the Meridian Street bridge and took the left onto Spruce. I was planning to turn onto Winnisimmet and head home, but I knew home just meant more tossing and turning—at least I convinced myself that it did. I kept going straight, through the Chelsea Produce Market, headed for the Sir Galahad Motel and Lounge.

The Sir Galahad is a down-and-out strip club with cinder-block walls, surrounded by wholesale fruit and vegetable warehouses. The girls don't wear fancy costumes. They don't even bother to lie about being college students. And no one pretends it's a gentleman's club.

I had gone to the Sir Galahad religiously when forensics had been my full-time occupation. I had needed to stay close to the naked truth about human beings, to keep resonating with lust and envy and hatred and all the other emotions that can drive violence.

I had also gone there to drink. And that fact kept me behind the wheel of my F-150 after I parked alongside the building. I sat and watched the pink neon dancer on the Sir Galahad sign as she flickered in the night. And I remembered how living so close to the raw edge of humanity had made me feel the need to take the edge off with scotch or cocaine or, more often, a combination of the two. I remembered how it was a sucker's strategy—letting the interest on my pain compound daily.

I can't be certain what made me get out of the truck. Maybe it was having seen Billy Bishop's scarred back, or having tried to imagine what it might be like for an infant to struggle for air and find none, or having revisited feelings I had once felt for Kathy. Or maybe it wasn't any of those things. Maybe I was just having my old trouble walking a straight line through a world with emotional minefields buried haphazardly all the way to the horizon.

Whatever the reason, I walked inside the Sir Galahad. Music blared from speakers that would have sufficed for a rock concert. Red and blue and purple lights doused the walls and ceiling with color. I took a seat up front, at the runway. A dancer with blond hair who might have been nineteen had stripped down to white panties. She hitched her thumbs inside the waistband, pulling them down a few inches, teasing the twenty or so truckers and bikers scattered around the room. They nodded and winked and smiled at her. Then she pulled them back up, all the way into her crotch. The men burst into applause.

"What are you drinking?" a waitress about fifty-five, wearing skin-tight jeans and a tube top over a stick figure, asked me.

I thought about ordering a Diet Coke—for about one second. "Scotch," I said. "Rocks."

"You got it," she said. She turned around and headed back to the bar.

The dancer peeled her panties to her ankles. She stepped

out of them and stepped over to the man two seats from me, who had folded five one-dollar bills over the brass rail. She bent over backwards, spreading her legs and holding herself on all fours, like a crab, opening herself up to him.

My scotch arrived. I paid for it, held the amber liquid up to the colored lights. It glowed rust blue, rust red, rust purple. A magic rainbow of calm. I brought the glass to my lips, smelling the aroma of my father, tasting his warm, alcoholic breath. Then, tilting my head back, I glanced at the dancer and noticed that the lowest part of her abdomen was scarred from a Cesarean delivery.

Part of me truly wanted to be numb, wanted to scramble the chemical messengers in my brain, to blur the images of cruelty floating through it. Because they were too sharp. Sharp enough to do serious damage. But another part of me had started to wonder where the dancer's child might be at that moment. With a grandfather? A boyfriend? Home alone? Dead? I stared at her as she grabbed her knees to spread herself wider, head turned to the side, eyes closed.

I put the drink down without swallowing a drop.

"Ain't she a fucking gem?" the man with the five-dollar bills called over to me. He was about forty, built like a weight lifter, wearing a New England Patriots football jersey and a black nylon skullcap.

"She's all of that," I said.

"What an ass on her," he said.

"What an ass."

"You're a spot welder, aren't you?" he asked.

In a certain way, I guessed I was, but I didn't think he was floating an elegant metaphor for piecing people back together. "No," I said. "Why do you ask?"

"You didn't do no work on the new Chelsea High School? Welding?"

"No," I said. "I'm a psychiatrist."

He burst out laughing. "Right on," he said. "Me, too." He reached into his pocket and pulled out more five-dollar bills for the rail.

I held my glass in both hands and looked into its depths,

still smelling my father, hearing the *clink* of his belt buckle coming loose. I thought about the countless times I had wanted to kill him. And I wondered what had stopped me. Why couldn't I bring myself to do him in? What makes a person finally cross the line? Was that the question that had drawn me to forensics in the first place? Was it the question—and not North Anderson's plea—that had brought me back into the company of murder?

I pushed the scotch away, caught the eye of the waitress, and ordered a coffee and a Diet Coke. It was going to be a long night.

I finally climbed into bed just after 3:00 A.M. I could sense the expanse of the king-sized mattress all around me. I felt dangerously alone.

Of course, I always had been alone. Isolated. At risk. But now the danger felt especially real. Because I couldn't dismiss what Carl Rossetti had told me; Darwin Bishop could be big trouble—bigger than anything I had faced before. A person with enough appetite and aptitude to accumulate a billion dollars can devour many things. I moved to one side of the mattress and dropped my hand to the Browning Baby semiautomatic tucked next to the bed frame. And with a fistful of cold steel as my pacifier, I fell into a restless slumber.

It didn't last. Not two hours later, the phone woke me. I fumbled for the receiver, dropped it once, then said, "Clevenger."

"Frank. It's North."

I squinted at my bedside clock. "It's four-fifty."

"I know that," he said. "I wouldn't call if it wasn't an emergency."

I sat up in bed. "What's happening?"

"Billy escaped from Payne Whitney two and a half hours ago."

I sat up. "Escaped? How?"

"Believe it or not, he just walked out of the emergency

room. He'd been complaining of a cough for hours. They sent him down with an attendant for a chest x-ray. As far as I can tell, the guy kind of lost track of him."

That was easy to believe. Psychiatry units that aren't built for violent offenders don't have true security protocols in place. I had seen inpatients wander away from "smoke breaks" when they were taken outside for a quick cigarette, from AA meetings that took place in another building on campus, and from "supervised" grounds passes to the hospital gift shop.

"I'm sure they've alerted the police in Manhattan and given them Billy's description," I said. "They can pick him up on a Section Twelve and rehospitalize him against his will."

"Actually, they can pick him up without a Section Twelve, if they find him. Billy's timing was flawless. As of seven P.M. last night, there was a warrant for his arrest. Tom Harrigan had everything set to go, including a court order for Billy's extradition back to Massachusetts. They planned to have New York Police arrest him on the locked unit at six A.M. today. Two officers would have accompanied him on a flight to Logan at seven-thirty."

"I'm having lunch with Julia Bishop today. She's coming to Boston," I said. "I'll find out if she has any sense where Billy might have gone."

"You called her, or she called you?" Anderson asked.

"She did," I said.

"Did she say why?"

"No. But she sounded a little panicked."

"She'll be missing Garret's tennis tournament," Anderson said wryly.

"He's in a tournament?" I asked. "Today?"

"The Bishops sponsor a charity competition at the Brant Point Racket Club. Garret Bishop is the top seeded player in his age group. According to the newspaper, he's set to defend his singles title from last year."

"Business as usual," I said. "All the way around Darwin's world."

"No stopping him," Anderson said. He paused. "Listen, you know I've never been convinced that Billy is guilty of murder. But I have to tell you, having him out of that hospital, on his own, really worries me. Because if he is the one who killed Brooke, he knows he has nothing left to lose."

Those words gave me a chill because I remembered Billy telling me the same thing at the end of our meeting. "If I were you, I'd add a few cruisers to those Range Rovers outside Bishop's 'watch house.' Billy wasn't happy with his father hospitalizing him."

"I tried," Anderson said. "Bishop thanked me for my concern and refused my offer."

"True to form," I said.

"I'll call you right away with anything new," he said.

"Same here." I hung up.

I lay back and stared into the darkness, my heart racing, thinking how I could really use that scotch I had set aside at Sir Galahad's. I wondered where Billy Bishop might be at that very moment. Would he have sought refuge at a homeless shelter? Would he bunk with a friend in Manhattan whose parents were out of town? Was he brazen enough to hide out at the Bishops' own penthouse? Or would he be huddled in a corner of the Port Authority, over on Eighth Avenue, waiting for a Bonanza Bus to take him back to Hyannis, where he could catch a ferry to Nantucket?

More important, what was he thinking of—escape or revenge?

7

I talked with Anderson before leaving my loft in the morning and learned that Billy was still at large. I had a couple hours before my 1:00 P.M. meeting with Julia, so I headed to Mass General for my third visit with Lilly Cunningham.

I expected to see her doing better, but she looked worse. Her skin was even paler than before. Her breathing was erratic. As her eyes followed me in from the doorway, she squinted to bring me into focus.

I pulled an armchair to the side of the bed and sat down. Above me, to the right of the window, the IV tree had grown new branches. A total of five hanging bottles and plastic bags dripped into the central line running into Lilly's subclavian vein. I looked at her leg, still suspended midair, and saw that another serpentine incision had been cut into the flesh to help her abscess drain.

"It's in my heart," she said weakly.

I knew she was talking about the infection having traveled to her heart, probably to the pericardial sac that surrounds it or to the valves deep inside its chambers. But I heard her words in another way, too. Because it was also true that the psychological trauma which had caused her to inject herself with dirt had reached the center of her being, the emotional toxin pumped now with the blood to every tissue, sparing only her central nervous system, walled off as it is by that baffle of membranes known as the blood-brain barrier. The lines of conflict were at last clearly drawn: Whatever had happened to Lilly as a girl had finally laid siege to the kingdom of her body, leaving the soul, and its own miraculous ability to heal, as her last defense—and my greatest ally.

I noted that, during my three meetings with Lilly, she had never had any visitors. Patients with Munchausen's often end up isolated; family and friends become enraged when they learn they have been caring for a person who has made herself sick. A wave of sadness—and, strangely, embarrassment—swept over me. The thought of Lilly suffering so terribly, without a hand to hold, made me want to reach out to her even more.

"*The sadness and shame you feel is hers, not yours,*" the voice at the back of my mind whispered. "*Help her own it.*"

"The last time I came to see you," I said, "you told me how frightened you were of being alone. Where does that fear come from, do you think?"

She cleared her throat. "Probably from losing my father," she said. She closed her eyes and slowly reopened them. "I haven't stopped missing him. I've thought of him every day since I was six."

"There are people you love today?" I said.

"Yes, of course. My husband. My mom and grandparents. A few good friends."

I leaned closer. I decided to gamble that Lilly's fear of being alone would translate into an even more imposing fear of death. "This is a very important moment, Lilly," I said quietly. "The infection is overwhelming your defenses. You could die. And that means saying good-bye to your husband and your mother and each of your friends. It means being completely and utterly alone." She seemed to be listening to me. "The only way to stay with the people you love is to open up to them, to let the truth flow. If you do that, I think all the stress you're under will start to fade away and your body will start to heal itself."

She looked away and shook her head. Several seconds passed. I sat still. Nearly a minute more went by. I was ready to gamble again by telling Lilly that I knew she had injected herself with dirt. But, of a sudden, she turned back toward me. Her eyes had filled with tears. "I did this," she whispered.

"Tell me what you mean," I said.

"I used a needle to inject . . . I caused the infection. I did this to myself."

I nodded. "I understand," I said.

She started to cry.

"I understand," I said again. I waited while she dried her eyes. "Can you tell me why you did it?" I asked.

"I don't know," she said. "I'm so ashamed."

"*But she does know. Ask about the shame*," the voice said.

"Is there something that happens to you around the time you inject yourself? Are there memories that bother you?"

She didn't hesitate this time. "I do it," she said, "when I feel filthy. I do it to punish myself."

"And what makes you feel filthy?" I asked.

"Nothing," she said, almost inaudibly.

"I'll never tell anyone," I promised.

She looked into my eyes, seeming to decide whether she could truly trust me. "I have bad thoughts," she said finally. "Terrible thoughts."

"Tell me about them."

She closed her eyes and stayed silent.

"Lilly, you have to let the truth out. You can't tie up your immune system any longer. You need it in order to stay with people you care about."

"I think . . ." She stopped herself.

"They don't want to lose you," I said. "They don't want to have to say good-bye."

"I think about my grandfather."

"What about him?" I asked. "What are the thoughts, exactly?"

"I think of myself . . . with him." She closed her eyes and shook her head. "Touching him. Him touching me."

"Were you ever close with your grandfather in that way? Physically?"

"Never." She opened her eyes and stared at the ceiling. "That's the strangest part." She looked at me. "I'm certain he never did anything like that." Her face was a portrait of confusion. "It feels so awful thinking that way about him."

"And thinking that way is what makes you want to inject yourself," I said.

"I would do it right now, if I could," she said. "It would make me feel so much better."

"To punish yourself," I said.

"Yes. The thoughts would stop."

So there it was, the pathogen attacking Lilly's heart. It had taken on the life of a bacterium, but it had been born in Lilly's psyche. Her guilt—and her infection—stemmed from her sexual feelings for the man who had taken care of her after her father's death. The only question that remained was what had cultivated that desire. Had she been the victim of sexual abuse she later repressed? Or could there be another explanation? "You have to be willing to feel all the pain without using a needle to chase it away," I said. "If you're brave enough to do that, then your stress will start to evaporate. The infection won't have a chance of winning. It won't be able to hide from your immune system."

"I want to try," she said. "Really, I do."

"Good."

"You'll help?" she asked.

"I told you I would stay with you through this," I said. "I meant it."

I made it to Bomboa about twenty minutes before my scheduled meeting with Julia Bishop. The place was unusually busy for lunchtime, but I'm a regular there, and K. C. Hidalgo, one of the owners, offered me my usual table right by the window. I told him I'd rather he find me a quiet table toward the back, and that I'd wait for my guest at the bar.

He looked at me with concern. "The bar? That's a new perch for you."

I'd eaten enough dinners alone at Bomboa for K.C. to hear my whole life story in two-minute installments. He was a slim El Salvadorian man in his early forties, with chiseled features and a smile that would have kept his restaurant full if the food was average. But the food was some of the best in Boston, and K.C. was getting rich. He ran his fingers through his thick black hair. "I thought the bar was off limits. 'Physician, heal thyself,' and all that."

"I'm drinking my usual brew," I said. "Coffee."

"Then my place is your place." He walked me to the bar and caught the attention of the bartender. "Coffee for the doctor," he said.

"You're taking good care of me," I said.

"Somebody ought to do it twenty-four, seven, dude," he said. "Somebody much prettier than me." He slapped me on the back. " 'Cause, let's face it, you don't have a great track record taking care of yourself." He smiled that smile, then headed back to his post near the door.

The bar was about twenty-five feet long, with every variety of alcohol stocked against a mirrored back. I could see my reflection, framed by bottles of gin and scotch and vodka. I didn't like the picture. But that didn't stop me from quietly asking for a Sambuca on the side when the bartender brought me my coffee.

He never came back, disappearing into the kitchen a few minutes, then tidying up the sink a few minutes more. I wondered whether I had whispered my order so softly that he had missed it. I was reluctant to approach him more openly for the booze, so I sat tight.

I was finishing off the last of my coffee when I caught Julia Bishop's reflection in the mirror. My heart started racing like a schoolboy's. She was wearing a whisper-thin, off-the-shoulder black cashmere sweater and hip-hugging tight black pants that flared slightly at the bottoms. Black sandals with three-inch heels made her look taller than I remembered her, like she had stepped out of the pages of *Vogue*. I glanced around the room and watched heads turning, including K.C.'s.

She walked up to me. "I'm glad you were able to see me," she said.

"Not a problem," I said, already adrift in that azure haze I had experienced the first time I met her. Julia's presence was so absorbing, in fact, that I felt removed in some measure from myself and heard my own words as I spoke them, almost as an echo.

"I don't think I've slept ten hours since Brooke. . . . And now, with Billy missing." She pressed her lips together to keep from breaking down.

The perfume Julia was wearing was more intoxicating than Sambuca. "We'll talk through everything," I said. "They're holding a table for us toward the back. It's quieter."

We moved to the table. Julia ordered a bottle of sparkling water. She said she had no appetite, which was understandable. But taken together with her sleeplessness, it made me worry she might be slipping into another depression. I ordered a few appetizers, to satisfy the waiter.

"I couldn't tell you much when you visited the house," she started, "but there's a lot you need to know about Billy. I think some of it will be critical when he goes to trial. Someone needs to make the judge aware of what he's been through."

"Anything you can tell me would be appreciated," I said.

"I'm sure my husband filled you in on Billy's background in Russia."

Listening to her use the words *my husband* bothered me. "He did. He told Captain Anderson and me about Billy witnessing the murder of his biological parents, then suffering abuse at the orphanage."

She seemed pained by what she was about to disclose. "What I doubt Darwin would have shared with you is how much trauma Billy has suffered since his arrival in this country."

"He didn't share any of that," I said.

She swallowed hard. "Darwin isn't the man you might think. He's very intelligent. He can be remarkably charming. But he's also very controlling. And he can be cruel."

I decided not to offer up the fact that Billy had shown me the welts on his back. I wanted to hear from Julia first-hand whether she believed Darwin Bishop was physically abusive. "Cruel, in what way?" I said.

"His demands on the boys are extreme," she said. "He expects them to be perfect—in school, athletics, at home. He interprets any emotion other than pride and self-confidence as a sign of weakness." She shook her head. "My son, Garret, is competing in a tennis tournament today, completely against his will," she said. "He pleaded with his father to let him drop out. He's beside himself about the baby, of course. And he's worried about Billy having left the hospital. Win wouldn't hear of him not playing."

"Garret wouldn't defy him?"

"Never," she said. "That's a difference between Garret and Billy. Garret wouldn't risk Darwin's temper."

"Tell me about his temper."

She dropped her gaze. "I called you because I sensed you were an extraordinary person, Frank. But this still isn't easy to talk about."

"Nothing shocks me anymore," I said.

She looked deep into my eyes—into *me*. "Why is that?"

"I've seen people at their worst, doing terrible things." Telling her about my pain felt like giving it to her, relieving myself of it.

She kept looking into my eyes as she nodded, her posture and expression inviting me to say more, to empty myself into her.

"I left forensics years ago," I said. "I wasn't doing well." That was as much as I wanted to yield, and Julia seemed to know it.

She took a deep breath. "I've always believed people

appear in our lives when we need them to," she said.

"I believe that, too," I said. Our eyes met, and I realized why models command the fees they do. Her luminous eyes promised to see the best in me and to help me see it. They made me want to be strong for her.

"The truth is," she said, "the boys and I have lived in fear of Darwin for years. He becomes physically abusive, unpredictably. It used to happen when he drank. I thought the alcohol was to blame. But it only got worse after he managed to stop drinking."

"He hits you?" I asked. I could feel my jaw tighten, my pulse rate start to climb. I knew some of my reaction had to be rooted in having watched my father beat my mother, but I didn't know how much of it. And I didn't know how to control it.

Julia looked embarrassed. "Let's say I've worn my share of dark lenses," she said. "I've hidden a lot over the years."

"And he's physically abusive to the boys?"

Her expression turned solemn. "That's as much my fault as anyone's," she said. "I should have left with them a long time ago."

"So you're saying he does abuse them," I said.

She nodded once. "Billy's gotten the worst of it," she said.

I noticed I was leaning into the table. I settled myself back in my seat. "Why?" I asked.

"Two reasons, I think. First of all, Billy's had a much harder time achieving. Win takes that as a direct challenge to his authority. He doesn't seem to understand that Billy's background may mean he always has to struggle. He literally believes that Billy willfully failed again and again in school—and in sports—to spite him."

That certainly didn't sound like the man who had made so much of Billy being ill, rather than evil—and so worthy of help. But I was learning that Darwin Bishop had at least two faces. "What's the other reason Billy is your husband's preferred target?" I asked. *Your husband.* I didn't like the words any better when I spoke them.

"Billy is the one who always seems to fight back. He won't give in. No apologies. No promises of more effort or better behavior—not even after setting the house afire. Obviously, that stubbornness makes Darwin angrier. He doesn't have anyone else in his life who stands up to him." Her eyes fell. "Myself included."

I decided to share what Billy had told me about being beaten with a strap. "When I visited Billy at Payne Whitney, he showed me his back," I said.

"He won't let me look at his back," Julia said. "He hides it from me."

"It's covered with welts. He told me that your husband whips him with a belt."

She winced.

"That happened some number of times?" I said. "What Billy described?"

She nodded.

"Do the boys try to protect one another?" I asked.

"No," she said. "They don't have a close relationship. They pretty much steer clear of one another. I've always thought that had something to do with Garret having come from Darwin's previous marriage. The boys didn't meet until Garret was seven and Billy was six. But I think Garret also avoids him because Billy's been the one acting out, getting into trouble. He doesn't want to be painted with the same brush."

"Or hit with the same strap," I said.

"Or that," she said.

"Darwin told North Anderson and me that Billy inflicted those wounds on himself," I said.

"That's absurd," she said. She looked directly at me again. "Listen to me. Part of me would like to see Billy spend his life in prison for what he did," she said, working to keep her voice steady. "Part of me wishes this state had the death penalty." Her chest rose and fell sharply with her breathing. "I've lost my baby."

"I understand," I said.

"You couldn't."

She was right. I stayed silent.

"I'm here because the other part of me knows that Billy isn't fully to blame for what he did—even though he did it to my daughter. My husband is also guilty. And I am, too, for not having done something about Win's violence." She took a few moments to steady herself. "My husband and Billy have been locked in a terrible struggle," she said. "It's nothing a boy should have had to deal with. Certainly not a boy with Billy's history. And I think it's the reason he struck out at Brooke. I think he really wanted to hurt Win."

That fit eerily with the theory I had shared with Billy during my hospital visit. It also answered a question for me; Julia Bishop obviously didn't think her husband was responsible for her baby's death. I wasn't at all sure she would consider moving Tess off the estate. I decided to slowly test the waters. "I happened to see the *New York* magazine article that ran after your wedding," I said. "The two of you were driving down Fifth Avenue in a Ferrari. You seemed very much in love."

"I thought I was," Julia said.

"Did you know a great deal about him before you married him?"

"I've learned a lot more. Why do you ask?"

"Had he shared his criminal record with you?" I asked.

"Yes," she said. "But I didn't make much of it. I knew about his drinking."

Not making much of marrying a man who had beaten his first wife—drunk or sober—seemed peculiar. "What exactly did he tell you?" I asked.

"He told me about a barroom brawl that led to an assault charge," she said. "It was around 1980, I think. There was mention of it in the paper when Win was arrested for drunk driving."

I shook my head. "That isn't what the newspaper was referring to," I said. "I pulled Darwin's record. Your husband pled guilty to assault and battery of his former wife, Lauren, along with violating a restraining order she had taken out. He got the year right, but that's about it."

She looked at me as if I must be joking. Then, seeing that I wasn't, she leaned toward me, incredulous. "I had no idea," she said. She let her head drop into her hands. "I've been so stupid."

It felt like the right moment to introduce the idea of Tess Bishop staying with grandparents. "The question I would ask yourself, Julia, is whether it's completely clear to you that Billy is the one who took Brooke's life."

She looked up. "What do you mean?"

"Billy denies hurting his sister."

"Of course he does," she said. "He never admits any of the destructive things he does."

"So you're convinced he's responsible?"

"Well, yes."

I took the leap. "It isn't possible your husband is involved?"

She squinted at me. "You're saying you think Win might have done this?"

"I'm saying the facts of the case aren't clear to me yet. Darwin does have an extensive history of being abusive— toward you, Billy, and Garret. And the pattern goes back even further, to his first marriage."

Julia seemed lost in thought.

"He's the only one in the house who has a known history of violence toward family members," I pressed.

"He never wanted the twins," she said blankly.

I relaxed a bit, thinking she might cooperate with the idea of getting Tess to a safer place. "Tell me more about that," I said.

"He never wanted children of our own. I mean, biological children. He made it very difficult for me when I was pregnant. I nearly went through with an abortion." She squinted down at the table, remembering. "I've wondered whether God is punishing me for that."

"You showed a lot of strength going through with the pregnancy," I said. "I don't know why you'd be punished."

"I wanted children so much," she said. She caught her lip between her teeth.

I waited a few moments. "Why didn't Darwin want them?" I said softly.

"According to him, it has to do with the war," she said, looking up at me. "He won't talk about Vietnam, except to say that he saw horrible things there, things that convinced him it wasn't fair to bring children into the world." She rolled her eyes. "It's a bit of a cliché."

"You don't buy it," I said.

"No. I don't."

"What do you think his real reason is?"

"It's about maintaining control," she said. "Win is incapable of intimacy. I think he felt having a son or daughter together—let alone twins—would connect him too closely with me, not to mention the child. No matter how much you love adopted children, they aren't blood. It isn't the same." She paused. "He sees me as a combination concubine and governess, not a wife and mother. Those roles would give me too much power."

"Did you object to adopting Billy?" I asked.

"I questioned Win's motives, that was all," Julia said.

"Why?" I asked.

"Win had driven Billy's father out of business," she said. "The two of them owned competing mining companies. It was a very tough time. Win almost lost everything, but he ended up on top, as usual. Then, about five months later, Billy's parents were murdered. I felt Win was playing Gandhi, adopting a rival's child."

I was stunned by the connection, particularly because Bishop had never mentioned it. Had he been silent out of humility? "It does sound admirable," I ventured.

"It may *sound* that way," she said. "But I'm quite certain he was just posturing for his business associates in Russia, faking his concern for Billy to impress them. He never showed Billy any love."

I could have told her even more about the real Darwin Bishop, including what I knew about his affair with Claire

Buckley. But it wasn't the right time. And I wasn't at all sure it was my place. "The question I want to raise is whether it might be safer to have Tess stay somewhere outside the house," I said. "Maybe with your parents, or with friends."

"I don't know if I could do that," she deadpanned.

"Why not?"

"Darwin would never allow it," she said.

Those words certainly spoke to Bishop's psychological control over his wife. "You could do it on your own. You have every right . . ."

"Rights don't necessarily hold up when you're dealing with someone like him," she said.

"Why is that?"

"The few times I've broached the idea of a separation, he's made it clear he wouldn't let it happen."

"What choice would he have?"

Julia smiled for an instant, as if she was about to explain something about the world to a child. Then her face fell again. "Being Darwin Bishop expands the range of possibilities," she said. "There could be a whole legal team filing endless motions for custody of our children, a media campaign to ruin my reputation and influence judges, months of travel with Garret and Tess to any one of a dozen countries Darwin does business in. He could probably pay Claire enough to convince her to go with him. He might even decide that they should never return."

"And Claire would stay with him?" I asked, wanting to see whether Julia would volunteer any suspicions about the affair.

"Everyone has a price, Frank," she said. "Claire isn't from money. She's very impressed by it."

Julia certainly didn't seem naive about her nanny. But her response didn't tell me exactly how much she knew about Claire's behavior. I didn't want to press her. "The bottom line," I said, "is that Darwin would go to great lengths to keep you from divorcing him."

"Or I suppose I could just disappear."

"You're saying he'd . . ."

"I'm saying I'm not brave enough to find out, Frank," Julia said. "At least I haven't been in the past. I've never had the courage to walk away."

"Maybe it's time."

"Maybe. Maybe that's one reason I called you. You make me feel like I could do it," she said.

The idea of rescuing a woman was a potent drug for me. "Only because you can," I said. "As soon as you believe it."

She nodded to herself, then focused on me with a new intensity. "Do you really think Tess could be in danger? You believe Darwin is capable of killing our daughter? His own flesh and blood?"

I hadn't had the question put to me so directly before. I thought about it for several seconds. I thought about Julia's belief that Bishop craved control, that he couldn't tolerate intimacy. I thought about the parts of his own soul he had snuffed out. "Yes," I said. "I think he is."

She kept staring at me. She seemed on the verge of agreeing to get Tess to a safer place. But then her gaze fell—maybe under the weight of so many years bending her will to Darwin Bishop's. "I have to think about this," she said.

"I hope you'll think about it sooner rather than later," I said. Later as in *too late*, I thought to myself.

She looked back at me, hopefully. "Will you be at Brooke's . . ." she said, then stopped, choked up. She waited a bit, took another deep breath. "Will you be at Brooke's funeral tomorrow? It's on the island. St. Mary's on Federal Street. Five P.M." She had to pause again. "Darwin wants the sun to be setting as the mass ends."

Another possible reason why Bishop would prefer an evening funeral mass occurred to me: the stock market closes at 4:30 P.M. "I'd like to be there," I said. "I'm not sure Darwin would be comfortable with my attending, given the ongoing investigation."

"I want you there," she said. "I need you there, whether Win has a problem with it or not."

"Then I will be."

"Thank you," she said softly.

I told Julia I would walk her to her car. I was on my way out of Bomboa, with Julia a few steps in front of me, when K.C. Hidalgo caught my arm. I stopped.

"She's terrific," K.C. said. "You look great together." He winked at Julia, who had stopped near the door.

"It would be mixing business with pleasure," I said, half to remind myself. "Probably a recipe for disaster."

"What a pleasure, though," he said.

K.C. was living with the night manager of his joint, a stunner named Yvette. "I'll take that from where it comes," I said. "Say hello to Yvette for me."

"You got it." He paused. "Hey, one other thing, champ," he said. He leaned toward me. "When you ordered that Sambuca? I had already told Stevie at the bar not to serve you any booze. Try sneaking another drink at my place, I'll lock you in the fucking basement and throw away the key until you're good and dry."

. I forced a smile.

"I mean it," he said.

"You're a good guy, K.C."

"Get a hold of yourself, will you?"

"Sure," I said. "I will. Trust me on this."

"Right," K.C. said. His tone made it clear he wasn't buying my bullshit. "I'm here if you need me."

I caught up with Julia. We walked outside.

"My car is in the Dartmouth Street garage," she said. We started down Stanhope, headed toward Dartmouth. But within several steps, Julia stopped. "I'm okay alone," she said.

"I don't mind the walk," I said.

She glanced across the street. "It's not a good idea."

I followed her eyes and saw a white Range Rover with smoked windows. I assumed it was one of Darwin

Bishop's. I felt a rush of adrenaline. "He's having you followed?" I said.

"Unlikely," she said. "He's probably having you followed." She held out her hand. "Shake," she said. "All very businesslike, right?"

I took her hand, but just held it. She looked into my eyes with what I read as a combination of tenderness and fear. "I'll see you tomorrow night," I said. I let go of her hand.

She nodded tentatively, turned around, and headed toward the Dartmouth Street garage.

I crossed the street and walked up to the Range Rover. I couldn't see through the driver's-side window, so I knocked on the glass. The window came down. A man who looked to be in his mid-thirties was in the driver's seat. His neck was weight-lifter thick, his face half-shaven. He was wearing a blousy silk shirt, but it covered an obviously large frame.

"Can I help you with something?" he said, without any emotion.

"I want to get a message to your employer," I said.

He didn't respond, but he didn't close the window.

"Tell Mr. Bishop I don't mind if he has me followed. I don't mind if he visits me, either. I live at Thirty-nine Winnisimmet Street in Chelsea. Top floor. Unit Five B. I'm there a fair amount, almost always in the late part of the evening."

"I'll be sure to do that," the man said.

I started to leave, but turned back. "One more thing: Since I'm not a kid and I'm not female, tell him he can expect to have a tougher time with me than his usual targets. He might want to bring someone like you along to give him a hand."

8

The telephone was ringing when I walked into my loft, but I got to it too late. I glanced at the answering machine. It had registered thirty-one calls, but used up less than a minute of talk time. That meant lots of hangups. I was about to scroll through them for caller IDs when the phone started ringing again. I grabbed it. "Clevenger," I said.

"How many psychiatrists does it take to change a light bulb?"

I recognized Billy Bishop's voice. "Where are you?" I asked.

"C'mon," he said. "How many?"

"Three," I guessed, to appease him.

"Just one," he said, "but the light bulb has to want to change."

"Okay," I said. "Pretty funny. Now, where are you?"

"I'm not locked up in that loony bin," he said.

I glanced at the caller ID. It read, "Unknown Caller." I figured Billy was probably at a pay phone. "Are you all right?"

"I'm fine, if you forget the part about my father trying to throw me in jail for life. It would take an awful lot of therapy to get my mind off something like that, don't you think?"

I smiled, despite the gravity of the situation. "I guess

you're right." I paused. "Tell me where you are," I said. "I'll meet you."

"No. And I can't stay on the line long," he said. "I need you to loan me a little money. I'll pay you back. I promise. I'm good for it."

I wanted to slow things down and coax Billy back into the hospital, even though he would certainly be arrested. As risky as navigating the judicial system might be for him, it was a lot safer than the streets. And Billy wasn't the only person in peril; I hadn't forgotten that his history of violence meant he might strike out in unpredictable, very destructive ways. "I think you made a mistake leaving Payne Whitney," I said. "I think you're better off going back and getting a lawyer to fight for you."

"Thanks for the advice," he said. "Will you do life with me?"

"They have to prove you're guilty," I said.

"I need money," he said. "That's all I need right now."

"Where can I meet you?"

"Like I said, you can't. There's a safe place where you can leave it for me. I have somebody who can grab it and bring it to me."

"Where are you?" I pushed.

"Can I have the money?" he asked. "You know I didn't kill Brooke. You *know* it."

He was starting to sound desperate. I gambled he was desperate enough to trust me. "Not unless we can meet face-to-face," I said.

"Impossible," he said.

"That's the deal, Billy. Take it or leave it."

He was silent a few seconds. "I'm at the end of my rope," he said finally. "You've got to come through here, Doc. I'm counting on you."

I closed my eyes, imagining how terrifying it would feel to be sixteen years old, all alone, facing life in prison. "I'm just asking you to meet me halfway. You get the money when I get to see you."

"That's it. Your final answer?"

"That's it."

"Then you're as much to blame for what happens as anyone else," he said bitterly.

"To blame—for what?"

"Read about it in the papers." He hung up.

"Billy!" I yelled into the receiver. I dialed *69, trying to be reconnected, but got the standard computer message telling me the callback feature wouldn't work. I slammed the receiver down. The phone crashed to the floor.

The end of my rope. I stared at the phone cord looped around one leg of the table. I could almost hear the call I had gotten years before from Anne Sacon, a social worker with the Department of Youth Services, after Billy Fisk had been found hanging from a noose in his parents' garage. Days earlier Fisk had reached out to me for what proved to be the last time, telling me how unhappy he was at home and asking whether he could come live with me. It hadn't seemed even remotely possible at the time. Patients don't move in with their psychiatrists, after all. But had I known how close he was to the edge, I would have agreed.

Was history repeating itself? Was God testing me to see whether I had learned to go all the way out on a limb for someone about to fall?

I flicked through the handful of numbers that had registered on my message machine. They were all in the 508 area code, which included Cape Cod and Nantucket. The only number I recognized was North Anderson's. I figured the others probably belonged to Billy, that he had run closer to home, rather than further away.

I listened to North's message. No emergency, but he wanted me to call him. I dialed his number at work. His secretary put me through.

"Billy's come up for air," I told him.

"How so?" he asked.

"He called me for a loan."

"I hope he's looking to buy a one-way airplane ticket to Russia instead of a stolen gun," he said. "I wouldn't give him any dough."

"He wanted the money dropped off so a buddy could run it to him. I told him no deal."

"Good. The last thing I want to do is tail sixteen-year-olds across two states—or two continents," Anderson said. "He'll circle back to you."

"He got pretty threatening at the end," I admitted. "He told me to watch the papers."

"All the more reason to keep him running on empty. Without a full wallet, he'll turn up sooner."

That made me feel better about my decision to withhold the cash, but not a whole lot better. "I got your message on my machine," I said. "What's up?"

"Nothing urgent. I just wanted you to know I'm starting to feel some political pressure from good old Darwin. We must be getting to him."

"What sort of political pressure?" I asked him.

"I serve at the pleasure of the mayor," Anderson said. "And the mayor serves all kinds of masters, including Darwin Bishop. He called to let me know he isn't pleased I have you on board. He doesn't see why we need a forensic psychiatrist involved in the case when there's an identified lead suspect and a clear path to prosecution once that suspect is apprehended."

"Translation: Leave the billionaire alone and close the case down," I said.

"You speak Nantucket very well."

"So what does that mean for us, in the short term?" I asked.

"It doesn't mean anything, short or long term, until they fire me, run me off the island, and set up a blockade to keep me away."

I had relied on North Anderson's loyalty before, but I didn't want to take it for granted. "You could cut me loose, and I could keep working on my own time," I said.

"Wow," he said. "You've come a long way. You didn't even want this gig, let alone wanting it pro bono."

"Things change," I said.

"Not everything," Anderson said. "If they want to shake

you off the case, they'll have to get me off the case. And that's not happening."

"Understood." I let myself linger a couple seconds on the good feeling that Anderson's camaraderie inspired in me. "I got my own message from Darwin Bishop today," I said. "He had me followed when I took Julia to lunch. Some gorilla in one of his Range Rovers was parked outside the restaurant."

Anderson was silent for a bit. "I think you ought to come down here for a few days," he said.

"You want to watch my back for me?"

"Why not? You've watched mine enough."

I had already started to feel myself being pulled back to the island, especially since Billy's calls seemed to place him a lot closer to Nantucket than Chelsea. "Any chance I could interview Darwin Bishop once more?"

"I can try to set it up," Anderson said. "He's already having you followed. He might actually like the chance to check in face-to-face."

"I'll take a ferry over tonight, provided they have space. If you get me that interview, I'll have a pretty full dance card. I'm attending Brooke Bishop's funeral tomorrow."

"At Julia's invitation?" he said.

"Yes."

There was a little longer silence this time. "Look, we go back a long way, right?"

I knew where he was headed. "You don't have to say it."

"I'm just going to tell you the way it is: You can't touch her."

"I haven't," I said.

"You haven't and you *won't*?"

I hesitated.

"Listen to me," Anderson said. "Whether you mess around with married women is your own business. I'm not about to give you any lectures on morality."

"Good."

"You can't touch her because it contaminates the case.

You can't see clearly from the inside of anything, if you know what I mean."

I knew exactly what he meant. Crossing personal boundaries in professional relationships is always ill-advised. As a psychiatrist, it's especially unethical. But my attraction to Julia was blurring all those lines. I didn't feel I could honestly make any promises or predictions about where my relationship with her was headed. "You're right," was all I told Anderson.

"And . . ."

"And I'll try to be on that ferry I mentioned."

"You're playing with fire, Frank."

"I hear you."

He let out a heavy sigh. "Call me when you hit the island."

"Will do."

I packed light, but then realized I was traveling a little too light, given the special attention Darwin Bishop was paying me. I walked over to the bed, reached down to the bed frame, and grabbed my Browning Baby pistol. I tucked it in my front pocket. It had been a long time since I'd needed to carry, but it was that time again.

I walked to the kitchen next. I looked up at the double doors of the cabinet over the refrigerator. I hadn't opened those doors for more than two years. But I hadn't emptied the cabinet, either. A collection of single malt scotches stood inside, waiting for a moment like this one, when some sort of trouble in the world would become my trouble again. There was a flask in the cabinet, too—a well-worn, sterling silver one with "FGC" engraved, front and center. *Frank Galvin Clevenger.* I was never one for monograms, but Galvin had been my father's first name, and it had seemed fitting that I include the "G" on a vessel that contained the spore of the illness we shared.

I reached up and opened the doors. I took down the flask and a bottle of twenty-year-old Glenlivet. I twisted the cap off each. Then, in a ritual that had sometimes reminded me of a transfusion, sometimes of bloodletting, I poured a thin stream of scotch from bottle to flask, listening to the familiar song of the liquid splashing into the hollow vessel. It was a deep, throaty tune at first and something more shrill toward the end. I remembered it with dread and—more ominous for me—nostalgia.

I put the bottle back in the cabinet and the flask in my back pocket. And I walked out of the loft that way, on a journey that would take me, in equal measure, into my future and into my past.

I planned to take the 7:00 P.M. ferry out of Hyannis and leave my truck in the lot there. But when the clerk at Steamship Authority told me a car reservation had opened up (something of a miracle in June), I happily paid the $202 and drove aboard.

North Anderson had reached me on my cell phone and offered me the guestroom at his house, but I had passed, not wanting to impose on him or his wife, Tina. Playing hostess, with no notice, when you're six months pregnant can't be much fun. I also preferred having my own base to work from. I gave Anderson my ETA and found a vacancy at the Breakers, part of the White Elephant hotel complex on Easton Street, which runs along the north side of Nantucket Harbor.

I napped for about an hour in my truck, then woke up and stepped onto the deck to get some air. It wasn't quite sixty degrees, chilly for late June. I stood near the stern, breathing in the mist and watching the ship's white cotton wake. I wondered whether Billy had made the same trip earlier. I imagined him laying low and stealing onto the island unseen or unrecognized, a cruel irony for a boy whose identity—including his biological parents, his native land, his first language, and his name—had already been stripped from him. Now survival required burying the rest of himself, at least temporarily. If that felt too much like dying, he might decide to make it official. Strangely, suicide is sometimes a person's way of taking control—the soul's last-ditch effort to free itself from overwhelming earthly influences.

I thought back to my first psychotherapy session with Dr. James. I'd been talking five or ten minutes about a nurse I was romancing. She wanted a commitment, I didn't feel ready to make one, and that seemed to mean I was going to lose her. Looking back on it, the whole affair was hopeless; I was nowhere near ready for a real relationship.

James stopped me midsentence. "We don't have a lot of time together," he said. "We shouldn't waste it talking about some conquest of yours. May I ask you a specific question, so we can begin, in earnest?"

I stopped jawing and nodded my head.

"When was the first time," he said, "that you thought of killing yourself?"

I sat there, stunned, looking at the gnomish, eighty-one-year-old man seated across from me, wearing a seersucker suit and two silver and turquoise cuff bracelets. "When was the first time I thought of *killing* myself?" I echoed.

He looked at his watch. Then he winked at me and smiled warmly, even lovingly. "C'mon, Frank," he said. "Give it up. What have you got to lose?"

And I did. Just like that. Such were the man's gifts. I told him that the first time I thought of ending it all was when I was nine years old. I had taken a beating from my father, and I had gone upstairs to my room and thrown a pair of jeans, my baseball glove, and a favorite model airplane into a duffel bag. Then I had walked downstairs, stopping in the tiny foyer outside the kitchen. A short staircase led to the front door.

My father saw me and walked out of the kitchen. "Going somewhere?" he asked.

I summoned all the nerve I could and stared up at him. "Good-bye," I said.

"What do you think you're doing?" he said.

"Don't look for me," I said, shaking with fear. "I'm not coming back." Translation: Tell me you're sorry, and that you want me to stay, and that everything will be different if I do.

He laughed at me. "So, go," he said. "You want to be a big shot? You don't want to live here? Take off." He walked back into the kitchen.

I glanced at my mother, cooking dinner. All the years she had stood idly by as my father meted out his brutality could have been overshadowed if she had had enough courage to come to me at that moment. But she didn't make a move, didn't say a word.

In truth, I had nowhere to go. I was nine. I had never felt as helpless. I dropped my suitcase, ran to my room, and started to cry. And I came up with a plan to wait until my parents were asleep, then use my father's belt as a noose to hang myself from a hook on the bathroom door.

Thinking about two things had kept me on the planet. The first was my best friend, Anthony, who sat behind me in homeroom and had an uncanny ability to finish my sentences. The second was my two-year-old turtle, Seymour, who surely would perish if left alone with my mother and father.

I wiped the mist from my face and took a deep breath of Atlantic air. The night seemed even chillier than before. I reached into my pocket and took out my flask. I unscrewed the cap, brought the metal to my lips, and swallowed a mouthful.

By the time the ferry reached Nantucket Sound, with Martha's Vineyard off to my right and the lighthouse at Cape Pogue just visible on Chappaquiddick Island, I had downed about a third of the scotch. More went as we slipped between the jetties that protect the channel into Nantucket Harbor. And once we had powered past Brant Point light, headed toward the wharf, the flask was empty. I held it up to the moonlight and focused on the monogram engraved in the sterling, pregnant with my father's "G" in its center. I rubbed it a few times with my thumb, picturing him standing outside the kitchen, telling me to leave if I wanted to. Then I tossed it into the waves.

• • •

I checked into the Breakers, walked over to my suite. Fresh flowers and a bottle of Merlot had been left for me, courtesy of the management. Fortunately, I was already feeling guilty about my drinking. I put the bottle in the hallway, just outside my door.

I hadn't been in the room fifteen minutes when North Anderson called from the lobby. He said he wanted to talk. I told him I'd be right down.

We walked over to the hotel's Brant Point Grill for a late dinner. From our table we had a sweeping view of the harbor and a good view of the rest of the dining room. Both of them were a little too pretty and made me uneasy. Looking at the tanned, well-dressed, bejeweled patrons, I wondered how the community was coping with a murderer at large. "Has the local paper covered the Bishop case?" I asked Anderson.

"I hear the Boston Globe's working on a long piece," he said. "But they've treated it like a car theft on the island. There was a two-paragraph story buried in the *Inquirer & Mirror*."

"See no evil, hear no evil," I said. "Funny thing how that doesn't seem to make it disappear."

Anderson nodded. "People use all kinds of escapes. You know that. This island, the way of life here—it's definitely one of them. To be honest, that's the reason I signed on as chief of police. I didn't think I'd be working another murder case the rest of my career. And I would never have missed it." He leaned a little closer. "For you, escaping still seems to mean booze."

I realized I must have had scotch on my breath. "Just a slip, you know? It happens."

"No, I don't." he said. "I don't know how it happens that you'd risk everything you've built over the last two years. Because I remember where your head was after the Lucas case. I wasn't sure you'd make it back." He looked away. "Maybe I was wrong bringing you on board."

I squinted at him. "Excuse me?"

The waitress had walked up to our table. I reluctantly focused on the menu and put in my order. Anderson did the same.

"Listen," he said, as soon as she had left. "I needed help, so I pushed you to get involved. But you might have had it right when you turned me down." He looked at me like a physician about to diagnose something incurable. "You may not be able to do this work anymore. It tears you up too much."

"Didn't you just tell me on the phone last night that they'd have to shake you loose from this case to shake me loose?" I said.

"I'm letting you off the hook," he said. "Think about it and let me know."

"I don't need to think about it," I said. "I'm into this too deep to back off."

He nodded unconvincingly.

"I won't touch the crap. All right?"

"Sure," he said.

I was feeling leaned on, so I leaned back. "Maybe my drinking isn't really the issue here," I said.

"What's that supposed to mean?"

"You're getting pressure from the mayor. You've got a nice job. You want to keep it. So I slip, and you say I'm down for the count. You make everyone happy."

"Like who?" Anderson bristled.

I shrugged. "Like the mayor and Darwin Bishop." Having said those words, I wished I could have stuffed them back inside me. I knew Anderson was just trying to help me. "I didn't . . ." I started.

He was already on his feet. "Hey, fuck you," he said, barely keeping his voice down.

"I didn't mean that," I said. "And I didn't start this whole thing."

The muscles in Anderson's jaw were tight, his expression telegraphing he was barely in control, but he managed to sit down. "All I want," he said, "is to solve this case without it ruining your life or mine. So when I see you starting to get close to a suspect's wife . . ."

"Is that what this is all about?" I said.

"Let me finish." He lowered his voice. "When I see you getting close with Julia, then starting to dive back into a bottle, I worry whether your vision is getting cloudy. Because I'm depending on it. Is there something strange about that? Or did you forget that her son and husband are the two lead suspects in this case?"

"There's nothing strange about it," I admitted. "I understand."

"Good." Anderson drank his entire ice water without a breath. He put the glass down with the decisiveness of a judge ruling on a case. He looked around the dining room self-consciously. "You're set for a second interview with Darwin Bishop tomorrow," he said.

I was a little surprised Bishop had consented to it. "What did he say, exactly?"

"Whatever he said, he didn't say it to me. I only got as far as Claire Buckley. She handles Bishop's schedule."

"I guess she handles a lot of things."

"No question about it," Anderson said with a wink. "Sal Ferraro, my private investigator friend, the one who tracked down Bishop's hotel and travel receipts, tells me they've got another trip planned next month. July in Paris. Bishop reserved a very pricey suite, for one full week, at the George V, right near the Champs Elysées."

"Why wouldn't they book two rooms?" I said. "Just for appearances?"

Anderson smiled. "Why did Gary Hart pose for a photograph on *Monkey Business*? Why did Clinton use the Oval Office?"

"Good questions. I guess it seemed worth the risk at the time. Or it seemed about time to self-destruct."

"Exactly. That was my point about you and Julia," he said.

"Point made," I said, hoping that would be enough to get him off the topic.

He seemed satisfied. "Are you going to tell Darwin about Billy having contacted you?" he asked.

I thought about that. Strictly speaking, it was Bishop's right to know—not only because the information involved his son, but also because Billy's tone at the end of our call meant Darwin Bishop's own safety and that of other family members could be at risk. "I have to tell him," I said. "Until we're absolutely certain who the murderer is, I don't want to keep anyone's secrets."

"I agree," Anderson said. He pressed his lips together and nodded to himself. "Does that include Julia?" he said.

"You're relentless," I said.

"Does it include her?" he persisted.

I stared back at him. "Asked and answered," I said flatly.

"Not really," he said. "But let me ask a different question." He paused: "Why haven't we talked about her as a suspect?"

"Julia?" I said.

"She wouldn't be the first woman to murder her child," Anderson said. "She was at home the night Brooke died, just like everyone else."

"We haven't talked about her because neither one of us has a gut feeling she was remotely involved," I said. "We haven't talked about Billy's brother Garret, either."

"Stay with me on Julia for a minute, okay?"

"Sure."

He gathered his thoughts. "Some women get depressed after they have a kid, don't they? Postpartum depression?"

Postpartum depression, an illness that descends within six months of giving birth, affects tens of thousands of women in the United States alone. The cause isn't known. It might be hormonal, neurochemical, or psychological—or some combination of the three. "Of course," I told Anderson.

"And women who've killed their kids have used postpartum depression as the basis for insanity pleas, haven't they?" he said.

I knew what he was getting at, but I wasn't in the mood

to admit it. "You sound like a prosecutor," I said. "Am I on trial here?"

"Just answer me."

"In some cases, women with postpartum depression have pled not guilty by reason of insanity after killing their babies," I allowed.

"In a few cases, it even worked," he went on. "They successfully argued that they were so depressed they lost contact with reality."

"I had one of the cases," I said. "A woman down in Georgia who shot her daughter and killed a neighbor's kid. The jury let her off."

"And Julia Bishop has a psychiatric history. Depression."

I thought back to my lunch with Julia, particularly to my worry that her lack of sleep and lack of appetite might reflect a recurrence of that depression. "What you're saying makes some sense," I said, "but—"

"But she has pretty eyes and a great ass, and Frank Clevenger loves the ladies, especially the broken ones." He grimaced. He knew I hadn't gotten over losing Kathy to mental illness. "Sorry," he said. "Now it's my turn to apologize."

Part of me wanted to grab Anderson by the throat, but another part of me knew he was right. I couldn't exclude Julia Bishop as a suspect in the murder of little Brooke. "Don't worry about it," I said.

He still wouldn't let go. "Meaning what, exactly?"

"She goes on the list," I said. "I don't think she filled Brooke's throat with plastic sealant, but I can't prove it right at this moment, okay? Satisfied?"

"Yes." Anderson relaxed. He sat back in his chair. "Don't get me wrong. I'd be blown away if she were the one, Frank. But I've been blown away before."

Dinner arrived. Swordfish for me, sirloin for Anderson. I thought to myself how I would love a glass of Merlot to go with the whole spread. I meditated a bit on those words. I would *love* a glass of Merlot. Maybe Anderson wasn't off base at all. Maybe addiction was at the heart of my romantic feelings for women, including Kathy—and Julia. Maybe it truly was the broken parts of them that attracted me, because they spoke to what was broken inside me.

We finished dinner and made plans to meet in the hotel lobby at 10:00 A.M. the next morning. Anderson would be driving me to a ten-thirty appointment with Darwin Bishop. I offered to get myself there, but he reminded me that an official backup wasn't a terrible idea, so long as white Range Rovers were following me around.

I headed back to my suite. The bottle of wine was waiting for me in the hallway, where I'd left it. I looked straight at it because my impulse was to look away. Then I walked into the room, quickly closed the door, and slid the dead bolt home.

9

As soon as Anderson and I had reached Wauwinet Road, we picked up a tail—one of Bishop's Range Rovers. It followed us down the road and pulled up behind Anderson's cruiser when he parked in the semicircle in front of the Bishop estate. "Take your time in there," Anderson said. He grinned. "Doesn't look like I'll be lonely."

"I won't be long," I said. I walked to the door alone and rang the bell. I looked out toward the tennis courts and saw two men crossing the grounds on ATVs, rifles strapped to their backs. Security had obviously been beefed up around the complex.

Half a minute later Claire Buckley greeted me, holding Tess Bishop in her arms. The infant was wrapped in a pale yellow blanket, asleep. "She was fussy," Claire said dreamily. "She wouldn't let me put her down." She moved aside. "Come in."

I stepped into the foyer. Seeing Tess in Buckley's arms made me anxious, but I tried not to show it. I focused on Tess's delicate fingers where they curled around the edge of her blanket. Her tiny fingernails were cotton-candy pink. Her skin had the luster of silk. "She's beautiful," I said.

Claire looked down at the baby, smiled, and nodded to herself.

Our life stories begin to take shape very early, and completely without our consent. At five months, Tess had lost her twin sister to murder and was being nurtured, in part, by her father's mistress. She was being weaned on violence, duplicity, and danger. I wondered whether she would ever overcome her first twenty weeks on the planet. "I feel badly for her," I said automatically.

"At least she never really knew Brooke," Claire said quietly. "It's better that way."

I supposed that was true, but I didn't think it was Buckley's place to say it. I wanted to remind her that Tess belonged to someone else. "Do you plan to have children of your own?" I asked.

She looked up at me, seemingly taken aback by the question. Maybe she actually felt Tess was hers, or maybe she just felt I was getting too personal. "I haven't thought that much about having kids," she said. "I'm still young. You know?"

I had noticed. So had Darwin Bishop. Claire's youth was hard to miss. Her straight brown hair, which she had worn in a braid on my last visit, was loose this time and hung halfway to the small of her back. Her body, more visible now in shorts and a simple light blue, sleeveless blouse, had the muscle tone of a gymnast. I let my gaze linger on her face and realized that she was more than pretty; she was a natural beauty, with deep brown eyes, full lips, and high cheekbones that mixed elegance and sensuality. She had the looks of a freshly minted high school English teacher who makes half the class—the male half—daydream about being kept after school. "You're right," I said. "You have plenty of time. And you're certainly needed here."

"I'm glad I can help. The Bishops have been wonderful to me," she said. Tess stirred in her blanket, stretching her arms so that Claire had to readjust her own. "She'll need a bottle soon. I'd better bring you to Win."

We started toward the study. "Is Julia at home?" I asked.

"I gave her the day off," Claire joked.

"Nice of you," I said flatly.

She stiffened. "Actually, she went to the Vineyard to visit with her mother. The two of them will come back together by late afternoon." She paused. "Brooke's funeral is at five."

"I plan to stop by," I said.

"I'm sure the family would appreciate that," she said. "I'll be here with Tess. I think we can spare her the mood at the church."

"Probably a good idea," I said, even though I didn't think it was the best one. I would rather have seen Tess stay close to Julia or Julia's mother.

Darwin Bishop was working on a laptop computer when Claire and I got to the door of his study. Looking at him, I felt a surge of loathing. The intensity of the emotion took me by surprise.

He glanced at me over half-glasses. "Please, come in," he said.

"I'll see you on your way out," Claire said to me.

I watched her leave with the baby, then walked into the study. I lingered a few moments on the portraits of Bishops' polo ponies, buying time to calm myself.

"Doctor," Bishop said, motioning for me to take the seat in front of his desk. I did. He kept watching the computer screen.

"Do you need another minute?" I asked.

"I need another year," he said, pulling his eyes away from the screen. "Acribat Software is down forty-five percent since last March. I have a rather substantial position."

It bothered me that Bishop was tracking his portfolio on the day of his infant daughter's funeral, but it didn't surprise me. "Sorry to hear that," I said, trying to filter the sarcasm out of my voice.

"Not as sorry as I am." He glanced back at the screen. "Do you follow the markets?"

"Not much," I said.

"You're better off." He removed his glasses and focused on me for the first time. "It's a rough game. Like a lot of things in life, you don't want to get into it unless you can stand to lose. You can get hurt badly."

I didn't think Bishop was talking about the market. He was warning me to stay away from the murder investigation—or from Julia. "Thanks for the advice," I said. "I'll keep it in mind."

"For whatever it's worth." He put on the fake Bishop smile. "What brings you?"

I decided to start with what I needed to tell Bishop about Billy. "Your son called me last night," I said.

He didn't show any surprise. "Were you able to trace the call?" he asked.

Bishop hadn't asked whether Billy was all right, or living on the streets, or about to do himself in. His first question had been a strategic one about whether Billy could be tracked down. "He wasn't on the line long enough," I said. "I wasn't set up for a trace, anyhow."

"What did he have to say?"

"He wanted me to loan him money, which I refused to do."

"I think that was wise," Bishop said. "Maybe he'll get hungry or scared and head back to the hospital." He shook his head. "I wish he had stayed put. We would have done our best for him."

"He wasn't convinced of that," I said.

"He never has been," Bishop said. "It isn't easy to trust anyone after you lose your parents the way he did."

"No question," I agreed.

"*It's also hard to trust anyone*," the voice at the back of my mind said, "*when your adoptive father is whipping you with a strap*."

"You should know that he's very angry," I told Bishop. "I had the feeling he might lash out at you or your family."

"We've struggled with Billy's rage a long time," Bishop said. "Since Brooke, we're taking every precaution. It's a little like Fort Knox around here. We'll be just fine."

"Do you have any idea where his anger stems from?" I asked.

"I would say that emotion is displaced from tragic losses he's suffered in his life," he said. "But you would know better than I."

"Did you know the police were set to arrest him early this morning?" I asked.

"I did," Bishop said. "Their plan actually helped me focus my thoughts." He folded his thick arms.

"How so?"

"Given that they've decided to arrest and try Billy, his best chance for acquittal is a straightforward plea of innocence. His mental state and his trauma history should be irrelevant because no case for insanity or diminished capacity need be made. As I've said before, there were several of us at home the night Brooke was killed. I don't see any way the police and the District Attorney can prove that Billy was the one responsible."

That was a simple strategy: Billy would stand trial for murder and either be acquitted or do life. Either way, the chances of suspicion settling on any other family member would be close to zero. Judging from what Laura Mossberg at Payne Whitney had told me, that had always been Bishop's plan. He had never really intended to keep Billy out of the courtroom. I decided to play my hand more aggressively. "If you believe the D.A. won't be able to prove Billy is guilty," I said, "why are you so certain he is?"

Bishop looked at me like he didn't understand.

"Why do you think he's the one who did it?" I asked, more directly. "Did you see him?"

Without a word, Bishop stood up, went to the door, and closed it. Then he walked back to his desk chair and sat down, staring at me. "Do you have another theory?" he deadpanned.

"You've said yourself, five people were at home that night. Billy, your wife, Claire, Garret—and you."

He nodded to himself, gazed out his window at the rolling lawn behind the house, then looked back at me. "I've learned to be straightforward whenever possible," he said. "I'll tell you what I'm thinking. You went to see my son at Payne Whitney, and he spun such a compelling fantasy that you've lost track of reality."

"I'm hopelessly deluded," I said.

"I'm not saying that," Bishop said. "But it took me years to understand how manipulative and skilled in deception Billy is."

"I believe he's both those things," I said.

"Yet whatever lies he told you," Bishop went on, "led you to seek out my wife, to learn more about this family."

That wasn't completely accurate. Julia had called me, not the other way around. But I wasn't about to share that fact with Bishop. "I certainly wanted more background," I said. "Your wife and I talked briefly over lunch in Boston. But you already know all that." I paused. "Just out of curiosity, if you're going to have me followed, wouldn't a Chevy sedan or a 4Runner be a little less conspicuous than a Range Rover with smoked windows?"

"I wasn't trying to be coy," he said.

"Neither was I," I said. "Do you always have people followed?"

Bishop kept his game face. "Not infrequently. More information is better than less." He ran his fingers through his silver hair. "Let's get to it, Dr. Clevenger: What tall tale did Billy fabricate that would lead you to believe someone else might have harmed Brooke?"

That felt like an open door to Bishop's truth. I couldn't resist walking through it. "It's hard to fabricate welts all over your back," I said.

Bishop smiled, nodded. "Ah, so that's part of the equation here," he said. "He claimed I beat him. That's been an ongoing refrain."

"Whereas you would claim his wounds are self-inflicted," I said.

"I didn't any more use a belt on Billy than bite him or cut him or pull the hair out of his head. All that was his doing."

"Maybe," I said. "But his version does fit pretty well with your history."

Bishop shouldn't have had to ask what I meant by that comment. The message I'd given his driver about Bishop preferring to fight kids and women wasn't subtle. But he must have wanted to hear what I had to say firsthand. "What history do you mean, exactly?" he asked.

I didn't mind hitting the highlights. "I mean the trouble with your first wife, Lauren: you know, the little problem with violating a restraining order. That, and the conviction for assault and battery."

He didn't flinch. "I was a different person then," he said.

"Oh?" I said.

"For one thing," he said, "I was a drunk."

I hadn't expected him to admit that—certainly not so plainly. "You were a drunk," I said. "An alcoholic."

"A drunk," he said. " 'Alcoholic' makes it sound like I had fallen victim to some fancy illness over which I had no control. Take a trip to the Betty Ford Center, and all's well. The truth is I was making the decision to drink every day. Because I wasn't willing to look at myself in the mirror. No detox program, no matter how much it cost per day, would have done me any good. I needed to face facts."

Bishop's apparent candor didn't square with the lie he had told Julia about his prior criminal record or with his having savaged Billy with a strap. "What is it that you weren't willing to face?" I asked skeptically.

"Who I was," Bishop said. "And some things I had done."

I nodded once, letting him know I was prepared to keep listening.

"I didn't grow up with much in the way of material possessions," he said.

"You were poor," I pushed.

He didn't back away from the word. "Yes. Not enough to eat, if you really want to know. Secondhand clothes to wear to school. Nights without heat. And those things bothered me for the longest time. It's pathetic to admit it, but I was embarrassed about where and what I had come from. It made me angry. And hateful. I kept it all inside as a kid and a teenager. Then, when I went to Vietnam, I suddenly had carte blanche to express all that negative emotion." He pursed his lips, took a deep breath, and stared through the window again. "I did things over there that I'm not proud of." He looked back at me. "For a long time, I tried to obliterate the memories with booze. I was out of control. And my wife Lauren was in that line of fire. God bless her, she's a friend of mine today. I don't know why. I don't deserve it."

I couldn't tell whether Bishop was leveling with me or playing me. What he was saying sounded good, but I couldn't see any reason why Julia would lie about witnessing Billy's beatings. "Thank you," I said. "That gives me more insight. There aren't many people who can talk about themselves that way."

"Neither could I, for a long time," Bishop said. "It's still a struggle opening up."

That last sentence missed its mark, coming out hollow and contrived. I think Bishop knew it. My gut told me he was painting himself in the kind of light he thought a psychiatrist would favor. "Let me tell you a little about me," I said, "as long as we're opening up here."

He cocked his head slightly to listen.

Even that movement looked scripted to me. "I have one real skill," I said. "It's the only thing people pay me for."

"And what's that?" he asked.

"I'm a burrower."

"A burrower."

"Yes," I said. "I just keep going deeper and deeper, kind of like a screwworm, until I get to the truth."

Bishop must have heard me loud and clear: I didn't intend to stop working the investigation. "In that regard," he said, "despite how much I might value your relentlessness in other circumstances, I should tell you that my plan for Billy to plead innocent—rather than entering an insanity plea or putting forward a diminished capacity defense—makes your services unnecessary."

"To whom?" I asked.

"This family," he said.

That certainly could have been debated, given that Billy—and Tess—were members of the family, but I had a simpler point to make. "The family isn't my client in this case," I said. "The Nantucket Police Department is."

"And I'm sorry if they gave you the impression this would be a long and involved piece of work," Bishop said. "I'll make good on that expectation. I'm happy to cover a month of your time. Two months. Whatever you think is fair."

Bishop obviously felt the police department and he were one and the same. It was also obvious he wanted me off the case badly enough to pay for it. I wondered how badly. "Two months, full time, bills at fifty thousand dollars," I said.

"That's a rich fee," Bishop said.

"Too rich for you?" I said, forcing a smile.

"I didn't say that. If your expectation was for two months' employment, you should be compensated accordingly. I'll arrange everything." He held up his hand. "There is one condition: You're to have no further contact with Julia."

Maybe I had missed the point. Maybe I was being bribed to stay away from Bishop's wife, more than from Billy's case. Regardless, it was time to end the charade. I stood up. "No deal," I said.

Bishop's face hardened. "I met your price."

"The thing is, once I start burrowing," I said, "I can't stop. Not for any price. It's a little like your drinking."

"*Or yours*," the voice at the back of my mind said.

"I wish you would rethink your decision," Bishop said.

I nodded. "Thank you for your time," I said. "I can show myself out." I started toward the door.

"Last chance," he called to me. Something in his tone had changed dramatically, becoming mechanical, with no effort to connect or persuade in it.

I stopped in front of the portraits of Bishop's horses again. "How can someone as open and sensitive as you are not fall for these animals?" I said. "It seems inhuman."

"If you were a stock," Bishop said, "I'd be selling."

I walked out of the office.

Claire Buckley caught up with me before I reached the front door. "I hope you got your questions answered," she said.

"Some of them," I said.

"Is there anything I can help with?" she asked.

I slowed my pace. I decided to increase the anxiety level in the house another notch by letting Claire know I had my doubts about Billy being the assailant. "Do you think Billy is the one who killed Brooke?" I asked. I watched her face, expecting a replay of the same confusion with which others, like Laura Mossberg and Julia Bishop, had greeted that question—as if they had never considered any other possibility. But Claire bit her lower lip, looked down at the ground, and said nothing. "Do you think Billy's the one?" I repeated, finally.

She took a deep breath. "Is this confidential?"

"Just between you and me," I said. "It won't go any further."

"Not even to Win."

"You have my word."

"You need to understand," she said, "there was a reason I got so involved with Brooke and Tess."

"Okay," I said.

"I never expected to be a full-time nanny, you know? It just sort of happened. I was mostly helping with decorating, arranging parties, setting up some of Win's business meetings at the house."

"What changed?" I said.

"Julia did, actually."

"What do you mean?"

"As long as I've known her, she's always been very upbeat and vibrant. She's a wonderful woman. I have a lot of respect for her."

That had to make it more gratifying to sleep with her

husband. "You have respect for her, but . . ." I prompted Claire.

"But after she gave birth to the twins, she went downhill. She took no interest in the babies. She didn't want to be around them."

"And you picked up the slack." I tried to keep my tone even, but cynicism crept in.

"Because Mr. Bishop asked me to," she said.

He was "*Mr. Bishop*," all of a sudden. My putting her on the defensive was shutting her down. I backtracked. "To be honest, they're lucky you were here—and willing to step in. A lot of people would have said, 'Hey, it's not in my job description.'"

"I could never do that," she said. "Win was beside himself."

"Of course," I said. "What was Julia like, exactly?" I asked. "Was she sad and tearful, or . . . ?"

"More irritable. Win called it a 'black mood.' They'd hired a baby nurse for the twins—a woman named Kristen Collier—but Julia argued with her and fired her a week after the twins were born."

"Do you remember where she was from?" I asked.

"Yes," she said. "I helped find her. She's from Duxbury."

Duxbury is a suburb of Boston, about twelve miles south of the city. I took a mental note of Kristen's name and hometown. "Did Julia ever mention hurting herself?" I asked. "Or anyone else?"

Claire shook her head. "I don't want to make more of this than it is. I mean, it's probably not that uncommon. Right? I think a lot of women feel the way Julia did and just never say anything. And her moods had been getting better over the last month."

"*A lot of women never say anything*," the voice at the back of my mind prodded me, "*but what did Julia say?*"

"I understand," I said. "But did Julia share anything specific about her feelings—anything, in particular, that concerned you?" I asked.

Claire looked away and said nothing.

"Claire?"

"Well, she told me once that . . ." She fell silent, again.

"Go on."

"She told me . . . She said she wished she never had the twins." She dropped her voice to just above a whisper. "She said she wished they were dead."

My heart fell. It is true that many women feel overwhelmed after childbirth and wish they could go back to their lives without the constant demands of a new infant. They may even fantasize about the baby not surviving. The most honest and brave of them might even confess their private thoughts to doctors or close friends. But given Brooke's death—her murder—the question had to be asked whether Julia had acted on those thoughts. My whole being told me that that wasn't the case, but I couldn't completely trust my instincts where Julia was concerned.

"I wasn't going to say anything," Claire went on, "but when they took Billy to the psychiatric hospital, he really did seem shocked."

"Tell me what you mean," I said.

"I've heard him lie plenty of times," she said. "He's very convincing. He could have your wallet in his pocket and tell you flat out that he hasn't seen it. That happened to me once with him. He even helped me look for it after he'd stolen it. And I remember him swearing he was nowhere near any of the neighbors' pets, even when he had scratch marks all over his arms from one of the cats." She toyed with her shiny Cartier love bracelet. "But the night he left for Payne Whitney, he seemed just plain scared. Like he didn't know what had hit him."

"Are you saying you don't think he did it?" I asked.

She bit her lower lip again. "I'm not sure what I think. I just wanted to get all this off my chest."

"I appreciate that, Claire," I said. "I really do."

"If I think of anything else, should I be in touch with you?" she asked.

"I'm staying at the Breakers overnight," I said. "Feel

free to call me there. And you can always reach me on my cell phone." I gave her the number. She walked me to the door. "By the way, where's Garret today?" I asked.

"In his room," Claire said. "He's having a lot of trouble coping. He's lost his sister *and* his brother. It's a chore to get him to come out of there for meals."

"But he makes it to his tennis matches," I said.

"Reluctantly," she said, "to say the least." She glanced at her watch. "Actually, he has to defend his singles championship at twelve-thirty."

"On the day of his sister's funeral?"

She rolled her eyes. "I don't get involved in any of that," she said. "That's between Garret and his father."

I looked up the staircase, then glanced back toward Darwin Bishop's office. "You think Garret would mind if I talked with him a few minutes?" I asked.

"He won't speak with anyone," she said. "I don't think you'd get anywhere right now."

"I don't mind trying," I said.

She hesitated. "I would have to run that by Win."

I knew how that would turn out. "Don't bother," I said. "I'll catch up with him another time."

"Learn anything?" Anderson asked, as we drove away from the Bishop estate.

"You're right about one thing. Bishop wants this investigation to end," I said.

"What did he say?"

"He offered me fifty grand to cut bait."

"I hope you took it," Anderson said.

I looked over at him. He was grinning. "He wasn't happy when I turned him down," I said. "He's not pretending we're on the same team anymore."

"So he still sits at the top of your list? You think he's the one."

"I think if we keep the pressure on him," I said, "he'll let us know, one way or the other."

"I'll buy that," Anderson said.

I didn't want to hold anything back. "Claire stopped me on my way out," I said. "She wanted to tell me a few things about Julia."

"Like?"

"Julia did get quite depressed after the twins were born." I kept any alarm out of my voice. "I guess she even made a stray comment about wishing they hadn't been born."

Anderson raised an eyebrow. "All worth hearing," he said. "I'm glad you made the trip."

"Me, too," I said.

"I reviewed that data you e-mailed about the risk of a second infanticide when one twin has been killed," Anderson said. "Seventy percent. I'm going to press the Department of Social Services to intervene and get Tess out of there."

I didn't like the idea of forcing Julia's hand, but the risk to Tess was too high to worry about hurt feelings. "It's the right thing to do," I said.

As we passed Bishop's "watch house" another Range Rover pulled behind us.

Anderson glanced into the rearview mirror, then over at me. "You should get out of that hotel and head to my place for the night."

I instinctively felt for the Browning Baby in my front pocket. "Not a bad idea," I said. "Maybe I'll head over after the funeral."

"Why just maybe?" he asked.

"Because my room is nonrefundable," I joked.

Anderson shook his head. "If you're planning anything with Julia, you're not thinking straight."

"I'll probably come by," I said, feeling the urge to close down the discussion.

"You've been warned," Anderson said.

10

The Brant Point Racket Club on North Beach Street is the kind of place you'd expect people of leisure to spend leisure time. The fences around the outdoor courts are hung with green nylon sheeting intended to protect the players not only from the sun but from the paparazzi. The clubhouse is understated and elegant, with deep armchairs to linger in and talk about this shot or that shot, this racket or that, all the while nursing a gin and tonic, maybe checking a stock quote on a Palm VII.

I had driven over to Brant Point after Anderson left me at my hotel. I thought I might get a few minutes alone with Garret Bishop. My gut told me that something other than grief was keeping him scarce.

I got to Garret's singles match just before 2:00 P.M. The temporary bleachers around the court were filled with spectators. Garret was already winning the third set 4–1. He'd taken the first two 6–2, 6–4. He was serving for another game point. He leaned back. Beads of sweat flew off his brow. He tossed the ball over his head, tracking it with his eyes like a hunter. Then he reached to the sky and funneled every ounce of strength in his powerful body to his arm and wrist. A dull thud broke the silence, his opponent swung and missed, and, just like that, it was 5–1.

What sort of young man, I wondered, can perform with excellence on a tennis court when his baby sister's funeral is to be held four hours later? And what had it cost Garret to buckle to Darwin Bishop's demands for performance and grace under any pressure, no matter how intense? Where had all his anxiety, sadness, and fear gone?

The match ended just five minutes later—6–2, 6–4, 6–1. Garret scored match point, moving in for a weak lob, posturing to slam the ball down the right baseline, making his opponent back up to defend against his power, then tapping the ball ever so gently, so that it dropped just over the net.

As applause filled the air, Garret simply turned and walked off the court—no fist raised in triumph, no nod to the crowd, no handshake at the net.

I tried to get his attention when he was about halfway to the clubhouse. "Garret," I called out, from a few steps behind him. He didn't stop. I quickened my pace until I was walking beside him. He kept staring straight ahead. "Garret," I said, a little louder.

He turned to me, a blank expression on his face. "What?" he said, without any hint that he remembered we had met.

"I'm Frank Clevenger," I said. "I met you with your mother at the house. I was with Officer Anderson."

He kept walking.

"The psychiatrist," I prodded him.

"I know who you are," he said, without breaking pace.

"I'd like to talk with you for a minute," I said.

"I don't need to," he said. He picked up his pace. "I'm getting through it."

It dawned on me that he might think Julia had sent me to help him with his feelings about the murder. "No one knows that I've come here," I said. "Your father and mother didn't send me. I came because I need information."

"Such as?" he said.

I didn't think I had the luxury of being subtle. "I want you to tell me what you can about your father."

That stopped him. He turned to me. "My father," he said, with palpably fragile patience.

"Yes," I said.

"What do you need to know about him?" he asked.

I had the feeling I would get more, rather than less, information from Garret if he knew I suspected his father of involvement in Brooke's death. Maybe he'd relish the chance to get out from under Bishop's thumb. "I'm not comfortable with the party line that Billy killed your sister," I said. "I'm looking at other possibilities."

He looked at me doubtfully. "Isn't Win the one paying you?" he asked.

I remembered that Billy had asked me the same question. I also noted that Garret called his father by his first name. No terms of endearment anywhere in sight. "No," I said. "I work for the police."

"They usually work for Win, too."

Garret's statement gave me a moment's pause about whether North Anderson had always kept himself at arm's length from the Bishop family. But the doubt didn't last more than that moment. Anderson and I had been through hell and back together. "Nobody investigating this case is on your dad's payroll," I said. "That may be a problem for him."

He glanced at the ground, then back at me, sizing me up. "Okay," he said. "So, talk."

"Do you think Billy killed your sister?" I said.

"No," he said.

"What do you think happened?"

"I think she was born dead."

"Excuse me?"

"Stillborn," he said.

I shrugged. "I don't get it."

"Not just Brooke. Her and Tess."

"What do you mean?" I said.

"I mean we're all walking dead people in that house," Garret said. "Only one person matters. Darwin Harris Bishop."

"He made you play in the tournament today," I said. "Claire told me that."

"Claire," he repeated with scorn. He shook his head. "You don't get it," he said.

"Get what?"

"It's not this tournament. It's not tennis. It's everything. What I wear. Who my friends are. What I study. What I think. What I feel."

In some ways, Garret's complaint sounded like one that most seventeen-year-olds would have about their fathers or mothers. And that probably explained why I responded with an unfortunate cliché. "You don't have your own life," I said.

"Right on," he said. "I'm going through a phase."

"I'm sorry," I said immediately. "I didn't mean it that way."

Garret looked at the ground again, kicked the sand, and chuckled to himself.

"I really do want to know what it's like in that house," I said.

He looked back at me. His lip curled. "It's like being eaten from the inside out, until there's nothing left of you," he said. "Dad's kind of like Jeffrey Dahmer. Only he doesn't have to pour acid in your head to turn you into a zombie. He does it in other ways."

Garret clearly thought of his father as psychologically fatal to him, but I wanted to know if he had any direct physical evidence that would link him to Brooke's murder. "Did you see anything the night Brooke died?" I asked. "Do you think your father . . . ?"

He looked away. "You still aren't getting the point," he said.

"I want to," I said. "Give me another shot at it."

"There's only air in our family for Win. The rest of us have been struggling to breathe our whole lives. So it doesn't matter if he suffocated Brooke." He looked at me more intensely. "It really doesn't. In a way, it's better. Less painful. Quicker."

Garret was speaking the language of learned helplessness, the mindset that takes over in prisoners who, seeing no chance of escape, stop struggling to achieve it. "You still might be able to help Billy," I reminded him. "I know you two aren't close, but he could spend his life behind bars."

"He'll have more freedom there," Garret said. "And I doubt the guards would beat him as badly."

I heard that loud and clear. Julia, Billy, and Garret all seemed to disagree with Darwin Bishop's claim that the wounds on Billy's back were self-inflicted. "If Billy is innocent, and you can prove it," I said, "then you must have seen something the night Brooke died."

"And if I step out on a limb and testify against Win, and Win goes free," Garret said, "then what do I do?"

I didn't have a good answer to that question. In the seconds I took to try to think of one, Garret started to walk away. "Where are you going?" I called to him.

He turned back toward me, but didn't stop moving. "Think about it," he said. "None of us can get away from Win. Billy still doesn't understand that. Otherwise, he'd head right back to the hospital." He turned, broke into a jog, and headed to the clubhouse.

I climbed into my truck and checked my home machine for a message from Billy, but he hadn't left one.

I had time before I needed to be at Brooke's funeral. I felt like I should use it to get my thoughts clear on what I had learned about the Bishop family. I downed a sandwich and two coffees at the 'Sconset Café, then drove out to the Sankaty Head Lighthouse, opposite the Sankaty Head Golf Club. The light, perched on sandy cliffs, is visible from twenty-nine miles at sea. It was built in 1850 to help sailors navigate the treacherous Nantucket shoals, a beautiful but shallow graveyard of ships.

I parked near the lighthouse and walked a quarter mile into the tall grass that surrounds it. The sun was warm and bright, and the ocean stretched endlessly before me. There are those who insist it is impossible to walk the bluffs from

the center of Siasconset to the lighthouse and arrive with a
single negative thought in mind. Maybe I should have taken
that route, because my mind was full of them.

The list of suspects in Brooke's murder was getting
longer, not shorter; it now included every person in the
Bishop house the night she was killed.

Certainly, Darwin Bishop headed the list. He was the
only one with a history of domestic assault, a history that
stretched back decades and reached all the way to the raw
welts on Billy Bishop's back. He was the only one who
had threatened me or tried to shake me off the case. It was
he, so far as I could tell, who had not wanted the twins.
He may have been enraged by their intrusion on his plans
for a fresh start with a new love—Claire Buckley.

But then there was Billy. Anyone with a history of firesetting, torturing animals, destruction of property, theft,
and, yes, bedwetting had the pedigree of a true psychopath.
Add to that the pent-up rage reflected in his self-abuse—
biting himself, cutting himself, and pulling out his hair—
and the prescription for disaster was complete.

My mind moved on to Claire Buckley. How draining
was it for her, after all, to serve as a glorified baby-sitter
when being the lady of the household seemed within reach?
After traveling the world with Darwin Bishop, sharing luxury suites and rare bottles of wine, how did she feel when
Julia announced she was pregnant again—and with twins?
Had Darwin told her that leaving his wife would have to
be put off? Beneath the care and concern Claire had shown
the infants, did she look upon them with bitterness, as living embodiments of her billionaire lover's continuing bond
with his beautiful, supposedly estranged wife?

I thought back to Claire's revelation of Julia's ambivalence about having had the twins, including Julia's statement that she "wished they were dead." Had Claire truly
given me that data reluctantly? Or had she scripted the dis-
closure in order to distract me from her own motives? How
could I be certain that Julia had made the statement at all?

That brought me to Julia herself. Would I take her more

seriously as a suspect if I wasn't moved by her? I had to admit that Julia's postpartum depression, complete with feelings of estrangement from Brooke and Tess, increased the risk of her harming them. But it didn't increase that risk dramatically. The vast, vast majority of women with postpartum depression, after all, never strike out at their infants.

Finally, Garret himself had begun to worry me. Growing up with Darwin Bishop had seemingly sapped him of any hope for a real future. I wondered whether his prison camp mentality might lead him to put other family members "out of their misery." Could he have killed Brooke, I wondered, in order to free her?

I shook my head. Darwin Bishop had vowed that neither the police nor the District Attorney would be able to prove Billy's guilt because anyone at home the night Brooke was killed could be the murderer. It almost felt as though the family was actively organizing to make Bishop's case, choreographing a dizzying dance to keep me off balance.

There was another way to think about the maze of possibilities. It was true that every member of the family had had the opportunity to kill Brooke. But each might also have had part of the motive. The family's collective psyche, working largely unconsciously, might have silently spurred one of its members to act on behalf of the group. Maybe that was the dynamic making it so difficult to settle on a lead suspect.

Some students of the Kennedy assassination, for example, discount the theory that an organized conspiracy existed to do in the president. Instead, they say, a convergence of interests from many different venues—including, but not limited to, the military, the CIA, and the Mafia—worked silently and almost magically to place the president in jeopardy. According to this vision, Lee Harvey Oswald acted alone, but as the culmination of those myriad dark forces, in the same way that a great and popular leader can express and achieve goals that represent the culmination of our collective hope and courage.

That vision of how Brooke had come to die bothered

me more than any other. Because the same forces that would have emboldened her killer still existed. And, most likely, their next target would be Tess Bishop.

I took out my mobile phone and dialed North Anderson. His office patched me through to his cruiser. I asked him whether he had made any progress getting Tess off the Bishop estate.

"No go," he said. "I talked personally with Sam Middleton, the executive director of the Department of Social Services. He told me what I guess I already knew: Regardless of the statistics, kids aren't yanked out of a home just because there's been a murder, especially when somebody has been charged with that murder. You didn't see Jon-Benet's brother placed in any foster home after she was killed."

"That's just DSS policy Middleton is parroting," I said. "Isn't there a creative way around it?"

"I tried Leslie Grove, the medical director of Nantucket Family Services. She could file a 'child at risk' petition with DSS, but says she won't go near it without evidence that Tess has been directly threatened."

"Then I guess Julia is the only one who can make the difference," I said. "I'll see if I can get a minute with her at the funeral. Her mother's coming in with her from the Vineyard. Maybe they could go back together, with the baby."

"Sounds like you're comfortable the baby would be safe with them," Anderson said.

In my heart, I was comfortable with that. But I knew Anderson was still concerned I had lost perspective where Julia was concerned. "We don't have a way to isolate Tess from the entire family," I said. "The next best thing is to keep her away from as many family members as possible. For my money, that should include Darwin Bishop."

"Fair enough," Anderson said. "Hell, if it made anyone feel any better, the kid could stay with Tina and me."

"Thanks," I said. "I'll make the offer. I wouldn't hold my breath, though."

"Did you get to talk with Garret?" he asked.

"For five minutes. He goes on the list. He said Brooke was better off dead than living with Darwin. I didn't like the sound of that."

"Any more good news?" he said sarcastically.

"Absolutely," I said. I needed to let Anderson know we should at least touch base with the baby nurse Julia had fired. "When I spoke with Claire, she mentioned a private duty nurse Julia had hired to care for the twins. Kristen Collier, from Duxbury. Julia argued with her and fired her about a week after Brooke and Tess were born. I guess it's worth talking to her. She still might have a key to the place. I'd just like to know she was somewhere other than Nantucket when Brooke died."

"Will do," he said.

"I think that about covers it, then," I said. "I'll talk to you later, after the funeral."

"At my place?" he asked pointedly. "Sacrificing your room deposit?"

"Sure," I said, mostly to avoid arguing. "Your place it is." I hung up.

I looked out at the Atlantic, then turned and took in the whole panorama at Sankaty Head. The cliffs seemed literally to dissolve into beach, then beach into sea. Birds dove out of the sky to skim the cresting waves. It was a scene of awesome beauty, and the thought occurred to me that I had once lingered in such places myself, having lived with my girlfriend Kathy in Marblehead, another yachting town that had spawned a guidebook for tourists. The quiet danger in such places, I had learned, is that the combination of their wealth and physical beauty keeps pain from surfacing, forcing it to cut its own repressed geography of underground dark rivers. Thus, one can easily believe all is well, that the terrain of life ahead promises solid footing, when it is actually ripe to give way.

I walked to my truck. As I reached it, I noticed one of Darwin Bishop's white Range Rovers parked about fifty yards away, closer to the road. I waved. Then I climbed in

and headed back toward town, to watch a Nantucket family
of fortune bid farewell to an infant daughter.

Darwin Bishop's colleagues turned out in numbers to pay
their respects. A line a quarter-mile long stretched from the
door of St. Mary's Our Lady of Hope down Federal Street,
onto cobblestoned Main. I waited in that line over an hour,
behind a group of men talking about the competitive nature
of the oil business and in front of another group planning
a trip to India to recruit software engineers. Granted,
Brooke hadn't been their daughter, and people will do their
best to distance themselves from tragedy, but something
about the tone of the conversations felt especially removed,
as if we might have been in line to attend a convention or
watch a movie. After about thirty minutes, the banter really
started to bother me. At the forty-five-minute mark I
couldn't help interrupting a particularly energized, bow-tied
fellow, about forty, with thick, sandy hair, who had been
jawing about the "fucking SEC." I touched his arm gently,
noticing the fine cotton of his pinstriped shirt. Sea Island
cotton, they call it. "Excuse me," I said.

He looked at me, a little put out to be interrupted.
"Yes?" he said, with a synthetic amiability.

"Is it true that the little girl's windpipe had been blocked
off?" I said.

"What?"

I noticed that his friends were still talking about the markets. "It's what I heard, but I wasn't sure. I'm not from the
island. I'm a friend of Julia's from way back. I heard her
baby was—essentially—strangled."

"I guess that's right," he said tightly.

"I was just thinking how terrible that would be," I went
on, "not being able to breathe. Suffocating."

"Then don't think about it." He let that linger a beat,
then turned away.

I listened to hear whether my little intervention would
resonate for a while, keeping Mr. Bow Tie quiet, if nothing

else. But he was right back in the fray, arguing that the SEC rules were vague and unevenly applied. He got pretty heated about it.

Dozens of limousines were lined up closer to the church steps. Whispers had it that they had transported some of the most powerful guests, including Senator Drew Anscombe and famed financier Christopher Burch of Links Securities. Assistant Secretary of State William Rust and Russian ambassador Nikolai Tartokovsky had supposedly been fast-tracked to the family's side aboard Darwin Bishop's Gulfstream jet.

The atmosphere inside the teak doors of the weathered gray church was far more solemn. A marble statue of Mary, hands down, palms open, stood near the entrance. A stained-glass window of gold, ruby, emerald, and sapphire panes, depicting her in the same posture, glowed behind the altar. Between the two lay a tiny casket covered by a white pall, emblazoned with a deep red cross.

A *tiny casket* is a non sequitur, a wrenching failure of all God's magnificent intentions.

Julia will bury her baby come morning, I thought to myself. *She will put her baby in the ground and leave her there.* My throat tightened as I pictured Julia walking away from the burial plot, pictured Brooke curled into a ball, shivering. I shook that image out of my head, but it lodged like a fistful of earth in my throat.

All the pews were full. I stood to one side of the hall. Looking around the room, I saw not only Anscombe and Burch but a host of luminaries, from newscasters to rock stars.

The priest, a surprisingly young man with wavy black hair and tanned skin, offered the opening prayer:

> *"To You, O Lord, we humbly entrust this child,*
> *so precious in your sight. Take Brooke into*
> *your arms and welcome her into Paradise,*
> *where there will be no sorrow, no weeping nor*

pain, but the fullness of peace and joy with your
son and the Holy Spirit for ever and ever."

My eyes looked up at Mary, another mother who lost her child to murder. I wondered whether that connection, or anything that could be said inside these four walls, or anything that could be said anywhere, ever, would provide real solace to Julia.

Darwin Bishop was the next to offer a prayer. My jaw tightened as I watched him climb the stairs to the altar. He gripped each side of the lectern and slowly took stock of the room, much as he might at a corporate gathering. His eyes were dry. "Wisdom 3:1–7," he said. In an unwavering voice, he read:

> *"But the souls of the just are in the hands of*
> *God and no torment shall touch them.*
>
> *"They seemed in the view of the foolish to*
> *be dead and their passing away was thought an*
> *affliction and their going forth from us utter*
> *destruction.*
>
> *"But they are in peace."*

Brooke had died, horribly. It was Bishop who seemed at peace. I felt my blood pressure rising as he went on:

> *"Chastised a little they shall be greatly blessed*
> *because God tried them and found them worthy*
> *of himself.*
> *"As gold in the furnace, he proved them, he*
> *took them to himself.*
> *"In time of their visitation they shall shine*
> *and shall dart about as sparks."*

I turned and walked quietly out to the lobby, not wanting to watch Bishop or listen to him or risk seeing Julia kiss him when he took his seat.

I did want to offer Julia my condolences. I waited until the end of the mass, when the family formed its receiving line.

The Bishops stood to one side of the altar, accepting a seemingly endless stream of sympathies. Julia, in a simple black fitted dress that I am embarrassed to say made my heart race even in the presence of tragedy, stood next to the priest. Darwin stood on his other side.

I shook Garret's hand first. His grip was firm and, as I looked at him, his gray-blue eyes met mine with composure, if not chilliness. I stepped in front of Julia's mother next. She was an elegant and slim woman, about sixty-five, battling tears. I took her hand. "I'm sorry about your granddaughter," I said, recognizing how inadequate the words inevitably sounded.

"Thank you," she said, leaving her hand in mine. "You are?"

"Frank Clevenger," I said, not expecting the name to register with her.

"I thought you might be," she said, glancing toward Julia, a few feet away.

I moved on toward Julia. I couldn't help feeling that it was appropriate for me to have met her mother, that there was some small chance I might become important in both of their lives, even after the investigation was over. It was a warm feeling, but I fought it. I wanted to maintain my balance until Brooke's murder had been solved. But in the instant I took Julia's hand, my plans for equanimity evaporated. Darwin Bishop had moved off several feet, obviously not wanting to greet me, and I found myself locked in a private moment with his wife, at their daughter's funeral, staring into her eyes as she stared into mine. "I'm so . . ." I stumbled, wanting to avoid the cliché.

She took my hand, moving her thumb along the inside of my wrist. "I appreciate your being here. I know it was asking a lot of you."

"You could ask for more," I whispered, drunk with her presence. Her black hair and green eyes, together with skin as smooth and radiant as I ever expect to see or touch, made me feel further than ever from the tenement house I grew up in. Add the chaser of feeling just a little outclassed by Julia's wealth, a little lucky to be smiled upon by a woman with so many options, and my balance was truly put to the test.

"Are you staying on the island?" she said.

"Yes," I said.

"Where?"

I could feel myself falling. "The Breakers," I said. Letting go of her hand was an act of will, but I sensed that if we lingered any longer, it would raise eyebrows. I instinctively glanced at Garret and saw that he had already registered the emotional exchange between his mother and me. He shot me a look full of confusion and anger. "I hope I see you soon," I told Julia, and walked away, headed toward the back of the church.

I wasn't quite to the door when someone behind me grabbed my arm. I whirled around and found myself face-to-face with Darwin Bishop. His face had a look of fragile indulgence on it. "There's a part of me that likes your audacity," he said, still holding my arm.

Half of me wanted to share my condolences with him. The other half wanted to break his hand. "I don't think this is a good place to talk," I said.

"It's not the place I would have chosen, especially for you to romance my wife," Bishop said.

"That's not . . ." I started.

He let go of my arm. "You're in over your head," he said, in a tone that was almost fatherly. "Your instincts aren't serving you."

"Thanks for the advice," I said, and left it at that. I turned to go, but he grabbed hold of my arm again. I turned back to him.

"You know how you told me you have one skill?" Bishop said. "You're a burrower. Nothing more, nothing less."

"That's what I told you."

"I thought about that. And I realized I've really only got one skill myself."

"Which is?" I said.

"I pick winners from losers. In anything. It doesn't matter whether it's stocks, people, businesses, ideas. It's like a sixth sense with me."

I thought back to Bishop's bet on Acribat Software, down forty-five percent in a year. But that fact was a petty distraction; his billion-dollar fortune obviously meant he could see things other people would miss—in the markets, and perhaps elsewhere. "That's a valuable skill," I said.

"I rely on it," he said. "And my sixth sense tells me you're about to lose everything." He smiled. "I can smell it coming." He turned and walked away.

I watched him take his place again in the receiving line. My pulse was racing, and the muscles in my right arm were tense from holding back with the right cross I would have liked to deliver to his chin. But thinking about it now, what probably bothered me most was that I knew he was right, at least about one thing: I would have told anyone else in my place to stand back from the boundaries I was starting to cross.

11

I got back to my room at The Breakers at 9:40 P.M. I had grabbed takeout shrimp and arugula gourmet pizza for dinner—nothing being regular *anything* on Nantucket—and eaten it on my way back to the hotel. The night had turned windy and rainy, and that, together with the late hour, gave me a good excuse to bow out of spending the night at North Anderson's. I called him at home and got the customary urgings toward safety that I would expect from a friend. Double-lock the door, no unexpected midnight repairs to the plumbing, and so forth. I sidestepped them, told him I'd be fine, that I was leaving the island in the morning and not returning for at least a day. I had business to attend to back in Boston, including another visit to Lilly at Mass General.

The management had left my bottle of wine back inside my room, on my nightstand. I smiled at its persistence, grabbed it, and was about to bring it far down the hall, where it couldn't find its way back to me, when the phone rang. I picked up. "Clevenger," I said.

"It's Julia."

"Where are you?" I asked.

"Downstairs."

I didn't know exactly how to respond. "In the lobby . . ." I said, for filler. Thinking of her just three floors away—alone—made me start to think what it would be like to hold her, without worrying that we might be seen.

"I need to be close to someone I trust," she said. "Just for a few minutes. I . . ." A moment of silence. "I want to tell you what it was like for me at the church tonight, what I really felt."

I knew the smart thing to do would be to join her in the lobby or meet her for coffee at the Brant Point Grill. But knowing what to do and actually doing it are different things. "I'm in room 307," I said.

When I heard a knock at my door, I resolved not to let things get too far, to keep some therapeutic distance between the two of us. I opened the door. Julia stood there in her black dress, her hair damp from the rain. She had been crying, but her eyes still glowed. I offered her my hand. She took it and walked into my arms. I pushed the door closed and let her cry as I held her. The feel of her delicate shoulder blade against my palm, the rising and falling of her chest against mine, a tear that ran off her cheek and down my neck were all intoxicating to me. No less so was the music playing in the background of our lives: her cruel husband, my cruel father, her need to escape a bad marriage, my boyhood fantasies of rescuing my mother.

Julia raised her head off my chest, turning her face up toward mine, with her eyes closed. And I did what might be forgiven, but not excused. I moved my hand to her cheek and kissed her, gently at first, then more passionately, sensing not the crossing of boundaries but the melting of them, their obliteration. Our mouths became one. And it seemed to me—and I believe to her—that our futures had also, mystically and immeasurably, been joined. My unconscious seemed to be saying that if these were the worst of circumstances in which to have found one another, they were, unavoidably and irretrievably, *our* circumstances. The rules of decorum that governed the great mass of relationships would have to yield. We were inevitable.

I have kissed many women in my life, but none of them made me feel the way Julia did. She ran her fingers up the back of my neck, then pulled me toward her, inside her, receiving all my passion, then pulling back, barely brushing her soft, full lips over mine, catching my lip between her teeth, gently pulling, making me feel she was hungry for me. Then her lips traveled up my cheek, and I heard her excited breathing louder than my own, felt her warm tongue slip inside my ear, move deeper, speaking about all the warm ways our bodies and souls could join into one.

Only after we had kissed a long time did I gather a fragile resolve to ease her away from me. "You wanted . . . to talk," I said.

She took a deep breath, let it out. She slowly opened her eyes and nodded. I took her by the hand and guided her to a couch that looked onto the harbor. The aluminum masts and gilded stems of a hundred or more sailboats caught the moonlight and swayed like a glittering crop of silver and gold on a field of blue. "Tell me," I said quietly, still holding her hand. "What was it like for you at St. Mary's tonight?"

She looked at our hands laced together, then placed her other hand on top of them. She looked back at me. "Like burying a piece of myself," she said. "I kept wishing it could have been me who died. Since the day she was born, I've had a feeling about Brooke—that she was someone extraordinary." Tears began streaming down her face. "It's horrible to say, but I felt much closer to her than I do to the boys. Even closer than I do to Tess."

Julia's recollection of her earliest reaction to Brooke was light-years from the estrangement Claire Buckley had described. Part of me wanted to resolve the discrepancy with a few questions, but it didn't seem like the time to ask them, partly because I didn't want to hear answers that would replace any part of my affection for Julia with new doubts about her. I wiped the tears off her cheek. "What other feelings did you have today?" I asked simply.

"Anger. Wanting someone to pay." She cleared her throat. "Most of all, guilt," she said.

"How so?"

She hesitated.

"You don't have to tell me anything, you know," I told her. "It's up to you."

She squeezed my hand. "I should never have exposed the girls to Billy. They didn't sign up for that risk."

Julia's suspicions clearly hadn't shifted substantially from Billy to her husband. "I understand," I said. "What do you think you should have done?"

"I should never have allowed the adoption. We weren't prepared to handle a boy with Billy's problems. And Darwin wasn't interested in being a father to him, anyhow."

"Darwin insisted," I said.

"Then I should have left," she said. "For that reason, and the others."

I felt like I had another chance to press my case for Tess's safety. "Aren't those other reasons still valid?" I asked gently. "Billy isn't at home, but the rest of the stresses still affect Tess—and Garret."

"You mean Darwin's temper," she said. "The control issue. His violence."

"Yes."

"I've talked with my mother," she said. "I may go back to the Vineyard with her and the children."

"Good," I said.

"There's just no telling how Darwin will respond."

"I think Captain Anderson would provide police protection," I said. "At least for a while."

"Right." She didn't seem satisfied with that safety net.

"And I would be around," I said, "if you needed me."

She squeezed my hand more tightly. Then she raised my hand to her lips, kissed it. "How can I feel this close to you this fast?" she asked.

"I've asked myself the same question about you," I said.

"Any answers?"

"Blind luck," I said.

She closed her eyes and slowly moved my hand inside the "V" of her dress, so that my fingers slid naturally under the lace of her camisole and onto her breast. When they reached her nipple, it rose up for me and she made a sound

of exquisite pleasure, like she had just awakened and was
stretching in a warm feather bed.

Every man dreams of finding a woman who will not
only yield to him, but one who will embrace and confirm
him, matching every iota of his masculinity with an equal
or greater measure of femininity. Julia was this rare woman.

Touching her made me want to touch her everywhere. I
moved one hand to her knee, just above her hem, and the
other to the back of her neck. I drew her toward me, so
that I could unzip her dress. She rested her head on my
shoulder, waiting and willing. But I couldn't allow myself
to undress her. I ran my fingers down the edges of her
spine, over the cloth. Then I kissed her cheek and sat back
on the couch. "This isn't the right time," I said. "With you
coming here from the church, feeling everything you're
feeling, we couldn't be sure what it meant."

She nodded, almost shyly. "It's late, anyhow. I should
be getting home."

We stood up. There was an awkward moment, re-
adjusted to the fact that we wouldn't be making love.

"You're here for the night, or longer?" Julia asked.

"I'm leaving in the morning, but only for a day. Then
I'll be back."

"We could meet somewhere Friday night," she said.

That felt like throwing caution to the wind. "The fact
that I'm being followed won't scare you away?" I said.

"It didn't tonight," she said. "I'm more frightened by the
thought of not seeing you."

"Paranoia," I said. "A fear with no basis in reality." I
smiled. "I treat it all the time."

Thursday, June 27, 2002

I woke just after 5:00 A.M. with my heart racing. I flicked
on the bedside light and searched for something amiss, but
nothing had disturbed the elegant furnishings of my room

or the peaceful harbor outside. I got up and walked to a set of sliding glass doors that gave onto a small deck. The sailboats still swayed in an easy breeze. I walked out and breathed deeply of the ocean air. The day was already warm. It was calm enough to make me nervous, and I wondered whether the quiet was the thing weighing on me. Maybe I was missing the throaty drone of tugs and barges working Chelsea's Mystic River, the smell of overheated petroleum, the firefly headlights of the occasional early morning commuter crossing the Tobin Bridge. But something made me reject that easy answer. I walked back inside and, still thinking of Chelsea, instinctively dialed my home phone for messages. One had been left just forty-one minutes earlier. It was from Billy. My heart raced faster.

"What I don't understand," he said, "is why they always leave the second-floor bathroom window unlocked." His speech was staccato—pressured speech, we call it in psychiatry. "They don't even lock it when we leave the island for Manhattan—which, I guess, is also an island, but I forget that, sometimes. I mean, it's like they figure no burglar will notice the window because it has frosted glass, which is just . . . stupid. Unless they think nobody would notice it behind the oak tree, which actually makes everything easier, if you can climb. 'Cause no one can see you once you're into the branches. Not that Darwin's Range Rover robots are exactly Secret Service." He laughed, but it was a quick, anxious laugh that made me think he was high or very scared or manic. "Anyhow, that takes care of my immediate cash crunch. I won't need to bother you." He laughed again. A couple seconds passed. "I think you believed me at the hospital. That's why I'm calling. I want you to know I believe what you said, too. I don't think I really ever wanted to hurt anything or anyone other than my father." He hung up.

I started to pace. I ran my hand over my shaved scalp again and again, a nervous habit that only manifests itself when I sense things have gone very wrong. Billy was on the island—or had been. And, unless he was bluffing, he had managed to slip into the Bishop house and steal something of value. I thought back to our discussion at Payne Whitney, when I had pressed Billy on a potential motive for killing Brooke. And that made a crown of shivers ring my scalp. Because Billy was right: I had argued that his violence had always been about taking things away from his father. I prayed that this time it had been a watch or a ring or a lockbox stuffed with cash, and not little Tess.

I showered and pulled on a fresh pair of jeans. Then I called North Anderson at home. It was only five-twenty, but I had to let him know that Billy was close by—or had been, and that he had apparently invaded the Bishop home.

Tina answered the phone after half a dozen rings. "Hello?" Her voice still had sleep in it.

"Tina, I'm sorry to wake you. It's Frank Clevenger."

She skipped the pleasantries. "Hasn't North called you?" she said.

"No." I picked my cell phone off the bureau and saw that it was registering "Out of Range." "Was he looking for me?" I glanced at the ceiling, cursing the layer of steel or concrete blocking my signal.

"He left for the emergency room about an hour ago. There's something wrong with Tess Bishop."

I felt lightheaded. "Something wrong? Did he say anything else?"

"She stopped breathing," Tina said.

"Where's the hospital?" I asked.

"On South Prospect Street, at Vesper Lane," she said. "Nantucket Cottage Hospital. It's only about a mile out of town. There are little blue hospital signs all over that will point you the right way. You can't miss it."

"Thanks, Tina," I said.

"Sorry to give you bad news, Frank. I'd love to see you. Maybe when this whole thing settles down."

"You will," I said.

I ran down the stairs to the lobby. The woman at the front desk gave me directions to the hospital, but as I raced from street to street in the darkness, I realized I actually

could have connected the little, fluorescent "H's" and gotten there just fine. Another thing about Nantucket: Nothing
is random. Everything has signage. Over the course of four
hundred years, Nantucketers have slowly worn away all the
island's rough edges, and all possibility for surprise, so that
the island now has its metaphor in every piece of beautiful,
smooth, dead driftwood that washes up on its shores.

In such places, I reminded myself, things must happen
to let people know they are alive and human. Love affairs
take root—complicated ones, full of jealousy, pain, and revenge. Deep depression strikes. Addictions flourish. And,
occasionally, some very ugly variety of psychopathology,
which has had time to twist on itself grotesquely—like a
gnarled, forbidding tree—begins to bear poisonous fruit.

North Anderson's cruiser was parked near the emergency room, next to an ambulance and two black Range
Rovers. I parked alongside them and hurried through the
sliding glass doors.

Darwin Bishop, in khakis, a pink polo shirt, and black
Gucci loafers, was pacing the lobby, talking on his cell
phone. Two of his security guards stood nearby. He turned
away and, keeping his voice just above a whisper, said,
"Sell all of it at fifty-eight."

I walked up to the receptionist, a blue-haired woman
who was obviously beside herself. "I'm Dr. Clevenger," I
said. "I'm here to see Captain Anderson."

"He's in Room Five, with Mrs. Bishop and the baby,"
she said, wringing her thickly veined hands. "I hope you
can do something. She's so tiny."

"You're not going in there," Bishop said, from behind
me.

I turned around. He was standing with his two goons.
"What happened to Tess?" I asked flatly.

He ignored the question. "You're not welcome here," he
said.

I started past the receptionist. But I hadn't taken more
than four steps when someone grabbed my wrist and jerked
it, hard, behind my back, his arm falling across my neck.

I looked over my straining shoulder and saw one of the bodyguards had hold of me. It was an amateur move that made me question whether Bishop had hired him away from a Kmart. I leaned slightly forward, then drove my free elbow into the man's rib cage. A sharp crack told me I had hit home. He groaned and let go. Then his friend started coming at me.

"That's the end of it!" Anderson yelled from the hallway, half a dozen yards past the reception desk. He walked toward us.

Bishop pointed at me, but kept his distance. "I want him out of here."

Anderson walked up to me. "Let's go outside. I can bring you up to speed."

I took a mental note of that minor surrender and followed him back through the sliding glass doors, over to his cruiser.

"What the hell is going on?" I said. "What happened to Tess?"

He leaned against the hood. "Cardiac arrest," he said. "They got her back, but her heart's still not beating the right way. They're not sure if there's damage to her brain from lack of oxygen."

"My God."

"The Bishops rushed her to the ER at about three A.M." he explained. "I guess she'd been crying for about an hour before she stopped breathing. Julia and Claire were with her the whole time. When she passed out, they called 911. Actually, they had Darwin place the call."

"What does the doctor say?"

"She drew a toxic screen and found a high level of nor . . . trip . . . something."

"Nortriptyline," I said.

"That's it."

Nortriptyline is an antidepressant medication that can be fatal in overdose. Too high a concentration in the bloodstream slows electrical conduction through cardiac muscle, making the heart skip beats, then spiral into chaotic rhythms that pump no blood. "Where did the nortriptyline come from?" I asked.

"It's Julia's, prescribed by a psychiatrist in Aspen," Anderson said. "She was skiing there with Darwin a year or so back and was really feeling low. She says she felt better when they got home, so she stopped using it."

"But she kept the bottle?" I said.

"Right."

"So what are you thinking?"

"Actually, Frank," Anderson said, "it's looking like Billy's our man."

I hadn't even broached the news about Billy having broken into the Bishops' home. "Why do you say that?"

"He snuck into the house through a bathroom window during Brooke's funeral, stole some cash and jewelry. I guess he must have decided to take a little side trip to the nursery and feed Tess the pills. Claire had been writing letters in Darwin's study most of the night."

"How did you know he'd been in the house at all?" I asked.

"He left a note," Anderson said.

"What did it say?"

"Payback's a bitch. Love, Billy."

"Where did he leave it?" I asked.

"In an empty bank envelope Bishop says was full of cash—about five grand. The envelope was in a little antique desk in the master bedroom. I guess that's where he keeps his spare change."

"Interesting." I shook my head, thinking how peculiar it would be for Billy to tie himself so clearly to a murder scene. "Billy left me a message on my Chelsea machine about an hour ago. I tried calling you to tell you about it just before I headed here."

"What did he say?" Anderson asked.

"That he went in through that window, stole some things. That's all."

"I've got officers combing the house for evidence. We'll

see what turns up. All hell is going to break loose on the island now."

"Meaning?"

"I've asked the State Police to help with a manhunt for Billy," Anderson said. "They're bringing in thirty troopers, dogs, infrared search devices, the whole nine yards. And that's the tame part. Bishop may have used his contacts to keep the press at bay so far, but that dam won't hold. Reporters will start pouring in as soon as word about Tess filters through the wires. One rich kid murdered at home sounds like yesterday's news. Another attempted murder in the same family, and you've trumped the Ramseys."

"And raised them about nine hundred million," I said. "How's Julia?"

"Stunned," Anderson said. "She hasn't said ten words in there."

I wanted to be with her. More, I felt it was my *place* to be with her. But I was troubled by the fact that it was Julia's medication Tess had overdosed on. "Anyone in that house could still be the killer," I said. "The signs of nortriptyline toxicity can show up many hours after an overdose. Tess could have been poisoned before the funeral." Another thought occurred to me. "I'm not sure Billy would even know a nortriptyline overdose can be lethal. The only ones who talked to the doctor in Aspen were Darwin and—"

"Julia," Anderson said. "Agreed. Nobody's cleared yet. But anybody would say Billy is the lead suspect, by a country mile."

"Why would he leave a note *and* a voice message about breaking into the house, if he knew he would be connecting himself to another murder?" I asked.

Anderson shrugged. "We're not talking about a normal kid."

"No," I said, "we're talking about a sociopath. They usually don't make our work easy, do they?"

"I didn't say to stop poking around," Anderson said, "to the extent Bishop lets you."

"He could have poisoned Tess as easily as anyone else,"

I said. "For all we know, he might have decided Billy's break-in was the perfect cover. So, tell me: When, exactly, did he start deciding who investigates what?"

Anderson stiffened. "Don't go there again, Frank. I'm paying him the same deference I'd pay anyone. He doesn't have to give you access if he doesn't want to. I'm sure you can figure a way around him."

"Great," I said. "I'm on my own, all of a sudden. This wasn't a case I exactly lobbied you for, if you remember. I took it because you said you needed help."

"And I still do." He winked. "We're waiting on a helicopter from Mass General. Tess will be flown to their ICU for observation and treatment. Julia's going along for the ride, not Darwin. He meets her there tomorrow."

"So if I had a few questions for Julia, I should get to Boston sooner rather than later," I said.

"That sounds right," Anderson said. "Once Bishop lands in Beantown, I'd head back here to touch base with Claire and Garret. She was home alone with Tess during the funeral, and he strikes me as one very angry young man."

"Not a bad plan," I said.

"For a guy abandoning you." He looked out over the hospital's expansive lawn. "You know, I wanted to give Billy a real chance. He just didn't read like a killer to me." He looked at me. "I think I may have read him wrong."

"Maybe," I said. "Maybe I did, too. But my gut tells me to dig deeper."

"Then that's what you'll . . ." He caught himself. "That's what we'll do."

12

As I waited for a space to open up on the ferry back to Hyannis, three ferries came in carrying some of the state troopers North Anderson had requested for the manhunt. More than twenty drove off in cruisers, SUVs, and ATVs. Reporters from local networks, and a few of the nationals, had traveled on the same boats. I spotted R. D. Sahl from New England Cable News, Josh Resnek from the Independent News Group, and Lisa Pierpont from *Chronicle TV*, all cozying up to Jeff Cooperman, from *Dateline NBC*. The skies hosted not only the usual commuter planes but more than one State Police helicopter, no doubt fueled to crisscross the hidden forests and ponds and cranberry bogs that make up the Nantucket Moors, better known as the Commons.

On any day in late June, Nantucket has no shortage of celebrities strolling down Main Street, but the Bishop tragedy was one of those island events that felt like it might resonate for generations. People who were not impressed by many things seemed to want to be part of the spectacle. Or perhaps, collectively and unconsciously, they were intent on making it into a spectacle, draining it of its terror and tragedy, in order to tame it into an entertainment event that could fit neatly inside a twenty-inch television. Then it could be labeled on-screen, over a ten-second clip of ominous, computer-generated music: "Infanticide on Nantucket: Day Four." The murder of a baby and attempted murder of another would be inscribed in something as innocuous as *TV Guide*.

I finally made it onto the 3:00 P.M. ferry, which landed me in Hyannis at 4:40 P.M. I caught the 5:00 WRKO news broadcast, driving up Route 3. The Bishops were the lead story. About fifteen seconds were devoted to the facts of the case, and the next minute or so to Darwin Bishop's billionaire lifestyle. Money sells better than murder and almost as good as sex. If the press had only known about Bishop sleeping with Claire Buckley, we might not have heard any other news for days.

North Anderson was interviewed at the end of the piece and said the department was "still investigating," but had identified a lead suspect. He explained that the individual's name was being withheld because he was a minor.

I got to Mass General at 5:50 P.M. and headed to the Pediatric Intensive Care Unit—PICU, for short.

Few places could inspire more reflection. The space looks like a miniature mall from hell, with tiny glass storefronts along all four walls. Each room holds a child at risk of death or awaiting certain death. The nurses' station sits at the center, a kiosk of pathos, with monitors beeping out the weak rhythms of hearts meant to beat strong for the next seventy or eighty years. Below the monitors, a row of looseleaf charts holds a collection of short stories detailing God's limitations, with the first names of patients written on white tape along the bindings.

I found Tess's name and matched the number above her chart with one posted outside the furthest room to my right. Just as I did, I noticed John Karlstein, the pediatrician in charge of the intensive care unit, walking toward the nurses' station from one of the other rooms. He spotted me, too, and headed over.

Karlstein is a huge man, with a full beard, who stands six foot four in his trademark black alligator cowboy boots. He had been hired when the previous PICU director refused to dance to the tune of managed care companies and was eased into a full-time teaching position. Since then, the PICU had become a cash cow. "How are you, Frank?" he said in his bass voice. "It's been a while."

"Okay. You?"

"Can't complain," he said. "We're full. That's the good news. The bad news is that everybody's length of stay keeps getting shorter and shorter."

I nodded. "I guess it depends how you look at it—from our side of the bed, or the patients'."

He smiled, not seeming to take any offense. "I look at it the end of every month to make sure we're meeting our projections. We're on life support ourselves." He slapped my shoulder. "Someone file a psych consult?"

"Not this time. I'm involved in the Bishop case—forensically," I said.

"I didn't know you were back in that game."

"I'm not. A friend of mine with the Nantucket Police called me in. I took this one case."

"I can see why," Karlstein said. "What a story, huh? First one twin, now the other. And this guy Bishop is a billionaire. Brilliant, they say. A financial genius."

"That's the word," I said. I nodded toward Tess's room. "How's she doing?"

"The baby?"

"Right."

Karlstein's face turned serious. His left eye closed halfway, a reflex that seemed to kick in whenever his intellect engaged. As much as John Karlstein watched the bottom line, and as much as that could get under my skin, he was still one of the best pediatric intensivists in the world. Maybe *the* best. "Here's the deal," he said. "The nortriptyline is a cagey sonofabitch, especially in children. After overdose, you can still see fatal cardiac arrhythmias crop up days later. Tess's QRS interval was point fourteen seconds, which you know is too long. The electrical impulses traveling through her heart are still sluggish. That means she's still very much at risk. We've done what we can—meaning large-volume gastric lavage, followed by charcoal to really go after any pill fragments or trace medicine still in her gut. I don't think they were aggressive enough with that down on the island."

"It's a small hospital," I said.

"No crying over spilt milk." He winked. "The only other thing that worries me is whether there could be another toxin in her system that wouldn't show on the blood and urine screens."

Plenty of substances don't turn up on toxic screens unless you go looking for them, with precise chemical probes. "Do her symptoms suggest another poison?" I said.

"No, but I don't want to be blindsided by anything." He glanced over at Tess's room. "We've got her monitored, on all the right IVs, crash cart one foot from the bed." He looked at me with the kind of brash confidence everyone should pray for in a doctor. "No fucking way I'm letting this kid go, Frank. Period."

Doctors don't pat each other on the back much, but I was moved by Karlstein's determination. "She couldn't be in better hands," I said. "Not for all the money in the world."

Karlstein wasn't a man to take a compliment. "She's where the chopper dropped her off." He turned serious again. "I don't want to mix metaphors here. I know you're working on the investigation. But you might consider taking a quick look at the mother for us. She's not dealing well."

"Tell me what you mean."

"I just have a bad feeling about her. She hasn't said more than a couple words since she arrived, which is understandable—shock or whatever—but she's glued to the bedside in a way that worries me. She hasn't left for more than a minute. Hasn't eaten. No phone calls. Not a question about her daughter's care." He paused. "I guess none of this is very specific data, but she reads to me like somebody about ready to lose it."

"I came here to talk to her," I said. "But I can't do it as

an official consult for the hospital—not when I'm involved in the investigation."

"Fair enough," he said. "We'll get someone else from psychiatry to see her if she goes downhill."

We agreed on that, and I walked to Tess's room. Julia was sitting with her back to the glass wall, staring at the baby, so she didn't notice me standing there at first. That gave me a minute to steady myself at the sight of Tess's three-month-old body with EKG leads stuck to her chest, two IVs running into her tiny arms, and a nasogastric tube snaking into her nose. Her arms were taped to boards designed to keep them from flexing and dislodging the IV needles. She was breathing, but mercifully, she was asleep.

I have seen many ugly things in my life, including the grotesqueries that had driven me from forensic work, but Tess's plight took a backseat to none of it. I was trying to find words to share with Julia when she turned around and saw me in the doorway. She looked lost and beyond panicking over it, resigned to wandering aimlessly, like a ghost of herself. Yet whatever emotional vacuum had stripped her of affect had left her beauty intact. She looked almost of another world—her shiny black hair even more captivating without her attending to it, her green eyes shimmering even under the fluorescent lights. Maybe it was the backdrop of sterility and death that made her seem so incredibly vibrant. Or maybe it was simply that I had fallen in love with her. I stepped into the room.

She spoke before I could, which was a relief. "You were right," she said blankly.

"About?" I said.

"Win."

"What do you mean?"

"He did this to Tess." She turned back toward the baby.

My pulse quickened. I walked in and stood on the opposite side of the bed, watching Tess breathe. "Why do you think that?" I asked.

"He asked me where the pills were."

"The nortriptyline?"

She nodded.

"When?"

"Yesterday." She closed her eyes. "Before we left for Brooke's . . . funeral."

"Did he say why he wanted them?"

She looked toward the corner of the room, at nothing. She seemed to be lost in thought.

"Julia," I prompted her. "Did Darwin say why he wanted the nortriptyline tablets?"

She took a deep breath.

"Julia?"

"He said he was worried I'd take them. All of them. That I'd kill myself."

"Were you thinking about suicide?" I asked.

"I was upset, that's all," she said. "I mean, I said goodbye to my daughter. Shouldn't I be allowed to show some sadness, shed a tear or two?"

"Of course," I said softly.

"I promised him I wouldn't hurt myself. But he still wanted the pills." Her face moved a few degrees toward sadness. "The bottle was in the side pocket of a carry-on we had taken with us to Aspen last year," she said. "I had a bad feeling about the whole thing. I thought about telling him the pills were lost." Her voice fell to a whisper. "But I gave them to him." She looked at Tess.

"Are you willing to tell North Anderson all this?" I asked.

"Yes," she said. She stared through me. "I gave Darwin the medicine he used to poison my baby. You begged me to keep her safe."

"She'll make it," I said.

"At the hospital on Nantucket they said she might have brain damage."

I knew Julia's statement was actually a question, but I didn't have the answer. Tess was at risk for neurological complications, but I didn't know how grave a risk. "Give her a little time," I said. "There's every chance she'll make a full recovery. She could look much better in a couple days—or a couple hours."

"I'm not leaving," she said.

"No one's going to try to make you. You can stay with her as long as you want." I walked over to her and crouched beside her seat, so that our faces were on the same level. "You do need to keep yourself well for her."

Julia looked at me directly for the first time.

"She's going to need a healthy mother more than ever," I said.

"Can you stay with us a little while?" she asked. She offered me her hand.

I took it. Her hand was trembling slightly, like a delicate, frightened bird, and holding it made me feel needed and strong. I thought of North Anderson's warning about getting too close to see the truth about the Bishop case, but, at that moment, it seemed to me that there were two clear-cut suspects—Billy and Darwin Bishop. "I'll stay here a while," I said. "I have another patient to visit in the hospital a little later, but I can stop back after that."

She caught her lip between her teeth in a sad and seductive, little-girl way. "I meant, will you stay with us when we leave here? I'm not going home."

"What's your plan?" I asked, sidestepping the original question.

"I'll take Garret and Tess to my mother's," she said.

I nodded.

"I want you to come with us," she said. "Just until I feel safe." She shrugged. "Who knows? Maybe we'll both end up feeling safer together."

Looking back, I heard those words with a part of myself injured in childhood and unhealed as an adult, despite the good work of Dr. James in trying to piece my psyche back together. Because the pull toward rescuing an unhappy woman—a wife and mother—who would simultaneously rescue me was nearly overpowering. It was a dream I had stored away in my unconscious for forty years. And it was all I could do to remind myself that Julia had had equal access to Tess—and to the nortriptyline—as Darwin. "I promise not to leave you in danger," I said, leaving the door open for any and every possibility.

I called North Anderson and told him about Julia's suspicions. He said he would have a detective from the Boston police force take her statement. "I got to tell you I'm being shoved toward the sidelines," he said. "I guess you got to be careful what you ask for. The state's pulling out all the stops to find Billy, but the resources come along with a State Police captain named Brian O'Donnell. He's hot to run the whole show."

"What sort of guy is he?"

"Nobody we'd want to have a beer . . ." Anderson said, stopping himself.

"It's okay," I said. "I can take a joke, without taking a drink."

"Let's just say he's by the book. Very focused. Very serious." He paused. "Megalomania is probably the right diagnosis, if that's a diagnosis at all."

"It's been replaced with Narcissistic Personality Disorder," I said.

"Sounds about right," Anderson said. "When are you back?"

"Early tomorrow. I'll check in with Claire and Garret, like you suggested."

"I'd do it as soon as you can. O'Donnell has the Governor's ear. He could pull the plug on both of us."

"Understood."

"Call me when you hit the island."

I headed to Lilly Cuningham's room and was surprised to find her sitting up in bed, reading the *Boston Herald*. Her leg was still packed with gauze, but it was out of traction. I walked closer and saw that the Bishop story had made it onto the front page of the late edition, under a massive headline that read: "TWIN TERROR." A photograph accompanying the story showed Julia and Darwin at a black-tie event. A smaller inset showed the Bishop estate. I tried to focus on Lilly. "You seem to be on the mend," I said.

She lowered the paper and smiled at me. "They finally found the right antibiotic," she said.

I glanced at the IV pole. It had been pruned down to one hanging plastic bag. "I guess so."

"I'm glad you came back," she said.

"I told you I would." I sat down.

"I've been thinking about my grandfather."

The way those words rolled off Lily's tongue made me wonder whether the antibiotics had done all the good work on her leg, or whether her mind had opened up enough to let some of the toxins drain. "What about him?"

"These thoughts I have," she said. "I don't think they're flashbacks—or some sort of delayed recall. I don't think Grandpa ever touched me."

"Okay," I encouraged her, "where do you think the thoughts are coming from?"

"My imagination," she said. "They're things I've dreamt up—nightmares during the day. Don't all little girls have funny feelings for their dads?"

Freud did believe that all young girls have unconscious sexual feelings toward the men in their families. But those feelings generally evaporate by adulthood and never fuel serious psychiatric symptoms. I wondered why Lilly's impulses had survived childhood and adolescence intact. Why did they surface on her honeymoon? And why were they so threatening that she had to resist them by doing something as distracting and destructive as injecting herself with dirt?

"*Because she couldn't count on anyone else to resist them*," the voice at the back of my mind said.

That seemed like the right path to journey down. "How would your grandfather have responded," I asked her, "if you had made the first move?"

"The first move?" she said.

"If you asked him for sex," I said.

A hint of a smile played across her lips. "I don't want to think about it," she said.

"That's always up to you," I said. "But if you choose to confront the thoughts, they may not sneak up on you anymore. You may find you can turn them on and off, without using a needle."

She looked as if she was on the fence about trying.

"Try it for ten seconds. No more," I said.

She looked at me to see if I was serious, then rolled her eyes and shook her head.

"Would he have been angry with you?" I led.

"No," she said. "He was an understanding man."

"Embarrassed?"

She shook her head.

"Shocked?"

She blushed, giggled. "God, I honestly don't know how he would have responded."

Those words, taken literally, sounded like they came directly from the heart of the problem. Lilly couldn't predict whether her grandfather would have taken her as a lover, had she asked him.

Healthy psychosexual development unfolds in an atmosphere in which children know the adults around them would never take them up on their sexual feelings. When a little girl asks her father whether he will marry her, a good answer is, "I'm married to your mother. I love her. Someday I know you'll meet someone who loves you that way." The father (or grandfather) should not respond with a suggestive wink or a playful pat on the backside—or with silence.

Unconsciously fearing that an offer of romance would be accepted by her grandfather, Lilly reacted by burying her sexuality. When it emerged on her honeymoon, it emerged with all the guilt and anxiety of a little girl trying to steal away the man of the house. Her sexual impulses were taboo. Worthy of punishment. Dirty.

"Did he have other women?" I asked.

"Oh, I would think so," she said. "Almost certainly."

"Why do you say that?"

"They argued about it—he and my grandmother. He worked late a lot. Some nights he didn't come home at all. There was a real scene over a woman he had hired as his secretary."

"Did he ever mention these women to you?" I asked.

"I don't think so," she said. "At least not directly. But I knew he was unhappy with my grandmother."

"How did you know that?"

"He used to talk about old girlfriends he dated before he got married. One, in particular. A woman named Hazel. She was Jewish, and my grandfather was Irish Catholic, and that ended that. The times were different. But he told me she was the one he was meant for."

"How old were you when he shared that with you?" I asked.

"Probably eight. Maybe nine." She paused. "Weird, how I remember that."

People often cling to single, vivid childhood memories as symbols of larger psychological issues. By age nine, after all, Lilly knew plenty of toxic facts about Grandpa. He wasn't completely in love with his wife. He was available to other women. Most important, he was willing to share intensely personal, very adult information with her. Perhaps, nine-year-old Lilly might have reasoned, she could one day replace her grandmother and make her grandfather complete. Keeping him content was important, after all, since she had already lost her father.

"It sounds like you don't know what your grandfather would have done, had you offered yourself to him," I told Lilly. "That means he seduced you, without ever laying a hand on you."

"That's so hard for me to believe," she said. "He wasn't mean or predatory. He was . . . loving."

"I doubt he set out to do you any harm," I said. "But he was empty emotionally and looking everywhere to be filled up—even by the romantic fantasies of his granddaughter.

You played along, because that's what little girls do at eight or nine or ten." I let that sink in a couple seconds.

"And that's why I feel so guilty?" she said.

"Yes," I said. "That guilt may have been protective, for a time. When you were little, it may have kept you from getting yourself deeper into a relationship that was bad for you." I leaned closer to the bed. "Now that emotion—the guilt—has outlived its purpose. It's time to let it go."

She glanced at her leg. "What do I do when these images come up, and the feelings come back? Is there something I can take?"

"My opinion might be a little different from what other psychiatrists would tell you," I said.

"Why? What would they say?"

"I think most would tell you to take an antianxiety medication, like Klonopin, or a combination antidepressant/antianxiety medication, like Zoloft. Or both. And you could do that. Your symptoms would decrease or even disappear, at least for a while."

"What would you recommend?" she asked.

"I say, run into the images, not away from them. Find a psychiatrist to help you watch the scenes as they unfold in your mind. My guess is that your guilt will turn pretty quickly to anger. And that's a much easier emotion to deal with."

"Can't I do that work with you?" she asked.

No doubt Lilly wanted to win over every male authority figure she came across. Her grandfather. All her surgeons. Why not a psychiatrist? Her case fascinated me, but I had a chance to demonstrate that I was willing to do the right thing for her, not the gratifying thing for me. Seeing that I, unlike her grandfather, could draw that distinction might be the first baby step on her long journey to recovery. "I'd recommend someone older than I am," I said.

She looked away. "I'm not sure I could open up to anyone else."

"It's someone I have tremendous respect for," I said.

"You said you'd stay with me through this."

Normally, I wouldn't have divulged what I was about to tell her, but I felt that Lilly needed a special, continuing connection with me. Without that, I feared she wouldn't follow up. "I'm referring you to a psychiatrist who helped me," I said. "My own analyst."

She looked at me. "Your own analyst? You'd share him with me?"

"Yes," I said. "I will."

"Who is it?" she asked.

"Dr. Theodore James. He's your grandfather's age."

The PICU was in crisis as I walked through its sliding glass doors. Nurses ran for IV bags, and John Karlstein barked orders from Tess's glass cubicle. Someone had pulled the blinds closed.

Julia was standing in a far corner of the central room, crying, as a nurse tried to comfort her. "Frank!" she yelled when we made eye contact. She ran to me. I held her, her chest heaving so hard she was barely able to speak. "She stopped . . . breathing. Tess . . . Please, God."

"Hang a tocainide drip," Karlstein ordered. An alarm sounded on the bank of monitors at the nurses' station. I looked over and saw Tess's tracing had gone flat. "Hold the drip. We're going to shock her again," Karlstein yelled. "Stand back!"

Julia crumpled in my arms. "No!" she pleaded. "Frank, please help."

I eased Julia into a seat by the unit secretary's desk, with no view of Tess's room, and motioned for the nurse. "Stay here," I told Julia, as the nurse arrived. "I'll find out what's happening."

I walked to the edge of the group of five or six figures huddled over Tess. She had been intubated, and one of the nurses was squeezing a rubber ambu bag to force air into and out of her lungs. Karlstein looked like a battlefield general, a towering figure amidst a tangle of hanging bags and bottles and rubber tubing, the paddles of the cardioverter still in his hands.

He glanced at me. "We've got a pulse," he said. "Maybe we got lucky."

Several members of the team nodded to themselves, drinking in that bit of reassurance. Unlike Karlstein, who still looked crisp, they were sweat-soaked, whether from working feverishly or standing so close to the abyss.

"Let's start that tocainide now," Karlstein said.

I noticed a full surgical tray had been opened at the bedside. I knew what that meant: Karlstein had been prepared to open Tess's chest and pump her heart by hand. I felt a surge of admiration for him.

"Try letting her breathe on her own," he said.

The nurse at the head of the bed untaped the breathing tube from Tess's lips and slowly pulled it out of her throat. Tess coughed, weakly at first, then more vigorously. Then she began to cry.

Smiles broke onto the faces of the men and women who had, at least for the moment, beaten back death.

"Strong work," Karlstein said. "Let's order in some Chinese. My treat. Just make sure we get plenty of those potstickers. Fried, not steamed." He walked out of the room and motioned for me to follow him. I did. He headed over to Julia, who was standing, wide-eyed, where I had left her. "Her heart's beating, and she's breathing," Karlstein told her.

Julia started to weep again. "Thank you so much," she managed. She leaned against me in a way that would have made it natural for me to put my arm around her—something I wanted to do, and would have done, were we somewhere else. When I didn't move to hold her, she straightened up.

"We're going to watch Tess like hawks," Karlstein said. "What I'd advise is for you to take, say, five, ten minutes with her, then go and get some rest. There's a decent hotel across the street. Check in. Nap. She'll be here when you get back."

"I'm not leaving," Julia said, looking to me for support.

I saw Karlstein's left eye close halfway, his mind chewing on something. "Why don't you give Dr. Karlstein and me a minute?" I said to Julia.

She took a deep breath, wiped her tears away. "I'm doing fine," she said. "I won't get in anyone's way. I promise."

I nodded. "One minute," I said. "I'll be right back." I stepped away and headed to a corner of the PICU, with Karlstein lumbering behind me.

"Talk about touch and go in there," I said, nodding toward Tess's room.

"I'm gonna call one of the cardiac boys and have him thread a temporary pacemaker," he said. "I don't like the way she crapped out on us. Ventricular tachycardia, out of nowhere."

"What do you think her chances are?"

"Impossible to predict," he said. "If we can get her out of here okay, she's still at increased risk for a year or more."

"From sudden death," I said.

"You got it. Twenty-five percent of people who make it back after cardiac arrest drop dead during the first year after discharge from a hospital. Take it out four years and you go up to about thirty-one percent. No one knows exactly why."

"That's still better odds than she had about three minutes ago."

Karlstein smiled. "Thanks for reminding me." He shook his head. "This place could get to you, if you were a half-normal person, you know?" He chuckled.

I did know. I also knew Karlstein couldn't think it was all that funny. "You can always give me a call," I half-joked, trying to take the edge off the invitation.

He slapped me on the back. "I'm one of those guys

who'd fall apart if I gave myself fifty minutes to think," he said. "Better to keep on chugging."

I didn't respond, which was enough of a response to let Karlstein know I wasn't a big fan of that strategy.

"Two things I do need to tell you," he went on, "seeing as you're involved in the Bishop case—forensically, at least." The way he said "*at least*" made me wonder whether he intuited that Julia and I were more than professionally involved.

"Shoot," I said.

"I'm gonna go ahead and file that psychiatry consultation on the mother. I've been at this long enough to know she's having a tough time."

"Fair enough," I said. "I'm sure you're right."

"And I'm ordering a sitter, as well," he said.

"A sitter?" I said. "You want the baby on one-to-one observation?"

"One of the nurses suggested it, but I was already batting the idea around in my head." He took a deep breath, glanced at Julia, then looked back at me. "She hovers, you know? She's got that stickiness to her."

Those were code words for parents who seem *too* close to their kids. "You're not sure she has the baby's best interest at heart," I said. "You want someone to keep an eye on her."

"*At heart*, that's a good one." He smiled.

"I didn't mean it that way," I said.

"Freudian slip, maybe," he said. His voice turned serious. "Let's face it, Frank, there's been a murder in this family already. If Tess codes again, I damn well want to know it's because of the nortriptyline from last night, not something in Mommy's purse."

"She's lost one daughter," I said. "Another may die. I'm not arguing against the sitter, but I don't think there's any 'normal' way to respond in a situation like this."

"Granted," he said. "I'm being extra-cautious. It's my way."

I swallowed hard at the realization that another person I

respected was red-flagging Julia as a suspect. "No. You're doing the right thing," I said. "I'll let her know to expect company."

I walked back to Julia. "Staying here around the clock isn't going to change Tess's prognosis," I said. "There's a hotel across the street. Let me check you in. You can eat, maybe sleep a little. Then you can come right back here."

"I don't trust them to keep Darwin away," she said.

"I'll stay here myself until you're back," I said.

She shook her head. "I'm not leaving."

"Okay . . ." I wanted to let her know about the one-to-one. "There's going to be someone watching Tess, anyhow," I said. "They're ordering what's called a 'sitter.' "

"What's that?"

"Usually a college kid, or a student nurse," I said. "The person sits by the bedside, twenty-four hours a day."

"What for?" she asked.

I thought about fibbing that the reason was to monitor the baby's breathing, but decided to be straight with her. "With the investigation ongoing, the hospital needs to protect Tess from anyone who may have had access to her before the overdose," I said.

"Including me," she said.

"Right," I said, watching for her reaction.

"Good," she said. "That makes me feel a little better. At least they're taking her safety seriously."

Julia's comment made me feel a little better, too. Typically, a parent who has caused a child's injuries will resist close monitoring by the staff, sometimes insisting on a meeting with the hospital's patient rights advocate, or even calling in an attorney. "Does that mean you'll think about the hotel?" I asked.

"I'll get a room a little later," she said unconvincingly.

"You know, I live ten minutes from here, in Chelsea," I said. "You could always—"

"Thanks." She reached for my hand and held it a few

moments. "You've been incredible," she said. "I need you with me to make it through this."

"You've got me," I said.

"Just blind luck, I guess," she said.

13

I stopped at Café Positano for a quick, late dinner. Mario steamed my milk and handed me a cappuccino while I waited for three slices of the best pizza outside of Rome. It felt good to be back in familiar territory. When Carl Rossetti walked in, I actually started to relax for the first time in days.

"You're buying," he said, striding over to me at the espresso bar.

"The two-carat stone tap you out?" I said.

"I got some information for you. But it's gonna cost you. A double espresso, a nice bottle of Limone soda, and a cannoli."

"Done."

He laid his hands on the bar, his pinkie still dancing with excitement about the ring. "I would have called you, but this is news to me, like two hours ago, so I sat on it, seeing I was on trial in Suffolk Superior, and you can't carry a cell phone in there. That, and I was thinking I might bump into you here."

"How'd you do in court?" I asked him.

"Not so good this time. Statutory rape case. The guy's an accountant, twenty-six years old, never so much as a traffic ticket. He meets a girl who says she's seventeen—according to his version of events—when she's really fourteen, almost fifteen. I'm sitting there, looking at this girl, who's drop-dead gorgeous, built like a centerfold. And I'm thinking how many of us would turn it down, right? Not Roman Polanski. Not Elvis. Not Jerry Lee Lewis. Probably not me. I would have liked to ask the judge and court clerk what they'd do."

"I bet you didn't," I said.

"No," Rossetti said. "I asked for six months house arrest."

"What did you get?"

"Judge Getchell came down on him like a ton of bricks, sent him to MCI Concord for two years. He gets listed as a pedophile on the state registry, probation for five years. That's if he makes it out of Concord alive. The inmates get word he's a sex offender, they'll be waiting for him."

"That's the kind of verdict you get when the judge has to wonder whether he'd commit the crime," I said. I caught Mario's eye. "Double espresso for the counselor," I told him.

"And . . ." Rossetti said.

"And a Limone and cannoli," I said.

"Thank you, Franko."

"Exactly what am I paying you for?" I asked.

"I heard back from my buddy Viktor in Russia," he said. "The one who runs an oil refinery."

"Right . . ."

"He snooped around, asked his globe-trotting friends about Darwin 'Win' Bishop—who, by the way, I hear had another tragedy in the family."

"Tess, the other twin, is at MGH," I said. "I just came from there. She was poisoned. She went into cardiac arrest."

"She made it, though? She'll pull through?" he asked.

"Looks that way."

"Good. Good for her."

"They're saying the Russian boy did it," he said.

"They're not supposed to say anything publicly," I said. "Billy's a minor."

"Yeah, well, it's all over the news, as of ten minutes

ago, anyhow. He broke into the Bishop estate, blah, blah, blah. They're gonna leak everything on this kid. Harrigan wants him. Like any D.A. would. Another notch in the prosecutorial belt." He shrugged. "Myself, I don't buy the party line here. Everything I hear about this Darwin Bishop makes me more convinced he's the killer."

"What did Viktor find out?" I asked.

"Long and short of it, Bishop isn't Trump—if Trump is even Trump."

"I'm not sure I follow." I was sure I didn't.

"Bishop might have a billion in assets, but he's got that and maybe fifty, sixty million in debts. This guy's further over the edge financially than I am. And that's saying something."

Mario brought Rossetti's espresso, Limone, and cannoli, and set them down in front of him.

"How would Viktor know that?" I asked.

Rossetti bit off half the cannoli, keeping his eyes closed as he chewed it. "Oh, baby," he purred.

"You doing all right there?" I said.

He held up a finger, sipped his espresso. "Heaven," he called out to Mario, then focused on me again. "These guys all hear about it when someone's hemorrhaging," he said finally. "According to Viktor, it's common knowledge that Bishop's scrambling. He invested most of the cash he netted from Consolidated Minerals and Metals in four Internet plays: Priceline.com, MicroStrategy, Inc., CMGI, and Divine InterVentures. They all plunged about ninety-five percent after he bought in. Priceline dropped from $136-a-share to a buck. Okay? Bishop's looking to liquidate some of his art, a property he owns in Cannes and another at Turnberry Isle in North Miami."

"That may explain why he's trading stocks every time I see him," I said.

"And you know what that means. More trouble. It's like grabbing at waves when you're drowning."

"Especially if he's been reaching for more technology plays," I said. "Tide's been going out a long time."

"One question to ask is whether he insured the kids," Rossetti said.

"Brooke and Tess? Life insurance on infants?"

"You can write a policy on anyone."

"We'll look into it," I said.

"Are they getting any closer to finding Billy?" Rossetti asked.

"I haven't heard anything. But if he's still on the island, they'll track him down. They've got dogs, helicopters, and a small army of state troopers."

"Let's hope he doesn't resist and doesn't have a weapon."

I hadn't thought of the possibility of Billy being harmed by the police, let alone killed. "If he were to take a bullet to the chest," I said, thinking aloud, "everyone would assume the case was closed and go home happy."

"Like I told you before," Rossetti said, "you're in the ring with heavyweights now. A man like Bishop can decide to make things happen—especially if he's on the ropes himself."

I finally made it home at 10:55 P.M. There were no distressing messages or strings of hangups on my machine, for a change. I called North Anderson's mobile phone to bring him up to speed on the information I had gotten from Carl Rossetti. "A lawyer friend of mine named Carl Rossetti has a high-level, corporate connection in Russia. The word on the streets—or in the boardrooms—is that Bishop is in financial trouble," I told him. "Bad stocks, lots of debt. He's got a bunch of art and real estate up for sale."

"You never know whether people are what they seem to be," he said.

"No argument there." I paused. "Rossetti thought we should check whether Brooke and Tess had life insurance."

"Will do. I already sent that detective by to speak with Julia at MGH," Anderson said. "Terry McCarthy. I'll get a report on the interview soon. And I had someone on the force down in Duxbury check in with Kristen Collier, the baby nurse Julia fired."

"Come up with anything?"

"Nothing earth-shattering. She told me she was enraged with Julia when she was let go. Now she feels bad about the whole thing, like she was partly to blame. I guess Claire Buckley had given her a whole song and dance about how Julia's depression could get worse and worse, how she might not be able to think clearly, might end up not being able to care for the twins at all."

"Nice borderline move there," I said. "Splitting off the baby nurse from the mother. Claire keeps control of the household that way."

"And this Collier kind of lost sight of who she was really working for," Anderson said. "She started double-checking Julia's plans for the twins with Claire—even things that sound pretty routine, like which baby formula to order up, when to schedule doctors' appointments."

"Those things may seem routine to us, but not to a woman who's expecting," I said.

"Tell me about it," Anderson said. "Tina's rereading every baby and parenting book she can lay her hands on. There are no small details."

"And when you have a woman like Julia suffering with postpartum depression, she's going to want to appear strong, not ill," I said. "She could be hypersensitive to people treating her like a basket case."

"Apparently so. She axed Collier with no notice."

"What does Kristen Collier look like, anyhow?" I asked.

"Young and pretty, just like Claire," he said. "And if you're headed where I think you are, I did get the feeling that her relationship with Win didn't help things any."

"Tell me more."

"I guess working as a baby nurse was her way of biding time. She's got her R.N., but she's back in school for an MBA. During the week or so she lived with the Bishops, she took the opportunity to ask Darwin for his thoughts on her career, the economy, what-have-you. They spent some time together."

"Julia might not have liked that," I said. "Claire would have hated it."

"Claire has called her from time to time over the past few months, saying she was checking in, wanted to make sure she'd landed well. But Collier had the feeling she was checking her out, making sure she hadn't had any more contact with the man of the house."

"Had she?" I asked.

"She says no."

"And is she carrying a grudge?"

"I don't think so," he said. "Not the kind that leads to murder, anyway. She seemed pretty straight up."

"At least someone does," I said.

"Will I see you tomorrow on the island?" Anderson asked.

"Definitely. We'll talk then."

He hung up.

I walked around my loft, putting things in order. I stopped in front of the Bradford Johnson canvas that Justine Franza had taken a liking to—the one with a rope tied between two ships' masts, as a storm threatens not only the distressed vessel but the rescuing craft as well. The painting had always spoken to me, but I wasn't sure any longer that the only reason was the bravery of men putting their lives on the line to help others. This time I read another message in it—something about being bound to trouble, treating it almost as ballast, as if I would feel unstable on calm waters. Did that mean I was forever destined to have pained and broken people as my constituency? Or would I gravitate toward safety once I had healed more of the broken parts inside me?

I looked up toward the liquor cabinet, then forced myself to look away. I turned on the television, hoping for distraction, but caught the last thirty seconds of a report by David Robichaud on WBZ that took viewers live to the manhunt for Billy. Huge spotlights swept over dunes as

state troopers with dogs combed the dense foliage of the
Nantucket moors. State Police Captain Brian O'Donnell,
the man North Anderson had told me was pressing to run
the entire investigation, promised: "Wherever he is, we'll
find him. I've assured Mr. Bishop, the mayor's office, and
the Governor that an arrest will be made in this case—and
soon."

I noted the order in which O'Donnell had ticked off his
allegiances. Bishop first.

I was about to surf for something mindless when the
buzzer sounded, signaling someone at my front door. I
walked to the intercom. "Yes?" I said.

"Frank, it's Julia. I'm sorry I didn't call first. I . . ."

I hit the SPEAK button. "No reason to be sorry," I said.
"Please come up." I hit the buzzer to let her in. Then I
stood there, feeling anxious and excited and, strangely, exposed. Having someone you care for visit the place you
live is like stripping naked. My place was a loft in gritty
Chelsea, after all, not an estate in Nantucket or a two-story
penthouse in Manhattan. I was a lot more comfortable as-
sessing the lives of others than laying mine bare. I listened
to Julia's footsteps as she took the flights of stairs. When
she knocked on my door, I opened it slowly, as if I could
better control things if I could make them unfold gradually.

Julia stood there in blue jeans, a white T-shirt, and a
short black leather jacket, looking as beautiful as I had ever
seen her. "I felt a little better about leaving Tess once the
sitter came, so I checked into that hotel and tried to nap,
but I couldn't," she said. "I thought, maybe, here—with
you. I mean, if it isn't putting you out, or putting you in
an awkward position. Because . . ."

I took her hand and gently pulled her inside. We kissed
deeply. The warmth of her lips and tongue, the press of her
hands against my back, the smell of her hair transported
me to an emotional state in which passion and peacefulness
not only coexisted, but fed one another. I felt strangely
comfortable with wanting her, as if, from all time, she had
been destined to be my object of desire. We separated and

stood in silence, each of our hands in one another's, like schoolkids on a dimly lighted front porch. "I'm glad you came here," I said.

"A little variation on the traditional house call," she said. "I was surprised you're listed, like a regular person, in the telephone book."

"I'm pretty regular, when you come right down to it," I said.

"No, you're not," she said. "Far from it. The people you've worked with, the violent ones . . . can find you so easily."

"That's the best way to let them know I'm not afraid of them."

"Are you, sometimes, though?"

"No," I said. "Never. But that may just mean there's something wrong with me."

She brushed past me, into the living room.

I walked toward the kitchen. "Can I get you anything? A drink? Dinner?"

"I grabbed something at the hospital cafeteria," she said, wandering around the loft. "Please go ahead, though."

I watched her as she checked out the loft, taking in the art, touching some of the furniture. She stopped in front of the plate-glass windows. "This is one of the most beautiful views I've ever seen," she said. "How did you find this place?"

"A friend of mine used to live in this building," I said. "I liked watching the tankers."

"From her place," Julia said. She smiled.

I nodded.

She took off her jacket and walked over to my bed. "I need to sleep for half an hour or so. I'm exhausted. Do you mind?"

"Of course not," I said.

She laid down on the gray linen comforter, curled up like a cat. "Hold me?" she asked.

I walked over and climbed onto the bed, spooning myself against her, my face lost now in her hair, my hand laced into hers, held close to her breast. I could feel her engagement ring against my skin, but that seemed an artifact from a life she had lived before ours intersected.

"A psychiatrist—a woman—came by the intensive care unit to talk with me," she said.

"And . . ."

"I told her I won't want to go on if Tess doesn't make it," she said. "I couldn't bear to survive, thinking I let this happen to her."

"Dr. Karlstein is fighting like hell for Tess," I said.

"I believe that," she said. "And I believe she'll pull through. Otherwise, I could never have left her, not even for an hour."

We lay together as Julia slept. Before dozing off myself, I let my mind wander three, four months into the future, past the investigation, which I now believed should end with Darwin Bishop's arrest. And I could actually see Julia and myself making a life together, somehow offering Billy and Garret safe harbor from the storms they had weathered. I actually thought I might have the chance to redeem myself for losing my adolescent patient Billy Fisk to suicide.

We awakened at the same moment. Julia rolled over and faced me. "I want to know that we're together," she whispered. "I want you to make love to me."

I propped myself on an elbow and brushed her hair away from her face. "This is a complicated time to start," I said.

"We started the first time you touched my arm," she said. "The day you met me outside the house, with Garret."

"I just . . ."

"You can't control what you feel for me," she said, glancing at my crotch, full with my excitement. She unbuttoned and unzipped her jeans, guided my hand into her panties and between her legs. She was completely shaved, and her impossibly soft skin was warm and wet. "Not any more than I can control what I feel for you."

Julia's sexual desire in the face of losing Brooke and nearly losing Tess troubled me, but I silently chastised myself for judging her. What textbook reaction, after all, would have satisfied me? Bitter rage? Isolation? Did I want to see her slip deeper and deeper into depression?

My head was swimming. Why resist Julia's needs, I asked myself, when the gods of chance and love might be giving me my one shot at happiness? Why deny my own needs? I looked into Julia's eyes and ran the tip of my finger along the cleft between her delicate folds. She sighed. And as she opened herself to my touch, it seemed a part of my soul, lost a long time, was being returned to me.

Friday, June 28, 2002

I started driving Julia back to Mass General at 1:30 A.M. We had fallen asleep again, after making love. I checked my rearview mirror a few times to make sure we weren't being followed.

"Worried about Win?" Julia asked.

"Shouldn't I be?"

"I've worried about him for so long, I sometimes forget to."

"Why do you think you married him in the first place?" I asked. "You've said you thought you were in love, but why did you fall for him? What attracted you?"

She took a deep breath. "I'm not sure it was about Win," she said. "He was charming, handsome. All that. But it was more about me. I think I was actually using him."

That sounded pretty up-front. "How so?" I asked.

"I come from a large family," she said. "Four brothers and myself. Dad was an attorney, but not a real name in his profession, nothing like that. My mother was quiet. A homemaker. She didn't have any dreams to speak of and she never seemed terribly interested in mine. Darwin was larger than life—certainly larger than my life seemed at the time."

"Your relationship with your father?" I asked. "How was that?"

"I loved him, but he spent most of his time with my brothers—their athletics, their schooling. I started modeling at fourteen, probably to compete for his attention. It grew into a lot more than I expected, but he never really cared about it. And I never developed real self-confidence from it."

"Your marriage provided that?"

"In a way," she said. "Or it seemed to. Being Win's wife meant I didn't have to figure out what else I was. Mrs. Darwin Bishop was a good enough label for my parents and friends. For most people. And for a long while, it was good enough for me, too. I borrowed his success. I even fooled myself into thinking I was contributing to it. The power behind the throne. That kind of thing."

"But you had achieved a good deal of success yourself, in modeling," I said.

"I always understood that was skin-deep, and that it would end." She looked out the window at the Boston skyline as we crossed the Tobin Bridge. "I knew from the first time Darwin hit me that our marriage would end, too. But I was . . . paralyzed. I never took the time or had the strength to find my own way."

"Yet," I said.

"Yet." She smiled. "Enough about me, already, Dr. Clevenger. How have you happened to stay single?"

"I was with a woman for years who was ill—mentally," I said.

"Who was she?"

"A doctor," I said. "An obstetrician."

"Is that what brought you together?" Julia asked. "Medicine?"

"That was part of it. But, in a certain way, I was using her, too," I said. "She was fragile, so I was the one in control. My being with her gave me the chance to say I was in a relationship when I was really avoiding relationships. Hiding out."

"Why hide?" she said.

"Because I had to hide—emotionally and physically—

in the house I grew up in. I guess it got to be a habit."

She looked at me as if she wanted more of an explanation.

"My father used a belt, just like Darwin," I said.

"I'm so sorry, Frank," she said. "I had no idea."

"It was a long time ago," I said.

Julia was silent several seconds, sitting and looking through the windshield. Then she turned to me. "You don't have to hide anything, anymore," she said.

I wanted to believe the heart of what Julia had said—that I could be known and loved at the same time. Because, deep down, I had always suspected the two were mutually exclusive. I glanced at her as she looked at me, with eyes full of acceptance and warmth. And I felt, truly, as though I had arrived at a new and better place.

I parked in the MGH garage and walked Julia the two blocks to the door of the hospital. We played it safe—no parting kiss, no long good-bye. She walked into the lobby, and I turned and started back for the truck. It was just before 2:00 A.M.

The MGH garage is a five-story cement structure, the back of which overlooks the Charles River. The building runs two city blocks, with the wall furthest from the hospital sitting on Cambridge Street and the wall closest to it bordering a darkened alleyway that leads to Storrow Drive. I had just started to walk across that alleyway when someone pushed me, hard, from behind. I lurched forward and, struggling to stay on my feet, felt a sudden and odd twisting sensation at the bottom of my rib cage, about halfway between my spine and my side. It burned red-hot for the first second or two, then flipped into a penetrating ache so severe it made me double over and fall to the ground. I tried reaching for the Browning Baby in my pocket, but my arm didn't seem to be taking instructions from my brain.

"What could she have done," a husky, peculiar-sounding voice said, "being what she is?"

I struggled to see the figure jogging away from me, but

only caught a glimpse of black, army-style boots. I groped for the painful place on my back that was making me see double. I felt something warm and slick. Then everything went black.

"Frank!" Colin Bain called to me. "C'mon, man, stop ignoring me." I felt my sternum being assaulted by Bain's knuckles—a sternal rub, they call it, which is actually more of a brutal sternal raking, designed to wake the unresponsive and separate them from the dead.

"Christ! I'm fine," I muttered, twisting away from him. I opened my eyes and tried to sit up, but a searing pain reached through my back and yanked me down to the mattress by my ribs.

Bain was standing by the bed, wearing his round wire-rimmed glasses. He swept his longish red hair away from his face. "Welcome, friend," he said.

I was naked to the waist. Bandages circled my torso like a half-wrapped mummy. "What the hell happened to me?" I said.

"Someone jumped you in the alleyway near the garage," he said. "Stuck you good. A five-inch blade, so far as I can tell. At least, that's how deep it went." He smiled. "You slept through the best parts. I already explored the wound, cleaned it up, sewed you shut. You were so out of it I didn't even have to use lidocaine."

"The mind is a wonderful thing," I said. "Thanks for the help."

"No problem," he said.

"Did they catch the guy?" I asked.

"Not even close," he said. "They didn't find you for five or ten minutes, judging from the amount of blood you'd lost."

I checked out the space around me and spotted a unit of packed red blood cells hanging from an IV pole. A length of red IV tubing ran into my arm. I shook my head.

"Hospital security said they thought you were some

Compulsion

195

"They didn't notice the blood all over your jacket until they
flipped you onto a gurney to sleep it off in the lobby." He
winked. "I do have their names, if you want to catch up
with them."

I started to chuckle, but choked on a bolt of pain that
shot straight through my abdomen, then up into my throat.

"You're gonna be in a fair amount of discomfort for a
couple days," Bain said.

"Discomfort's a nice word for it," I said, catching my
breath.

"An MRI showed the blade sliced through the latissimus
dorsi and internal oblique," he said. "I threw in about sixty
stitches. The tip just missed your portal artery, by the way.
If that had been severed, you'd have bled out for sure.
You're lucky to be alive."

"Thanks for letting me know."

"It wouldn't be a bad idea to be admitted overnight, for
observation. Just to make sure nothing got nicked in there
that we don't know about."

"No way," I said. "I don't have the time."

"You were almost out of time—for good," he said.
"What's a day or two?"

Now it was a day *or two.* "I'm in the middle of a forensic case," I said. Saying those words helped my still-
foggy brain make the obvious connection between the
Bishops and my being stabbed. "This probably has something to do with that."

"So maybe it would be good to lay low for twenty-four,
forty-eight hours, you know?"

"I can't," I said.

"Suit yourself," he said. "I'll write you a scrip for some
Keflex. Hopefully, that'll prevent any infection. Percocet
for the pain. Just let me know when you need more."

The addict in me perked up. Downing three, four Percocet would be like taking a chemical vacation from the
whole Bishop mess. I actually caught myself wondering
how many refills Bain would write for me. Luckily, I re-

alized what a great excuse he was giving me to fall apart. "I'd better skip anything abusable," I said. "I've had problems with that stuff before."

He took the revelation in stride. "I didn't know. We'll make do with Motrin, then."

"Thanks."

"If you get any fever, chills or swelling, come right back here. Agreed?"

"You got it," I said.

"The external sutures come out in ten days. The internal ones dissolve," he said.

"I'll see you in ten days, then." I gritted my teeth and sat up. My side felt as if it was ripping away from the rest of my body.

"The cops want to talk to you, by the way," Bain said. "Should I let them know you're awake?"

"Sure."

"These guys are Boston cops," he said. "But I did take the liberty to let a friend of yours from Nantucket know your condition. North Anderson? He told me he heard what had happened to you from colleagues of his on the force up here. I hope I didn't step out of line filling him in."

"No," I said. "I'm glad you talked with him."

Bain looked at me with concern. "You're sure you won't stay the night? A couple very pretty nurses on Blake eight."

"Maybe I'll take a rain check after I'm healed up," I said.

I told the Boston patrolmen everything I could remember, which was nothing much. Even the black boots had temporarily slipped my memory, let alone the odd turn of phrase spoken by my assailant. They had no clues, either. There'd been a mugging in the same spot about eight months before, but that didn't amount to much of a pattern, and it didn't do anything to push Darwin Bishop—represented, of course, by one of his thugs—out of my mind as the most likely culprit.

I waited for the rest of the blood to drip into my arm, swallowed three Motrin, and pulled myself together enough to roll off the gurney and maneuver into a big white button-down shirt I borrowed from Bain. I steeled myself for the elevator ride up to the ICU, but every jostling stop made me break out in a cold sweat.

I found Julia seated next to Tess's bed, with a twenty-something male sitter on the opposite side of the mattress, reading what looked like a law school textbook. He and I exchanged the standard greetings.

"What happened?" Julia said. "You look awful."

I told her.

She went pale. "This is my fault," she said. "I should never have taken the chance coming to your place."

"It could have been a random attack," I said, even though I knew better.

"We have to be much more careful," she said, shaking her head. "This is what I was afraid of."

I was feeling more determined than scared, which I probably should have taken as a warning sign that I was losing perspective. "I'm going to the island later today," I said. "I have to finish some work with North Anderson."

"When will you be back?" Her eyes filled up.

"A day. Maybe two."

"Win flies in today," she said. "I'm going to tell him I don't want him to see Tess. If he tries to, I'll file a re-straining order with the court."

"I have someone who could help you with that," I said. "Carl Rossetti, a lawyer from the North End." I took her in my arms and held her a moment, trying to keep my breathing steady, despite the searing pain that gripped me whenever I raised my hands above waist-level. "I'll call to check in," I managed. I let go.

She leaned closer. "You know that I love you," she said.

Those words took me by surprise, not because I didn't feel the same way, but because I wasn't used to anyone keeping pace with my emotions. "I love you, too," I said.

:   .   .

I was headed out of the hospital lobby when Caroline Hallissey, the MGH chief resident in psychiatry, caught up with me. Hallissey, a gay activist, was around thirty years old, under five feet tall, and about 250 pounds. Her face might have been pretty at one time, but her features were swollen now. She wore a silver hoop through her right nostril and a silver bolt through the skin over her left eyebrow. I had heard that she and her partner had just adopted a daughter of their own. "Got a minute?" she said.

"Sure," I said.

I must have looked as bad as I felt. "You okay?" she asked.

"I'm fine. What's up?"

"I did the consult on that woman in the ICU. Julia Bishop? You're involved in that case, right?"

"Right," I said. "What do you think?"

"She's depressed, that's for sure," Hallissey said. "She has numerous neurovegetative signs. Sleep loss. Lack of appetite. Difficulty concentrating. Low self-esteem. The symptoms were even worse just after her twins were born, but she's very resistant to being treated for any of it."

"It's a tough time for her to think clearly about herself," I said.

"Agreed," she said. "I wouldn't force anything on her. She's not suicidal, in the classic sense—just alluding to not wanting to go on if her daughter should die." She paused. "The thing that troubled me more was that I felt a lot of hostility from her."

"Meaning?"

"She asked a lot about my credentials. What undergrad school did I graduate? Where did I go to medical school? Who supervises my work with patients? The whole nine yards."

I wondered if that had anything to do with Hallissey's appearance. "She's in the middle of a homicide investigation," I said. "She doesn't know exactly who to trust."

"That could be part of it," Hallissey said. "But this felt more personal than that. Like she had an issue with *me*." She looked away, her eyes thinning as she struggled for words to describe her interaction with Julia. "I got the same feeling from her that I used to get from male patients who didn't respect female physicians. The ones who wanted to make sure I knew it."

"Not every psychiatrist-patient interaction is a love match," I said.

Hallissey looked directly at me. "I don't mean to step out of line, but it doesn't sound like you want to hear any of this. Maybe it's not a good time to talk."

I shook my head. Hallissey was right. I was automatically discounting her negative feedback about Julia. "I do want to hear it," I said. "Please. Tell me what else you noticed."

She hesitated.

"I'm listening," I said.

"Maybe it's the way she is with women," Hallissey said. "I mean, I've seen her be very cordial with Dr. Karlstein. And you don't seem to have any problem with her. But a couple of the female nurses in the ICU told me she treats them like she owns them. They definitely get bad vibes." She shrugged. "She supposedly modeled, right? Someone mentioned *Elite* or something."

The word *supposedly* stuck out like a sore thumb. I wondered whether jealousy was blurring Hallissey's therapeutic vision. Psychiatrists call it *countertransference*—the clinician's own feelings boomeranging back as if they had something to do with the patient's inner world. "She did model," I said. I pushed further to gauge Hallissey's reaction. "I guess she was pretty successful at it. The cover of *Cosmo*, *Vogue*, all that. Big time."

"Of course she was successful," Hallissey said. "It's textbook. She's magnificent-looking, but she has no real self-esteem. She exists for men. She needs them to adore her because she loathes herself. And that's why she immediately feels hatred toward me. Because I'm a woman."

The idea that Julia might harbor ill-will toward females troubled me. She had given birth to twin girls, after all. "Do you think she's a risk to the baby?" I asked Hallissey. "You feel the sitter is necessary?"

"I don't see what good it would do," she said. "I mean, if the kid's going home with her within a couple days, what's the sense of one-to-one observation now?" She rolled her eyes. "She'd probably end up taking advantage of the coverage to run to Gucci for a pair of shoes, or something. Beef up the wardrobe."

That comment increased my suspicion that jealousy or ill-will might be coloring Hallissey's perspective on Julia. I nodded and relaxed, but only a little. I couldn't afford to ignore her theory. "Will you be checking in with Ms. Bishop again?" I asked.

"Dr. Karlstein asked me to stop by tomorrow," she said.

"Would you page me if you come up with anything else interesting?" I asked.

"I'll do that," she said.

"And congratulations on your child," I said. "Hopefully, she won't end up modeling."

Hallissey's face lighted up. "No way," she said. "I can promise you that isn't going to happen."

It was 7:20 A.M. when I pulled myself into my truck and headed home to throw a few things together for my trip to Nantucket. The day was sunny and heating up the way Boston can in late June. I took the curves on Storrow Drive slowly, avoided potholes where I could, and slowly climbed the stairs, pausing every half-flight to gather courage.

I was most of the way to the fifth floor when a few frames of my experience in the alleyway visited me. I remembered being pushed, feeling a flash of pain, then losing my balance and pitching forward. I closed my eyes and stood motionless on the steps, trying to coax more of the attack back into consciousness, but nothing would come.

I grabbed fresh jeans and a black T-shirt in my apartment and was about to pull them on when I noticed the gauze around my abdomen had bled through. I walked to the bathroom and unwrapped myself.

Colin Bain had worked hard on me. The surface of the wound was more of a jagged laceration than a simple puncture, as if my assailant had ripped the knife upward, trying to gut me from behind. Bain's handiwork was impressive— tiny stitches, the mark of a surgical craftsman, ran in a lightning bolt shape along the bottom of my rib cage. I turned toward the sink, doused the wound with cold water, and blotted it dry. Then I rewrapped myself with a roll of gauze Bain had thrown in an emergency-room doggy bag, along with samples of Motrin, my prescription for Keflex, and my wallet. I swallowed three more Motrin, stuffed the wallet in my jeans, and got dressed.

My chances of making it to Hyannis conscious, then having the luck to get a seat (let alone space for my truck) on the ferry, were vanishingly slim, so I drove to Logan and waited for the ten-fifteen Cape Air flight. I tried North Anderson on his mobile, but got his voice mail. I left him a message that I'd be arriving at eleven and hoped he'd meet me at Nantucket Memorial—an intriguing name, I've always thought, for a very pleasant airport on a very beautiful island.

14

Anderson was waiting at the gate when I arrived. We'd had some turbulence in the last fifteen minutes of the flight, and I was bent toward my right side, trying to keep the muscles on that side slack. "You look great," he said, with a tight grin.

"Thanks a lot," I said.

The grin dissolved. "Truth is, you should be laying low, letting yourself heal up."

"I feel fine."

"Half of me thinks we should get out of the way," he said, "let the state cops handle the whole investigation from here."

"They'll let it begin and end with Billy," I said. "Bishop's too wired politically."

"I don't want it to end with you in a box," Anderson said. He shook his head, let out a long breath. "You're sleeping at my place tonight, period."

"Your place it is. Better safe than sorry." I winced as I straightened up.

"You didn't get a look at whoever did this? Nothing?"

"Not that I can remember."

"I guess it could be a random attack," he said. "The ER at Mass General draws a tough crowd."

"Could be," I said.

"It doesn't feel that way, though," Anderson said. "I'd

lay hundred-to-one odds that whoever did this was looking to do *you*."

"Maybe we're making somebody nervous," I said. "Maybe that's not such a bad thing." I didn't add that I had done more than enough to make someone jealous, namely, Darwin Bishop.

Anderson nodded to himself. "How's Tess?"

"Her heart stopped again. They got her back, and they're putting in a temporary pacemaker. I think she'll pull through."

"Julia hanging in there?" he asked.

"As well as anyone could," I said. "No question, she's depressed. She'll need help down the road."

"From a disinterested third party, I hope," he said.

I sidestepped that comment. "She says she'll take out a restraining order on Bishop if he tries to visit Tess in the hospital."

"We'd see the fireworks from that day in court all the way down here," he said. "I spoke with Lauren Dunlop, Bishop's first wife. She's remarried, three kids. Lives in Greenwich, Connecticut, now."

"What did she have to say?" I asked.

"She confirmed everything," he said. "Said she put up with physical and emotional abuse from Bishop for years, finally found the backbone to get the restraining order and file for divorce. It was a long haul. She was terrified of him."

"Did you ask her why she didn't end up with custody of Garret, under the circumstances?" I asked.

"According to her, it was out of the question," Anderson said. "Bishop would have fought the divorce tooth and nail, if it meant surrendering Garret. He was obsessed with the boy. Like some *Prince and the Pauper* thing. He wanted to take an abandoned baby and raise him to be a nuclear physicist or pro athlete or President of the United States. He even did what he could to interfere with Lauren's visitation rights. She doubts very much that he'll let Julia leave with the children. Not without a huge battle."

"I don't think Julia's going to back down," I said. "She doesn't plan to go home when Tess is discharged. She says she's leaving for her mother's—with the children."

"Good for her. Terry McCarthy filled me in on her statement, by the way. I think he's the best detective on the Boston force."

"And?"

"She came through with flying colors," Anderson said. "Everything was consistent with what she told you: Bishop took the nortriptyline from her just before Tess was poisoned." He paused. "Tommy found her convincing. He got no bad vibes, even when he bluffed and asked her if she'd sit for a polygraph."

I thought back to Caroline Halverson's comments and wondered how well Julia would have fared with a female detective. "What did she say?" I asked.

"She said, 'How about we do the polygraph right now?' "

"Good for her," I said, feeling relieved. I smirked. "I wonder whether Win would sit for one."

"I asked him to," Anderson said.

"You asked Bishop to take a polygraph?"

"Obviously it wouldn't be worth jack at trial, but I wanted to gauge his reaction."

"And . . ."

"He told me to talk with his lawyer," Anderson said.

"He may need one."

"He retained John McBride about an hour after I made the polygraph suggestion."

McBride, based in Boston, was one of the best criminal defense attorneys in the country and a master at excluding physical evidence against his clients. "Better be careful how you conduct the search of the Bishop estate."

"White glove, all the way." Anderson smiled. "I heard from McBride personally this morning. He wanted to put me on notice that his client won't be available for questioning until charges are filed against him."

"Is McBride representing anyone else in the family?"

"He didn't say he was."

"So what's the plan? We just drive onto the Bishop estate and ask for Claire and Garret?"

"Just like that, the way I figure it," Anderson said. "I still have an active search warrant for every inch of that property, and they're both on the grounds right now, according to the patrolmen I stationed on Wauwinet Road. Either one of them can refuse to talk. But I don't think they will."

"Why not?" I asked.

"The family is full of agendas," he said. "Garret's got one. Claire has her own. They're all using this tragedy to get things done—jockeying for more power, more freedom, whatever."

"So let's get over there while we can." I bent to pick up my overnight bag, sending the muscles of my back and side into spasms that nearly brought me to my knees.

Anderson grabbed me under the arms. "Easy," he said.

I closed my eyes and gritted my teeth, waiting for the pain to end. When it had died down, I stepped back and forced a smile. "Sudden movements are not what the doctor ordered," I said.

Anderson leaned and picked up my bag. "Let me do the heavy lifting for now," he said.

We met three cruisers on the drive up Wauwinet Road. Television vans lined the road, starting half a mile from the estate. Reporters leaned dangerously toward Anderson's car, waving hands for us to stop for interviews. Photographers snapped photos as we drove by. I heard the sound of a helicopter, looked up through the windshield, and saw a State Police chopper and another from Channel 7 News crisscrossing the sky.

"Big change," I said.

"The press is loving this," Anderson said. "As soon as they find out Tess is at MGH, they'll send an army over there, too."

A couple Rovers were parked at Bishop's "watch house," and a couple more sat in the semicircle in front of the main house, but no one tried to stop us when we headed for the front door. I checked out the grounds and noticed that Win's security team was outnumbered by State Police SUVs and ATVs. "Are they here to search the grounds or defend them?" I asked Anderson.

"You got me," he said, shrugging. "It depends how cozy Bishop really is with Captain O'Donnell. You'll meet him, eventually. I'd love your take on him."

Claire Buckley answered the door, as usual. She seemed nervous. "No one let me know to expect you," she said, with a tight smile. "Win headed to Boston."

"We won't take much of your time," Anderson said. "Just a few questions."

"I guess that would be fine," she said. "Come in."

Anderson glanced at me and winked. His prediction that we wouldn't meet with much resistance from Claire seemed to be holding up.

As we followed her toward the living room, she glanced back at me struggling along. "You seem like you're in pain," she said.

"I had a little problem in Boston," I said. "Someone jumped me."

She stopped and looked at me with what seemed like real concern. "Are you all right?" she said.

"I will be." I smiled. "Pulled muscles." And a few slashed ones.

"Can I get you anything?"

"Thanks, no."

She invited Anderson and me to take seats on the couch. She took a floral wingback chair opposite us. "How can I help you?" she asked, twisting her diamond pinkie ring back and forth. She noticed me noticing her nervous hands and laid them unnaturally still on her thighs.

Anderson motioned for me to take the lead.

I didn't know exactly what I was after, so I started with a very general question. "Claire, when we last met," I said,

"I didn't ask you directly whether you actually saw anything the night Brooke was murdered—anything that might shed light on the investigation. Now, with Tess in the hospital, I need to ask about both twins."

"What sort of thing do you mean?" she said.

"Anything peculiar," Anderson interjected. "Something that got your attention. Maybe seeing the tube of plastic sealant or the bottle of nortriptyline or hearing one of the babies in distress."

"If I had had anything like that to share," she said, "I already would have." She paused. "And the police finished searching the house, right?"

"*She has nothing* like that *to share*," the voice at the back of my mind said.

"Claire, did you see or hear *anything at all* that we should know about?" I said. My mind replayed the question she had just asked Anderson about the search. "Or maybe you found something . . ." I added.

She cast a worried glance my way, as if she and I shared knowledge that shouldn't be extended to North Anderson. She started twisting her pinkie ring again.

"I've told Captain Anderson about Julia's feelings toward the twins after they were delivered," I said, prompting her. "We share all the information about the investigation. Anything you would tell me, you can tell both of us."

"I didn't see anything directly related to the attacks," she said.

"Okay," I said. "What did you see?"

"I found something," she said. "Something weird."

"Weird . . ." Anderson said.

"A letter," Claire said. She looked down and shook her head. "I only bring it up because of Tess—because Julia is still with her." She let her head fall into her hands. "God, I don't know if I should be mentioning any of this."

My skin had started to crawl. I was either about to hear a baseless attack on Julia, fueled by Claire's desire to take her place in Darwin Bishop's life, or something that would topple my vision of Julia and rocket her forward on the suspect list. "If there's something weighing on you related to Julia and the twins," I said, "please tell us—especially if it can help us keep Tess safe."

Claire looked up at the ceiling, glanced at Anderson, then focused on me. "Wait here." She got up, walked out of the living room, and headed upstairs.

"What do you figure she's up to?" Anderson said.

"No way to know," I said. "I think the whole, 'I don't want to tell, make me tell' routine is a bunch of crap, but that's my only read so far."

"She's a gold digger," Anderson said. "I don't trust her."

I nodded, but my anxiety about what Claire was about to reveal kept growing. I tried to keep it in check by getting up and walking around the expansive room. I lingered on some of Bishop's trinkets: a vintage Chelsea ship's clock, a set of Daum torsos in subtle shades of blue and green and rose, a collection of enamel fountain pens in a glass-topped, mahogany box.

I stopped wandering the room when my gaze crossed an empty space on the wall. I stood still, looking at the spot. Bishop's Robert Salmon painting of a ship at sea had been hanging there when I last visited. I scanned the walls and saw that the beach scene by Maurice Prendergast was gone, too. Carl Rossetti and Viktor Golov, I thought to myself, must have been right; Bishop was liquidating his art collection. Those two canvases alone could bring several million at auction.

Claire Buckley walked back into the room clutching a folded piece of stationery. I returned to my seat on the couch. She took hers in the wingback.

Anderson leaned forward, staring at the sheet of paper.

"I found this in Julia's closet," she said. "I was straightening up."

"The closet?" I said.

"I'm compulsive that way. Inside closets. Under beds. Behind bookcases. I can't relax until every nook and cranny is spotless."

I resisted making a diagnosis. "And what did you come across?" I said.

"It was tucked inside a hatbox," she said. "The box seemed like it was empty, so I was going to use it to store some loose hair ties and so on, but then I found this." She held up the stationery. "I read it. I shouldn't have, but I did."

"So what does it say?" Anderson asked, a little irritation sneaking into his voice.

"I don't know how important it is," she said, letting out her breath dramatically. "That's why I'm giving it to you." She shook her head. "I don't feel good about this."

I couldn't stomach Claire's manufactured reticence much longer. I walked over to her, held out my hand. "Thank you," I said. "We understand."

She placed the folded sheet on my palm with exaggerated care, as if it was a wounded bird. Then she looked away.

I took my seat back on the couch, unfolded the stationery, and saw that it was a page of a letter, written in a feminine hand. My eyes flicked to the bottom of the sheet. It was signed by Julia, and dated June 20, 2002, the day before Brooke was murdered. My heart fell. As Anderson watched for my reaction, I kept a game face and read in silence.

> I wish this marriage had never happened. I am bound to it by my worst qualities—fear, dependency and—pathetic as it is to admit—attachment to material things. To complicate matters further, there are the twins. Darwin is still enraged about them.
>
> Since the day I first saw you, you have sustained me. I think constantly of our time together. What I need now is the courage to leave everything else behind, no matter how much suffering that causes in the short term. Ending

everything can't be worse than what we have
already lived through.

I cry every day, don't sleep, hardly eat, and
often lack the will to go on . . .

Except when I think of seeing you. Which
is enough to give me hope, for now.

My temptation is quiet.
Here at life's end.

—*Julia*
June 20, 2002

My heart was racing. A wave of nausea overshadowed
the pain in my back. The most optimistic reading of the
letter was that Julia had another lover. The more sober reading was that she had grown desperate enough to strike out
at the twins. The last line of the letter, "Here at life's end,"
struck a particularly ominous note. I handed the sheet of
paper to Anderson.

Anderson's jaws worked against each other as he read.
His eyes ran up and down the page a few times. Then he
folded the letter back into thirds and slipped it into his shirt
pocket. "What do you make of it?" he asked Claire.

"I don't know what to think," she said. "I was shocked."

"Having read it, do you think Julia attacked the twins?"
he pressed. "You think she killed Brooke?"

"I can't believe she would," Claire said, "but with her
depression and, now, this . . . I'm not sure of anything anymore."

Anderson glanced at me, then looked back at Claire. "I'll
ask you again: Are you holding back any information? Did
you see something important the night of Brooke's death
or Tess's poisoning?"

"No," she said, rather unconvincingly.

"Okay, then," Anderson said. His cell phone began to
ring, but he ignored it. "What about your relationship with
Darwin Bishop? Do you feel that contributes to Julia's de-

pression? Or don't you think she even knows what's going on?"

I looked at Anderson, unsure where he was headed.

"I don't know what you mean," Claire said. "I'm close to both the Bishops."

"Let's level with one another, Claire," Anderson said.

She squinted and shook her head as if she had no idea what he might be getting at.

"I'm talking about your romantic relationship with Darwin Bishop," he said. "The suites you've shared abroad. The expensive wine. All that."

Her face flushed. She stood up. "I think you should leave," she said. She looked at me as if I had betrayed her. "Both of you."

Anderson stayed seated. "We're not in the business of screwing up anyone's life," he said. "The secret stays with us. One interview with Garret, and we're on our way. That's all we have on our agenda."

Now I realized what he was up to. He was pushing Claire to get us face time with Garret.

Claire looked like she was barely keeping control of her anger.

I wasn't sure whether we'd get our interview with Garret or get thrown out. "You can count on us not to leak any of this to the press," I encouraged her, nodding toward Wauwinet Road. I let the veiled threat sink in a moment. "They're lined up for half a mile out there. We should just talk with Garret and be on our way."

A few seconds passed before Claire responded. "I'll tell him you're coming up to his room to see him," she said finally. "Then, I'll trust you to leave."

Anderson waited until she was gone. "With John McBride, Attorney-at-Law, on retainer and Captain O'Donnell taking over," he explained, "we may not get another shot at Garret. I think it's time to shake things up a little bit, anyhow. See if anything falls out."

I nodded, then pointed toward Julia's letter in Anderson's pocket. "That doesn't read so good," I said. I pictured

Julia seated at Tess's bedside. All of a sudden, I wished Caroline Hallissey hadn't decided to discontinue the one-to-one sitter.

"I warned you," Anderson said.

"I know," I admitted. "I should have listened."

"It's hard to hear anything but violins around a woman like that," he said. "Don't beat yourself up over it."

Claire came back and walked us to the door to Garret's room, then turned around and left again without a word. Garret was hunched over a desk covered with books, writing on a pad of white, lined paper. The walls of the room were floor-to-ceiling bookcases, overfilled with titles. Unlike the uncreased, unread volumes in his father's study, Garret's were well worn. There were dog-eared classics by philosophers from Plato to Kerouac, scientific texts by Albert Einstein and James Watson, volumes of poetry by Eliot and Yeats, religious works by the Dalai Lama and William James and St. Thomas Aquinas. The room had none of the trappings of a seventeen-year-old boy. No model of a Porsche or Corvette could be found on any of the shelves. No poster of any teen sex goddess hung over the bed. There was no phone. And the room contained absolutely nothing to do with sports—including tennis.

"Garret," I said from the door, "It's Dr. Clevenger. I'm here with Captain Anderson."

He kept writing.

"Garret?" I said. I took a few tentative steps into the room. I felt almost dizzy from a potent cocktail of physical and emotional pain. Part of me wanted to rush back to Boston, to Julia, to get at the truth.

Garret's hand stopped moving across the paper. "Jesus. Have some respect," he said. "Did I say you could come in here?"

I backed up one step. "We won't take a lot of your time," I said.

He let out a heavy sigh and spun around in his desk chair. "What do you want?"

"Just to talk," I said.

"So, talk," he said.

I wanted to lighten the mood. "Nice collection, by the way," I said, motioning toward the walls of books.

He ignored the compliment. "If this looks like it might go long, we should move it somewhere else," he said. "I'm only allowed to stay in here two hours a day. I don't want to waste it."

"What do you mean, you're only allowed to stay in here two hours?" Anderson said. "This is your room, isn't it?"

"Darwin's worried I'll become a recluse, a bookworm, maybe a fag," he said, sounding half-bitter, half-amused. "Even worse, I might start 'thinking too much,' as he puts it. Much better to swat a fuzzy ball back and forth over a net or ride a horse within an inch of its life, swinging a long stick."

"I take it you're no fan of polo," I said.

"Not much, lately. I used to like watching this one horse. Her name was Brandy," he said. "She was special."

"In what way?" I said.

"Her coat was unbelievable—kind of a cinnamon brown, very soft to the touch. Every muscle on her was perfectly cut. When she ran, it was like poetry. And she was sweet. She'd walk right up to me whenever I came around the stables, look at me with these big, brown eyes, almost as if she knew we were in the same tough spot."

"What spot is that?" Anderson said.

"Being ridden by Darwin," Garret said.

Garret sounded more human and vulnerable than he had the other two times we had met. "Is Brandy still around?" I asked him.

"Glued, dude." He winked. The hard edge had come back into his voice.

"She died?" Anderson said.

"She stopped winning. Then she disappeared." Garret shrugged. "It's all very Darwinian. Survival of the fittest."

He looked at me. "Are you all right?" he said. "You look like death yourself."

The muscles in my back had tightened, and I was trying to stay on my feet. "I'm fine," I managed. "Sprained muscles." I paused, shifted gears. "Captain Anderson and I are here because I haven't had the chance to speak with you since I saw you at the tennis club," I said. "That was the day before Tess was rushed to the hospital."

"And . . ." he said.

"And I want to know if you can help us," I said.

"Help you, like, how?"

"For starters, if you saw anything strange before you left for Brooke's funeral, or when you got back, we'd be interested in hearing about it," I said.

"You would," he said.

"Of course," I said.

"Enough to pay for it?" he said.

Anderson and I glanced at one another.

Before either of us could answer him, Garret smiled broadly. "Just kidding," he said. "The last thing I need is money. Would you shut the door, please?"

Anderson took care of it. "Anything you tell us stays confidential," he said.

"Right," Garret said. "I've already told Dr. Clevenger I'm not testifying at any trial, if there ever is one. Dad's got Johnny McBride working for him now, you know."

"We know," I said.

"There aren't even any bloodstains in this case," Garret said. "How hard do you think it's gonna be for McBride to make jackasses out of the police and D.A.?" He looked at Anderson. "The search of the house was bungled, by the way. UPS dropped off two packages *inside the foyer*, and the State Police sergeant let the driver use the upstairs bathroom to take a leak—the one Billy snuck into."

"I'll look into that," Anderson said.

"You'll want to, before they carve you up on the witness stand," Garret said. "Better you than me."

"Did you have something to tell us about that night?"

Anderson said, nudging the discussion back into line.

"All I heard was another argument between Darwin and Julia," he said. "It got just as hot as the ones they used to have about the twins—how Darwin wanted to abort them."

"Was Claire around to hear it?" I asked, wondering whether she had edited her memory of that night.

"I'm not sure, but I don't think so," Garret said. "I think she had gone to the store to buy formula for Tess." He shrugged. "I wouldn't swear to it, but that's what I remember."

"What was the argument about?" Anderson asked.

"The nortriptyline," Garret said.

"What about it?" I said.

"Darwin wanted the prescription bottle from Julia. He was screaming at her for most of an hour before she gave in."

"Did he say why he wanted it?" I asked.

"He said she should find some other way to kill herself," Garret said, "like she was about to take an overdose, or something."

"And did you think your mother might try to hurt herself?" I asked.

"I think Darwin had something else in mind," Garret said, smiling.

"What?" I said.

"An overdose for little Tess, of course."

Anderson let out a long breath. "So you think it's a coincidence your brother broke into the house that night?" he said.

"A lucky break for Darwin, the way I see it. Win was already going to do the deed, but Billy's daring move—which I give him a lot of credit for, by the way—made it the perfect crime." He paused and looked at me with an intensity that made me uncomfortable. "Or nearly perfect," he said.

"Why *nearly*?" I asked.

"Because I have the prescription bottle," Garret said matter-of-factly.

"You . . ." I started.

"*Where?*" Anderson asked anxiously.

Garret turned around and pulled open the lowest drawer of his desk. He reached all the way to the back of it. His hand emerged holding a key. "My locker at Brant Point," he said. He tossed me the key. "Number 117, top shelf. Back, right-hand corner. Inside a tennis ball can."

"How did you get it?" I asked.

He winked. "Darwin left it in the top drawer of his desk in the study. Pure arrogance." He glanced at Anderson. "Of course, when you figure you have the local police and the state cops in your back pocket, you get heady."

Anderson ignored the comment.

"When did you find the bottle?" I asked.

"The day after Tess's overdose," Garret said. "But that's not the important part. The important part is that you won't find Billy's fingerprints anywhere on it."

Claire Buckley showed us to the door. Her demeanor was ice-cold. Before stepping outside, I tried to think of something to say to reassure her that Anderson and I had no intention of revealing her secret, but all of us got distracted by a State Police cruiser barreling into the circular drive. It stopped short behind North Anderson's car. A tall and broad fellow, about fifty, wearing a State Police uniform decorated with elaborate, embroidered patches and enameled pins, bolted out of the car and headed for us. His face was one of those sharp-angled, weathered ones that looked like it would stay ruggedly handsome forever. His salt-and-pepper hair was full and wavy.

"Told you you'd meet him," Anderson said. "That's Brian O'Donnell."

"Got a minute?" O'Donnell called gruffly to Anderson.

"Sure," Anderson said.

Claire turned around, walked back inside, and closed the door.

"I should introduce Dr. Clevenger," Anderson said, as O'Donnell reached us.

O'Donnell nodded at me, but didn't extend a hand. "What are you guys doing here?" he asked.

"Conducting an investigation," Anderson said. "What did you think we might be doing?"

O'Donnell frowned. "I *thought* we decided you'd clear things with me. I had no idea you were arranging another set of interviews for the doctor here."

"I don't think we ever came up with a hard-and-fast rule about what got cleared with who," Anderson said. "I agreed to work closely with you. And I will."

"Look, if you need a call from the Governor's office to make it official, I'll get that done for you. From here on out, the investigation is being run by my department. That means *me*."

"Maybe that call from the Governor would help clarify things," Anderson said.

"Well, let me make this much clear right now," O'Donnell said. "If you just interviewed the boy, you did so without his parents' consent. That means his statements aren't freely given and can't be used at Billy's trial."

Billy's trial. I heard that loud and clear.

Anderson didn't say whether we'd interviewed Garret or not. He also didn't mention the key to Garret's locker.

"As for Ms. Buckley," O'Donnell said, "I just don't see why she's on the suspect list at all. I know you have your thoughts about her supposed relationship with Darwin Bishop, but that hasn't been proven, and it's a pretty weak motive for a double homicide, to begin with."

"We're just dealing with the one homicide right now," I reminded him. "Hopefully, it stays that way."

"Whatever," O'Donnell said, shooting me an annoyed look. He collected himself. "North, I'm not trying to clip your wings here," he said. "I'm trying to get things done right so the case doesn't fall apart. First things first, let's get Billy and go from there."

"You any closer?" I asked.

"We think we're closing in," O'Donnell said. "We're moving as fast as we can, but not so fast that we ignore the potential dangers. The Commons are surprisingly tough terrain to search. And we don't know if Billy is armed or not."

That comment made me think back to Carl Rossetti's fear that the cleanest way to bury the truth in the Bishop case would be to bury Billy. "He's never used a gun before," I said.

"He hadn't asphyxiated one sibling and tried to poison another before, either," O'Donnell said.

"If he did this time," I said.

O'Donnell smiled. "I know you interviewed Billy at Payne Whitney. That went, what, half an hour?"

"It went long enough for me to use what I learned to learn more," I said.

"Just so you know something about me, Doctor: I've gotten to be a quick study, too. I've led twenty-six homicide investigations. And my take here is that everyone else in this family who might land on somebody's suspect list is no more than a red herring," he said. "Billy Bishop looks like, smells like, is the killer. Period. He worked his way up to murder in the usual manner, with stops along the way at destruction of property, theft, arson, and cruelty to animals. There's nothing very special about him."

"Sounds open and shut," Anderson said.

"Think what you want," O'Donnell said. "But please do what you say you will. And you *said* you'd clear your moves with me."

I saw Anderson's jaw set. His breathing moved into a Zen-like study in self-control.

O'Donnell made a visible effort at relaxing himself. "This is the way it always goes, North," he said. "I know it doesn't feel good yielding your home turf to the state, but we'll be out of your hair soon enough." He paused. "We found a swatch of cloth from one of Billy's jackets about a half-mile into the Commons. So we know we're headed in the right direction. It's just a matter of time now."

Anderson nodded. "I'll talk to you later, then." He walked toward his car.

I started to follow him.

"Good meeting you, Dr. Clevenger," O'Donnell said, extending his hand just as I moved past him.

I shook it. "I'm sure we'll see each other again," I said.

15

I braced myself as Anderson accelerated away from the Bishop house, but my back still screamed at me to stop moving. I fished in my pocket, came up with four Motrin, and swallowed them.

"Claire must have called O'Donnell while we were talking with Garret," Anderson said. "If I wasn't sure before, I am now: He's got to be in Bishop's pocket."

"All the more reason to keep pushing," I said. "I didn't like his comment about Billy being armed."

"Neither did I."

Anderson and I seemed to be on the same page again, which felt good. "After we grab the bottle of nortriptyline, I should pay Julia another visit in Boston," I said. "I'd like to see her reaction to that letter, not just hear it."

"Agreed," he said, dialing a call on his cell phone. "See how things go today. You can take a flight late tonight or catch the first one in the morning." As we sped past the gauntlet of reporters, Anderson squinted through the windshield, listening to his phone. He clicked it off, shook his head. "Your lawyer friend is no slouch," he said.

"Rossetti? Why? What's up?" I asked.

"The detective I assigned to check out the Bishops' life insurance policies left me a message while we were at the estate."

"The twins were insured?" I said.

"Ten million apiece," he said. "A guy named Ralph Rotman at Atlantic Benefit Group set them up with Northwestern Mutual."

"Twenty million dollars is a lot of money, even to Darwin Bishop," I said.

"Especially when your stocks are in the gutter," Anderson said.

I thought of Bishop's Gatsbyesque rise out of Brooklyn, all the distance he had put between himself and the poverty and hunger he had faced as a child. If his cash crunch made him feel he was headed back there, he might do anything to keep his inflated sense of himself alive—even kill Brooke and Tess. He might even convince himself that their lives would have been worthless with a disgraced, bankrupted father. Why not sacrifice them to the greater good, let their blood transfuse the rest of the family?

Some people do that kind of strange calculus when they feel besieged, whether the panic is rational or not. I once testified at the trial of a man who had murdered his wife because, he said, she was overly domineering toward him and the couple's two daughters. He believed they would all be better off without her, even if it meant his spending his life in prison. After pretending to leave for work one day, he circled back home and stabbed her thirty-six times. He went grocery shopping as she lay bleeding and unconscious on their bed. He filled the refrigerator and tidied up his kids' rooms. He wanted them to feel a little more organized amidst the impending chaos—his arrest, his wife's funeral, his trial. Then he put on a fresh shirt and pair of slacks, called the police, and confessed what he had done.

A nineteen-year-old man I evaluated was upset that his cousin—a South Boston gang member who disliked blacks—had been stricken with leukemia. To fuel the cousin's recovery, he approached a fourteen-year-old black boy in Roxbury and emptied four bullets into his chest. "I was sort of doing what my cousin would do, kind of like that might bring him back," the man told me.

Strange calculus, indeed. And none of it surprises me,

anymore—certainly not after what I was to learn about the Bishops.

Anderson and I made it to the Brant Point Racket Club just after 2:00 P.M. There was enough activity in the place that we attracted little attention as we located Garret's locker.

I had a moment of trepidation after North put the key in the lock. "Hold on," I said.

Anderson stopped and looked at me. "What?"

"We're following Garret's road map without a thought. Any chance this thing could be rigged?" I said.

Anderson looked at me askance. "Like, with explosives?"

I shrugged.

"I guess there's a chance." He turned the key and pulled the door open, partway. "I think it's slim." He grinned. "You've been hanging with the paranoids too long. You need to take some time when this is over."

"No kidding," I said. But I didn't think the symptoms of my patients at MGH were rubbing off on me. More likely, the vector was my feeling deceived by Julia, my worry over what else might be hidden in *her* closet.

Garret's locker was a window on his soul. A single racket was angled against two walls of the lower compartment, but there were none of the accouterments favored by tennis fanatics—no lambskin glove, no athletic tape, no sweatbands, no Bollé glasses, not even a pair of sneakers. The back wall of the lower compartment was wallpapered with very competent black-and-white photographs of Nantucket. There were shots of the harbor, the Commons, dunes, beach.

"The kid can use a camera, if these are his work," Anderson said, admiring the images.

"They're beautiful," I said. I lingered on the photographs for several seconds, then my gaze moved to the locker's upper compartment and the dozen or more old books haphazardly stacked there—works by Kafka, J. D. Salinger, Steinbeck.

Anderson took out a paper bag and used it to cover his hand. A plastic bag might cling to the bottle and rub away fingerprints. He glanced at the books. "Garret loves the classics," he said.

"There are worse escapes than photography and literature," I said, thinking of my own.

He reached past the books to the back, right-hand corner of the top shelf, where Garret had said the nortriptyline bottle would be hidden in a tennis ball can.

I realized we might be on the brink of evidence that would help exonerate Billy. The excitement of that possibility dulled the pain in my back, at least for the moment. Maybe it was my own strange calculus, but I felt as if I had the chance to discharge a debt I had been carrying for years—what I owed Billy Fisk and the cosmos and, ultimately, myself for losing that decent young man to suicide. And no doubt I felt that another debt was about to be satisfied. If Win Bishop were ultimately exposed as a murderer, part of me would feel I had paid back my father what I owed him: trial, conviction, and sentencing for stealing my boyhood.

"Got it," Anderson said, bringing down the tennis ball can. He used a piece of tissue to open the lid, then dumped the nortriptyline bottle—one of those typical orange-brown plastic affairs—into his bagged hand. He turned the bag inside out, securing the bottle inside it. "If Win's fingerprints are all over this, and Billy's aren't," he said, "the old man will wonder a long time why he didn't toss this over the cliffs." He smiled. "You were heading to Boston, anyhow. Why don't we bring the bottle to the State Police crime laboratory? I could grab prints off it right at the station, but I'd rather get it done by the experts."

Anderson arranged for a chopper to fly us directly to the crime lab in Boston. I was glad to be headed in Julia's direction—and fast—not only to confront her about the letter Claire had shown us, but also to protect her from Darwin, who would have arrived in Boston hours earlier. The latter motivation was the stronger of the two. Even with her shining more brightly as a suspect, even with my new doubts about what, if anything, our "love" really meant to her, I felt moved to rescue her. She was the most powerfully seductive woman I had ever met.

While we were in flight, Anderson radioed the New York City Police Department to arrange a computer transfer of Bishop's fingerprints, first logged when he was arrested during 1980 for the restraining order violation. We didn't expect Darwin to deny handling the prescription bottle, but we didn't want to take any chances with documentation; evidence can disappear at the worst possible moments, especially evidence against an influential suspect.

Billy's prints had been stored by the U.S. Department of Immigration and were already part of the investigation file. Anderson was carrying a set with him.

We met with Art Fields, director of the crime lab, who agreed to let Anderson and me watch the testing. Fields is a short, bulky man of about sixty, with bushy black eyebrows and a permanent mischievous smile that looks as if he's just heard a witty, off-color anecdote. "What are we looking for?" he asked Anderson.

"The main question is whether Billy Bishop's prints are on the bottle," Anderson said. "If not, then one big piece of evidence points away from him as a suspect."

"Is this kid slow, or something?" Fields said. "Mentally, I mean."

"No," I said. "He's extremely bright."

"He couldn't think to wear gloves?" Fields asked.

"Of course he could," Anderson said, "but his prints are all over the crime scene: the window and window frame he boosted himself through, the twins' room and cribs, even the antique desk he stole five grand out of. He left a note, too. It starts to stretch the imagination to think that his only effort to avoid detection would be slipping on a pair of gloves when he poisoned the baby."

"I don't think it would stretch Captain O'Donnell's imagination," Fields said. "He's certain the boy is guilty. And he's pretty sharp."

"Certainly seems to be," Anderson agreed, obviously wanting to avoid a conflict.

Fields smiled even more widely than usual. "Very political of you," he said to Anderson. "Personally, I can't stand the fucker."

Anderson chuckled. "That makes two of us," he said. He looked at me. "Maybe, three."

"What bothers you about O'Donnell?" I asked Fields.

"I'm a pathologist, not a prosecutor," he said. "I go after facts, not any particular slant on them. I don't get convinced that blood just *has* to be on a piece of clothing. If I find it, I find it. If I don't, I don't."

"Whereas O'Donnell . . ." I prompted.

"He lobbies for the evidence to conform to the case he's building. He campaigns for a particular outcome. Not that he'd tamper with anything, but his absolute certainty that things ought to come out one way, rather than another, can infect the technicians. And he tends to hang around them. So if they get clumsy, I worry they'll stumble toward the results he expects of them, without their even being aware of it."

That was pretty high-end psychological reasoning, especially for a pathologist.

The expression on my face must have telegraphed what I was thinking. "I have my Ph.D. in psychology," Fields explained. "This is a second career for me."

"That's quite a change," I said. "What motivated you to switch?"

"I got tired of coaxing the truth out of people," he said. "When I want the facts from a hair sample, I don't have to worry about creating a safe, therapeutic environment. I just toss it in a blender and run its DNA on a gel."

"You really can't do that with psychotherapy patients," I said, with a wink.

"Not if you're depending on repeat business," he said.

Fields walked us from his office into the laboratory. We stood with him at a long black lab bench outfitted with chrome gas jets and faucets, watching Leona, a fifty-ish wisp of a woman no taller than four feet, her hands disfigured by rheumatoid arthritis, as she used an ostrich-feather duster to powder the prescription bottle. Every movement seemed to tax her, and she winced frequently, apparently from the pain in her joints. She took nearly twenty minutes to lift half the prints off the bottle, using two-inch lengths of special tape. When she seemed about to cry, Fields asked her whether she wanted him to take over. "No," she said tersely. "This has to be done right."

Fields laughed and backed off, and we waited another fifteen minutes for Leona to finish up.

"We'll bring the whole set down the hall to Simon Cranberg," Fields told us. "He'll let us know if the prints match whatever's on record for Darwin Bishop and Billy."

We were already headed out the door for that session when Leona called to us. "I think I should have dusted the inside of the bottle, too," she said.

We looked back at her.

"The suspect might have been careful not to touch the outer surface," she said, "but not as careful removing the pills."

"She's right," Fields said.

We walked back to the lab bench. Anderson surrendered the paper bag with the bottle inside.

Leona pulled it out, twisted off the cap, and squinted inside. "Hmm," she said.

"Hmm, what?" I asked.

She didn't answer, instead picking up a pair of tweezers and fishing inside the bottle with them. When she pulled them out, a two-inch photographic negative was caught in their pincer grip.

"What the hell is that?" Anderson said.

"It was curved flush to the inside wall," she said. "The color's so close to the orange plastic that we wouldn't have seen it if we didn't take our time and go the extra mile." She pointed a crooked finger at Fields. "Let that be a lesson to you." She held the negative up to the light so we could all get a peek at it. The image was small and shadowy, but it looked like a beach scene, with tiny people in the foreground.

"Let's get a print made," Fields said. "It won't take more than a couple minutes."

We left the bottle with Leona so she could lift any prints from the interior wall. Then we dropped the negative with the photography department and headed to Cranberg's office.

Simon Cranberg turned out to be a lumbering man in overalls, with lamb chop sideburns and half-glasses—a cross between Ben Franklin and Attila the Hun. He had already loaded Darwin Bishop's prints onto his computer, so we started by looking for their match on Leona's pieces of tape. Cranberg scanned each length with a magnifying glass, checking his computer screen now and then. Within a minute he decided to run one of the strips through a scanner that transferred the lifted prints to a split screen next to the ones from Bishop's criminal record. "That's a match," he said with certainty. "Darwin Bishop's prints are on that bottle."

That was no surprise to me. I glanced at Anderson, expecting him to look reassured, but he looked oddly unsettled. "What's wrong?" I said.

"Nothing," he answered unconvincingly. "It's going like we thought it would."

"Let's look at the boy," Fields said.

Cranberg went over each length of tape meticulously, loading every image onto the screen next to Billy's fingerprints from Immigration. A few times he went back to pieces of tape he had already looked at. After he had scanned the last of them, he shook his head. "None of the lifted prints belongs to Billy Bishop," he said.

"You're certain," I said.

"A bunch of people barehanded that medicine bottle," Cranberg said. "Billy definitely isn't one of them."

"That's it, then," Fields said. "You've got your answer. I can tell you, it isn't the one Captain O'Donnell will want to hear."

I felt a real sense of relief for the first time since taking the Bishop case. Because I believed what Anderson had said: If Billy had tried to kill Tess, he wouldn't leave prints everywhere except the prescription bottle, not to mention leaving a note. And if Billy hadn't poisoned Tess, it was highly unlikely he had killed Brooke. I hoped a jury would see it that way, too.

I looked over at Anderson again, expecting a mirror image of my mood. He winked and nodded his head tentatively. No sign of triumph anywhere. Maybe, I told myself, he had simply run out of steam getting us where we needed to go.

A young man from the photography department appeared at the door, holding a manila envelope.

"Perfect timing," Fields said. "Let's get a look at that photograph. Maybe we're on a roll here."

"Did you want to review it first?" the young man asked Fields. He sounded like he was making a suggestion.

Fields either didn't pick up on his discomfort or he ignored it. "No need," he said. "We're all friends here." He took the envelope, opened it, and pulled out a five-by-eight black-and-white glossy. Then he stood there staring at it, his face losing its permanent smile for the first time since I had met him. "What's this about?" he said quietly.

I walked over and looked at the photograph. My heart fell. The muscles in my back felt like they were knotting themselves into a noose around my gut. I looked at Anderson, who had hung his head. No doubt he had recognized the beach scene even when Leona had held up the negative. Because he and Julia were the only two figures in it, holding each other close on a deserted stretch of Nantucket beach. Before I could think what to say to him, he walked past Fields and me, and out of the room.

I followed Anderson, concentrating to keep my legs moving. Waves of emotion were crashing inside me. I felt betrayed, enraged, and foolish, all at the same time. I also felt unnerved. I was lost in the geography of the Bishop case. If North had lied to me about his connection with Julia, what else had he lied about? Could I rely on any of the data he had fed me about Bishop? He was the one, after all, who had told me about Bishop's affair with Claire Buckley. He was the one who had confirmed Bishop's having taken out life insurance on the twins.

My mind upped the ante. Could Anderson, I wondered, have been directing my seduction from the beginning? Might he and Julia be partners in crime, using me to help focus suspicion on Darwin Bishop, to get him out of their way?

And what about my having been attacked outside Mass General? Anderson knew my itinerary better than anyone. Was it possible I was winning over a woman he wanted badly enough to have me killed? Was the letter Julia had written meant for him?

I couldn't believe I needed to do it, but I checked for the Browning Baby in my pocket as I headed down the hallway toward the exit to the heliport.

I didn't get there. As I passed an open door to my right, a few feet from the exit, Anderson called my name. I stopped and looked into what seemed to be an anatomy lab, full of gleaming, stainless-steel dissection tables. Anderson was seated on one of them. I walked cautiously inside.

Anderson stared up at the ceiling, shook his head, then looked at me. "I'd explain, but I can't," he said. "It was just something that happened. I never would have . . ."

"I didn't want this fucking case!" I seethed. "I didn't need this case! Do you understand? You dragged me into it." My stitches pulled viciously at my insides. I closed

my eyes and tried to catch my breath as the pain died down
slowly. I looked back at Anderson. "Why the hell didn't
you tell me about this?"

"I tried, in my own way," he said. "I kept warning you
to keep your distance."

"That's not the same as telling me you were with her,"
I said.

"I was never *with* her," Anderson said, holding up his
hands. "We were headed there—maybe. I can't even say
that was in the cards." He dropped his hands to his thighs.
"Let me try to tell you exactly what happened."

I stared at him.

"I met her about a month after I took the job down here.
That's going back about a year and a half. She and Darwin
hosted a fund-raiser for the Pine Street Inn, the big shelter
in Boston. All the heavy hitters around here turned out,
including all the local politicians. I was new in town, so I
spoke to the crowd for ten, fifteen minutes about my plans
for policing the island. She called me up, maybe three
weeks later, said she wanted to talk about trying to help
some of the kids on the island who were struggling with
drug problems—maybe start some kind of community action group."

I looked at him askance. "She called you?"

"Not that that's any excuse." He paused. "Things at
home weren't the best for me. Maybe we were going
through what every married couple goes through, but Tina
and I were certainly having a rough time. We weren't talking as much. We were fighting more. And I was second-
guessing the move here. I was pretty upset about it for a
while."

"Why?" I asked, unable to resist the therapist's mantle,
even in my rage.

"I loved Baltimore. That city was part of me. I came
here because of what you and I had been through on the
Lucas case and because I thought it would be better—safer,
cleaner, prettier—for Tina and Kristie."

I wasn't about to let him off the hook. "So Julia called you. Then what?"

"After meeting a couple times for coffee, she told me how unhappy she was. And I started to talk a little bit about what was bothering me. We'd take walks, trade phone calls." He glanced down, let out a sigh. "I felt good. I really did. For the first time in a long time. She's amazing to look at, and that was certainly part of it. But it was more than that. Her voice, the way she looked at me, the way she listened . . . I thought I'd found someone who could help me change my life."

I didn't like hearing how close Anderson felt to Julia or how similar his emotional experience with her was to mine. "When did you first have sex with her?" I asked, trying to chase the misty look out of Anderson's eyes. "And how has that affected the investigation?"

Anderson's eyes thinned. His expression hardened. "Never did, on the first question. Never would, on the second."

"Sure, and give me a break, in that order," I said.

"I never had sex with her, Frank," Anderson bristled. "I'm not *you*."

I shook my head. "Take the girl and the case and—" I started to walk out.

"Wait a second, will you?" he said. "Look, I'm sorry. You didn't deserve that."

I stopped, turned around.

"Okay," he said. "I'll tell you the whole story. About ten weeks into my . . . relationship with Julia, Tina told me she wanted a divorce. She didn't know about Julia, but she could see I was getting more and more distant. I didn't want to see the divorce happen, so I tried to stop things cold with Julia, but I found myself thinking about her all the time, wanting to talk with her, to hold her hand. So I kept meeting her." He rolled his eyes. "The most we ever did was kiss, Frank. It must sound childish, but that's all that happened. And you know the strangest part?"

"What?" I said flatly.

"Somehow, holding her and kissing her was enough. I didn't even care that we hadn't shacked up. I didn't want to risk what I thought we had." He fell silent.

I could hear the sadness in Anderson's voice. "You're not over her," I said.

He looked straight into my eyes. "No," he said. "I don't expect I ever will be."

"So your warning to me to steer clear of her—that was . . . what?" I asked. "Jealousy?"

"Maybe, a little. Mostly, not." He leaned forward. "I meant what I said. I knew firsthand how my feeling close to her was making it hard to keep my vision clear on the case. I didn't want yours to get cloudy, too."

"Noble," I said.

He ignored the comment. "There's something else, too. And this may sound strange. But the way I felt . . . maybe, still feel about her, I'm not sure it's even normal. I mean, I was on the verge of leaving my wife a week after I sat alone with Julia for the first time. Take it for what it's worth: I was worried for you. That's why I came down on you so hard about your drinking."

Part of me wanted to tell Anderson he was full of crap, but another part of me resonated with what he had said. It was the same issue I had struggled with in my relationship with Julia: How had my feelings for her grown so strong, so fast? Why was I willing to go out on a limb for her when I wasn't certain who she was? Why had I crossed professional boundaries I would have counseled others to respect?

I looked at Anderson, trying to decide whether I could ever trust him again. All the questions that had visited me as I had walked down the hall were still in play. He could easily be carrying on a sexual relationship with Julia and secretly be furious at me for doing the same. The two of them could truly be using me to paint Darwin Bishop as the killer. "Was the letter Claire Buckley handed over to us meant for you?" I asked. "Are you the one Julia was going to send it to?"

"I don't think so," Anderson said.

"You don't *think* so," I said.

"I can't know for sure, but it's just not the tone we used with one another," he said. "It's much more flowery. It would have come out of left field, if you know what I'm saying. Not only that; we hadn't been in touch for weeks before Brooke's murder."

"So you think there's someone else in her life, besides you and me."

"I do," Anderson said. "I think that's why I went off a little on Claire back at the Bishop estate, leaning on her about her affair with Darwin." He shrugged. "I was pissed off about what I had just read. I killed the messenger."

I was split between feeling as if I were with a blood brother who had been through the same war as I or with an enemy caught red-handed sticking a knife in my back. Maybe, literally. "When you asked me to get involved with this case," I said, "did you do it because you wanted to help Julia, because you were in love with her?"

"She let me know she didn't believe Billy was guilty," he said. "My gut told me the same thing."

"That doesn't answer my question."

He hesitated, but only for an instant. "Yes," he said. "I called you because I wanted to help her."

"And . . ." I said, prompting him to answer the second part of my question.

"And because I thought I . . ." He stopped, corrected himself. "And because I loved her." He shrugged. "You wanted an answer. You got one. It sounds crazy, but I loved her."

I nodded. That honest response brought me a bit closer to feeling like Anderson was on the level. But it still left me with doubts. I focused intently on Anderson. "If I didn't think Darwin Bishop belonged at the top of the suspect list, would I still be on this case?"

"What are you asking me, Frank?" Anderson said, struggling to keep his voice steady. "You want to know whether

I'd try to jail a man for the rest of his life in order to steal his woman?"

That was what I was asking, even though it sounded horrible when Anderson said it. I stayed silent.

"When I told you they'd have to bounce me off the case to get you off the case, I meant it," he said. "It may be hard to believe that now. But if you'd told me Billy had all the traits of a murderer, he'd be at the top of our list, not Darwin. I wouldn't railroad someone into a murder conviction. Not even for Julia Bishop."

16

Anderson flew to Nantucket. I took a cab from State Police headquarters to Mass General. While we needed space and time to make sense of how to go forward together, we both knew we had to keep moving. With all the complications in the Bishop case, one thing hadn't changed: Someone had tried to kill five-month-old Tess Bishop—and might well try again.

As the taxi sped down Storrow Drive, with the Charles River off to my left and the Boston skyline to my right, I began to wonder who had placed the photographic negative in the medicine bottle. The obvious candidate was Garret, given his penchant for island photography and the fact that he had turned the bottle over to Anderson and me. But it was also remotely possible that Darwin Bishop had put it there—storing away part of his motive for attempting to kill Tess right along with the means he had used to try to kill her. The answer was on its way; Leona would be dusting the negative for prints.

It was after 6:00 P.M. and getting dark when I walked through the hospital's main entrance. I had the fleeting impulse to stop in at the emergency room and grab a Percocet prescription from Colin Bain, to dull the pain from the injuries to my body and psyche—my savaged back, my hurt pride, my broken friendship. Any addictions counselor would forgive me the slip, given the circumstances. Luck-

ily, I realized that staying sober might be one of the few
things still within my control. No sense burying a knife in
my own back when other people were doing such a good
job of it.

I took an elevator up to the PICU and instinctively
walked toward Tess's room. But I stopped short, noticing
that a five- or six-year-old Asian child was lying in that
bed. I scanned the other rooms around the PICU perimeter,
but Tess wasn't in any of them. My mind jumped to the
most dire conclusion—that her heart had given out. I
stopped a young, female nurse walking by. "I'm a doctor
working on the Bishop case," I said. I couldn't bring myself
to ask the obvious question. "She was here yesterday," I
said.

"Do you have identification?" the woman asked.

Her response seemed to confirm my fear. She wanted
proof I was a staff member before delivering bad news. I
felt lightheaded.

"Are you all right?" she said. "Do you need to sit
down?"

Before I could answer, John Karlstein strode through the
PICU's sliding glass doors. "Frank!" he called out, from
behind me.

I turned quickly, without thinking, and stretched my lac-
erated muscles. "Jesus," I muttered, between clenched teeth.

"My mother thought I was," Karlstein said. "Nobody
since."

I straightened up, as best I could.

"It's good to see you," Karlstein said. "Bain told me
what happened in the alleyway out there. You should sue."

The nurse apparently got the idea I was part of the team.
She smiled and walked away.

"Sue?" I said. "Who? For what?"

"They've had trouble in that spot before," Karlstein said.
"Remember? A mugging less than a year ago. They should
have lighted it like day. Sue the hospital, man."

"I think I'll pass," I said.

"It's a payday from some goddamn insurance company,"

he said. "What do you care? They've been sticking it to us pretty good, haven't they? You should give me a finder's fee for suggesting it."

Karlstein was probably joking, but I could never quite tell with him. My mind focused back on Tess. "What happened to the Bishop baby?" I said. I steadied myself for the worst. "Bad news?"

"Only for my census," he said. "We transferred her to Telemetry. She's out of the woods. Pacemaker's working like a charm."

Telemetry is a "step-down" cardiac unit where patients' hearts are still monitored, but in a more laid-back setting. "Thank God," I said.

"We did have a little trouble before she left," Karlstein said.

"What sort of trouble?"

"The billionaire. He wanted to see the baby—badly."

"Who was stopping him?" I asked.

"Your friend. She turns out to have some real backbone of her own."

"My friend . . ."

"Julia. The mother." Karlstein winked, making it obvious he had intuited she was special to me. "She had already hustled down to Suffolk Superior Court a couple hours before her husband arrived. Picked up a temporary restraining order against him. She had all the paperwork in a neat manila folder. Security showed him and his bodyguards to the door."

"He came here with his bodyguards?" I said.

"I assumed that's who they were. They were bigger than I am."

I knew we hadn't heard the last of that confrontation. "How did Julia handle things?"

"She was a rock while her husband was here. Then she fell apart. Just wracked with tears. I had Caroline Hallissey visit with her again, just to make sure she would be able to pull it together."

"And?"

"Hallissey is her own person," Karlstein said evasively.

"What did she have to say?" I pressed.

"Nothing sensible."

"C'mon, John. Just tell me."

"She thought Mrs. Bishop was *acting* upset," he said, "manufacturing her emotions to manipulate us into doting on her."

"Did you think so?" I asked.

He shook his head. "If that was an act, she deserves an Academy Award. You know me, I'm no bleeding heart. For me to call in a psych consult, *twice*, you have to be in pretty bad shape."

"Well, thanks for letting me know Hallissey's take on things, anyhow," I said. "The more information I have, the better." I paused. "And thanks for helping Tess."

"Don't thank me. Sue the hospital and cut me in." He smiled in a way that made it clear he was pulling my leg. Then he leaned closer and dropped his voice. "Get some rest," he said. "You look like you're about to collapse. And we really can't afford to lose you around here."

I took the stairs up to Telemetry, a unit that looks a lot like any other inpatient ward, with private rooms off a central corridor. I stopped at the nurses' station, found Tess Bishop's room number, and walked to the doorway. Julia was seated by Tess's bedside, watching her intently, just as she had been in the PICU. I monitored my internal reaction to seeing her. The expected anxiety was there, along with a flash of anger, but those negative emotions were eclipsed by another feeling, which I hadn't anticipated—an edgy sort of comfort. It was something you might experience arriving home in the midst of a family tragedy, when you know things have gone bad, but you also know they are *your* things, together. Owning a share of trouble can be an oddly warm and centering experience.

As for Tess, she looked more like a normal infant than before, with fewer leads and lines emerging from her extremities. Her sleep seemed substantially more restful than in the PICU. Her respirations were less labored and more regular, centered in her chest rather than her abdomen. And her color had moved toward pink from ash.

Julia turned and saw me in the doorway. She stood up, took her own deep breath, and smiled. "How long have you been standing there?" she asked.

"I just got here." I walked into the room. I nodded at Tess. "Dr. Karlstein told me she's doing well," I said.

"He was remarkable," she said. "I couldn't have asked for anything more." She looked down at the ground, then back at me. "Darwin came to the hospital. Luckily, we were the second item on his agenda, as usual. He called before he went into a board meeting at some company headquartered here in Boston. That gave me time to go to court and get a restraining order."

"Karlstein told me about that, too," I said. "Good for you."

She started to smile, catching her lower lip between her teeth. "There's no way I would have had the strength to do anything like that if it weren't for you."

I wanted to believe her, which told me how hard I had fallen for her. I was fresh from learning of at least one other romance of hers, with North Anderson. And there was probably a third man in the mix, assuming the letter Claire Buckley had shown us was intended for someone other than North. Yet I still felt like her relationship with me was of a different order and exponentially more important to her. "Didn't you ever see *The Wizard of Oz*?" I said. "No one can give you courage—or a heart or a brain. You must have had it all along."

"Hold me?" she said.

I walked closer, coming within a few feet of her, then stopped and just stood there.

"What's wrong?" she asked.

"We need to talk," I said.

She tilted her head. "What about?"

"North Anderson," I said. "For starters."

She nodded, as if she had known we would eventually arrive at this moment. "He told you we spent some time together," she said.

"Yes," I said. I held off mentioning the photograph.

"And I hope he told you that nothing happened," she said. "Because it didn't. I mean, we didn't . . ."

"But you got close, emotionally," I said. "And maybe you still are. I don't know."

"No," she said. "We're not. Not the way you're thinking. I still care for him, but not in a romantic way."

I shrugged, unconvinced. "All right," I said.

"Can we sit down, please?" she said.

I took one of the armchairs by Tess's bed. Julia took the other.

"You know how difficult my life has been with Win," she started. "I mean, you believe what I've told you—what I've been through?"

"Yes," I said. "I do." And I did. But I also found myself thinking about Caroline Hallissey's assessment of Julia as someone who manufactured emotions.

"I met North at a fund-raiser for the Pine Street Inn in Boston," Julia went on. "I thought he might be able to help me with a project I wanted to start—reaching out to kids who were into drugs. There are more of them on the island than anyone will admit, and I thought, with North having come from Baltimore, he would be a lot less naive than his predecessor."

I noticed how little I liked hearing Julia use North's first name, not much more than I liked her referring to Darwin as her husband. "There's nothing naive about him," I said. "He's seen it all, at least twice." I gestured for her to continue.

"We started meeting about the drug issue, and I started feeling drawn to him," she said. "But we never connected in anything like the way you and I do." She leaned closer. "You have to believe me. I felt safer with North in my life, and I admired him, but I wasn't in *love* with him."

Meaning, she *was* in love with me. I heard that loud and

clear. And I still liked hearing it. "I saw a photograph of the two of you on the beach," I said.

"On the beach?" she said.

"You were holding one another," I said. "Kissing." I cringed at my own tone of voice, which reminded me of a jealous high school kid hassling his girl about going parking with someone else.

She looked at me in disbelief. "Win actually gave you that photograph?" she asked.

I stayed silent. I wanted to hear Julia's version of where the photograph might have come from, without any prompting from me.

"I can't believe he'd do that," she said. "He's so sick."

"Tell me what you mean," I said.

"One of Darwin's security guards took that photograph," she said. "Win was having me followed. He actually used it to try to force me to have an abortion."

"What?"

"He said if I didn't terminate my pregnancy, he'd turn the photo over to the newspapers and let them have a field day with it," Julia said. "That scared me. Obviously, I didn't want to be embarrassed myself, but I was also worried North would lose his job or his marriage or both. So I booked an appointment at a family planning center."

I felt relieved that Julia's story sounded at least remotely credible. "Did Darwin talk about divorce once he knew you had spent time with North?" I asked.

"Never. I think he actually liked the fact that he had something to hold over my head. It gave him even more control over me," she said. "He feeds on that."

"And he never turned the photograph over to the press," I said.

"I should have known that was a bluff," she said. "Advertising my infidelity would have hurt his ego more than it would have fed his need for revenge." Her eyes filled up. "I guess he just waited to get back at me—through Brooke and Tess."

I hesitated to push Julia further when she was close to

tears, but I needed to ask her about the letter Claire had given North and me. "There's something else," I said.

She wiped her eyes. "What? I'll tell you anything you want."

That was a disconcerting turn of phrase. Was Julia, I wondered, just telling me what I wanted to hear? "A page of a letter you wrote surfaced," I said.

"Surfaced?" she said.

"Maybe when the police searched the house," I lied.

"Really," she said.

I didn't feel right lying to her. And I figured turning up the heat between Julia and Claire might not be such a bad idea. "Actually, we got it from Claire Buckley," I said. "She found it—in your closet."

"A letter I wrote," she said, without any trace of anger.

"Yes," I said.

"What did it say?" she asked.

I had made a photocopy of the letter at State Police headquarters. I reached into the back pocket of my jeans and took out the sheet of paper. I unfolded it and handed it to Julia.

She looked at it for several seconds, her face a blank. "What did you want to know?" she said finally. There was no anxiety in her voice.

"It certainly sounds like a letter you would have written to someone you were involved with," I said.

"It is," she said matter-of-factly. "And I am."

I am. Her use of the present tense felt like an assault. My hope that Julia would explain everything away evaporated. My back started to ache again. "Who was . . ." I stopped myself. "Who *is* he?" I said.

"*She*," Julia said pointedly.

It took me a moment to convince myself I had heard her correctly. "You're . . . seeing a woman?" I said.

"Does that shock you?"

"Well, yes. I mean, not that she's a woman." Now, I had lied. "That you have someone else in your life. And it doesn't sound like something casual or meaningless to you."

"Not at all," she said. "She's sustains me. Like the letter says: From the day I first saw her."

"When did it start?"

"Six or seven months ago."

"And it's still going on?"

"Yes."

"Why didn't you tell me?" I asked. "Is she from the island?"

"She lives in Manhattan. I fly to see her once a week during the summer, when I can." Julia smiled. "Otherwise, we talk by phone, for fifty minutes."

"For fifty . . ." I stopped short.

Julia shook her head and looked at me as if I was being foolish. "She's my therapist," she said. "Marion Eisenstadt. That's who I wrote the letter to. I never sent it because I thought it was . . . well . . . inappropriate, and a little morbid."

I was stuck back on the punch line. "The letter was to your therapist?" I said skeptically.

"I can give you her number if you want to check it out," she said. "I've written to her before."

Could it be? I wondered. Might Julia simply have been reaching out to anyone she could, including North and her therapist? Was it possible that she really had chosen me for a different and much more complete role in her life, the same way I had chosen her? I desperately wanted it all to be true. "I don't need her number," I said.

She read over the letter, then looked up at me. "I was feeling really down that day," she said.

That comment gave me a nice bridge to the second half of my concern. "The verse you wrote at the end makes it sound like you might have been dwelling on death," I led.

"Is that an elegant way of asking me if I was thinking about killing my daughter?" she asked.

"Please understand. I need to ask these . . ."

"I felt like my life was over, Frank. I felt like I had sold myself to Darwin. Does that answer your question? I didn't know how much worse things could get—until . . ." She was fighting back tears. "Until I lost Brooke," she said, choking on the words.

"We can talk about this later," I said.

She cleared her throat. "Maybe I asked for this," she went on. "Maybe God is trying to teach me a lesson. All I had to do was leave. But I was weak. Pathetic. And I cared about the goddamn house and the art and all that garbage."

"And you've learned what matters," I said. "You got further than most people get in their lives." I marveled at how quickly I had started taking care of her again.

"If I've already lost you, you should tell me now," she said.

That felt like an ultimatum. Or maybe Julia was simply putting me on notice that she couldn't cope with uncertainty from me. She had lost Brooke. Her marriage was over. Billy might be imprisoned forever. Tess's health was fragile. Wasn't it understandable that she needed to know if she could count on me? Why should I be coy when my heart had an answer for her? "You haven't lost me," I said.

She moved into my arms, running her fingers gently over my back, holding me in a way no other woman ever had, something on the razor edge of raw sexuality and pure nurturance. Each force spoke to a deep and equal need in me. "Stay with me tonight?" I asked.

She glanced at Tess. "I want to stay here a while longer," she said. "I'll grab a cab later and meet you in Chelsea."

"I'll see you later, then," I said.

I was dead tired, but decided I should visit Lilly before leaving the hospital. I planned to be on Nantucket the next day and, with the progress Lilly had already made, I wasn't sure how long she would be an inpatient.

I found her seated in an armchair by her bed, staring out the window. Her blond, curly hair was tied back with a little black bow. I knocked at the door to her room. She glanced at me, then resumed her vigil.

"Mind if I come in?" I asked.

She shrugged dismissively.

I felt as though I might have done something wrong, something to shake Lilly's trust in me. But I couldn't imagine what that might have been. I hadn't breached her confidence by talking to her family members. I hadn't even shared detailed clinical impressions of her with her internist or surgeon. I'd shown up every time I had said I would. Was she still upset I hadn't agreed to continue seeing her as an outpatient?

"*Just because you feel she's lost trust*," the voice at the back of my mind said, "*doesn't necessarily mean she's lost trust in you.*"

That was true. Even during the briefest psychotherapy, the psychiatrist is a blank screen onto which a patient will project feelings he or she harbors for other important figures in their lives. Lilly's silence and standoffish body language might be meant for me, but might be a reflection of her anger toward someone else, like her husband or grandfather.

I walked in. I saw that Lilly was connected to just two IV bottles. Her leg was still wrapped in gauze, but it looked less swollen. She was less pale. She was getting better.

Without turning her gaze from the window she took a deep breath, let it out. Her sky-blue eyes thinned in a way that hinted at stormy thoughts. "That fucking bastard," she said. "All those years. He really screwed me up."

I sat down in the armchair next to her. "Who are you thinking about?" I asked, already pretty sure of the answer: Lilly's mind had begun to channel her self-loathing into rage at her grandfather.

She shook her head. What looked like a wave of nausea swept over her beautiful face. She swallowed hard. "I was a little girl," she said. "He was getting his rocks off manipulating a child."

"You've been remembering your grandfather," I said.

"His stupid comments," she said, still looking straight ahead. "The way he checked me out."

I waited to see if she would share her memories.

She looked at me. Several seconds passed without a word.

I didn't break the silence. I wanted her to know she was the one in control of what she revealed and what she kept private.

"My friend Betsy was turning nine," Lilly said finally. "I was nine, too. I remember getting dressed for her birthday party. It was summer, and my mother helped me put on a pale yellow, blowzy dress. It had little butterflies embroidered on it in white thread. I guess you could see my underwear through it. Pink cotton underwear." She rolled her eyes. "I remember my grandfather looking at me, some stupid smile on his face." Her hands closed into fists. "And then he said, 'Keep wearing dresses that show your panties, and all the boys will be staring at you. I know I would be.' "

He would be. He would be staring at his granddaughter's panties. "Do you remember how you felt at the time?" I asked.

"I've been trying to bring it all back," she said. "Because you told me to run into the images, not away from them." She paused to collect her thoughts. "Partly, I think I felt foolish, because I didn't really understand what the hell he was talking about. Why would anyone care about my underwear? But the way he looked at me, I knew I was doing something he liked, or at least something that got his attention. And I was sort of proud of it, but embarrassed, too." She shook her head again, in disgust. "The way he said *panties*. I remember that. He lingered on the word, like he was . . . tasting it."

I wanted Lilly to keep her disgust flowing, to keep her emotional wound open and let her infection drain. "He liked saying it," I said. "It excited him."

She closed her eyes. Instead of growing angrier, she blushed. "Here's something weird: It's one of the things that my husband likes, too, I guess. On the honeymoon, he asked me to let him look at me in . . . my panties."

"Did you let him?" I asked.

She nodded bashfully.

"He just wanted to look at you dressed that way?" I said, inviting her to divulge more.

Her cheeks turned crimson. "While I touched myself," she said quickly.

I felt as though we were only halfway to the core of the problem. Lilly hadn't attacked her husband for admiring her body. She had assaulted herself, injecting herself with dirt. The trigger for her pathology was her shame. "How about you?" I asked. "Did you like it when he watched you that way? When you were touching yourself?"

"I guess I did. I mean I . . ." She stopped herself mid-sentence. "You know."

"You had an orgasm," I said.

"But then, like a minute later, I felt so disgusting," she said.

"Right," I said. Lilly's trouble was in separating her adult sexuality from the confused, frightened, disgusting sexual intimacies shared by word and glance with her grandfather. "It's going to take time to get enough distance on your past experiences with your grandfather to feel good enjoying the present with your husband. You've got to expect a lot of conflicted emotions. And you've got to give yourself the time to feel them and to get over them."

"But I will?" she asked. "I will get over them?"

"Yes," I said.

"I called Dr. James's office," she said. "We have an appointment in a week."

"I'm glad." I felt gratified that she had followed up with Ted. I also felt a pang of regret that I hadn't continued seeing him myself. I missed him—his clear thinking and steady hand. I would have liked his advice on Julia. "He can help you as you remember more. You can trust him completely."

"I'll try to," she said. She looked at me in a way that

showed she was still very needy and very vulnerable. "Will you stop by before I leave?" she asked. "They told me I'll be here a few more days. It would just help to know I'm not on autopilot until discharge."

"You'll handle the controls better and better," I said. "But, yes. I'll see you before you leave."

17

I grabbed a cab back to Chelsea and walked through the door of my loft at 9:17 P.M. By 9:22 I had already gotten the number for Dr. Marion Eisenstadt from Manhattan Directory Assistance, dialed her up, and convinced the woman at her answering service to page her. I hung on for her more than five minutes.

"Dr. Eisenstadt," she said finally. Her voice was younger than I had expected.

"This is Dr. Frank Clevenger, in Boston," I said. "I'm a psychiatrist working with the Bishop family, on Nantucket."

"Yes?" she said.

"I'm calling to . . ."

"You're a forensic psychiatrist," she said. "Is this a police matter?"

Having a reputation isn't always an advantage. "Not formally," I said. "The Bishops allowed me to evaluate their son, Billy. Now I'm learning as much as I can about the entire family, so I have a complete picture of him when I testify at his trial."

"Okay," Eisenstadt said tentatively.

"And Julia Bishop told me you've treated her. She suggested I call you."

A few moments went by. "I don't think I can tell you much without a release of information from Ms. Bishop."

I felt as though a weight had been lifted from my soul. First of all, Eisenstadt actually existed. Secondly, Julia was clearly her patient. "I completely understand," I said. "We haven't had time to dot our i's or cross our t's. You probably know Billy is still at large. I've had contact with him by phone. Anything you can share with me could help me—either to reach out to him now, or to help him in court later."

"Such as . . ." she said.

"Such as where you think he fits, in terms of family dynamics," I said, as a throwaway line. "Have you treated Ms. Bishop a long time?"

"Sporadically," Eisenstadt said, still sounding cautious.

"She summers on Nantucket, of course," I said.

Several more seconds passed. "More sporadically than that would explain. I think we've met four, possibly five times, in total. But that's really all I can say."

My confidence in Julia's story plummeted and all that weightiness settled right back inside me. I sat down. "I didn't know it was that infrequent," I said. "Perhaps you still feel you know her well enough to—"

"If you do get that release, I'd be happy to share the file."

"Would that include her letters?" I asked, reaching.

Eisenstadt was silent.

"Ms. Bishop mentioned she's written you, from time to time," I said. I could hear my tone of voice drift toward an investigator's, and I knew Eisenstadt would hear it, too.

"Without a client's written permission, I can't confirm or deny the existence of any specific item in the medical record," she said flatly. "That's the law. I'm sure you're familiar with it."

"I understand," I said. I tried taking another tact. "Shall I have Ms. Bishop specifically authorize release of the letters, or would a general release of information suffice?"

"I can't say any more," she said, coldly this time.

"Of course. Thank you for your time. I'll be in touch."

"Not at all. I'll be happy to talk with you again." She hung up.

I stood there, holding the phone in one hand, rubbing my eyes with the other. It seemed beyond the realm of possibility to think that Julia could have bonded so closely with Eisenstadt in four or five hours as to have written that Eisenstadt "sustained" her, that she meditated "constantly" on their time together, and that she had the will to live only when "I think of seeing you." Eisenstadt was female, after all—the wrong gender to inspire that kind of intimacy from Julia.

Julia had another lover. I didn't know whether that fact itself, or her lying about it, troubled me more. In any case, the investigation had missed a critical beat: Interviewing whoever she had been sleeping with at the time of Brooke's murder.

There was no telling what such an interview would yield. What if Julia and her lover had plans to run off together—plans her lover abandoned when she became pregnant with the twins? What if Julia had come to see Brooke and Tess as the only barrier between her and a fresh start with another man?

Conversely, what if her lover had come to see the twins as an obstacle? A man might do anything to have Julia.

A dull headache had cropped up at the base of my skull. I needed better news. A little relief. Ballast. I dialed State Police headquarters and asked for Art Fields, feeling like I was pulling the lever on a one-armed bandit that had just swallowed my last coin. He picked up a minute later. "Frank Clevenger calling," I said.

"Glad you called."

"Do we know whose prints are on that negative yet?" I asked.

"Just one person's," Fields said tentatively. "Darwin Bishop's."

I felt like I had hit the jackpot. But Fields's voice didn't have celebration in it. "You don't sound satisfied with that," I said.

"There aren't any other prints," he said. "Not Billy Bishop's. Not *anyone's*. I would have liked to see one unidentified stray—from whoever processed the roll, some clerk in a store, whoever shot the film for Bishop and turned it over to him. Somebody."

"Wouldn't those people be trained to hold the negatives without touching the surfaces?" I asked. "Don't some of them wear gloves?"

"But a lot of them screw up, don't care, or whatever," Fields said. "So you have to wonder whether someone went to the trouble to keep the negative extra clean before it made its way to Bishop. And you have to wonder why."

"Unless it's a coincidence," I said. "I mean, one of Darwin's security guards could shoot the film, turn it over to a lab for processing, and bring the negatives back neatly tucked in an envelope, with no one ever touching their surfaces."

"Sure. That's possible. Sometimes you get perfect pitch out of a choir, too. I just would have been reassured by a little background noise."

"Agreed," I said. "Did you call in the results to Captain Anderson?" I said.

"Should I?" he asked.

That question had to be about whether Anderson was to be trusted, given what Fields had seen in the photograph. And the question helped me see that I still had faith in Anderson. I believed his story about having been magnetically drawn to Julia and having lost his bearings in the relationship. She had that power. That was more obvious to me than ever. "Yes," I said immediately. "He's the one to funnel all the information through."

"Will do then," Fields said.

"I appreciate it. Thanks for your help."

"No problem," he said. "I do the work for whoever comes through the door with credentials, but I actually like doing it for people who want to hear the truth. Take care." He hung up.

I agreed that the photographic negative would have been

an even more convincing piece of evidence had it been a little dirtier. But the portrait of Darwin Bishop as the killer was compelling, nonetheless. His *were* the only fingerprints on that negative. He had lobbied Julia to abort the twins. He had taken out life insurance on them, had a history of domestic violence, and had asked Julia for her bottle of nortriptyline.

It was just past 10:00 P.M. Julia would probably be arriving soon. I needed to sleep, even for half an hour. I dropped into a tapestried armchair that looked out at the Tobin Bridge, enjoying the silent, firefly traffic arching through the night, then closed my eyes and actually drifted off.

Ten minutes later, my phone rang again. I glanced at the caller ID and saw North Anderson's mobile phone number. I figured he was calling to touch base after Fields shared the news about Bishop's prints with him. Part of me wanted to let it ring. But I knew that avoiding Anderson wouldn't solve anything. I grabbed the receiver. "It's Frank," I said.

"How are you doing?" he said.

"Okay," I said, a little more stiffly than I wanted to. "You?"

He skipped the question. "They picked Billy up," he said. "He wants to see you."

"Picked him up?" I said. "Is he all right?"

"Other than being worn out, from what I hear. He hadn't eaten or slept much."

"Where did they find him?" I asked.

"Queens. LaGuardia Airport," Anderson said. "He was ready to board a flight to Miami."

"How did he manage to get off the island without the police stopping him?"

"He probably made a run for it right after the break-in."

"I'll fly to New York on the first shuttle," I said.

"Stay put. He's headed back your way," Anderson said. "The State Police are picking him up by van and transporting him to the Suffolk County House of Corrections, right downtown in Boston. I can get you in there as soon as you want. He's under arrest, charged with one count of first-degree murder, one count of attempted murder, and a laundry list of lesser charges—breaking and entering, grand larceny, fleeing the jurisdiction. A grand jury will decide whether to indict sometime tomorrow. If they go for it, Billy stands trial as an adult. He could get life."

"Does he have a lawyer?" I asked.

"Court-appointed, so far. Darwin Bishop didn't want to pay for private counsel, assuming he still has the cash to swing it. I thought you might talk to Julia. See if she can help."

I could recognize an olive branch when somebody held one out. Anderson was yielding Julia to me. "I'll mention Carl Rossetti to her," I said. "He's brilliant. And I've known him almost as long as I've known you. We can trust him."

Anderson heard my handshake loud and clear. "Thanks, Frank," he said. He let a few seconds pass. "Billy's going to need somebody like Rossetti. O'Donnell and the D.A. are both convinced they've got their man. They'll paint Billy as such a monster in the media that he'll be public enemy number one by the time he steps into court."

Their *man* happens to be a boy, I thought to myself. If they can try kids as adults, why don't they try immature fifty-year-olds as juveniles? Another one-way street paved by the state. "Have you talked to Fields?" I asked, switching gears.

"I did. There are a lot of things pointing in good old Darwin's direction—including that negative—but it's all circumstantial. The way the D.A.'s office is looking at this case, the break-in is the place to hang their hats. If they can convince a jury that the timing of Tess's cardiac arrest and Billy's B & E is too close to be a coincidence, then they prevail. Billy fleeing the jurisdiction doesn't look good, either."

"No," I agreed. "It doesn't."

"That it?" he said.

"I talked to Julia about the letter," I said.

"What did she say?"

"She told me she wrote it to her therapist, in Manhattan. Marion Eisenstadt."

"Can you check that out?"

"I already called her," I said. "She wouldn't really open up without a release from Julia, but she did tell me the two of them had only had four or five sessions together."

"And?"

"And Julia's letter sounds like something you'd write to a therapist after four or five sessions *a week*, for a lot of weeks."

"Sounds that way," he said. "But don't forget who we're dealing with here."

"Meaning?"

"Julia brings out incredibly strong feelings in people, incredibly quickly. Maybe that kind of thing cuts both ways."

"That she'd bond that quickly in therapy herself? Instant transference?"

"You're the psychiatrist," Anderson said, "but it seems possible."

"Possible," I agreed. "But, more likely, that was a love letter to another man."

"A man we'd want to talk to," he said.

"If we ever find out who he is," I said.

Anderson was silent a few seconds. "It doesn't make you feel very special, does it?"

"No," I said. "I guess not." Saying that, I didn't quite believe it. Remarkably, I was still holding on to the slim chance that Julia was a woman with a complicated past who had firmly settled on me for her future. I wanted to forgive her—almost anything.

"Are you headed back to the hospital to talk to her?" he asked. "I'd like to know what she has to say when you tell her you talked with her doctor."

I didn't want to tell him that Julia was headed over to my place. "I'll get to her one way or another," I said. That didn't sound great, even to me.

"It's your call," Anderson said. "Just keep being careful. You lucked out last time. You could have been killed."

"I hear you," I said. I paused, noticing that a hint of paranoia about Anderson had crept back into my mind. From his tone of voice, I wouldn't have been able to say whether he was warning me or threatening me. *You lucked out last time. You could have been killed.* "Can you get me an interview with Billy at eight A.M.?" I asked.

"You got it," he said.

"Let's talk soon," I said, and hung up. I was physically and emotionally exhausted. On empty. I closed my eyes again, thirsting for sleep.

I woke with a start, not knowing where I was for the first few seconds. I checked my watch—1:20 A.M. and still no Julia. I dialed Mass General to see if she had left the Telemetry unit.

The unit clerk answered the line. "This is Dr. Frank Clevenger," I said. "I'm calling to see whether Ms. Bishop might still be with her daughter Tess."

"Can you hold?"

"Of course."

Almost a minute passed. I started getting nervous, wondering whether something had happened to Tess. John Karlstein finally picked up the phone. "Frank?" he said.

"Right here." I wasn't sure why he was still following the case outside the intensive care unit, but I knew it couldn't be for any happy reason.

"They had a little problem down here with Tess," Karlstein said. "I was still upstairs tying loose ends, so I came by."

I closed my eyes. "What sort of problem?"

"Her breathing slowed. Respiratory rate went down to eight. We watched her blood oxygen concentration fall all the way to seventy-seven. I didn't want to put her on a face mask because I worried we'd suppress her respiratory drive even more. We kind of held our breath, along with her, for

twenty minutes. Then everything drifted back toward normal. Now she seems fine. Her pO_2 is back up to ninety-
five."

"What happened?"

"Honestly, I don't know," he said. "It could be that she's
got a little residual neurological damage somehow affecting
her respiratory rate. It could be the nortriptyline wasn't the
only toxin in her bloodstream when she was admitted. Or
it could be one of those things that happens out of the blue,
like I warned you about. Patients who code once tend to
code again."

"Is Julia Bishop there?" I asked, tacking on her last name
to make the relationship sound professional.

A new note of worry entered his voice. "She left a while
ago—just before this happened," he said.

"You're still concerned about her and the baby, their
interactions, I mean?" I said.

"I don't know if I am or I'm not. But I have found
myself thinking once or twice about Caroline Hallissey's
assessment. Long and short of it, I figure there's no harm
having her attending physician down here order up another
twenty-four-hour sitter." He cleared his throat. "Chances
are, this was a fluke. It happens. I've had patients look like
they were about to code, then bounce back and never have
another problem."

"Or it might not be a fluke," I said, half to myself.

"There are lots of medications that can suppress your
breathing," Karlstein said. "Ativan. Klonopin. They're all
commonly prescribed to people with depression." By which
he meant Julia. "We'll grab a toxic screen of Tess's blood,
just to be on the safe side."

"That's the right thing to do," I said.

"I knew you'd see it that way, Doc. Check in, any time,"
Karlstein said. "I'm hoping to be out of here in a few, so
I'll let the house officer know to fill you in on any changes.
You on beeper?"

"Sure am," I said.

"You're the man," he said.

We hung up. I didn't like the fact that Julia had left the unit just before Tess had run into respiratory trouble. Karlstein obviously didn't like it, either. But there wasn't any clear reason—let alone evidence—to believe the two events were causally linked. At least not yet. The toxic screen would show any new prescription medication in Tess's bloodstream.

Less than two minutes later, the buzzer at the front door sounded. I walked over to the intercom. "Hello?" I said. I hit the LISTEN button.

"Sorry I'm late," Julia said. "Still have time for me?"

"You know I do," I said. I let her in.

When she walked into the apartment, Julia seemed more relaxed than I had ever seen her, which I took to mean she hadn't heard about Tess and probably hadn't heard about Billy being arrested, either. I was anything but relaxed myself. I didn't linger with her at the door. "Can I get you coffee? A drink?" I asked, walking toward the kitchen.

She strolled through the loft, stopping in front of the plate-glass windows. The Boston skyline shone before her.

"Anything?" I asked again.

She turned slowly around. She looked like a goddess against the night sky. "Just take me to bed, okay?" she said, in a tired, needy way that, even under the circumstances, had me thinking about helping her out of her clothes.

I studied her for any sign of anxiety. There was none. Was it even remotely possible that she was fresh from trying to kill her daughter? "We need to talk," I said.

She took a deep breath and sat down at the edge of the mattress. "I've told you everything about North there is to tell," she said. "Go ahead, ask away."

"It isn't about North," I said. I walked over to her and, like a reflex, like there was no question of maintaining any real distance, held out my hand. She took it. I nodded toward the couch. "Let's sit."

The mother in Julia must have read the part of my mind that was preoccupied with Tess's difficulty breathing—

unless she already knew about it, having caused it. "Is something wrong at the hospital?" she said.

"Not anymore," I said. "Everything's fine." I helped her up and guided her to the couch. We sat down close to one another.

"Something's happened," she said, her voice straining. "What? Tell me."

"Things are fine. I called looking for you on the Telemetry unit. I ended up talking to Dr. Karlstein."

"Doctor—"

"He was there because Tess had had some trouble breathing."

Her head fell into her hands. "Is she all right?"

"She is," I said definitively. "Her breathing is completely back to normal."

"I'm going there right now," she said. "Will you drive me?"

"Hold on. She's fine. Really." I moved my hand to her knee and felt my own breathing quicken. Strange. With all the fires burning around us, the energy between us still felt the most incendiary. "Give me a minute to finish," I said.

Julia's panicked eyes searched my face. "Oh, God. You're not telling me everything."

"It's not about Tess," I said. I paused. "They found Billy. He was at LaGuardia, waiting for a flight to Miami."

She let out a sigh of relief. "At least he's safe."

"They're bringing him to the Suffolk County House of Corrections, in Boston. I'll see him there tomorrow morning."

She shook her head. "He shouldn't have to spend a single day in a place like that," she said. "He's innocent. I'm sure of it now."

I took back my hand, nodding to myself.

Julia looked at me with concern. "What else could be wrong?" she asked.

"Nothing," I said. A sigh that escaped me said otherwise. "I had a chance to call Marion Eisenstadt," I said.

She stared at me a few moments. "You're kidding."

"You can tell me if that letter wasn't written to her," I said.

"I can't believe you actually bothered her with this. Behind my back."

"She told me you've had four or five sessions together. That's all she'd say."

"She didn't tell you about the letters?" Julia asked.

Was she bluffing? "She wouldn't," I said. "Not without a written release of information from you." I let that not-so-subtle hint hang in the air.

"You want me to sign some form to let you look at my psychiatric records, to prove I haven't been fucking someone else? Are you joking?"

"I just want you to be honest with me. I want you to know that you can be."

She shook her head in frustration. Her eyes filled up.

"If that letter was written to someone else, I have to talk to that person, as part of the investigation. I can't let it—"

She looked back at me, a new anger in her eyes chasing away any hint of sadness. "That's right. You can't let it go. You can't let go of the past and let us have a life together. You'll see phantom lovers of mine everywhere you turn. Because jealousy doesn't take any courage. Acceptance does. Loving someone does. And you can't really love anybody."

I pressed ahead, even though Julia's diagnosis of me gave me pause. "It's still hard to understand how after four or five . . ."

"It's not my job to convince you of anything," she said. "You'll believe what you want." She stood up. "This is foolishness. We're foolishness. I need to be with my daughter."

I wasn't at all sure I wanted her to leave—the apartment or me. Because even if Julia was lying, all she was probably lying about was her complicated past with men. And my own romantic life had been anything but simple. Maybe she was right. Maybe I was hesitating at the threshold of an emotion that had evaded me my whole life—the feeling of unconditional love for a woman.

She started toward the door.

"Don't leave," I said.

She stopped, but didn't turn back to me. "You're the one who left," she said. She started walking again.

"It's late," I said. "At least let me drive you."

She pulled open the door and slammed it behind her.

18

I paced the loft for a few minutes, careful to avoid stepping close to the liquor cabinet, deciding whether to run after Julia. I stayed put. Barely. Whether she had lied to me or not, seen into my soul or not, I was finally starting to believe in my heart what North Anderson had been telling me all along. I couldn't see the case clearly with her dominating my line of vision.

I picked up the phone and dialed Anderson at home. I wanted to update him on how Julia had responded. He answered after one ring. "Anderson."

"It's Frank," I said.

"I'm glad you called," he said. "Things are getting ugly all of a sudden."

"How so?" I said.

"Mayor Keene called me about an hour ago. He wants me in his office first thing tomorrow. I think he's gonna let me go—or at least threaten to."

"Let you go?" I said.

"District Attorney Harrigan and Captain O'Donnell figure they've made their arrest," he said. "They want everyone to line up behind them. They know I'll stick out like a sore thumb."

"Jesus," I said. "Is this Keene guy really just a front man for Bishop?"

"Worse than that," Anderson said. "He'd do the same dirty work for any one of twenty of his campaign contributors. I should have thrown him a grand myself." He paused. "I'm worried Bishop might have passed that photograph of Julia and me to him. He mentioned being concerned about my 'sense of propriety.' "

"They'd blackmail you?" I said. "Maybe you should wear a frigging wire when you go in there."

"I don't particularly want to start a federal case right now, literally or figuratively. What I want is to get you in to see Billy one more time, then get you in front of some reporters here and in Boston. I think you should go public with your doubts about his guilt—provided you still have them after the interview."

"When can I see Billy?" I asked.

"I've got you scheduled for three A.M. Billy will be in a holding cell. Friends of mine are working the front desk and prisoner intake tonight. You're all approved for a face-to-face with him."

"I'll be there," I said. "But what about you? What's your plan for tomorrow morning?"

"I can't say it's exactly great timing to hit the unemployment rolls," Anderson said. "Not with another baby on the way."

"No." I wanted to give Anderson permission to back off and let me take the heat. "Why don't you keep a low profile? Let me go public with what I think. Tell them you can't control me anymore. You could even fire me, if that looks better. I'll just keep moving ahead. I'm sure Billy's defense attorney will call me as a witness, anyhow."

"I guess I could back off at this point," he said. "Trouble is, I'm not in the mood. So I'm going to tell Keene something slightly different."

"What's that?"

"I'm going to tell him that you and I have worked cases every bit as tough as this one, in much tougher places, like

Baltimore, that we've met men who make him and Darwin Bishop and O'Donnell and Harrigan look like dimestore thugs, and that, thank you very much, sir, Frank Clevenger and I like our odds of coming out on top of this case a lot better than we like yours. Have a nice fucking day."

I smiled. "I don't think that's going to save your job," I said.

"I have more important things to keep," he said. "My self-respect, for instance. Like I said, I've got a baby on the way."

"I'm with you," I said.

"Never doubted it," he said. "Three A.M. with Billy. You're all set up."

I tried for a little more sleep, but ended up lying in bed, fully clothed, thinking. Billy was about to stand trial for murder and attempted murder, even when no one in the Bishop household could be entirely excluded as a suspect. Beyond Darwin Bishop, a shadow of doubt still hung over Garret, Claire, and, whether I liked it or not, Julia.

I continued to worry that Tess Bishop's life was dangling from a thread—partly because of her medical condition, partly because she had been poisoned right under the spotlight of the investigation into Brooke's death. Her attempted murder, together with my stabbing, proved that whatever motive was driving the murderer, it fueled violence even when the risk of detection was high. He (or she) was driven to kill. That irresistible impulse wouldn't go away with Billy's arrest or his conviction. It wouldn't disappear until the desired goal had been achieved.

The clock read 2:26 A.M. The Suffolk County House of Corrections was only a fifteen-minute drive from my loft. I pictured Billy being dragged into that place in handcuffs and leg irons, being tossed into a cold cell for the first of many nights until he stood trial. The advice I had given him when he had called me, to surrender and let the justice system work, would probably seem absurd to him now.

Maybe he had had the right idea, after all—to run away from odds stacked so high it would take a miracle for North and me to beat them.

A flash of paranoia again invaded my restored goodwill toward Anderson. I would be leaving my loft in the early hours of the morning, driving to Boston, parking somewhere near the jail, then walking a deserted street to the entrance. If Anderson were behind my assault at Mass General, if he really hadn't gotten over Julia . . . "Stop ranting," I said aloud. I forced my mind to abandon that train of thought, but the mood of caution stayed with me, probably because my radar screen was tuned to a sensitivity that would twist even the most benign set of data into proof of an invasion.

I actually fell asleep for about fifteen minutes, which left me feeling more tired rather than less, and did something very bad to my back, the middle of which felt as if a clamp had been applied to the base of my right rib cage and tightened until my diaphragm ballooned up into my chest cavity.

I pulled myself out of bed and struggled into the kitchen. I gulped down a glass of milk to calm my stomach, so I could tolerate another couple Motrin. I swallowed them, then gritted my teeth and stretched a little to each side, which nearly brought me to my knees before it started to bring me down to a tolerable level of pain.

I got in my truck and headed toward Boston. Route 1 was empty, and I flew over the Tobin Bridge, around the curves of Storrow Drive, and off the exit ramp to the Suffolk County House of Corrections.

Boston's Big Dig construction had chewed up most of the parking near the place. The rest was reserved for Corrections Department personnel. I took a spot about five blocks away. I felt for my pistol, then realized I had left it back at the loft. Great timing.

I got out of the truck and walked, more quickly than I would have in daylight, checking around me now and again. I smiled to think what Laura Mossberg would have to say about my behavior—more evidence of post-traumatic stress disorder, my condition having deteriorated after being jumped.

A homeless man stepped into my path about a block from the front door of the jail. His face was covered with a couple days of beard, his eyes were bloodshot, and his breath stunk of alcohol. "You have my money," he barked.

I took a step back. That had to be the most interesting way I'd been asked for a handout in my life. I told him so, reaching into my pocket, watching his hands to make sure they didn't disappear into his clothing and reappear with a weapon.

"You gotta be different," he said. "Everybody's heard it all these days."

We weren't more than a quarter mile from MGH. "I guess you could grab a coffee and head in for a detox," I said.

"I'd rather grab a beer," he said. He winked.

A lot of people would have taken that bit of honesty as a good enough reason to keep their money, but I knew what it was like to need a beer. "Here you go." I handed him two dollars.

"I gave you a five," he said. "Where's my five?"

I smiled. "Now, you're pushing it. Good luck." I walked by him.

I hadn't gotten ten yards down the sidewalk when I heard footsteps behind me. I turned around and saw the same man walking toward me at a good clip, his eyes more focused than before, one of his hands down by his side, clutching something that glittered in the light drifting down from the street lamps. I thought of running, but he had closed to within five feet of me.

He smiled, his mouth full of perfect-looking, glistening white teeth, a mouth that seemed to prove he had been laying in wait for me, pretending to be homeless. He raised his arm above his head.

I reared back, cocked my fists karate-style, and waited for him to come a foot or two closer. If all he had was a knife, I'd have him on the ground before he could use it.

He stopped, dropped his arm. "I'm sorry," he said. "I scared you." He slowly held up a silver crucifix. "I forgot," he said. "Thank you. And God bless you." He smiled that toothy grin again, then pointed at his mouth with the crucifix. "Tufts Dental. Free clinic," he said, as if reading my mind. "Got 'em today." Then he turned around and started walking away in the direction of Charles Street, probably to get that beer he wanted, celebrate his new teeth, who knows?

I took a deep breath, talked my heart down to a regular rhythm, and headed for the jail. Maybe a call to Laura Mossberg, I thought to myself, wouldn't be such a bad idea, after all.

Within a couple blocks of the building, I saw television crews starting to swarm into position. I quickened my pace. I didn't want to talk about Billy's case until I had come up with just the right message to counter the story Bishop, O'Donnell, and Harrigan were spinning.

North Anderson had done his job paving the way for my visit with Billy, so I got my visitor's badge at the front desk without any trouble. I signed in, walked through the metal detector, then passed through three separate iron doors, each of which opened as the one behind it slammed closed.

Despite all the times I have visited prisons, I have never lost the feeling of melancholy that coming and going from such places provokes in me. I feel as if I am drowning in questions. By what twists of fate are these people locked up? Who still remembers them as little boys, full of innocence and wonder? And this, getting to the heart of the matter: By what good fortune do I walk the streets a free man? Because I do not feel the great distance between myself and these rapists and murderers and thieves that I presume most others do. I feel separated from them by something wafer-thin and translucent. I think they sense it, too. I carry the scent of their pack. But for the occasional

kind words from my unpredictably violent father, but for a
teacher in sixth grade who took a liking to me and told me
I would amount to something, but for who knows what
other myriad, minuscule details of my life story, I can easily
imagine that I would be an inmate, too. And I feel this
especially when leaving a prison's barbed-wire walls, returning my visitor's badge and retrieving my medical license. I half-expect a dubious stare from an omniscient
front desk clerk, a finger raised, *Just one moment*, then an
alarm sounding, a rush of booted feet coming my way, my
sentence shouted at me as I am carried off to a cell, the din
all but obscuring my plea: "Guilty. Guilty as charged.
Guilty as hell."

I took a long, wide corridor toward the interview rooms.
The fluorescent lights made my skin look cadaverous. The
floor, a high-gloss, gray linoleum, translated every one of
my steps into an ominous echo bouncing off bright white,
cinder-block walls.

A guard met me at the end of the corridor and brought
me to Billy Bishop, already seated at a small table, inside
a six-by-eight-foot room with a glass door. He was wearing
the standard-issue orange jumpsuit, with a black number
stenciled across his chest. He stood up. He looked every
bit as wiry as he had at Payne Whitney, but all the brash-
ness had drained out of his posture. "I wish you had lent
me that money," he said, forcing a grin. "I could have been
long gone."

The guard and I exchanged reassuring glances, and he
left. I stood just outside the room. "I'm glad you're all
right," I said.

Billy made a display of looking around him. "I wouldn't
say this is all right," he said.

I nodded toward the table. "Let's talk," I said.

He sat down. I took the seat opposite him. I noticed that
the fingers of his hands were laced together so tightly that
his knuckles had gone white.

"Strange place," he said, his voice suddenly a sixteen-
year-old's, full of worry.

"It is." I paused. "Tell me how you're doing."

"How am I doing? I'm done," he said, his eyes showing none of their old fire. "Win won."

"Not yet," I said. "We're still working."

He closed his eyes and nodded. "They have me in protective custody, because I'm accused of hurting . . . killing a baby. I guess that ranks me with the guys who like sex with kids. If they could get at me, they'd—" He stopped and looked straight into my eyes.

Being imprisoned is more stressful than many men can stand. But being imprisoned as a pariah, a target, makes everything else look tame. "I want to ask you straight out," I said. "Did you have anything to do with what happened to Brooke or Tess?"

He kept looking right at me, never blinking, and shook his head.

"You didn't," I said. I wanted him to speak the words.

"I felt bad for the twins," he said. "They were born at the wrong time, into the wrong family. Like me, losing my parents. I didn't have any desire to hurt them."

I nodded. "I'm going to help find an attorney to represent you," I said. "In the meantime, you've got to try to keep your mind busy while you're in here. And you've got to try to stay hopeful."

"That's a long yard," he said. "Game's about played, don't you think?"

"It's not over. I promise you."

Billy's eyes filled up. He looked away while he struggled to hold back his tears. Then he took a deep breath and looked back at me. "I've got one idea," he said. "It's my last shot, or I wouldn't even mention it."

"What's that?"

"If Garret saw something the night Brooke was murdered, something about Darwin, would his word mean anything in court? Would a jury ever believe what he had to say?"

I thought about all the circumstantial evidence linking Darwin Bishop to the crime. An eyewitness, especially

Bishop's son, might well be enough to make jurors believe Billy had been wrongly accused. "I think his testimony could change everything," I said.

"You should ask him, then," Billy said.

"I did," I said.

"That was before they caught me. Ask him again."

"Why don't you tell me?" I said. "What will Garret say that he saw? He must have told you."

Billy shook his head. "That's not up to me to talk about."

I wasn't sure why Billy would maintain a code of silence around something that might get him off charges of attempted murder and murder. "Why not? Why can't you talk about it?"

"Because I figure there's a good chance the jury won't budge, even with Garret's testimony, and then I'll get put away for life, and he'll be all alone with the devil. Just Garret and Darwin. If it were me, I don't think I'd take that risk. I mean, we're not that close. I'm not his real brother. And I've done some rotten things since I moved in with him. The stealing and all that. He would have been better off without me there."

My heart went out to Billy at that moment. He had lost his family in Russia and hadn't ever really been a full member of the Bishop family. Julia hadn't really favored his adoption, after all. Maybe that was part of the reason he'd started getting into trouble in the first place. "I'll ask Garret to think about it," I said. "You should ask him, too. Because it really could turn the key and get you out of here."

He nodded to himself, glanced at me, then looked down at the table. "If I did get released . . ." he started, then stopped short.

"Go on," I encouraged him. I was glad he could at least entertain the possibility that he'd go free.

"Nothing," he said. "It's stupid."

"Try me," I said.

He just shrugged.

"I've said more stupid things in my life than I can

count," I assured him. "You'll never catch up."

That got him to smile. He glanced at me again, a little longer this time. "Well, if I ever did get out of here, I wouldn't have anywhere to go. They'd never take me back home." He cleared his throat. "Not that I'd go there, anyway."

"That can all get worked out," I said. "Between the Department of Social Services and Nantucket Family Services there are . . ."

"What I'm getting at is . . . Well, maybe I could kind of crash with you a while," he said. " 'Cause I think I could be different than the way I've been. If I had someone around I trusted. You know?" He looked at me, for my reaction.

I was slow to respond because at least half my mind was occupied with thoughts of Billy Fisk, how things might have been different for him if I'd been willing to go out on a limb.

Billy looked embarrassed. "It is a stupid idea. I mean . . ."

"I'd be willing to give it a try," I said.

"You would?" His voice was equal parts surprise, doubt, and relief.

"Sure," I said. "Why not? What have we got to lose?"

Billy and I said our good-byes, and I headed out of the prison. A prison guard friend of Anderson's escorted me to a back exit so I could circle around to my car without being hounded by the media. "They'll be waiting for you," he explained, handing over copies of the *Boston Globe* and *Boston Herald*. Both papers, apparently worried about exhausting their readers' appetites for the Bishop family saga, had run stories about me. The headlines were typical tabloid trash: "Doc in Hostage Drama Back for Billionaire Babies" and "He Doesn't Shrink From Murder." The photographs of me that accompanied the articles had been shot during my testimony years ago in Trevor Lucas's very public murder trial.

All in all, I knew the coverage wasn't a bad thing. The media would be primed to listen to the message about Billy that Anderson and I hoped to get out. I just had to be careful to pull the trigger at the right time.

It was 4:10 A.M. En route home, I called the chemistry laboratory at Mass General to check on Tess's blood work. The laboratory technician told me the toxic screen had been negative; no new substance had been found in the baby's bloodstream. That ruled out Julia having slipped Tess anything to slow her breathing—at least anything recognizable by routine testing.

I called North Anderson next. He'd been in touch with Art Fields about the prints Leona had lifted from inside the prescription bottle. Three individuals—including Darwin Bishop, but *not* Billy Bishop—had touched the inner surface. No surprises there. "I would guess the other sets belong to Julia and maybe to the pharmacist who filled the prescription," Anderson said. "So that's another chink in the armor of Harrigan's case against Billy." He paused. "How did your visit go with him? They let you in, didn't they?"

"I just finished," I said.

"How does he look to you? Is he holding up?"

"He's lost some weight. And he's scared. But he hasn't lost hope."

"Good for him," Anderson said. "He's a tough kid, then. Did he give us anything we can use?"

"He thinks Garret may be holding something back," I said. "He wants us to ask him one more time whether he saw anything the night Brooke was killed."

"It's going to be hard to get access to him, but we can give it a shot."

"It's the best one we have," I said.

"You're headed my way then?" he asked.

"First thing."

"Call me before you leave. I'll swing by the airport and pick you up."

"Will do."

I took the left onto Winnisimmet Street, heading to my loft. Luckily, I happened to glance down the first cross street, called Beacon. I noticed two of Darwin Bishop's Range Rovers parked halfway down the block, engines running. That was a very bad sign. I drove past my building and saw a couple of Bishop's men huddled in the entryway, either politely buzzing my apartment or, more likely, getting ready to jimmy the front door.

With my wound still howling at me and my gun on the coffee table five stories up, I wasn't about to go looking for trouble. I figured I'd travel real light to Nantucket, buy myself a change of clothing on the island. I needed a new pair of jeans and a new black T-shirt, anyhow. My favorite set was bloodstained, and the T-shirt had a nasty tear across the back, to boot.

I turned up Front Street and drove straight for Logan Airport and the first Cape Air commuter flight of the morning.

Anderson picked me up at 7:30 A.M., an hour before his scheduled meeting with Mayor Keene. We headed over to the temporary State Police headquarters for the Bishop investigation, a specially decked out trailer that had been sited next to the Nantucket Police Station.

Brian O'Donnell greeted us cordially enough, maybe because he figured Anderson was about to be fired, anyhow.

As we walked through the strategy room, its conference table loaded with maps of the island, its walls covered with aerial photographs of the varied terrain, I managed to hold back from needling O'Donnell about the fact that Billy had apparently escaped the island before all the ATVs and choppers started scrambling through cranberry bogs and hidden forests.

Anderson showed less restraint. "Did they use infrared

heat-seeking devices out there in the moors?" he asked O'Donnell.

"I believe so," O'Donnell said, without breaking stride.

"Anything turn up? A lost dog or cat, or something? That might make an interesting human interest story for New England Cable News, trigger some goodwill toward the department. You always want to have something to show for a production as expensive as what went down around here."

"We got what we were looking for," O'Donnell said, turning to smile at us for the briefest moment. "That's all that matters."

O'Donnell's office occupied the last third of the trailer. He took a seat behind a folding aluminum table he was using as a desk. We each took one of the plastic chairs opposite him. He laced his fingers behind his neck. "Gentlemen, how can I help you this morning?" he asked.

I got right to the point. "I'd like to interview Garret Bishop one more time," I said.

"Impossible," O'Donnell said.

"Why is that?" Anderson asked.

"You already know why. The investigation is wrapped up. Garret's given his statement. We have a suspect under arrest. Billy will be indicted by the grand jury within a day or so."

I heard O'Donnell loud and clear. *Don't rock the boat.* "I think Garret may be able to add critical information about what happened in the Bishop household the night Brooke died," I said.

"We have a clear picture," O'Donnell replied, with a grin. He glanced at Anderson in a way that seemed to telegraph that he'd seen the photograph of him with Julia on the beach. He let his not-so-subtle double meaning sink in for a few seconds. "The picture's been developing ever since Billy Bishop tortured his first animal. From there, he's escalated. Breaking and entering. Destruction of property. Arson. Murder. We've been over this ground."

"That picture doesn't fit with the fingerprint evidence I

shared with you from the state laboratory," Anderson said.

"It doesn't need to fit that data," O'Donnell countered. "Unless you're a Navy Seal, you're not going to get into and out of a property with no evidence you were ever there. The important thing for Billy, given that his hands had been all over that house for years anyhow, would be to keep his prints off anything directly linked to the mayhem he committed while inside. It's simple enough. He wore gloves. End of story."

"I don't think you'll get a conviction with the information you have," I said. "Garret might actually make that easier. If he tells us anything, it might cut against Billy, not for him. I have no idea."

"We'll get a conviction," O'Donnell said. "Billy Bishop will do life. Mark my words."

"Any decent defense lawyer is going to depose me and figure out I have doubts about Billy's guilt," I said. "The jury will hear those doubts. Let me address them now and get them out of the way."

"Mark Herman from the Public Defender's office has been court-appointed to defend Billy," O'Donnell said. "I'm sure he'll be in touch with you. He's a good man. The Bishops aren't retaining private counsel."

I didn't know Mark Herman, but O'Donnell's tone of voice made me wonder whether it was possible Herman was in the bag, too. Maybe he wouldn't press for an acquittal. Maybe he'd try to convince Billy to plead to a lesser offense, like second-degree murder. I exchanged a look with Anderson that conveyed my cynicism. It was obvious to me that we weren't ever going to get anywhere with O'Donnell. I decided to burn the bridge. "I actually have a great deal of sympathy for people like you," I said.

"Is that so, Doctor?" O'Donnell said.

"It's harder to see a sociopath when he's wearing a uniform," I said. "But I know you must have gone through something terrible that ruined you. Nothing comes out of nowhere."

"I guess we're done with our meeting," O'Donnell said.

"The only question left is what that something was," I said.

He stood up.

"What was it? What was so hurtful in your life that the badge hasn't been enough to help you turn your hatred around?"

O'Donnell walked out of the office. "See yourselves out," he called back to us.

The rest of the day felt like running into wall after wall in an endless maze. Anderson's meeting with Mayor Keene went down pretty much the way he had thought it would. Keene handed him a copy of the photograph of him and Julia embracing by water's edge, then handed him a three-month suspension, without pay, for inappropriate conduct.

Anderson and I tried driving to the Bishop estate to see if we might stumble on Garret again, but were intercepted by State Police vehicles and turned back.

I called Julia Bishop at MGH to ask her to intervene and arrange a meeting with Garret, but she hung up on me before I could say three words.

Finally, I contacted Carl Rossetti to see if he could get a court order allowing Garret's interview with Julia's consent. He went to the trouble of finding Julia at MGH and getting her written permission, but then learned that Darwin Bishop's team of lawyers had already gotten a preemptive order from the court prohibiting any access to Billy or Garret unless *both* parents allowed it.

I had to admit things were looking worse for Billy. It felt as if a particular version of the facts was congealing around him, casting him permanently and inescapably as the killer in a drama that would not yield, even to the truth.

19

North Anderson and I decided to weigh our options over coffee at Brotherhood of Thieves, a favorite haunt of his. We settled on going to the media with the information we had, hoping to bring enough facts to light that Billy would go to court still enjoying a shadow of a doubt as to his guilt. If we were quickly and wildly successful getting our message out, the D.A.'s office might even start worrying about their prospects for a conviction and wait a while before asking a grand jury to indict. That would buy us more time. In any case, I was almost certain Carl Rossetti would agree to represent Billy—pro bono, if necessary. The exposure would pay him back a hundred times over.

The strategy was anything but surefire. Anderson had left his badge with the mayor. That meant I was officially off the case, too. O'Donnell would probably try painting us as exiled, disgruntled former members of his team. And that might be enough to keep our version of the evidence largely out of print and off the airwaves. These days, maverick reporters are as few and far between as maverick investment bankers.

We were waiting for the check when my cell phone rang. The number on the display was for MGH. I thought it might be Julia, apologizing for hanging up. I felt a little uncomfortable answering the call with North at the table, but I didn't want to miss any important news.

Anderson intuited the reason I was hesitating. No doubt Julia was still on his mind a good deal of the time. "If it's her, go ahead," he said. "I'll take a walk, if you want."

"Stay." I picked up. "Frank," I said.

"Frank, it's John." John Karlstein. His voice sounded more solemn than I'd ever heard it.

The background noise in the restaurant seemed to disappear. I could feel, even hear, my galloping heart. Tess was dead, I told myself. I stared at North Anderson, not looking at him as much as looking *for* him. For more ballast. I felt I had sailed too far into the storm. After bearing witness to Trevor Lucas's butchery, I had barely pieced my psyche back together. Failing to prevent the murder of Julia's baby felt like it might snap the mast of my life once and for all, leaving me adrift forever. That had always been the risk in taking this case. I had spoken the fear to Justine Franza, the Brazilian journalist I'd met at Café Positano, who had seen so much beauty in my Bradford Johnson painting of men from one ship trying to save another at risk. *What if both ships end up sinking?*

Anderson gave me a reassuring nod of his head.

"You there, Frank?" Karlstein asked.

When people use your name while talking to you—especially when they use it two times in as many sentences—it is because they feel the need to reach out to you, to take care of you. "Bad news," I said.

"Afraid so," he said. "This really came out of left field."

I closed my eyes. "Tell me."

"Julia's been hurt," he said.

My eyes opened to a squint. "Julia? What happened to her?"

Anderson looked at me, a lover's worry in his eyes. "Jesus Christ," he said. "Is she all right?"

I looked down, listening to Karlstein. Guilt clawed at my insides. I had left Julia alone, in harm's way.

"Keep in mind, I'm getting this secondhand," he was saying. "I wasn't on the Telemetry floor when the whole thing went down. Long and short of it, her husband came back. I guess he wanted her to sign legal papers of some kind. She did the right thing—reminded him there was a restraining order against him and asked him to leave. He wouldn't budge, so she asked one of the nurses to call the police."

"And . . ." I said.

"And then he just lost it," Karlstein said. "It took a bunch of staff to drag him off her."

I looked at North. "Darwin beat her up."

"That fucking bastard," Anderson said.

I had a sinking feeling that Karlstein was letting me down easy. "She made it, though? I mean, she's alive?"

"Yes. Yes," he said. "Of course."

"How bad off is she?" I asked.

"She's stable," Karlstein said, "but she took some serious punishment. There's a good deal of facial swelling from a fractured zygomatic arch. She's also got four broken ribs and a liver laceration. I put her in the ICU, just to be cautious. Grabbed a CAT scan of her head, which came back normal. I'll order a repeat before she leaves here, make sure she hasn't started to bleed intracranially. Ophthalmology came by to check out her eye; the right one is swollen shut. Doesn't look like there's any retinal damage." He paused. "She'll heal up, physically. Emotionally, it's got to be a longer mile."

"Is she with it?" I asked.

"I put her on a fair amount of Darvocet, so she's drifting in and out. But when she's awake, she's holding her own. She's completely oriented. She knows who I am, what day it is, where she is, who the president is—all those questions you guys throw at people."

"How about Tess?" I asked. "Darwin didn't hurt her, did he?"

"He didn't go near her," Karlstein said. "I mean, this wasn't one of those things where the father can't stand being away from his kid and goes berserk. The one-to-one sitter said Bishop never even went to Tess's bedside."

"Was he arrested?" I asked.

"Security held him until the police got here. He left in cuffs," Karlstein said. "I'm no lawyer, but I'd say he's gone for a while, even with his connections. There's no shortage of witnesses to what he did. And the way they say he went after her . . . He was trying to kill her."

"Tell her I'll be there as soon as I can," I said. "Me, and my friend North Anderson."

"I'll tell her right now," Karlstein said.

"Thank you, John," I said. "Thanks again."

"No problem," he said. "See you later."

I hung up.

"Will she be all right?" Anderson asked. "What the hell happened?"

I told him everything Karlstein had told me. "It sounds like Bishop cracked," I said. "I guess he really had the subsoil to lose it. He's looking at charges of violating a restraining order and attempted murder. He could go away twenty years." Saying that made me see more clearly that Darwin Bishop really had been battling to keep parts of himself buried. But marrying a model, accumulating a billion dollars, and buying his way into Manhattan and Nantucket society hadn't freed him of his underlying rage— not any more than alcohol had.

"This makes it a lot harder for O'Donnell to close the investigation," Anderson said. "And even if he does, your friend Rossetti should be able to raise doubt in a jury's mind about whether the D.A. put the wrong person on trial."

Anderson was right. "It's certainly not the way I wanted to score points, but I'll take 'em."

"I wonder what those papers he wanted her to sign were all about." Anderson said.

"I guess we'll find out from the Boston cops who arrested him," I said. "Coming with me?"

"If you'd rather go alone, all you have to do is say so."

"I know that," I said. "That's the biggest reason we should go together."

• • •

Even with John Karlstein's description of Julia's injuries, even with his tipping his hand by telling me she needed to be observed in the ICU, I wasn't prepared for what I saw when I visited her there. Maybe it was the fresh memory of her extraordinary beauty, or maybe I had simply summoned a level of denial to make it through my phone conversation with Karlstein, but the swelling and discoloration of Julia's right eye, cheekbones, and lips shocked me. So, too, did the nasogastric tube that ran into one of her nostrils, down her throat, and into her stomach, draining blood-tinged fluid, and preventing her from speaking clearly. Yet, seeing all that, I wanted nothing more than to hold her and stroke her hair and promise her that everything would turn out all right. I tried to keep my smile bright and my voice steady, because I could tell that she was watching North and me for our reactions.

Anderson was good enough to take the first shot at humor. "I'd like to see the other guy," he said. It was a twist on a tired cliché, but he delivered it with warmth and reassurance, and it seemed to give Julia something she needed. She smiled.

"I talked to Dr. Karlstein," I said. "You'll heal up. It's a matter of time. All you have to do is rest."

Julia tried to say something, but choked on the nasogastric tube and fell into a coughing fit.

I bent over the bed and helped her sit up, relishing the chance to put my arm around her shoulders.

"Let me get a pen and paper," Anderson said. "You can write down whatever you need to tell us." He walked off toward the nurses' station.

I brushed my lips against Julia's ear and felt her move her hand to the side of my thigh. "I'm sorry I wasn't here," I said. "I'll be here for you from now on." A single tear escaped her eye. I dried it with my shirtsleeve.

Anderson walked back into the room. He handed Julia

a pen and pad of paper. She wrote just three words: *Is Tess okay?*

My throat tightened. Julia's concern for her baby, while she nursed her own battered body, began to paint as absurd the notion that she could be responsible for Brooke's death or Tess's cardiac arrest. "Dr. Karlstein said she's absolutely fine. I'll check in on her."

She nodded weakly. Then she held up a finger, signaling us she had more to write. *Good to see the two of you together*, she wrote.

Anderson and I looked at those words and both nodded. It *was* good that our friendship had survived wanting the same woman. It meant it could survive most things.

I took particular comfort in what Julia had written because it seemed to say she was openly choosing me, despite her affection for North, that she was willing to acknowledge our being a couple, even in his eyes. Maybe she really could commit to one man. Maybe Brooke and Tess's father really was out of her life for good. And maybe someday she'd be able to admit that the letter Claire Buckley had found was written to him, not to her therapist. It didn't have to be that day. Or the next. "You rest up," I said, helping her lay back on the pillows.

Her brow became furrowed. "Billy," she mouthed.

"North and I will take care of Billy," I said.

She looked at North for confirmation.

"We're not going to let him down," he said.

We left Julia's room about 6:30 P.M. and were walking out of the ICU when Garret Bishop appeared in the hallway leading to it. We stopped. He walked right up to us. "What are you doing here?" he fumed.

"Checking on your mother," I said. "I take it you know what happened to her."

He glared at North Anderson. "Do they still have the bastard under arrest or have they let him go on a couple hundred thousand bail?"

"He's in jail, right here in the city," Anderson said.

Garret's lip twitched. He was grinding his teeth.

"If you were willing to tell us everything you know about the night Brooke died," Anderson said, "the bastard might stay locked up, forever. If you're not willing to stand up to him, I can't guarantee anything."

Garret looked away, then back at us. He took a deep breath. "Can I get any kind of protection?"

My heart leapt at the thought that Garret might finally be willing to take on his father.

"Police protection?" Anderson asked. "That could be arranged, under the circumstances. I'm sure of it."

"Who would I be giving my statement to?" Garret said, visibly trying to settle himself down.

"I'd set up an interview for you with three people: a Boston police officer, a State Police officer, and the District Attorney. Dr. Clevenger and I would be there, too." He glanced at me, then looked back at Garret. "We might even be able to get you in front of a couple reporters. That way you'd get to speak your mind to the whole state. The whole country, really."

Garret hung his head for several seconds, apparently mulling over the offer. Then he looked at us again. "Set it up," he said. "I want that animal gone for life. He isn't going to lay a hand on my mother ever again."

"Consider it done," Anderson said. "We'll meet you in the lobby in one hour and drive you over to the Boston Police Station. I'll start getting the audience together right now."

"See you in the lobby," Garret said. He walked past us, headed for the ICU.

"That could do it," Anderson said. "An eyewitness connecting Darwin to Brooke's murder makes the case against him. Let's hope he doesn't flake."

"What about that court order against interviewing Garret without both his parents' consent?" I asked.

"Call your buddy Rossetti and get him to shoot back to Suffolk Superior Court," he said. "With Darwin jailed for attacking Julia, he ought to be able to get a quick hearing with a judge and have that order reversed. I'll set the rest of the gears in motion."

"Will do," I said.

"The lobby, in say forty-five minutes, then?"

"Forty-five," I said.

It took until 10:00 P.M. to get the relevant players into an interview room at Boston Police headquarters on Causeway Street: Detective Terry McCarthy from the Boston force; State Police Captain O'Donnell; District Attorney Tom Harrigan; and Carl Rossetti, now officially chosen by Julia to represent her, Garret, and Billy.

Two hours earlier, Rossetti had worked his magic with Judge Barton at Suffolk Superior, getting us an emergency court order to take Garret's statement.

Darwin Bishop's assault on Julia had dissolved most of the animosity between the players in the room. Bishop was beyond rescue, and his henchmen knew it. The papers he had demanded that Julia sign at MGH turned out to be forms closing out two bank accounts in the twins' names, each of which held $250,000. He also happened to have been carrying two one-way tickets to Athens, Greece, a nice stopover on your way to disappearing forever. The tickets had been issued in his name and Claire Buckley's.

We chose Terry McCarthy to conduct the interview. McCarthy, a soft-spoken man of forty-two years who looks about fifty-five, is a former Boston College hockey player. He leans into every step with his right shoulder, half-lifting, half-sliding his feet, as if still on the ice. And, despite his smooth voice, he can still get this look in his eye that makes you think he's about to crush you against the boards or drop gloves and pummel you. That dichotomy may be the reason he can coax the truth from just about anyone.

McCarthy sat catty-corner to Garret at the conference table, the rest of us taking seats a respectful distance away. He turned on a tape recorder.

"Why don't we start with your name?" McCarthy said to Garret.

"That's easy," he said. "Garret Bishop."

"Your date of birth?"

"October 13, 1984."

"And today's date?" McCarthy asked.

"June 29, 2002."

"And, Garret, are you giving this statement voluntarily? Of your own free will?"

"Yes," Garret said.

"No one here has coerced you in any way—offered you anything?"

"No, sir," Garret said, with a hint of a smile. "I wish they would."

Captain O'Donnell chuckled.

Garret laughed a nervous laugh.

McCarthy got that look in his eye.

"Just answer his questions," Rossetti told Garret. "No jokes."

"Let me ask you again," McCarthy said, leaning into the table, his voice especially kind. "Has anyone offered you anything for what you are about to say?"

"No," Garret repeated.

"Very well. Let's get started, then. Tell us what you saw on the night of June 21, 2002."

Garret stared at McCarthy, seemed about to answer, then slumped a little in his seat and looked down at the table. Several seconds passed.

"Garret?" McCarthy prompted him.

No response.

I glanced at Anderson, who looked just as worried as I was that Garret was losing his nerve.

"Garret, if you don't want . . ." McCarthy started.

"Tell me again how I know I'll be safe," Garret said, still staring at the table.

"Okay, let's go over that," McCarthy said. "A state trooper is being assigned to you as a bodyguard. That person will be with you for at least six months, much longer if anyone you implicate in a crime is ultimately brought to trial. It's important you understand, though, as we've informed your mother and your lawyer: There are no guarantees. Nothing we can do will take away every bit of risk."

Garret pursed his lips, apparently pondering what he had just heard.

All I could do was sit there and wait. I scanned the faces in the room. Tom Harrigan rolled his eyes and shrugged.

"Are you reconsidering, Garret?" McCarthy said. "You shouldn't feel pressured to say anything." His tone suggested otherwise. "We can call it a night right now, if you want. Everyone will go home, like this never happened."

Garret looked up at him, glanced at me. A few more seconds of silence, then: "I was reading in my room. It was about eleven-thirty or so."

I felt my whole body relax. I sensed victory. I looked at Anderson. His fist was clenched. This was the moment we had worked for.

"I was reading and I heard something downstairs—from the basement," he went on. "It was a crash, like something had fallen."

McCarthy nodded encouragingly.

"I thought everyone else had gone to bed, so I was like, 'That's weird,' you know? So I started going down to the basement." He squinted, as if visualizing the scene. "I got as far as the family room and I was walking toward the kitchen, where the basement door is. But before I got there I heard footsteps coming toward me. So I stopped. And Darwin walked into the room." Garret paused, looked directly at McCarthy. "He had a tube of plastic sealant in his hand."

Every trace of sound seemed to evaporate from the room. What Garret had said was enough to help Billy, but he wasn't finished.

"I told Darwin I had heard something in the basement," Garret continued. "He said not to worry about it, he'd knocked something over, to go back to my room."

"And what did you do?" McCarthy said.

"I went upstairs. But I had a bad feeling about the whole

thing. Eerie, like. Darwin never goes down to the basement, first of all. And he seemed, like, out of it."

"Out of it," McCarthy repeated.

"Major league stressed or angry, or something," Garret said. "I couldn't tell."

"What happened next?"

"I heard him walk past my room, toward the nursery. So I waited until he'd gotten all the way down the hall, then I sneaked out of my room and followed him."

"And?" McCarthy said.

Garret closed his eyes. "I saw him take the tube of caulk and . . ."

"What did he do with the caulk?" McCarthy said.

"He put it in Brooke's nose. First on one side, then the other," Garret said. "Then down her throat." He opened his eyes. They were filled with tears.

It was the first time I had seen Garret cry. And for the first time, he seemed his age to me. He looked like an emotionally awkward, adolescent boy struggling to be a man, under the worst of circumstances.

"Then what happened?" McCarthy continued, unfazed.

"I went back to my room," Garret said, wiping tears off his cheeks.

"And you didn't tell anyone about this until now?" McCarthy said.

"No."

"Why not?"

"I was scared," Garret said.

"Of what?" McCarthy asked.

"Darwin."

"Why?"

"Because I've watched him beat my brother Billy almost unconscious," Garret said. "Because he's threatened more than once to kill me if I disobeyed him—let alone . . . turning him in."

"So why go out on a limb now?" McCarthy asked.

Garret swallowed, took a deep breath. "I saw what he did to my mother," he said, his lip starting to twitch again.

"If I had had the guts to stop him sooner, that never would have happened. I'm not going to wait until she's dead to do the right thing."

Garret left the interview room with a police escort. The plan was for him to stay the night in Boston, then head back to Nantucket.

State Police Captain O'Donnell was the first to speak. "Officer Anderson," he said, "based on what I just heard, along with the fingerprint evidence you obtained and the other circumstantial evidence in this case, I plan to charge Darwin Bishop with the first-degree murder of his daughter Brooke and the attempted murder of his daughter Tess." He glanced at Tom Harrigan. "I would presume the District Attorney's office will ask the grand jury to indict Mr. Bishop for those offenses, along with the attempted murder of his wife Julia earlier today."

"We'll be in front of the grand jury as soon as they can convene one," Harrigan said.

"I hope we can arrange Billy Bishop's release in the same time frame," Carl Rossetti said.

"We'll drop the charges against him as soon as possible," Harrigan said.

"When would that be?" Rossetti asked, stonefaced.

"I'll take care of it personally tomorrow morning," Harrigan answered.

Terry McCarthy looked over at Anderson and me. "That means Billy goes free in the A.M.," he said. "Would you two be picking him up?"

Anderson turned to me. "You mind taking care of that, Frank?" he said, with a wink. "I should get back to the island tonight."

"I don't mind," I said. "I don't mind at all."

As the room emptied, I pulled O'Donnell aside. "I think you owe me one thing," I said.

"What?" he said, annoyed. "You want some kind of formal apology? I should contact the newspapers, tell them how fucking brilliant you are? You haven't had enough news coverage in your life, Doc?"

"No," I said. "I'm not looking for anything like that."

He didn't walk away.

"*He's gonna pay up*," the voice at the back of my mind said. "*He owes you the truth and he knows it.*"

"I meant what I said when we met at your office," I told him.

He smiled a surprised, good-natured smile. "That I'm a sociopath?" he said.

So he knew where we were headed. "Not that you're a sociopath," I said. "But that something got in the way of you doing the right thing here." I saw him stiffen. I shook my head and looked away, giving him a little space. "This is over," I said. "No hard feelings. All I want is the answer to one question." I looked back at him.

He took a deep breath, let it out. "Ask already." His eyes met mine and stuck.

"You've been through something painful," I said. "I want to know what it was."

The smile left his face. "Why? What does that matter to you?" he said.

"It does," I said.

"But why?"

"It just does." I could have said much more. I could have told him that, wherever I go, I keep searching for primary evil, out of the womb—the bad seed—but have never found it. I could have told him that everyone really does seem to be recycling pain, that empathy, properly harnessed, really does seem to stop the cycle of hurt—and heal people. And I could have told him that something about those two facts kept my mood from plummeting and kept me out of the gutter, because they reassured me we might be a worthwhile species, capable of more compassion than we seem to be. "If it turned out we were butting heads purely over some allegiance you've got to the mayor or

Darwin Bishop, I just wouldn't know what to do with that. I wouldn't *understand* it, you know? I—"

"You need to know why people act the way they do. You want things to make sense," he said.

"Yes," I said.

O'Donnell chuckled, looked away. The smile on his face vanished. "I had a sister less than a year old kidnapped and killed by some bum drifter out of Colorado." He shrugged. "Maybe I wanted this case to go away. Maybe I shut down on it. My mistake." He glanced at me, then walked off.

I closed my eyes. "Thanks," I said quietly.

20

It was after midnight, but I didn't drive right home. I drove to the Suffolk County House of Corrections.

Luckily, Anderson's friends were working the overnight again. Tony Glass, a spark plug of a man about thirty, thirty-five, wearing Coke-bottle lenses, ran the front desk. He asked me if I was there for another visit with Billy.

"No," I said. "I want to see Darwin Bishop."

"Strange, huh?" Glass said. "The father and the son in the same jail at the same time?"

"Not for long," I said. "Billy should be released in the morning."

"Good. He seems like a decent kid," Glass said. "A couple of the guards were saying so. They like him."

I smiled. Billy might be likable, but he was also destructive and manipulative. I hadn't forgotten that. "He can be charming," I said.

"The father's in protective custody," Glass said. "He got into it with another inmate, took a little beating. You might want to see him down on the cell block, if you don't mind."

"No problem." I wondered whether Bishop had had a run-in with another inmate, or whether he'd run into a guard who didn't stomach wife-beaters.

Protective custody was basement level in the jail, a cell

block like the others, but without access to any common areas or recreational activities. It was also cold and dark down there, maybe to remind the inmates that *protecting* them was an additional burden for the system, not something that got them any warm fuzzies.

Only a few of the cells were occupied. A guard walked me to the last one in the row. Darwin Bishop was lying on a cot, wearing the same anonymous orange jumpsuit that Billy had been wearing. "Got a visitor, Bishop," the guard said. He walked away, leaving me there.

Bishop sat up. His lip was split, but he looked okay otherwise. "Dr. Clevenger," he said, sounding weak. "What brings you?"

What, indeed? Did I want to see with my own eyes that the truth had caught up with a man who had run from it for so long? Or had Julia sparked such a primal, competitive instinct in me that I wanted to savor a rival's defeat? I had planned to take her from him, after all. I had been planning it at some level since the day I met her. "I'm not sure why I'm here," I told him.

"I didn't go to the hospital to hurt Julia," he said. "I love her, probably more than I should. I lost control. And you're partly to blame. You've been seeing her."

"Terrorizing your family isn't a great strategy to keep them faithful," I said. "Having affairs of your own doesn't help, either."

"That doesn't excuse you," he said. "I never took something of yours."

"Is that why you sent your bodyguards to my apartment yesterday?" I said. "To even the score?"

"Yes," he said. "I wish you had been at home. You'd look worse than I do."

"Too late now," I said.

"Possibly." He ran a finger over his lip. It was bleeding. He looked at the blood. "You're not her first, you know. Your buddy North had her, too. She doesn't discriminate."

I said nothing.

Bishop looked at me. "You don't even care," he said.

"You want her anyhow. You're addicted to her, same as he was." He paused. "Same as I am." He looked at the ceiling, took a deep breath, and shook his head, as if he still couldn't quite believe what had happened to him. Then his gaze drifted around the walls of the cell. He swallowed hard. "I've been here before," he said quietly. "Alone. With nothing. I always come back."

The way he said those words, almost as a mantra, to soothe himself, made me feel something like pity for him. "No one can stop you from getting rich inside," I said.

Drake Slattery, Lilly's internist, called me just before 7:00 A.M. to tell me Lilly would be going home later that morning. I told him I'd be by to see her off.

She was dressed in street clothes—white jeans and a simple, light green blouse—when I got to her room. She had swept her blond curls over one shoulder and put on pretty pink lipstick and was seated in one of the armchairs by her bed, reading. I knocked. She looked up, smiled. "Come in," she said.

I took the other armchair. "Anything interesting?" I asked, nodding at the magazine.

She held up the magazine so I could see the cover. It was a copy of *True Confessions*. "Appropriate, huh?" she said.

I smiled. "I suppose so."

"Discharge day," she said.

"How are you feeling?" I asked.

"Honestly?" she said.

"Of course."

"I would love to do it again," she said.

"Inject yourself," I said.

She nodded. "I think about it most of the day. Sometimes I dream about it at night." She looked directly into my eyes. "This isn't going to be easy."

Lilly was describing something similar to the craving addicts experience when they try to put down a drug. For

her, the injections and resulting infections had been intox-
icants, after all. They had numbed her mind so she couldn't
focus on her complex feelings for her grandfather. Now,
with painful reality pressing in, her mind was pleading with
her to keep the drugs flowing. "Have you thought a lot
more about your relationship with your grandfather?" I
asked.

"A little bit during the day," she said. "A lot when I'm
falling off to sleep."

She seemed reticent to say more, so I chose provocative
words. "What comes to mind while you're lying in bed?"
I asked softly.

Her face flushed. "I have these dreams. They're different
from the ones where I'm hurting myself. Very different."

"How so?" I said.

"I'm hurting . . . him," she said.

That didn't surprise me. The longer Lilly stayed away
from her habit, the more she thought about the inappropriate relationship that had sparked it, the angrier she was
likely to get. I wanted her to know that she didn't need to
be ashamed of that anger, that she could talk openly about
it—to me or her new therapist (my old one) Ted James.
"How are you hurting him?" I asked her.

"It's awful," she said.

"They're just feelings," I said. "The only person you've
really hurt is yourself."

She looked down at her leg for several seconds. "In the
dreams, I'm in bed," she said, tentatively. "Grandpa comes
into my room to kiss me good night." She looked back at
me.

"And then?" I said, keeping my voice even.

"I pretend I'm asleep, but I'm not. He comes closer and
closer. It feels like he's taking forever to get to me. Finally,
I see his shadow on the wall. I watch it as he leans over
to kiss me. And just as his lips are about to touch my
forehead, I turn over and . . ." She closed her eyes.

"And . . ." I said, encouraging her.

She kept her eyes closed. "I have a knife."

"What happens?" I asked.

She looked directly at me again. "I cut his throat." She looked horrified.

"And then?" I said.

"Then he just stares at me with this terrible confusion in his eyes. Like he has no idea why I did it. And that's the worst part. That look on his face. It's even worse than picturing what I did to him—you know, the way his neck bleeds. I can't get his expression out of my head."

"Make sure she can keep it out of reality," the voice at the back of my mind said.

"You don't feel the impulse to strike out at your grandfather that way right now, do you?" I asked. "While you're awake?"

She looked at me as if I had two heads. "My God, no. I don't ever want to hurt him."

"I didn't think you did," I said.

Lilly's nightmare was transparent. Her grandfather had strung her along, seducing her for years. He had come *closer and closer*, without ever laying a hand on her. To an adolescent girl's unconscious mind, it must have seemed that he was taking *forever* to claim her. But such a girl's rage at being manipulated would grow in tandem with her erotic impulses, hence the fantasy of killing her grandfather as she lay in bed, *just as his lips are about to touch her*. Even the grandfather's *confusion* seemed on the mark. He may never have consciously intended to harm Lilly, acting automatically on his own bent emotional reflexes—his *shadow*—born of who knows what childhood trauma.

Something Ted James had told me years before came back to me. He'd been trying to help me let go of my anger toward my father, which I was never fully able to do. "Eventually," James had said, "you'll realize there's no one to blame and no one to hate. Your father was a victim, just like you."

I looked at Lilly. "Maybe the reason your grandfather looks confused," I said, "is because he never understood why your relationship turned toxic—the dynamics that

drove it in a destructive direction. Maybe he didn't understand it any better than you did."

"In other words," she said, "he didn't *mean* to screw me
up?"

"Maybe not," I said.

She seemed to be grappling with that notion.

"Do you say anything to him when he's looking at you
with that confusion in his eyes?" I asked. "After you've cut
him?"

"No," she said. "That's when I wake up."

"What would you say to him?" I asked.

She shook her head. "I don't know."

"Think about it," I said.

She smiled, then squinted past me, presumably imagining the situation. After a few moments, she looked back at
me. "Sleep tight. Don't let the bedbugs bite," she said. She
laughed.

I let myself laugh with her, to drain the tension from the
moment. Were she a long-term patient of mine, her words and
the tone of voice in which she had delivered them—combining innocence, rage, and something vaguely sensual—would
have been a perfect launching pad for a longer flight over
the terrain of her trauma. That was a very good sign indeed.
"You're going to be okay," I said.

"Think so?" she said.

"I know so." I extended my hand. She took it. "Good
luck," I said. "I'll be thinking about you."

Billy was scheduled to be released later that day, but the
gears of the legal system always grind. He wasn't released
that day, or the next. He and I joked about him being set
free on Independence Day, but that didn't happen, either.
It took ten days for the relevant paperwork to flow between
the D.A.'s office and the jail. Finally, on July 10, I went
to the Suffolk County House of Corrections and watched
him walk through the two sets of sliding steel doors that
pretend to separate good from evil. He glanced back just

once as he half-jogged to me. "I can't believe I'm out of there," he said. "Thank you."

"If you really want to thank me," I said, "you'll worry with me."

"Worry about what?" he said.

"About yourself. The stealing, hurting animals, setting fires—it can't go on."

"That's past history," he said. "I'm not gonna screw up."

"Past is future, as long as you run from it," I said. "Losing your parents, leaving Russia, living with Darwin—I promise you every shortcut you take to avoid facing those things leads back here. I've seen it happen. Dozens of times. Kids with hearts every bit as good as yours."

He glowed with that last phrase. "Will you help me?" he said.

"I will if you want me to," I said.

"I really do," he said.

Treating a sociopath is much harder than treating someone with depression, or even psychosis. The trouble is that sociopaths don't think they're sick. *Everyone else* is the problem. If the world would just get off their backs, cough up what they've got coming to them, everything would be fine. "We'll give it a try," I said.

He held out his hand. We shook on it. "So where are we going?" he said.

The way Billy asked that question made it plain he remembered my promise that I'd consider letting him live with me. I remembered, too. It was easy to deliver on it, at least temporarily, because I had been staying with Julia and Garret at Julia's mother's West Tisbury house on Martha's Vineyard. Julia had been released from Mass General just three days before and was still feeling unsteady, physically and emotionally. "We're going to your grandmother's house on Martha's Vineyard," I said. "I've been staying in the guest cottage while things come back together."

"So we get to hang out, like you said," he said.

"Sure looks that way."

"Will Garret be there?" Billy asked.

"He's moved most of his things in," I said.

Billy nodded over his shoulder. "I have better memories of the House of Corrections than Darwin's house," he said. "At least everyone agrees this is a prison. You kind of know what to expect."

Garret testified before the grand jury two days later. Carl Rossetti was there, as was District Attorney Tom Harrigan.

Rossetti told me the scene was heart-rending. Garret had been a mess, trembling and sweating, needing much more reassurance than he had at Boston Police headquarters. Still, by the end of his testimony, he had nailed Darwin Bishop's coffin shut with an eyewitness account that put the plastic sealant in Bishop's hand and the bottle of nortriptyline in his desk. That complemented the fingerprint evidence perfectly. An indictment of Darwin Bishop for murder in the first degree, with extreme atrocity and cruelty (a special add-on in the Massachusetts courts), along with two counts of attempted murder (Tess and Julia) was issued within an hour of Garret stepping down from the witness stand.

"I've been in this business long enough that most things don't get to me, you know?" Rossetti had told me. "But when Garret broke down, crying how he still loved his father but couldn't understand why, I almost got choked up myself."

"Almost," I had said.

"Honestly, Franko, the only time I really lose it is when I lose at the track. I drop more than a grand, I cry like a baby. Anything else, it's no skin off mine, if you know what I mean."

"So you did get choked up," I said.

"Pretty much," he said.

When Garret returned home, I sat down with him. "I talked to Carl Rossetti," I said. "I know how hard it was for you today."

"I didn't think it would be," Garret said. "I thought it

would be easier than last time. Maybe it's that we're getting closer to the trial."

"And the trial itself will be even harder," I said. "With everything Darwin has done, it's normal for you to feel a strange sort of devotion to him."

"That's what I don't get," he said. "Why would you worry about what happens to someone who's tortured you?"

The answer to that question brings up another strange human calculus. Most children would rather preserve the fantasy of a loving connection with their fathers and mothers, at all costs, even if it costs them their self-esteem. When you're three or seven years old, it's less frightening to think of yourself as an unlovable, disappointing screwup than to recognize the fact that you're living with a monster. "Questioning your love for Darwin would mean questioning whether *he* ever loved *you*," I said. "That's a tough one, at seventeen or forty-seven. Take it from me."

"Was your father . . . abusive?" he asked.

"Yes," I said. "He beat me."

"Shit," he said. "I'm sorry."

"Thanks," I said.

He shook his head, took a deep breath, let it out. "With everything Darwin did to me, I've always assumed he didn't really mean it. But he must have. He couldn't have cared about me. Not in any normal way."

I could hear the guilt in Garret's voice. He was about to put his father away for life, after all. "It's not a question you can figure out in one sitting," I said. "But if you keep coming back to it, you'll get closer and closer to the truth. And you'll be less and less afraid of it. Even when it hurts."

We sat for several seconds, without saying anything else.

Garret broke the silence. "I'm glad you're here—living with us for a while, I mean," he said.

I reached out, squeezed his shoulder. "I am, too," I said.

21

Julia's mother's house was vintage Martha's Vineyard—an oversized, rehabbed barn on a lush hill within walking distance of the sea. The guesthouse where I was staying was a weathered, gray 1852 cottage that had been moved from Edgartown at the turn of the century. Wild blueberries and gooseberries and grapes grew all around the place, and the scent of sweet pepper bush filled the air.

The first couple of weeks there were Eden. Not only were Billy and Garret coming to me for advice on everything from sports to girls to careers, letting me play the good father, but Julia was combining her neediness and sensuality more magically than ever. There were evenings she wept in my arms over vivid memories of Darwin's cruelty and could be comforted by no one else. She would mix her tears with surprise caresses, the warm wetnesses mingling into a potion that leached to the center of my being. She might whisper she was scared at one moment, that she needed me inside her at the next. And when we made love, it was with such intensity that I lost the boundary between my pleasure and hers, so that I was moved equally by each. Transported.

Those days were like a drug, a drug I wished I could stay on forever. But on Sunday, July 21, just shy of three weeks after Darwin Bishop's arrest, the high ended, and everything began to crash.

The day had been my best on the Vineyard. Julia, her mother, Candace, the boys, and I had lingered over a late, gourmet brunch that drifted effortlessly into an easy day of Julia reading on the porch while I played a lazy game of catch with Garret and Billy, the three of us cooling off in waves that seemed custom-made for body surfing. As evening approached, Julia said she was feeling more herself and suggested we celebrate with her first real excursion— a sunset stroll along the cliffs at Gay Head. I agreed, and we drove there together.

The faces of the 150-foot bluffs glowed like the center of the earth in the day's last light. The tide was low, rhythmically washing the velvet sands below, leaving behind fields of iridescent bubbles.

Julia wrapped both her arms around one of mine as we walked. "For the first time in my life," she said, "I feel safe."

I stopped, turned to her, and kissed her forehead. Her emerald eyes literally sparkled. "Same here," I said.

"You do?" she said.

I nodded.

"You trust me?"

"Of course I trust you," I said.

"Then close your eyes," she said, with a sly smile.

I glanced at the edge of the cliff, three feet away. "If you're already bored with me, you can just tell me."

Julia laughed like a little girl. "You said you trusted me." She kissed me deeply and pressed herself against me, moving her hand to my crotch and moving us a foot closer to the edge. Two more steps, and I'd have been parasailing without a sail. "C'mon, close your eyes," she said, massaging me. "It'll be fun. I promise."

I took a deep breath and closed my eyes until Julia was just a shadow. One of my knees bent automatically, bracing me. An exhilarating combination of passion and fear gripped my heart. Beads of sweat ran off my chest, down the center of my abdomen. I could feel them pool in my navel, then spill over.

Julia's warm, quick tongue moved up my neck, then into my ear. "Keep them closed," she whispered. She let go of me.

I stood there several seconds in a kind of trance, listening to my own breathing and watching Julia back up several feet.

"Don't cheat," she said. She turned to run away.

I lost sight of her in the sun's glare. Fifteen, twenty seconds went by. All I could hear was the wind and rustling grass.

"Okay," Julia called to me, from a distance. "Find me."

I opened my eyes and looked around. The colors of the grass, ocean, sky, and cliffs seemed even more brilliant than before. The sun was a burning, red-orange beach ball hovering on the horizon.

Julia was nowhere in sight.

"Where are you?" I called out.

No answer.

A quarter-mile of low hills stretched before me. Julia could be lying in the wavy grass almost anywhere. I walked away from the cliffs, scanning the ground for footprints. When I'd gone about fifteen yards, I turned to face a small grove of tall, flowering sweet pepper bushes about ten, twelve yards to my right, a subtle path of matted grass leading to it. I had a feeling she was squirreled away inside. I walked toward the bushes. When I had closed to within several feet, I heard her giggle from inside the foliage. I slowly walked the rest of the way and cautiously pushed apart the screen of leafy branches. Then I stood there, staring at her.

Julia was lying on her back on a bed made of her clothes, naked, her feet planted wide apart, her knees bent and touching. She looked like a mermaid in a secret garden, resting between tides. Her silky, black hair moved in an easy breeze that rustled the branches all around her. She smiled bashfully and let her knees drift apart. "You gonna come inside?" she said.

• • •

We got back to the house just after 10:00 P.M. Garret's bodyguard, Pete Magill, was strolling around the front yard. We greeted him, then went inside.

Julia's mother, Candace, was sitting on a well-worn leather couch in the great room, reading a magazine. Beside her, a lighted curio cabinet held a sampling of each of her children's toys. An original Barbie. A GI Joe. A metal race car. A cap gun. She looked up when we walked in. "Did you two have fun?" she asked.

"*I* did," Julia said. "I *think* he did." She laughed.

"We did," I said.

"How's Tess?" Julia asked.

"Asleep," Candace said. "She was no trouble."

"Are the boys at home?" Julia asked.

"Garret is," Candace said. "Billy's at a movie with that boy he met on the beach last week. Jason . . ."

"Sanderson," I said. "Seems like a good kid."

"He could be Billy's first real friend," Julia said. She gave me a smile full of warmth. "Billy's turning a corner. We must have the right doctor in the house."

"I hope so," I said.

"I'm going to go check on Tess and head to bed," Julia said. She kissed my cheek, turned to her mother. "Why don't you two talk a little while? You never do."

Candace looked at me. "I didn't know she was watching us, Frank."

I winked.

"Maybe we will," Candace said to Julia.

I watched Julia walk upstairs, then I sat down in a luxuriously worn leather armchair, catty-corner to the end of the couch.

"She's come a long way," I said.

"She's tough underneath all that pretty," Candace said, her voice elegant, yet kind. Her thinning hands were folded on the magazine now. Her paper-thin skin showed the blue veins running beneath it. "She didn't have it easy growing up, you know."

"She told me a little about your husband," I said.

"That was terrible," Candace said. "Truly."

Julia had told me she had had to compete with her brothers for her lawyer-father's attention, that she hadn't been very successful winning him over. But that didn't sound catastrophic. "What was the worst of it, do you think?" I asked, fishing.

"His ignoring her," Candace said.

I nodded and stayed silent, in hopes she would say more.

She didn't need any encouragement. Maybe she had been anxious to have this discussion. "If Julia did the slightest thing that displeased him, he would stop talking to her, stop looking at her, like she didn't exist." She shook her head. "He wasn't that way with the boys. Not ever."

I glanced at the curio cabinet. A tin carousel with flying, hand-painted horses caught my eye. Next to it sat a little porcelain doll, with lifelike, blue crystal eyes. Such pretty toys. No one showcases the ugly memories. "How long would he ignore her?" I asked.

"It could go on for weeks." She started wringing her hands. "A few times, he kept it up for over a month."

No wonder winning the attention of men was so important to Julia. "You think that's the reason she chose modeling as a career?" I asked. "No one ignores the woman on the runway."

"I would think so," Candace said. "I think it's the reason she made a great many choices in her life."

"Such as?" I said.

"Her marriage, for one—staying as long as she did. I don't think someone else would have taken the abuse for so long."

Candace was right, of course. Julia had learned to tolerate marathons of abuse as a girl, when she was powerless to do anything about it.

"So, why didn't *you* leave?" I asked, surprised at the edge in my voice. It was a question I could have asked my own mother, which explained the anger I was feeling.

Candace looked down at her hands, shook her head. "I don't know," she said. "I was wrong. I should have."

That confession was all it took to swing me back toward empathy. No doubt Candace had her own traumatic life history that explained why she would let her sadistic husband stay in the house. "Julia got out, eventually," I said. "She filed that restraining order and enforced it. That took a lot of bravery."

"I think she's on the right track now," Candace said. She nodded at me. "She found you, after all."

Candace went up to bed, and I started walking back to the guest cottage. The night was cool, about sixty degrees, with a salty breeze off the ocean. The full moon glowed so round and white that it looked like a fake—some idealized version of reality from a kid's drawing.

Halfway to the cottage, I noticed the light still on in Julia's bedroom. Her shutters were open, and I could see Julia pulling her T-shirt out of her shorts. I stopped and stared as she arched her back and pulled the shirt over her head, exposing her perfect breasts. She unbuttoned the top button of her shorts and began to unzip them, the cloth on either side of the zipper falling away from the graceful angles of her pelvis. Even after touching and tasting her again and again, I still hungered to watch her step out of those shorts and the thong she wore underneath.

Just as Julia bent her arms, moved her hands to her waistband, and arched her back, I heard footsteps behind me. I wheeled around and saw Billy standing about fifteen feet from me, half in shadows. I felt like a peeping Tom, caught red-handed. But another part of me felt like I had caught Billy peeping. Had he been lurking outside Julia's window, waiting for her to undress?

"You okay?" I said, not certain what else to say.

He didn't answer.

"Billy?"

"I'm sorry," he said softly.

He sounded so embarrassed and frightened that my worry about his voyeurism was overtaken with worry for him. "We can talk this through," I said, walking toward him. I stopped short after just a few steps. What I saw made me lightheaded. "What the hell happened?" I said.

Billy looked down and ran a trembling hand over his blue and white pinstriped shirt, the front of which was covered with blood. His fingers and palm glistened ruby red in the night.

I broke into a sweat colder than the night air. "Are you all right?" I said instinctively. I stepped closer.

"I think . . . I might have killed somebody," he said. He started to cry.

I stopped moving. "Killed . . . Who?" I said. My eyes frantically searched Billy's other hand for a weapon. I didn't spot one. "Tell me what happened."

He looked at his own bloodied hand.

"What happened?" I shouted.

"I can't remember," he said.

I had to pull Billy toward the cottage. He stared ahead with vacant eyes, occasionally stumbling, nearly collapsing at the threshold. I caught him and helped him to the couch, then unbuttoned his blood-soaked shirt and peeled it off him. He was shaking badly. I was still shocked to see the scars Darwin Bishop's belt had left across his back. I wrapped a blanket around his shoulders. "Tell me what you *do* remember," I said.

He hung his head. "I messed up."

"Messed up, how? C'mon, Billy. Tell me."

He closed his eyes and shook his head.

I picked up the phone. "Tell me every single thing you remember, or I'll call the police, and you can tell them," I said.

He took a deep breath, let it out. He opened his eyes, but kept looking at the floor. "I was with my friend Jason," he said. "We went to the movies. When we got out, three guys from his school were waiting for him. They started bugging him, calling him names. Faggot, pussy, wimp, stupid shit like that. I should have just walked away."

"But you didn't," I said.

"I warned them." He shook his head, gritted his teeth. "I told them, 'Get the fuck away from us. Or I'll . . .' "

"Or you'd—what?"

His upper lip started to tremble. "*Kill them.*" He looked straight at me.

"Then what happened?"

"One of them came right up to me." A tear escaped his eye, ran down his cheek. "He spit in my face."

"What did you do?" I asked.

"I hit him. Then, I'm not sure. Everything just . . . went black."

I wish I had a thousand dollars for every assailant who claims amnesia for the attack. "How did you make it back home?" I asked.

"I guess I was, like, on autopilot. I don't remember much of anything, until I saw you."

I didn't want to call the police unless I absolutely had to. I needed to know what had actually happened. "Can you tell me Jason's phone number?" I asked Billy.

"508-931-1107."

That was quick recall, for somebody struggling with his memory. I picked up the phone and dialed.

"Hello?" a woman answered after a single ring, her voice thick with pretension—lingering too long on the l's, underpronouncing the o. *Hellllleeew?*

"This is Dr. Frank Clevenger," I said. "Is this Ms. Sanderson? Jason's mother?"

"It is," she said, tentatively.

"I'm a close friend of Julia Bishop and her mother, Candace," I said. "Billy's with me right now."

"Oh," she said. Her voice was chilly.

"He's pretty shaken up," I said. "I was hoping you could fill me in on what happened tonight."

"All I can tell you is what Jason told me."

Had I asked for more? "Please," I said.

Sanderson sighed, as if I were asking the world of her. "We've had a continuing problem with a group of boys at Jason's school. We're year-round here, you know, and they've teased him for an eternity—all the way back to second grade. Jason isn't a slight boy, but he has the habit of retreating when confronted."

I had a sneaking suspicion Jason had gotten into that habit at home, backing down from Mommy. "Children can be very cruel," I said. "And, tonight? What happened tonight?"

"More of the same, apparently. Just name-calling."

More of the same. Sanderson wasn't being very helpful. "Billy came home with blood on his shirt," I said, hoping to shift her mind into gear. "Did Jason mention a fight?"

"A fight. Well, yes, of course. If you want to call it that. Billy attacked the three boys," she said. "Bloodied noses. Split lips. Apparently, a broken arm."

Relief washed over me. At least it didn't sound like Billy had killed anyone. "Is Jason all right?" I asked.

"He's frightened. He said Billy flew into a terrible rage." She paused. "He was actually foaming at the mouth."

"Did Jason mention that one of the boys had spit at Billy first?"

"No," she said. "As I understood it, name-calling seems to have been the extent of it, until Billy—"

"Billy can't stomach bullies," I said. I glanced at the scars across his back.

"I understand," Sanderson said. Her tone suggested otherwise. She was silent a few moments. "I am glad you called, on another front," she said finally, her voice descending into an almost comical mixture of pretension and gravity, like William F. Buckley stammering that you had cancer and your situation was utterly hopeless.

"Oh?" I said.

"We had a very distressing thing happen with Billy before the boys went out for their movie tonight," she said.

A pregnant pause. "Would it be more appropriate to discuss it with Julia?"

"Julia's still a little under the weather," I said. "I'll certainly share whatever you tell me with her."

"Very well, then," she said. "My husband and I have started something of a second family. We have a new baby. Two months old."

"Congratulations," I said, not sure exactly where she was going, but not feeling good about the general direction. Not enough time had passed since Brooke's murder for infants to be linked with anything but with death in my mind. I looked over at Billy, who was trying to wipe the blood off his chest.

"Before the boys left, Jason had a few chores to finish up around the house—nothing major, picking up his belongings in the yard, and so forth."

"Right," I said, hungry for the punch line.

"While he completed them, he left Billy alone in his bedroom. Jason has a new Nintendo game the boys have enjoyed."

"Okay."

"And when Jason had finished up outside, he asked my husband to let Billy know to come downstairs, so the boys could be off."

My patience had worn thin. "So what happened?" I said, more pointedly.

"Just this: My husband found Billy in the nursery, next to Naomi's bassinet, staring at her. She was napping. I had put her down about an hour earlier."

Despite the fact that Darwin had been charged with Brooke's murder, it couldn't have been comforting for Mr. Sanderson to find the former lead suspect in the case eyeing his infant daughter. "What did Billy say he was doing?" I asked.

"My husband asked him that. He didn't respond. He seemed like he was—away, in some sort of trance. Nicholas had to lay hands on him—jostle him a bit—to bring him back to the moment."

She could have said Billy seemed dazed or in a fog. *Trance* is one of those code words people reserve for psychopaths. "You were worried about him harming your daughter?" I said, to cut to the chase.

Billy looked at me, his eyes sharpening.

"I'm not saying that, exactly," Sanderson said. She paused. "Friends of ours on Nantucket have told us that Billy had problems, long before the tragedy with his sister, Brooke. I'm speaking of his stealing. Hurting animals."

"That's true," I said. It didn't look like Martha's Vineyard was going to offer Billy a second chance.

"And one never knows what to believe these days," she said. "About anything. It seems that there's always another shoe waiting to drop. Another bit of intrigue."

Translation: The police could have screwed up and wrongly accused Darwin Bishop of infanticide when his crazed, Russian adoptee son was really the guilty one. Maybe Darwin even sacrificed himself to shield the boy from prosecution. "I understand completely," I said.

"So we—my husband and I—talked it over. We'd prefer Billy not visit our home, anymore. It's best he not spend time with Jason, either."

I felt in my own gut what I knew Billy would be feeling: disappointment, isolation, abandonment. Losing a friend can be tough for anyone, but for an orphan like Billy who has just lost a sister . . . "I'll certainly let him know," I said. "And I'll make sure he abides by your wishes."

"Thank you so much," she said. "It's a difficult thing to speak about."

"Have a nice night," I said, as kindly as I could manage. "I hope Billy taught those boys a lesson. Maybe they'll stop torturing your son."

"Yes, well. Good night, then," she said.

I sat down on the couch next to Billy. He started to weep. "Listen to me," I said. "You didn't kill anyone. But you did hurt those boys who were picking on Jason. The way it sounds, you hurt them pretty badly—maybe even broke a bone or two."

He nodded somberly, getting control of himself again. "I lost it," he said.

"There's something else," I said.

Billy had overheard enough of my phone conversation to know I was referring to the Sandersons' baby. "I was just standing there, trying to imagine what Brooke went through," he said. "I haven't let myself. Not once. But when I walked past Jason's sister's room and saw her sleeping, I couldn't stop imagining it." He squinted at the floor. "So I just went in there and watched her. I mean, think about it: Waking up and not being able to breathe. Suffocating in a little bed with your mother downstairs, while your father watches you die."

As much as I welcomed Billy empathizing with the suffering of others, I was worried he missed how inappropriate his behavior had been. "Mr. Sanderson had trouble getting your attention. He had to shake you."

"I was staring at her, but I saw Brooke."

When he looked at me, his eyes were filled with sadness, but I also thought I saw (Did I, though?) the slightest hint of morbid curiosity—something close to excitement. "You lost control with those boys," I said. "And it was wrong to go into Jason's sister's room without permission."

Billy nodded.

I looked out the cottage window, at the full moon, gathering the will to tell him the consequences. "The Sandersons are going to need time to feel comfortable with you again. They don't want you to visit the house—or to spend time with Jason."

Billy's eyes thinned. "Why not?"

"You worried them," I said.

"I stood up for Jason," he said.

"No. You went beyond standing up for him. You also wandered around the Sandersons' home, into the nursery and . . ."

"What are they saying?" he said, indignantly. "They think *I* killed Brooke?"

"The Sandersons are thinking about their baby," I said,

dodging the question. "The long and short of it is that you probably remind them that life is fragile. And they don't want to be reminded of that right now. They're new parents."

"Bullshit," he said. "They think I did it." His lip curled. No more trembling. No more tears. "Fuck them. They can all go straight to hell." He stood up. "I'm not going to stop hanging out with Jason, just because his parents are uptight assholes." He took a step toward the door.

I stood and held up a hand, hoping to coax him to talk through his anger. But before I could say a word, he shoved me out of the way and stormed out.

"Billy!" I called after him.

He broke into a jog and disappeared in the direction of the house.

22

I gave Billy a few minutes, hoping he would cool down, then followed him to the house. I let myself in, not wanting to wake anyone. But I found Julia, her mother, and Garret standing in the living room, all of them looking uneasy. Billy had woken everyone in the house when he burst in, slamming the door behind him, cursing me, the Sandersons, and his own miserable existence all the way to his room.

"What happened?" Julia asked me. She was dressed in the simple white T-shirt I had watched her taking off. It barely covered her. As I looked at her, she glanced self-consciously at the tops of her thighs.

"Why don't we talk about it privately?" I suggested.

"He screamed he wished he was dead," Garret said.

I wasn't sure which of the details Garret and Candace really needed to know. "He got into a fight tonight with some bullies. They're kids who bother Jason Sanderson all the time. Things got out of hand, and the Sandersons are worried about Billy's temper. They don't want him to spend time with their son anymore."

Candace shook her head in dismay.

"Was anyone badly hurt?" Julia said. "Did Billy . . . ?"

"A broken arm sounds like the worst of it," I said. "There could be legal charges, but"—I caught Julia's eye—"let's talk about this privately and decide what you think we should do."

"I think that's a good idea," she said.

We went into the dining room. Julia and I sat at the table, the lights dim in harmony with the early morning hour. I told her everything I knew. "Billy's so charming it's easy to forget how much help he still needs," I said.

"Do you think he should go somewhere?" Julia asked. "A private hospital or something? Wouldn't that help him if he's charged with something?"

The idea of putting Billy in another hospital, right after Payne Whitney, wasn't very appealing to me, but I knew it might be the only answer. "We should talk with him about it, when he's able to. And we should call Carl Rossetti, in case Billy needs a lawyer again." I glanced at the clock. Almost 2:00 A.M. "The police haven't shown up so far. That's a good sign."

"Is there anywhere he could go that's . . . comfortable?" Julia asked. "You know, not a locked psych ward type of thing. That would be so horrible for him."

I thought about that for a few seconds. A possibility came to mind. "I could talk to Ed Shapiro, a friend of mine who runs the Riggs Center in Stockbridge," I said. "It's more like a retreat than a hospital. They call it a 'therapeutic community.' The patients live in cottages and get psychotherapy every day." I took a deep breath, shook my head. "I just don't know if they'd take someone with a history of violence like Billy's, even as a favor."

"It seemed like everything was going so well," Julia said. She took my hand. "Not much of a honeymoon."

Not much of a honeymoon. If I had stopped to think about that line, I might have realized I had heard it before—from Lilly. And it might have started me wondering about one very important similarity between the two women. But the trouble we were having with Billy was making me feel even closer to Julia. My mind was already starting to conceive of him as our child. I ran my fingers up the underside of Julia's arm, then stopped, noticing Garret at the entryway to the dining room. I took my hand back. We'd been careful to avoid physical contact in front of the boys. "What's up, champ?" I asked.

"I think I better tell you something," he said.

"What?" I asked.

Garret walked closer to us, his face solemn.

"Garret?" Julia said. "What is this about?"

"Billy," he said.

"You want to sit down?"

"No." He seemed jittery. "I wasn't going to say anything," he said, glancing first at me, then at Julia.

"What's bothering you?" I said.

"I found something," he said, the nail of his third finger picking at the skin at the tip of his thumb.

I waited.

"I was just hoping," he started. "I don't know what I was hoping."

"What did you find, Garret?" Julia asked, kindly but firmly.

"A cat," he said, looking up at her.

"A cat," I repeated, intuiting the rest, but hoping I was wrong.

"I was on my way to the stream." He looked at me. "There's a stream in the woods, way in back of the guest cottage. I go there sometimes, to think. So does Billy. And I found this cat."

"Dead," I said.

Garret nodded.

Julia's face fell. I instinctively reached for her hand again, but she quickly pulled it away, flashing me a look that reminded me to keep our intimacies under wraps.

"Maybe it just died," Garret said. "I mean, you never know."

"Sometimes you do," I said.

"I'm glad you told us," Julia said. "Thank you."

"Sorry," he said, more to me than his mother.

I shook my head. "Nothing to apologize for," I said, giving him the best smile I could muster. "You did the right thing. We didn't get Billy out of prison to watch him get himself put back in."

The door to Billy's bedroom was closed. I knocked. No response. "It's Frank," I said. Still, nothing. I gently tried the door. Locked. "Billy, let me in," I said. A few seconds passed, then the springs of his mattress creaked. A few seconds later the door opened—a little.

"What?" he said, without looking at me.

"Got a couple minutes?" I asked.

He turned around and headed back toward his bed. But he left the door open.

I walked into his room. He was seated on the edge of his bed, arms crossed, rocking slowly back and forth. "This is so unfair," he said bitterly.

I sat down next to him. "I think it is fair," I said.

He stopped rocking and looked at me as if I were betraying him.

"I don't think there's any way for the Sandersons to get inside your head and figure out why you were staring at their daughter," I said.

He looked down.

"And I think you went way beyond defending Jason," I said. "I think you exploded."

He shook his head, swallowed hard, as if he was about to cry again.

I put a hand on his shoulder. "You blacked out. It's lucky you didn't kill one of them."

"What do we do?" he asked, holding back his tears.

I felt as though he had opened the door the rest of the way. "I want to talk with a friend of mine who runs a place called the Riggs Center."

"A fucking psych ward again?" he said.

"It's not a psych ward. It's a place, like a retreat, out in western Mass."

"Oh, sorry," he said. "My mistake. A funny farm."

"The medical director is a personal friend. He . . ."

"I'm not going anywhere," he said. "Leave me alone."

I hadn't planned to bring up the cat Garret had found, but I needed to convince Billy to help himself, without destroying all hope for a relationship between the boys. "I found a cat in back of the guest cottage," I lied. "On the way to the stream?"

Billy looked at me, blinking nervously.

"A dead cat," I said.

The blinking stopped. "And?" he said.

"And that worries me, too," I said. "It should worry you."

"Why?" he said. "You think I killed it?"

I didn't respond, which Billy and I both understood to be my answer.

Something went out of Billy's eyes, something I hadn't fully seen until it was gone—his faith in me. What I couldn't know was whether it was anything more than the faith of a sociopath who had counted on me never to break ranks with him. He stood up. "Leave," he said, obviously trying to control himself. His hands balled up into fists.

"Billy—"

"Please," he said, the muscles in his arms twitching.

I stood up. "Think about what I suggested," I said. "It's the right thing to do." I walked past him and out of his room.

When I went to sleep, just before 3:00 A.M., lights were still burning in the main house. At 3:45 A.M. someone knocked on my front door. For some reason I assumed it would be Julia, up worrying about Billy, wanting to talk things through. I pulled myself out of bed, pulled on my jeans, and went to let her in. But when I looked through the glass door, I saw Billy standing there. For the first time, seeing him made me picture where my Browning Baby handgun was tucked away—in the nightstand drawer. I opened the door.

"I didn't want this to wait until the morning," he said, sounding apologetic.

"It is morning," I said with a wink.

"Right," he said. "I guess it is."

I thought about inviting him in, but thought again. "What's up?"

He looked straight at me. "I didn't kill any cat."

"Okay . . ." I said.

"But I'll go to that Riggs place."

I nodded. One step at a time, I thought to myself. Part of me was glad Billy was at least shamed enough by destroying a defenseless animal to deny having done it. If he went through with treatment, he could take the step of admitting what he had done later. "What changed your mind?"

"Garret."

"Garret?" I said.

"We talked—really talked—for the first time," Billy said. "About being adopted and living with Darwin and the beatings and everything. How I got the worst of it." He shrugged. "Garret feels like he let me down."

Maybe it had taken another crisis to start another phase of healing for the Bishops—this one a healing of the divide between Garret and Billy. "I'm glad for you," I said. "Both of you. It would be wonderful if you ended up being close."

"I told him what you wanted me to do, and he said I should do it. He asked me to do it. For him."

I would have preferred Billy fully accept that he *needed* help. But I wasn't going to turn down the gift from Garret. "I'll set it up," I said.

"Good," he said. He looked away, then back at me, almost shyly.

"What?" I asked.

"Would you take me there? To Riggs?" he said. "You know the doctor who runs it. If you were hanging out nearby, he might let you visit me during the first week or two."

"Sure," I said.

"That was Garret's idea, too. So if it's asking too much, or . . ."

"It's a great idea," I said.

Monday, July 22, 2002

By 9:30 A.M., Ed Shapiro had cleared Billy for a July 25 admission to Riggs, cutting the usual four-month waiting list to four days. It pays to have friends in quiet places.

Garret and Billy actually took a turn making breakfast for Julia, Candace, and me, whipping up waffles and sliced fruit like the pros do. I had to remind myself again of Billy's pathology in order to see past the goodwill filling the house to all the hard work it would take to keep Billy safe.

We planned to charter a sailboat and spend a lazy day together as a family. I stopped back at the cottage to grab a few things. A large manila envelope was sitting in the woven straw basket that hung next to my door. I picked it up and saw that it had been sent by Dr. Laura Mossberg from Payne Whitney, postmarked July 18. I figured she had finally sent along one of the old medical records on Billy I had asked her for.

I opened the envelope on my way into the cottage, then sat down on the couch to read the cover letter:

> *Dr. Clevenger:*
> Herewith, records of urologic care rendered Mr. Darwin Bishop, which only reached my desk today. I would normally be prohibited from sharing these materials with you, but your visit to the unit was preceded by Mr. and Mrs. Bishop signing our standard (and blanket) release covering all family medical records at Cornell Medical Center/Payne Whitney Clinic. I do not know if the enclosed materials would have had any bearing on your investigation.

Unfortunately, I have not received prior treatment records for Billy Bishop from other facilities.

I would be happy to hear from you in the future.

All good,
Laura Mossberg

P.S. I have also enclosed a copy of *I Don't Want to Talk About It*, a very good book on men and trauma. I hope you won't take offense (and that you might even take the time to read it).

I smiled. Talk about not giving up on a patient. And I wasn't even paying her. I started to read through the packet of medical records. Two pages in, I stopped short on a form marked "Screening Assessment Tool." My pulse moved into my temples as I read the first paragraph:

Mr. Darwin Bishop, a 50-year-old, married, Caucasian male, father of two adopted boys, presents for bilateral vasectomy. The patient informs us that his wife is supportive and that his decision is based on a long-held philosophical position that "it isn't fair to bring children into a world like this one." Mr. Bishop states that his perspective took shape during his experiences in Vietnam, on which he refuses to elaborate. He has held his belief for many years and rates his likelihood of changing his perspective and wishing to father biological children at zero percent.

The form was signed by Paisley Marshall, MD, and dated April 15, 1999, about two years before Brooke and Tess Bishop were conceived.

My mind raced from one fact to the next, almost in disbelief. Darwin Bishop was infertile. Brooke and Tess Bishop were not his biological daughters. Julia had had an affair and become pregnant with the twins.

I flipped page after page, half-expecting to see a note describing Bishop's change of heart about the procedure, but instead stopped on a surgical note dated May 12, 1999:

> Patient reaffirms desire for complete steriliza-tion. All risks described, including infection, al-lergic reaction to medications, pain, bleeding.
>
> Patient declines cross-over procedure.
>
> Patient received local anesthetic 0.5% Mar-caine with epinephrine and Versed to induce calm.
>
> Vital signs stable at onset of procedure.
>
> At surgery, normal appearing bilateral sper-matic cords and vas deferens were dissected free, segmental resections performed, and the ends ligated with 3-0 vicryl suture and sealed with Hyfrecator.

Bishop's having declined a cross-over procedure, a more complicated vasectomy that can be reversed, meant his in-fertility would be permanent.

Suddenly, Julia's explanation about the letter Claire Buckley had found sounded even more incredible. Her ther-apist Marion Eisenstadt obviously hadn't been the intended recipient. Julia had written the letter to her lover. The father of her children.

The investigation into Brooke's murder hadn't simply failed to ferret out a romantic partner of Julia's. We had neglected to interview the twins' biological father—a po-tential suspect.

I thought of trying to reach North Anderson, but knew he would be in Paris for the next ten days, spending a seemingly well-earned vacation with Tina. And I wasn't sure I needed his help. I didn't have a shred of evidence, nor any real suspicion, that Darwin Bishop had been wrongly charged with Brooke's murder. My doubts centered on Julia; she had lied to me and left me in the dark. Her character was again in question.

I had a job to do, but this time it was for me to do alone: to find out exactly who I had fallen in love with.

I remember the rest of that day in snapshots: the sun-soaked vistas of Vineyard Sound, Julia's surreal beauty, Candace's quiet grace, Billy and Garret working the sails and rudder together, a strong breeze blowing the hair off their foreheads, making them look younger, stronger, more handsome than I had ever seen them. The scenes would have made perfect postcards, which should have made me wonder whether the serenity was real or staged. But my focus was on the big lie—Julia's lie. I turned it around in my mind, trying to find an angle that would allow me to explain it away, to excuse it without further inquiry. I was that in love with her.

There were parts of the lie I had already accepted. I had no illusion that Julia had been faithful to Darwin Bishop. I had no lingering expectation that she would fill me in on every chapter of her romantic life. And I could even accept a chapter that included her being impregnated by a man other than her husband.

What I couldn't dismiss was the fact that she had jeopardized the investigation into her daughter's murder by withholding information.

Something else bothered me. A lot. Why hadn't Darwin Bishop disclosed the fact that the twins were not his biological children? Wouldn't he have wanted the police to worry about another potential suspect? Or did he fear that a jury might more readily believe him capable of killing another man's child?

After a day chockful of photo ops, Julia, the boys, Candace, and I got back to the house just after seven. I would have waited until the next day to confront Julia, but she called the cottage just after midnight.

"Come see me," she whispered.

"In your room?" I said.

"The boys are sleeping," she said. "We wore them out."

"Why don't you come over here?" I asked.

She giggled. "Because I just showered, and my hair is wet, and I have no clothes on, and I'm already in bed."

"I'll be there," I said.

I let myself into the main house and walked up to Julia's room. Her door was open, but the lights were out, and the room was almost pitch black.

"Don't turn on the light," she whispered from bed. "Just close the door."

I did as she asked. "You like it when I can't see," I said.

"I'll be your eyes," she said. "I'm on my stomach. I have two pillows under my hips and another one I can bite down on, if I need to. Is that clear?"

I felt my way toward the bed and sat down on the edge of the mattress. I reached out. My hand glided over the velvety smooth skin of of Julia's lower back. I sighed. "We have to talk about something," I said.

"After," she said.

I let my hand move to the even softer curves of her ass before I summoned the resolve to pull away. "No," I said. "We need to talk first." I felt her pulling the sheet over her and reaching for the bedside lamp.

"What's going on?" she asked, squinting at me in the lamplight. She was holding the edge of the sheet just below her breasts.

I looked away, in order to focus my thoughts. The walls of the room were covered with pretty oil paintings of the ocean and marshes and with black-and-white photographs of Julia as a little girl and young woman. "I got some medical records in the mail from New York today," I said.

"And?" she said.

I looked back at her. She had drawn the sheet to her chin. I didn't see any reason to be subtle. "I know about the vasectomy," I said. "I know that Darwin didn't father the twins."

Julia looked at me blankly, as if she hadn't decided whether to respond directly or to be evasive.

"Why didn't you tell me during the investigation—me, or North Anderson?"

She nodded to herself, then looked back at me. "This may not make a lot of sense to you, but I didn't say anything because I promised Darwin I never would. I promised him before the twins were born, when he was pressuring me to get an abortion. Keeping what had happened a secret seemed to be the only thing that mattered to him." A bitter smile played across her lips. "I swore on Brooke's and Tess's lives."

"You should have told us," I said. "And not just so we could interview the twins' biological father. A man like Darwin might feel you forced him into a situation he didn't want to live with. He might have decided to fix things his own way. It goes to his motive."

"When you bury the truth the way Darwin and I agreed to," Julia said, "it's almost as if it becomes untouchable. Like it doesn't exist, anymore. I didn't even think of it as relevant to what happened. We were all so focused on Billy as the guilty one."

"When we had lunch together in Boston, at Bomboa," I said, "you asked me whether I thought Darwin was capable of destroying his 'flesh and blood.' Why did you choose those words?"

" 'Why did I choose those words?' You sound like a detective," she said.

"I'm no detective. I just want to know. Why those words?"

"No reason. I didn't mean it literally. It's a cliché. I meant his children." She paused. "They are, legally. I mean, we're married."

"And you still say the letter that Claire found . . . was to your therapist, not the man you got pregnant by."

She looked at me askance. "Now I get it," she said. "You

don't believe me anymore. About anything."

I didn't respond.

"Because I didn't tell you everything about my *sex life?*" she half-shouted.

"Quiet," I said. "The boys."

"Because I didn't tell you," she said, barely keeping her voice down, "that my husband was so soured on the world and so controlling that he wouldn't give me children? I didn't spill my guts and tell you how it feels being treated like a pretty thing that's fun to fuck, knowing you'll never be a mother?" She shook her head. "This may come as a news flash, Frank, but I've been lonely. And scared. It hasn't been easy living with Darwin. So when I met someone a couple years ago who seemed to care about me, I reached out to him. I thought there was a chance we could have a life together. I got pregnant, and he couldn't handle it. We stopped seeing each other."

"Who was he?" I asked.

"I can't say," Julia said. "He's an acquaintance of Darwin's. He's very well known." She paused. "He was at Brooke's funeral. We didn't even speak."

"I'm supposed to believe you had a sexual relationship with an acquaintance of your husband's, bore his children, and have no contact with him now?"

"You know what *I* can't believe?" she said. "Where do you get off thinking that everything that happened to me before you arrived on the scene is your business? Have I asked you for a list of every woman you've fucked?" She looked away. "Leave me alone," she said.

"Julia . . ."

"Get out," she said. "Just get out."

23

Garret was standing in his doorway when I stepped into the hall. "Rough night?" he said. He was dressed in blue jeans, no top. He had every bit of the muscular definition Billy did, including a chest like a welterweight fighter and a washboard abdomen. He seemed jumpy—maybe worried, maybe excited.

I wasn't happy that the heat I had generated with Julia had reached him. "Looks like that's how it's ending up," I said. "Sorry we woke you."

"I wasn't that tired," he said.

I nodded toward his room. "Want to talk?"

"You're probably all talked out," he said.

I wanted to reassure Garret that things weren't falling completely apart, even though I was worried they were—first with Billy, now with Julia. Both within about twenty-four hours. "Actually, I wouldn't mind a little company," I said. "I won't take much of your time."

"Cool," he said. He backed into his room.

I followed him. He hadn't gotten around to organizing his things; boxes overflowed with clothes, photo albums, a few long-lensed cameras, hundreds of film canisters. I took a seat at his desk.

"It's a total mess in here," he said. "Embarrassing." He started picking up, piling everything into his closet. "This is a hard time for my mother," he said, glancing at me.

"I would think so," I said.

"Not just recovering from the beating and all that," he said. He grabbed another overflowing box. "The changes. Darwin not being here, first and foremost. Even though it's a good thing, it's a big thing, you know?"

That was true. Bishop had occupied a lot of physical and emotional space in the household. His absence opened up a void. Even the loss of negative energy can be dizzying. "I guess it's a little like coming home from a war," I said. "The demons stay with you a while."

Garret jammed the box into the closet, forced the door closed, then turned and looked at me. "For instance," he said, "without getting shrinky with the shrink, she wanted you to hit her in there."

"What?" I said.

"She yelled," Garret said. "Darwin would have gone ballistic. She was testing you to see if you would hit her."

Garret's insight made some sense. I had asked Julia to trust me, to fully disclose her past. One way to interpret her extreme response was as a way of probing how far she could push me without me pushing back. "You know your mother pretty well," I said.

He shrugged. "I've noticed the same kind of thing about myself since you've been living with us," he said. "Like this room. I could never have left it this way with Darwin around. Not unless I wanted the strap. I think I've let it get this messy to see if you'd cut me slack."

"It's really not my place to tell you how to keep your room," I said.

"You're pretty much the man of the house," he said.

I wasn't feeling much like the man of the house. I nodded at his desk. "So what are you reading, anyhow?"

"Poetry," he said.

"Who?" I asked, looking at the title, *The Land of Heart's Desire*.

"Yeats," he said.

"Is he your favorite?"

"I don't really have a favorite," he said, easing himself

into a beanbag chair in the corner of the room. "I like Emerson and Poe just as much. Maybe better."

I glanced up at the bookshelves, the only space in the room that was neat and clean. The volumes were arranged alphabetically, by author. I scanned the names. Auden, Beckett, Emerson, Hegel, Hemingway, Locke, Paz, Poe, Shakespeare. Yeats was at the end of the shelf—seven, eight volumes strong by himself. "What do you like about poetry?" I asked.

"Saying more with less," he said. "People use too many words. They become meaningless."

"Agreed," I said. "You like to write poetry, too?"

"Some," he said. "Just for myself."

That seemed to say I shouldn't expect to read any of Garret's work any time soon. "You're the most important audience," I said.

"Darwin would get pissed if he caught me writing," Garret said. "He said it was for girls. That's one of the reasons he wouldn't let me stay too long in my room."

"That's ridiculous," I said. "Nobody thought of Hemingway as a girl."

"His mother did," Garret said.

I smiled. Hemingway's mother had dressed the budding author in girl's clothes from time to time, one reason he might have become almost hyperbolically male as an adult. "Except her," I said.

"Maybe I will show you some of my stuff, someday," Garret said tentatively.

"I'd love to see anything you write," I said.

He looked out his window, then back at me. "She just needs time—and some space. Maybe it's good you're taking Billy to that Riggs place."

"I want to thank you for helping him with the decision to go there," I said. "It's the right one. You think you can hold the fort down a couple weeks by yourself?"

"No problem," he said.

"I'm sorry to worry you—about your mom and me," I said.

"Don't be," he said. "I'll never have to worry the way I used to."

I left Garret's room just before 1:00 A.M. As I walked by Billy's room, his light went out. Had he been eavesdropping, I wondered, or had Garret and I simply been keeping him up by talking too loudly?

On my way out of the house I paused to look at the toys Candace had arranged in the curio cabinet. A little windup bear with brass cymbals caught my eye. It was the kind of thing that had probably kept Julia entertained for hours as a child. I smiled, thinking how delighted she must have been the first time she wound it up and watched it perform, how simple her pleasures were back then.

A chill blanketed me. Because in my heart I knew, without knowing exactly why, that everything really had started to unravel, and that she would never be mine.

My sleep that night was broken into naps. Each time I awakened, it was with another memory of Julia, Darwin, or the boys. I pictured the first time I had met Julia outside the Bishop estate, remembered our lunch at Bomboa Restaurant in Boston. I thought back to my visit with Billy on the locked unit at Payne Whitney, to my verbal altercation with Darwin at Brooke's funeral, to Anderson and me searching Garret's locker at the Brant Point Racket Club. I thought again of Claire Buckley's demeanor when she had turned the mystery letter over to North Anderson and me. And I reviewed what Anderson and I had each said to Julia at Mass General after she had been assaulted, what she had said to us. The sleep between memories became shorter and shorter, the images more and more vivid. It was as if my mind was replaying the last three weeks, looking for a window onto the Bishop family's secret.

At 3:47 A.M. that window opened wide, letting in an icy wind that literally made me shiver. I sat up in bed, my mind snapping to full attention with a memory not from days or weeks before, but just hours. It was something I had seen in the main house, and it felt like a stray, abnormal laboratory result on a patient, one that tells you that a cancer long thought vanquished has been quietly invading deep into the bone, eating away at the marrow.

A whole train of thoughts began moving through my mind. I stood, squinting into the darkness, starting to connect the dots in a very ugly picture. An almost unthinkable one. I started to pace. The thoughts came faster and faster, careening through the night. I felt nauseated and light-headed.

I did not return to bed until more than two hours had passed. I did not sleep at all. Because I was no longer convinced Darwin Bishop had killed little Brooke. I was growing more and more certain, in fact, that someone else had. Someone I had trusted. And for reasons that both saddened and sickened me.

A cold sweat covered me. If I was right, that person was still stalking Tess, who was sleeping in her nursery, not fifty feet from my door.

My mind raced until sunrise, refining a strategy to expose the killer. It was a strategy of psychological warfare designed to quickly strip away the person's emotional defenses, uncapping explosive rage. If it worked, whoever had taken Brooke's life would make an attempt on mine within the next twenty-four hours.

Tuesday, July 23, 2002

At 9:00 A.M. I called the Payne Whitney clinic and had the operator page Laura Mossberg. She answered a few minutes later.

"It's Frank Clevenger," I told her. "I need your help."

"Really," she said, that special, therapeutic kindness in her voice.

"With the Bishop case," I said, to keep her off mine.

"I thought the case was closed," she said. "I read about the father being arrested. I was shocked."

"You just never know with people," I said.

"*You* seem to," she said. "You never believed Billy was guilty."

I sidestepped the compliment. "There's one loose end I still want to tie," I said. "For my own peace of mind."

"What's that?" she asked. "Does it relate to the records I sent?"

"Yes," I said. "And I wondered if you could get me a little more information from the family's medical records."

"What is it that you need?" she said.

"I'm hoping you might be able to find blood types for each member of the Bishop family, including all the children," I said. "Julia, the twins, and the boys."

"That shouldn't be a problem," Mossberg said. "We have the surgical record from Mr. Bishop's vasectomy, his wife's obstetrical chart, and birth records for the little girls. I'm sure Billy and Garret were also blood-typed, given that they were adopted."

"Excellent," I said.

"I won't ask why you want the data," she said, her tone hinting that she really wanted to ask.

"Well, I appreciate the help," I said. "I don't expect the information to change anything, but I'll certainly let you know if it does."

She laughed at the way I had avoided her curiosity. "I'll always be interested to hear from you," she said.

After we'd hung up, I walked back over to the main house. I wanted to start tightening the psychological vise on the Bishops.

Luckily, I found everyone together, assembled in the kitchen for what were becoming routine family breakfasts. "Hey," Billy said, from his seat across from Garret at the breakfast nook. "Sleeping in these days?"

Garret gave me a good-morning nod. I returned it.

Julia was frying eggs. She didn't turn around.

I glanced at Tess, playing with Teletubbies in her Pack 'N Play, then walked over to Julia. She was wearing tight, white tennis shorts that showed the outline of her thong. I gave her a slap on the ass, hard enough to be certain the boys wouldn't miss it. Before she could move out of the way, I kissed her neck. "God, you taste good," I said.

She turned around, controlled rage burning on her face. I gently touched her cheek.

The eggs sizzled.

Julia cleared her throat. "Sleep well?" she said tightly.

"Great. You?"

"Yeah, great," she said. She glanced at Candace, who looked down and went back to cutting asparagus when I tried to make eye contact with her. It seemed pretty clear there had been a mother-daughter chat before I'd arrived.

I stepped away from Julia and walked over to the breakfast nook. Billy slid over to make room for me. I sat down. "What's on tap for today, champ?" I asked him.

"Not much," he said. "I was supposed to hang out with Jason." He shrugged. "That won't be happening."

"I'm trying to convince him to go fishing," Garret said.

"Where?" I said to Garret. "I'll give you guys a lift, if you want."

"We don't need a ride," he said. "We can fish the stream. There's nothing big running in there, but it's fun, anyhow."

I nudged Billy. "Why not give it a try?"

He gave me a fake half-smile.

I winked at him, nodded toward Julia, then got up and walked back over to her.

She saw me coming this time. The expression on her face told me to keep my distance.

I stopped a few feet from her. I held up one finger, mouthed, "I'm sorry," and saw her expression mellow slightly. "Forget those medical records," I whispered. "Forget the letter, too. I'll never bring them up again. No looking back."

She searched my eyes for sincerity, nodded once, tentatively.

I took another step toward her and took her hand gently in mine. I leaned and whispered into her ear. "Meet me at the cottage later."

She looked toward the breakfast nook self-consciously.

"I couldn't sleep last night," I whispered, even more quietly. "I couldn't stop thinking how much I wanted you."

She blushed. "Cut it out," she said, catching her lower lip seductively between her teeth.

"I'll be in the cottage," I said, raising my voice to a stage whisper. I backed away.

Candace smiled knowingly at me.

"I'm gonna take a quick walk," I said, looking at Billy and Garret. "Anyone up for it?"

Billy looked down at his food.

Garret stood up. "Sure," he said.

"Catch the rest of you later," I said, and headed out with him.

Garret and I hadn't gotten ten yards from the house when his bodyguard Pete appeared behind us. That was unusual. He and Garret had gotten sloppy and were rarely together on the property. I turned around. "We'll be fine," I called to Pete, waving him off.

We started down a path that ran about two hundred yards, curving toward the ocean, then turning back on itself to form a kind of ellipse, with Candace's house at one apex and the horizon at the other. "Your mom seems a little better now," I said.

"It's like I told you," he said. "She was testing you."

"I've been thinking about that," I said.

"What about it?"

"Maybe I'm being tested in more than one way. This whole thing with Billy—the trouble with the Sandersons and killing that cat—could be a test, too. To see if I'll stick by him, by the whole family."

"Could be," Garret said.

"So I'm thinking I need to define my role here."

"What do you mean?"

"Like I think we should be a real family," I said, watching for his reaction. "That way Billy can look to me as a real father. He'll be able to count on me. You, too."

Garret stopped walking and stared at me.

We were still within throwing distance of the house. I set the jaws of the trap I was laying: "I'm going to ask your mom to marry me," I said.

"Wow," he said. He looked confused. "Wow," he said again.

"How would you feel about that?" I asked him.

"Great," he said. He sounded like he meant it.

"I know it would take some getting used to, for everyone," I said. "I haven't even mentioned the idea to your mother. But, suddenly, it seems obvious that it's the right thing to do." I looked toward the ocean, a rippling blue-green blanket beneath the sun-soaked horizon. "I have to tell you, Garret, I've never felt the way I feel about her. When I'm with her, I feel complete. When I'm not with her, I want to be." I looked back at him. "Have you ever felt that way?"

"I don't know," he said. "Maybe."

"Then you haven't. You'd know for sure. It's the best feeling in the world," I said.

He nodded.

"You're leaving for Yale in a couple weeks?" I said. "Believe me, there'll be more than one coed who turns your head. I hope one of them moves you the way your mom moves me."

"I guess I'll find out," he said.

"And, I mean, there's another reason we should make it official: I don't feel good about—well, you know—sharing a room with your mom until we're married. Neither does she."

Even Garret, at seventeen, recognized I had invited him across a boundary deeper than a World War II trench. "That's between you and her," he said.

"We just want to be respectful," I said. I let a few seconds pass. "I'm thinking we should elope. I'm going to ask her to fly to Vegas with me—maybe leave tomorrow."

"She isn't divorced yet," Garret said, grinning.

"Nevada won't sweat the details," I said. "The paperwork will fall into place, eventually."

"Sounds . . . amazing," he said.

"Not a word to your mother," I said. I didn't mention keeping Billy out of the loop. I knew Garret would fill him in within the next five minutes. I wanted him to.

"I guess I'll head back," Garret said. "Pretty amazing news."

"I'll see you later?"

"Later," he said.

I watched him as he made his way toward the house. Out of the corner of my eye, I noticed Julia standing inside the picture window of the living room, staring at us. Then I sensed another pair of eyes on me, looked up, and caught a glimpse of Billy on the second-floor deck. He turned and walked back inside. When I looked at the picture window again, Julia was gone, too.

I lingered where I stood until Garret disappeared through the front door. As he closed it behind him, I could imagine how the psychosexual tension would begin to rise inside Candace's pristine island retreat, could almost see the flames of an emotional bonfire start to lick at the pristine windowpanes.

Dr. Mossberg called my cell phone from the medical records department of the Cornell Medical Center at 1:20 P.M. The data she had gleaned from the Bishops' charts supported my theory that Darwin Bishop, while a violent man, was probably not Brooke's murderer. It pointed directly, in fact, to the person I suspected. As I hung up, the weight of that fact weakened my knees. I had to breathe deeply and swallow hard to stop myself from vomiting.

One of the darkest dramas imaginable had resulted in Brooke's death, and I had unwittingly played into it.

I was still feeling shaky when someone knocked at the door to the cottage. I struggled to my feet and cautiously opened it. Billy, again.

"You look like you've seen a ghost," he said.

"I didn't eat yet," I said. "That's all."

He walked past me and sat right down on the couch. "Garret told me about you and Mom," he said.

As I expected. "Oh?" I said.

"You're eloping?" he said. "Tomorrow?"

"So long as your mother says yes," I said. "I haven't asked her yet." I walked over and sat at the other end of the couch.

"She'll say yes," he said.

"How do you know that?" I said.

"She has trouble saying no," he said.

"Meaning?"

"Meaning," he said, leaning toward me, "that not everyone around here is deaf, dumb, and blind."

"I'm listening," I said.

"I don't want to break your heart, but you're not the first guy she's hooked up with. Not even close." He paused, blinking nervously. "She doesn't stay interested very long. Okay?"

Keep the pressure on, I told myself. "I can handle it," I said.

"You'll ruin everything," he deadpanned. "She'll just freak out and leave you, and we'll never be able to live together."

"You're overreacting," I said. "Everything will work out. People change."

He tilted his head, squinted at me. "What are you trying to do here?" he said, studying my face. "Is this the real reason you wanted me out of the way, at that Riggs place? My mother has you that fucked up in the head that you need Garret off to Yale and me out on that funny farm?" He stood up. "You were never going to come through for me."

"You have it all wrong," I said.

"I can't believe I trusted you," he said, shaking his head.

"You can always trust me."

He walked out.

I stood at the window of my cottage and watched him walk away, in the direction of the main house. Then I picked up the phone and dialed the home of Art Fields, director of the State Police crime laboratory in Boston.

Fields confirmed that I had drawn a scientifically valid conclusion from the blood-typing data Laura Mossberg had provided me. That meant direct forensic evidence linked Brooke Bishop and her killer. Fields cautioned me that the evidence was still circumstantial, but allowed that it was powerful.

I hung up, glanced at the clock. It was 1:29 P.M. All I needed to do was wait for Julia.

Two o'clock came and went. So did 3:00 P.M. And 4:00. I started wondering whether my plan wasn't going to net me the quick result I had expected. But then, at four-fifteen, Julia finally called to me from just outside my door. I opened it to find her in a sheer, pale yellow sun dress. The shading of her nipples showed through the cloth. "No looking back," she said. "It's really a deal? The past is the past?"

"Deal."

"Cross your heart and hope to die?" she said.

I stepped outside, pulled her into my arms, and kissed her. I felt myself getting hard as she pressed against me.

"Let's go inside," she said.

I shook my head and ran my hand up her thigh, raising her dress to her hip. My fingers moved under the hem. She was wearing no panties.

"C'mon," she said, trying to wriggle away. "No public displays."

I let her dress drop back into place, kissed her more deeply. "Take me somewhere outside again. Somewhere out of the way. I have a surprise for you."

She glanced at my crotch. "You're giving it away."

"You once mentioned a private place," I said.

Julia smiled. "Okay," she said.

She walked me past her mother's house, through the backyard, then onto a path that cut through a dense grove of trees. An enchanted little forest. About thirty feet inside, I stopped her and pushed her against one of the slim trunks. I ran both my hands up her legs and under her dress, moving my fingers along each side of her inner thighs, not stopping until I had slipped one finger deep inside her. She leaned to kiss me, but I leaned away. I dropped my hands, letting her dress fall into place. I stepped back. "Not here. Take me wherever we're going."

Julia turned her face away from me. For a moment, she looked as though she might be angry. Then she grinned impishly. "Catch me," she said. She bolted down the path.

I chased her. She was moving fast. I had to run almost full tilt to keep up. But even with the sound of my own feet hitting the ground, the wind whistling in my ears, I thought more than once that I could hear footsteps behind me. I hoped they weren't an illusion. If my plan was unfolding perfectly, then Julia and I were being followed, and the cauldron was really starting to boil.

I had almost caught up with Julia when she ran into a clearing. A stream cut between two low hills, gurgling over its rocky bed. The air smelled of lavender. I stopped and watched her jog to the water's edge, then turn around, breathing heavily. Sun filtered through branches, painting her with ribbons of light.

She untied the lace at the neck of her sun dress, pushed it off her shoulders, and let it slide to the ground. She was naked. And perfect. Eve before the Fall. Sinfully beautiful.

I walked up to her, knowing in my gut that we were being watched, but also knowing that I was in no immediate danger; the eavesdropper would never strike out at me with Julia present. He couldn't risk being discovered. It was time to bring his pathological jealousy to a fever pitch.

I got down on one knee in front of Julia and forced myself to kiss the slopes of her abdomen, running my tongue into her navel, amazed I could still be excited by her, even with what she had done. I looked up, into her eyes, more luminous than ever. "I want you to marry me," I said. I moved my tongue to the top of her groin.

"Frank," she said, closing her eyes. She took a deep breath and trembled as I moved my tongue even lower.

I took hold of her wrists. I could feel her pulse racing. I stood up. "Marry me," I said again. I brushed my fingers along her cheek. I understood now that Julia was addicted to at least three things: sex, money, and glamour. I wanted to offer her a cocktail of all of them. "We charter a jet to fly us to Vegas tomorrow, get married, and spend the rest of the week in Paris. I already booked a suite at the Ritz. I want to spend my life with you."

She ran her fingers over my lips. "I want that, too," she said. "I just . . ."

"Just say yes," I said.

She looked into my eyes. Several seconds passed. "Yes," she said. Then, without another word, she melted to her knees and unbuttoned my jeans.

24

It was just after 1:00 A.M. I had turned out all the lights of the cottage at midnight. Only a hint of the crescent moon seeped through the slats of the window shutters.

I lay awake in bed, fighting exhaustion, fully clothed under a sheet. My Browning Baby handgun filled the front pocket of my jeans.

I was confident I had put enough bait on the hook. Julia had already begun to pack for our elopement. I was claiming the sexual prize Brooke's killer thirsted for. He had to come for me.

The cottage had a back door with a chain lock. I left it dangling. I also left the back two windows of the cottage wide open—invitations to murder.

I was pretty sure who to expect in my midst, but the forensic data at the heart of my theory wasn't foolproof. My own attempted murder would be the definitive piece of evidence.

My eyes were getting heavier by the minute. I had had no sleep the night before. I hadn't had any real rest in weeks. I got up, walked to the kitchen sink, and splashed cold water on my face. It didn't do much. I got back into bed, pinching my thigh now and then to stay awake.

That didn't work, either. I drifted off and woke in a

panic. Five minutes might have passed. Or fifteen. Or fifty. I couldn't tell. My heart raced, and my eyes darted left and right, searching the shadowy cottage. I saw nothing. I was alone, safe, for the moment.

I sat up and swung my legs over the side of the mattress. Maybe a very quick, very cold shower would help, I thought to myself. I stood and started toward the bathroom. But then I froze, hearing footsteps outside the cottage, somewhere beyond my back door.

I felt for the Browning Baby in my pocket and walked toward the sounds. Someone was stepping on the leaves and fallen branches outside. I listened a little longer. The sounds went away.

I stayed close to the wall and carefully pushed aside one of the little drapes that covered the window in the back door. I squinted into the night. Then my breathing stopped as my worst nightmare gripped me.

Garret was perched on the lowest branch of a majestic elm, about nine feet off the ground, fifteen feet from the door. The moon's glow barely illuminated his muscular torso and the noose around his neck.

I rushed outside, horrified to see my life repeating itself in the worst way. I had lost a young man to suicide only once—Billy Fisk, whose memory had finally drawn me into the Bishop case. Was I about to witness the lethality of my failings again? I had obviously pushed Garret too far, not to the edge of murder, but to suicide.

Seeing Garret's bookshelf the night before, stocked with titles by the poet Yeats, had clued me in to his guilt. Julia had quoted Yeats in the mystery letter:

> *My temptation is quiet.*
> *Here at life's end.*

I had finally realized that Julia had intended that letter for Garret, not her therapist or some business associate of Darwin's. She had taken Garret as her lover.

Garret had been the one who had attacked me in a jealous rage outside Mass General Hospital, uttering a line from Yeats before plunging a knife into my back:

What could she have done, being what she is?

"Good morning," Garret said softly.

I looked up at him. The muscles of his chest twitched. He was closing and opening his fists rhythmically. Wired. "Don't do this," I said.

"You need her so badly," he said. "Take her."

"Let me help you," I said.

He laughed a gruesome laugh, craning his neck toward the dark sky, like some sort of deranged animal. Then he looked down at me, his eyes wide. "You wanted this," he said. "You made this happen."

A wave of nausea swept over me. Was it possible my psychological strategy—increasing the sexual tension in the house to a fever pitch—had actually been an unconscious way of finishing off my last rival for Julia's attentions? Darwin was in prison, charged with murder. Garret might soon be dead. Had I designed to vanquish father and son alike? "Your mother used you, Garret," I said. "She manipulated you. Just like she did me and North Anderson and who knows how many other men. I see that now. I know you're not fully to blame for what happened to Brooke. Or Tess."

He stayed silent.

"I think I know what happened," I said, keeping my tone even. "After your mom had the twins, she stopped the 'special relationship' you two had. She had somebody else to love. Brooke. And Tess. And when she moves on, she moves on. Cold. It's brutal. And it's painful."

"Billy didn't kill any cat," he said. "You deserve to know that. You care about him." He lifted one foot off the branch.

"Please," I said.

"You asked for this," he said.

I looked down and shook my head, trying to come up with words that would give Garret hope.

"Good-bye, Frank," Garret said.

I looked up just as Garret leapt off the branch. I closed my eyes, picturing Billy Fisk's face, bracing for the sound of his spinal column fracturing with the force of the rope. But, instead, I felt the full weight of Garret's body drop on top of me, knocking me to the ground. My head bounced off the dirt, leaving me dazed. The partially healed muscles in my back gave way, and a searing pain ripped through me.

Garret crouched over me, smiling, holding a knife in one hand and the end of the rope in the other. He lifted the noose off his neck, dropped it. "It wasn't tied to anything," he said. "The proverbial loose end. You should have checked."

I reached for my gun, but Garret dove toward me before I could get to it. I barely managed to raise my knee as he fell, burying it in his abdomen and knocking the air out of him.

The knife landed between us.

We both scrambled for it. His hand found it first. I grabbed his wrist and forced him onto his back. I nearly had him pinned when he rammed his head into my chin. I lost my grip on one of his arms, and he rammed an elbow into my face and pushed me off him.

He climbed on top of me and drove the knife downward, toward my chest. I caught hold of his wrist again. He was even stronger than I had imagined. The tip of the blade was getting closer.

"*Those that I fight I do not hate,*" he said, pushing even harder on the knife. "Yeats. My favorite." His lip curled. "You had no business moving in on us, in the first place. If you had just left us alone . . ." He put everything he had behind the knife.

The tip came within a foot of my chest. There was only one move I could think to make. If I suddenly stopped struggling, Garret's momentum would carry him toward me. I could invert his wrist as he fell and bring him down on the blade. I didn't want to kill him, was horrified by the realization that I would be left the victor in a grotesque Oedipal tale, but I had no choice.

I felt myself getting weaker. The blade couldn't have been more than six inches from my chest. I had to act. I pushed with everything I had left against Garret, moving the blade a few inches further away, priming him for the fall. I looked into his eyes, reviewing the split-second move that would bury the blade in his chest, severing his aorta.

Just as I was about to let my arms give way, I heard a dull thud. Garret collapsed onto to the ground, moaning.

I looked up to find Billy standing over me, holding a bat. His face was a mixture of confusion and anger. I wasn't certain whether he was even conscious of what he was doing. He raised the bat over his head, his eyes thinning with rage as he stared back at me. I thought he was about to make sure I didn't send him off to any psych ward. But then his gaze shifted to Garret. He took a deep breath and reared back.

"Don't," I yelled. "It's not his fault."

Billy froze, the bat still cocked over his head.

I saw that his pupils had constricted to pinpoints. A rivulet of saliva ran from the corner of his mouth. Adrenaline had to be coursing through his blood vessels. This was the Billy I would have seen the moment he broke into a stranger's home, set fire to the Bishop estate, or strangled a cat. This was the Billy who had attacked Jason Sanderson's bullies. He was at one with his demons. "You're not a killer," I said. "Put the bat down."

He didn't respond.

I wasn't even sure he had heard me. I pulled my Browning Baby from the front pocket of my jeans. "Billy," I said, my voice shaking. "Put it down. Now."

He took a deep breath and arched his back.

I flicked the gun's safety to the off position, ready to fire. But I wasn't ready. Even as Billy snapped his wrists forward, I couldn't bring myself to pull the trigger.

The bat sailed past me and Garret, bouncing off a couple trees, landing in some leaves. Billy looked straight at me. "You got to trust someone," he said. Then he reached down and held out his hand for me.

As Candace comforted Julia, who was heaving with very real tears, the police took Garret away in cuffs.

The officers took some evidence along with them—things I'd found in Garret's closet before they arrived. Part of that evidence was an album filled with photographs of Julia. She didn't seem to be modeling, even though she looked model-perfect in every one. It seemed that Garret had taken the pictures without her knowledge. Some of them were benign: Julia walking around the grounds of the Nantucket estate, hailing a cab in Manhattan, riding a horse. Others were provocative: Julia sunbathing and swimming laps in a revealing bikini, pulling off a sweatshirt to reveal a see-through ribbed T-shirt, nursing Brooke. Still others crossed the line into the erotic: Julia sleeping naked, only half-covered by a white sheet. Julia in silhouette behind a steamed shower door. Julia, topless, shot through a window of the family's Manhattan penthouse. Julia locked in an embrace with North Anderson. And this last image, which still sends shivers up my spine and a pang of guilt through my heart: Julia and me kissing, inside my room at The Breakers.

The officers also took a stack of letters hidden deep in Garret's closet, each smelling of Julia's perfume, and each on the same heavy stock as the letter Claire Buckley had turned over to North Anderson and me. Garret's name, written across the front of the envelopes, was in the same delicate script.

The first of the letters I had opened was one from the middle of the stack. It had helped me see how blatantly Julia had romanced her own adoptive son:

Garret,
No one should have to bear what you went

through with Darwin today. His insistence that you leave your room and spend hours outdoors shows that he misses the fact that you have great gifts—your poetry chief among them. Even though we are all afraid of Darwin, you should know he is more afraid of you, though he would never admit it. You are becoming the man he could never be—strong, sensitive, intelligent. He sees it. So do I. Women dream about making a life with someone like you. I once did.

Your favorite, Yeats, said it better:

But I was young and foolish, and now am full of tears.

—*Julia*
April 12, 2001

The tone in every one of the letters was the same. Despondency. Desperation. Seduction.

The officers carried away something else, too. A pair of black, army-style boots. They were the same boots I had glimpsed the night I had fallen outside Mass General, a knife edging toward my portal artery. The heel of the left boot was stained with blue paint that would turn out to match a crosswalk painted near the garage less than an hour before I was attacked.

The blood types Laura Mossberg had dug up for me supported my theory that Garret and Julia had been lovers and that he was the killer. Julia's blood type was B negative. The twins' blood type was O positive. Only a man with A positive or B positive blood could be the father. Billy was A negative. Garret was B positive.

I am certain Garret never realized what genetic testing would later prove conclusively—that Tess and Brooke Bishop were his daughters. But Julia knew it, and that ended her affair with him. She recoiled from him, but kept the children, children she had desperately wanted.

All Garret knew was that Julia had cut him off from her affections after she gave birth to the twins, that her maternal love for them somehow excluded her erotic love for him. Enraged, desperate to restore himself to his rightful place in her life, he became an elegant and opportunistic killer.

Brooke's murder was simple enough. Billy would be blamed. And when Garret overheard Julia and Darwin arguing about the nortriptyline, he used the cover of Billy's break-in to poison Tess, careful not to get his own fingerprints anywhere on the medicine bottle. He had probably already left the photographic negative of North and Julia where his father would find it, look at it, and touch it. Then he had retrieved that negative and planted it for us to uncover.

Garret had even given his father an apparent motive—pathological jealousy, the desire for revenge on Julia for cheating with North Anderson. And he had concocted a little physical evidence to go along with it. But the main ingredient in the scheme came as a surprise, even to him. Once Darwin lost control and actually assaulted his wife—no doubt fueled by the double bind of her accusing him of murder, obtaining a restraining order against him, yet carrying on her own affair—he was ripe for the kill. All Garret had to do was offer up eyewitness testimony, then cry a little as daddy went bye-bye. For life.

One thing Garret probably hadn't expected was my falling for Julia, too. And that, he could not abide. That called for action. A knife in the back. He probably felt like I'd done it to him first.

EPILOGUE

Saturday, November 23, 2002

Lilly Cunningham's heroism was, ultimately, her willingness to face her emotional injuries—the pain of being seduced by her grandfather, the self-hatred and hatred of him that it had spawned. Until she could find the courage to do so, she literally reabsorbed her own potential destructiveness, injecting it back into her body—dirtying, infecting, and disfiguring herself, but hurting no one else.

Julia Bishop had no such courage. She failed to confront the feelings of humiliation and worthlessness her father had provoked in her, hiding out behind her beautiful face and beguiling manner, feeding herself erotic conquests. Call it an addiction. Call it sexual sadism. Whatever its label, its effect was to pass on her destructiveness—to Garret.

In the courtroom, after being tried as an adult for murder and attempted murder, convicted and sentenced to life in prison, Garret asked for one thing. He wanted Julia to hug him. She did. Now she visits him three times a week at the Massachusetts Correctional Institute at Cedar Junction.

Julia has never visited Darwin Bishop, but I have. He was sentenced to nine years for Julia's attempted murder at Mass General. If you believe what he has to say (and I do), he really did think that Billy had killed Brooke. He really did want to bypass the criminal justice system and get him help at Payne Whitney.

Julia still lives with her mother on Martha's Vineyard. After her relationship with Garret was revealed, she voluntarily surrendered custody of Tess to the Department of Social Services. She was charged with no crime, though Anderson, O'Donnell, and I all believe she suspected Garret was the murderer all along, but kept that suspicion from the police, to keep her secret buried. Proving that she was an accessory after the fact, however, would be nearly impossible. No physical evidence linked her to any crime. And not even District Attorney Harrigan had the stomach for that kind of uphill battle.

As for Claire Buckley, she's been promoted to Darwin Bishop's fiancée. She's waiting for him, in a tidy little Trump Parc studio apartment—all that's left of Bishop's wealth. She swears he'll build a greater fortune than ever when he's released from prison. She may be right.

It took me three months and calling in a lot of chits, but I finally got Social Services to agree to let Billy crash with me in Chelsea. Permanently. I'm playing single parent now, and liking it, most of the time. The dead cat was, of course, a ruse of Garret's, but I don't have any expectations that Billy will be able to shed all his psychological scars. I do have hope for him, though. And I pray that will help give him enough confidence to walk into the future, instead of the past.

Read on for an excerpt from Keith Ablow's next book
PSYCHOPATH
Coming soon in hardcover from St. Martin's Press

ONE

January 23, 2003
Route 90 East, 37 miles outside Rome, New York

Mahler's *Tenth Symphony* played on the BMW X5's stereo, but even that serene music did nothing to calm Jonah. His skin was hot with anger. The palms of his hands burned against the steering wheel. His heart pounded, squeezing more and more blood with each beat, flooding his aorta, engorging his carotid arteries, making his head throb inside the skull, somewhere within the temporal lobes of his brain. At last count, his breathing had risen to eighteen respirations per minute. He could feel a dizzying undertow of oxygen sucking him inside himself.

His hunger to kill always began this way, and he always believed he could control it, ride it into submission down a long highway, the way his grandfather had broken sinewy colts on the plains of the Arizona ranch where Jonah had spent his teenage years. So cunning was his psychopathology that it fooled him into thinking he was greater than it was, that the goodness in him could overpower the evil. He believed this even now, with seventeen bodies strewn along the highways behind him.

"Just keep driving," he said through gritted teeth.

His vision began to blur, partly from surging blood pressure, partly from hyperventilating, partly from the milligram of Haldol he had swallowed an hour earlier. Sometimes the antipsychotic medication put the beast to sleep. Sometimes not.

Squinting into the night, he saw the distant glow of red taillights. He pressed down on the accelerator, desperate to close the distance between himself and a fellow traveler, as if the momentum of another—of a normal and decent man—might carry him through the darkness.

He glanced at the orange neon clock on the dash, saw that it was 3:02 A.M., and remembered a line from Fitzgerald:

> In a real dark night of the soul it is always
> three o'clock in the morning.

The line was from a short story called "The Crack-Up," a title apropos to what was happening to him—fine fissures in his psychological defenses giving way, splitting into bigger clefts, then into each other, becoming a gaping, black hole that swallowed him, then rebirthed him as a monster.

Jonah had read everything F. Scott Fitzgerald had written, because the words were beautiful, and the places beautiful, and the people beautiful, even with their flaws. And he wanted to think of himself in exactly that way, to believe he was an imperfect creation of a perfect God, that he was worthy of redemption.

He was, at thirty-nine, physically flawless. His face suggested both trustworthiness and self-confidence—high cheekbones, a prominent brow, a strong chin with a subtle cleft. His eyes, clear and pale blue, perfectly complemented his wavy, silver-gray hair, worn just off the shoulders, pleasantly tousled. He stood six-foot-one and was broadly built, with long, muscled arms and a V-shaped torso tapering to a thirty-one-inch waist. He had the rock-hard thighs and calves of a mountain climber.

Yet of all his features, women commented first on his hands. The skin was tan and soft, covering tendons that fanned perfectly from knuckles to wrist. The veins were

visible enough to hint at physical strength, without being
so visible as to suggest destructiveness. The fingers were
long and graceful, tapering to smooth, translucent nails he
buffed to a shine each morning. A pianist's fingers, some
women said. A surgeon's, others told him.

"You have the hands of an angel," one lover had gasped,
sliding his finger into her mouth.

The hands of an angel. Jonah looked at them, white-
knuckled, clutching the steering wheel. He was within fifty
yards of the car in front of him, but felt himself losing
ground in his race against evil. His upper lip had begun to
twitch. Sweat covered his neck and shoulders.

He opened his eyes wide and summoned the face of his
last victim in that young man's last moments, hoping the
image would sober him, in the way the memory of nausea
and vomiting can sober an alcoholic, making repugnant the
bottle that beckons so seductively, promising relief and release.

Nearly two months had passed, but Jonah could still see
Scott Carmady's jaw drop open, utter disbelief filling his
eyes. For how can a weary traveler, feeling lucky to get
help with a broken-down Chevy at the side of a desolate
stretch of Kentucky highway, believe the raw pain of his
cut throat or the warm blood soaking his shirt? How can
he make sense of the fact that his life, with all the momentum of a twenty-something's hopes and dreams, is screech-
ing to a halt? How can he fathom the fact that the
well-dressed man who has mortally wounded him is the
same man who has spent the time not only to jump-start
his car battery, but to wait fifteen minutes with him to be
certain it will not die again?

And what minutes! Carmady had revealed things he had
spoken of to no one—the helplessness sparked in him by
his sadistic boss, the rage he felt clinging to his cheating
wife. Opening up made him feel better than he had in a
long, long time. Unburdened.

Jonah remembered how a plea had taken the place of
the disbelief he had seen in the dying man's eyes. It was

not a plea for the answer to some grand, existential *Why?* Not some cliché last scene from a movie. No. The plea was purely for help. So that when Carmady reached for Jonah it was neither to attack him, nor to defend himself, but simply to keep from collapsing.

Jonah had not stepped away from his victim, but closer. He embraced him. And as Carmady's life drained out of him, Jonah felt the rage drain out of his own body, a magnificent calm taking its place, a feeling of oneness with himself and the universe. And he whispered his own plea in the man's ear. "Please forgive me."

Jonah's eyes filled with tears. The road undulated before him. If only Caramady had been willing to reveal more, to peel back the last layers of his emotional defenses, to give Jonah the reasons *why* he could be victimized by his boss and his wife, what trauma had weakened him, then he might still be alive. But Carmady had refused to talk about his childhood, refused utterly, like a man keeping a locker full of meats all to himself—keeping them from Jonah, who was starving.

Starving, like now.

His strategy was backfiring. He had truly believed that summoning memories of his last kill would keep the monster inside him at bay, but the opposite was true. The monster had tricked him. The memory of the calm he had felt holding death in his arms and another man's life story in his heart made him crave that calm with every cell of his white-hot brain.

He glimpsed a sign for a rest area, half a mile away. He straightened up, telling himself he could go there, swallow another milligram or two of Haldol and put himself to sleep. Like a vampire, he almost always fed by night; first light was just three hours away.

He veered off Route 90, into the rest area. One other car was parked there—an older model, metallic blue Saab, with its interior light on. Jonah parked three spaces away. Why not ten? he chastised himself. Why tempt the beast? He gripped the wheel even more tightly, his fingernails digging into the heels of his hands, nearly breaking the skin. His fever spawned chills that ran up his neck and over his scalp. His ribcage strained painfully against his bulging lungs.

Half against his will, he turned his head and saw a woman in the driver's seat of the Saab, a large map unfolded against the steering wheel. She looked about forty-five years old. In silhouette, her face just missed beauty— her nose a bit large, her chin a bit weak. Crows' feet suggested she was a worrier. Her brown hair was cut short and neat. She wore a black leather jacket. A cell phone lay on the dashboard in front of her.

Just looking at her made Jonah hungry. Ravenous. Here was a living, breathing woman, not twenty feet away, with a unique past and future. No other person had had precisely the same experiences or had thought precisely the same thoughts. Invisible bonds connected her to parents and grandparents, perhaps siblings, perhaps a husband or lovers or both. Perhaps children. Friends. Her brain held data she had gathered, picking and choosing what to read and look at and listen to out of interests and abilities that were mystical and immeasurable parts of her. Of *her*, a being like no other. She harbored likes and dislikes, fears and dreams, and (this, more than anything) traumas that were hers and hers alone—unless she could be coaxed to share them.

Bolts of pain exploded into Jonah's eyes. He looked away, staring at the highway for most of a minute, hoping another car would slow to enter the rest area. None did.

Why did it always seem so easy? Almost prearranged. Even preordained. He never stalked his victims; he came upon them. Was the universe organizing to feed him the life force of others? Did the people who crossed his path come in search of him? Did they unconsciously need to die as much as he needed to kill? Did God want them in heaven? Was he some kind of angel? An angel of death? His saliva started to run thicker in his mouth. The throbbing in his head surged beyond anything like a headache, beyond any migraine. He felt as though a dozen drill bits inside his

skull were powering their way out, through his forehead,
his temples, his ears, down through the roof of his mouth,
his lips.

He thought of killing himself, an impulse that had visited
him before each murder. The straight razor in his pocket
could end his suffering once and for all. But he had made
only meager attempts on his own life. Shallow lacerations
to his wrists. Five or ten pills, instead of fifty or a hundred.
A drunken leap from a second-story window that fractured
his right fibula. These were suicidal *gestures*, nothing more.
Deep down Jonah wanted to live. He still believed he could
make amends in this life. Beneath all his self-loathing, at
the core of his being, he still loved himself in the unconditional way he prayed the Lord did.

He flicked on the BMW's cabin light and sounded a
short blast of his horn, nauseated at secreting the first sticky
strand of his poisonous web. The woman startled, then
looked over at him. He leaned toward her, and held up a
finger, almost shyly, then lowered his passenger window
not quite halfway, as if *he* wasn't sure whether to trust *her*.

The woman hesitated, then lowered her own window.

"Excuse me," Jonah said. His voice was velvety and
deep, and he knew it had a nearly hypnotic effect. People
never seemed to tire of listening to him. They rarely interrupted him.

The woman smiled, but tightly, and said nothing.

"I know this would be, uh . . . asking a lot. . . . But,
uh . . ." He stuttered intentionally, to sound unsure of himself. "My, uh—phone . . . " he said, with a shrug and a
smile, "kind of died." He held up his cell phone. It was
silver and looked pricey. He extended his arm and turned
his wrist, checking the time on his shiny, Cartier chrono-
graph, a cabochon sapphire at the crown. He knew most
people trusted others with money, either because they believed the rich didn't need to steal from them, or because
they assumed the rich valued society's rules too much to
break them. "I'm a doctor," Jonah went on. He shook his
head. "Left the hospital about four minutes ago, and they're

paging me already. Any chance I could, uh . . . borrow your phone?"

"My battery is getting . . ." the woman started, sounding uncomfortable.

"I'd be happy to pay you something," Jonah said. The offer was his way of leapfrogging the woman's better judgment by transforming his request for the phone into the question of whether she ought to charge him to use it. A generous person would offer it for free—which, of course, required offering it to begin with.

"Go ahead," she said. "Evenings and weekends are no charge."

"Thank you." He got out of his car and walked toward the woman's door, stopping a respectful distance away. Partly to trigger her instinct to nurture him, partly to discharge the electric energy coursing through his system, he stepped briskly foot-to-foot and shook his head and shoulders, as if freezing.

She reached out, handed him the phone.

He stood facing her, letting her take note of his chocolate-colored, quilted suede coat, his sky-blue turtleneck sweater, his pleated, gray flannel slacks. Nothing black. Everything soft to the touch. He dialed seven random digits and held the phone to his ear.

"You can use it in your car, if you like," she said.

Jonah knew the woman's invitation to take her phone into his car reflected her unconscious wish that he would take *her* into his car. He also knew that the more proper he was, the freer she would feel to fantasize about him and the more penetrable her personal boundaries would become. "You've already been incredibly kind," he said. "I'll only be a moment."

She nodded, looked back at the map and rolled up her window.

He spoke loudly to be certain she would overhear him. The words reverberated in his ears. "Dr. Wrens," he said, then paused. "A fever? How high?" He paused again. "Let's start her on some IV Ampicillin and see how she does." He nodded. "Of course. Tell her husband I'll see her first thing in the morning." He pretended to click the phone off and knocked quietly on the car window.

She lowered it. "All set?"

He had obviously finished using the phone. Her question meant she wanted something else from him, even though he doubted she would be able to put into words what that something was. He felt a stiffening in his groin. "All set," he said. "Thank you so much." He held the phone out, waiting to speak until she was holding the other end of it, until they were connected that little bit. "Maybe I can return the favor," he said. He waited another moment before letting go of the phone. "You seem uncertain where you're headed."

She laughed. "I seem lost," she said.

He laughed with her—a boyish, infectious laugh that broke the ice once and for all. The beast was fully in control. The pain in Jonah's head seeped into his teeth and jaws. "Where are you trying to go, if you don't mind my asking?" He rubbed his hands together, blew out a plume of frosty breath.

"Eagle Bay," she said.

Eagle Bay was a small town on the Adirondack Railroad, close to the Moose River recreation area. Jonah had hiked nearby Panther Mountain. "That's easy," he said. "I'll scribble out directions." He had chosen the word *scribble* to conjure the image of innocence, of a harmless man-child barely able to write, let alone plot and plan.

"I'd appreciate that," she said.

Jonah felt as though he had sufficiently weakened her defenses to push past them. The average woman lacked the internal resolve to protect her boundaries, except in the face of obvious danger. And this woman could not see him as an imminent threat. He was handsome and well-spoken. He looked wealthy. He was a physician. He had been called by a local hospital to help someone in distress. A *woman* in distress. Now he wanted to help her.

He came around the front of the Saab, hugging himself.

Walking around the back of the car, leaving the woman's field of vision, might make her wary. He waited beside the passenger door, making no movement toward it. The less overt his demand to be let inside, the better his chances.

She seemed to hesitate, again, her face registering what looked like a textbook struggle between the instinct for self-preservation and the quest for self-reliance. Self-reliance won. She reached across the passenger seat and pulled open the door.

Jonah climbed in. He held out his hand. It trembled. "Jonah Wrens," he said. "It must be ten below, with the wind chill."

"Anna," she said, shaking his hand. "Anna Beckwith." She looked confused as she let go, probably because Jonah's hand felt warm and clammy, not cold.

"Do you have a pen and paper, Anna Beckwith?" Jonah asked. Speaking her name would make them seem less like strangers.

Beckwith reached behind Jonah's seat and rummaged through her handbag, finding a felt-tip pen and leather address book. She flipped to a blank page and handed the open book and pen to him.

Jonah noted that Beckwith wore no engagement ring or wedding band. She did not smell of perfume. He started writing out random directions, to nowhere. *Stay on 90 East, to exit 54, Route 9 West* . . . "I take it you're not from around here," he said.

She shook her head. "Washington, D.C."

"Are you a skier?" he asked, still writing.

"No," she said.

"A hiker?"

"I'm just visiting a friend."

"Good for you." He glanced at her. "Boyfriend?" he asked, matter-of-factly. He went back to writing.

"College roommate."

No boyfriend, Jonah thought. No wedding band. No perfume. No lipstick. And not the slightest hint of homosexuality in her manner or tone. "Let me guess . . ." he said. "Mount Holyoke."

"Why would you guess a girl's school?" Beckwith asked.

Jonah looked at her. "I saw the Mount Holyoke sticker on your back window when I drove in."

She laughed again—an easy laugh that showed the last of her fear had melted away. "Class of '78."

Jonah did the math. Beckwith was between forty-five and forty-six years old. He could have asked her what she had studied at Holyoke or whether the college was close to her home or far away. But answers to those questions would not give him access to her soul. "Why a girls' school?" he asked instead.

"I really don't know," she said.

"You chose it," he pushed, smiling warmly to take the edge off his words.

"I just felt more comfortable."

I just felt more comfortable. Jonah stood at the threshold of Beckwith's internal, emotional world. He needed to buy enough time to cross it. "Do you know Route 28?" he asked.

"I don't," Beckwith said.

"No problem," Jonah said. "I'll, uh, draw everything out . . . for you." Without thinking to, he drew a line up the page, then another, shorter line intersecting it at something close to a ninety-degree angle. He noticed the rudimentary cross on the page and took it as a symbol that God was still with him. Hadn't Jesus, after all, absorbed the pain of others? And wasn't that Jonah's aim? His thirst? His cross to bear? "Why would a coed campus have made you uncomfortable?" he asked Beckwith.

She didn't respond.

He looked at her, saw a new hesitancy in her face. "Sorry to pry. My daughter's thinking of Holyoke," he lied.

"You have a daughter?"

"You seem surprised."

"You don't wear a wedding band."

She had been studying him. She was coming closer. Jonah felt his heart rate and breathing begin to slow. "Her mother and I divorced when Caroline was five," he said. Then he delivered Beckwith this talisman, harvested from Scott Carmady's soul, now a part of his own: "My wife was unfaithful to me. I stayed longer than I should have."

That fabricated self-revelation was all the license Anna Beckwith needed to begin revealing her true self. "I was always shy with boys," she said. "I'm sure that's the reason for Holyoke."

"You've never married," Jonah said.

"You sound so sure," Beckwith said playfully.

Jonah kept writing out his haphazard map, not wanting to interrupt the stream of emotion flowing between them. "Just a guess," he said.

"You guessed right."

"I wasn't exactly marriage material myself," he said.

"I had two brothers," she said. "Both older. Maybe that . . . I don't know."

Jonah heard a whole world within the way Beckwith had said the word *older*. There was resentment and powerlessness in it—and something more. Shame. "They made fun of you," he said. He couldn't resist looking at her again. He watched her face lose its mask of maturity and become open and innocent and beautiful. A little girl's face. He thought to himself that he could never kill a child. And with that thought, the pain in his head fell off to a dull ache.

"They teased me quite a bit," she said.

"How old were you?"

"The worst of it?" She shrugged. "Ten? Eleven?"

"And how old were they?"

"Fourteen and sixteen."

Beckwith suddenly looked anxious, in the same way Jonah's other victims had—as if she didn't understand why she would share such intimacies with a stranger. But Jonah needed to hear more. So he pushed ahead. "What names did they call you?" He closed his eyes, waiting for her emotional wound to ooze the sweet antidote to his violence.

"They called me . . ." She stopped. "I don't want to go there." She let out a long breath. "If you could just give me the directions, I'd really appreciate it."

Jonah looked at her. "The kids at school used to call me 'faggot,' 'wimp,' things like that." Another lie.

She shook her head. "From the looks of it, you've really shown them," she said. "No one would call you a wimp now."

"Nice of you to say." He looked out his window, as if pained by the memory of his childhood traumas.

"They called me . . . *prissy pussy pants*," Beckwith said.

Jonah turned back to her. She was blushing.

"I know it doesn't sound like the end of the world or anything," she went on, "but they just kept it up. They wouldn't let me be."

Jonah was with the eleven-year-old Beckwith now, seeing her in a pleated, navy-blue wool skirt, proper white blouse, white socks, cordovan penny loafers. It was no accident her brothers had teased her most intensely as she reached womanhood, when they would be, consciously or not, focused on her pants and the soft folds of skin beneath them. And he intuited more toxic goings-on—from the way Beckwith had said that they *wouldn't let her be*. That sounded like code for sexual abuse. He stared at her, hoping she would strip her psyche naked and bathe with him in the warm pool of her suffering. "And besides the name-calling?" he said.

Beckwith stared back at him, the color slowly draining from her cheeks.

"How else were your brothers cruel to you, Anna?"

She shook her head.

"They tried to look at you?"

"I really have to get going," she said.

"They touched you," he said.

Suddenly, the little girl Beckwith disappeared, and the forty-five-year-old Beckwith sat rigidly in her place. "Honestly, it really isn't any of your . . ."

Jonah wanted the little girl. He needed the little girl. "You can tell me," he said. "You can tell me anything."

"No," she said.

Jonah could almost hear a bolt sliding home, locking him out. "Please," he said.

"I need you to leave," Beckwith said.

"You shouldn't feel embarrassed with me," Jonah said. He was straining for air. "I've heard everything there is to hear." He tried to force a smile, but knew his expression had to look more wolfish than reassuring.

Beckwith squinted at him, then swallowed hard, as if she finally saw she was in the company of madness.

Jonah's head had started to throb. "Where was your father?" he asked, hearing the telltale anger seeping into his voice. "Where was your mother?"

"Please," Beckwith said. "Just let me leave." Yet she didn't try to escape.

"Why didn't they help you?" Jonah asked. He felt saliva drip from the corner of his mouth and saw in Beckwith's face that she had seen it.

"If you let me go, I . . ." she started to plead.

The drill bits inside Jonah's skull started grinding again. "What did those little bastards do to you?" Jonah yelled.

"They . . ." She started to cry.

Jonah leaned over her, bringing his mouth to her ear. "What did they do?" he demanded. "Don't be ashamed. It wasn't your fault."

Beckwith's face twisted into the panic and confusion that had seized Scott Carmady—horrified disbelief at what was happening. "Please," she gasped. "Please, God . . ."

Her pleading was simultaneously excruciating and exciting to Jonah, a terrible and irresistible window on the evil inside him. He pressed his cheek to hers. "Tell me," he whispered in her ear. He felt her tears stream down his face. And he began to cry himself. Because he realized there was only one way to enter her soul.

He reached into his front pocket for the straight-edge razor. He opened it mercifully outside her view. Then he placed a thumb under her chin and gently tilted her head back. She offered no resistance. He drew the blade quickly across each of her carotid arteries, severing them cleanly. And he watched as Beckwith wilted like a three-day-old flower.

Blood began to drip down his cheek, mixing with his tears. He could not have said anymore whether it was his blood or Beckwith's, his tears or hers. In this pure and final moment, all boundaries between him and his victim were evaporating. He was free from the bondage of his own identity.

He wrapped his arms around Beckwith, drawing her tightly to him, groaning as he discharged the seed of life between their thighs, marrying them forever. He kept her close as her frenzy faded to exhaustion, until he felt his muscles relax with hers, his heart slow with hers, his mind clear with hers—until he was completely at peace, at one with himself and the universe.

DENIAL

A novel of psychological suspense

KEITH ABLOW

He's in deep.

A series of grisly murders has forensic psychiatrist Frank Clevenger on the case of a lifetime and the fight of his life against a brutal killer with a horrific trademark and his own powerlessness over sexual compulsion, self-destruction and DENIAL.

Psychopath

KEITH ABLOW

Having achieved celebrity status with the handling of his last case, forensic psychiatrist Dr. Frank Clevenger is approached by the FBI in regards to The Highway Killer, an elusive murderer who has left a trail of twelve bodies in twelve states with no obvious link. But from the opening pages of *Psychopath*, the reader is privy to the killings and knows that the predator is Jonah, a prodigiously talented, and dedicated, psychiatrist who specializes in *locum tenens* work—temporary assignments to hospitals all over the country unable to support a full time psychiatrist. It is the perfect job for a serial killer. In an open letter to *The New York Times*, Jonah taunts and challenges Clevenger to catch him. Now Clevenger must embark on a bizarre kind of public therapy in which his goal is to stop the killings by either apprehending Jonah—or curing him. Using his brilliant mastery of the tools of psychiatry, Clevenger must match wits with a killer who knows all the tricks of the trade.

"Keith Ablow is king of the psychological thriller."
> —Dennis Lehane, author of *Mystic River*

"Keith Ablow's setting is the darkest of all—the twists and turns of the human mind."
> —Harlan Coben, author of *Gone for Good*

AVAILABLE WHEREVER BOOKS ARE SOLD
FROM ST. MARTIN'S PAPERBACKS